BANDIT AMBUSH!

Lean, ragged men who reminded Kairn of scavenging stripers darted among their prey, knives flashing. Even as he watched, one leapt upon Bat's back, pinioning his arms as another thrust a short spear into his belly.

Then three men attacked Kairn and he had no attention to spare. They hesitated at the sight of his longsword, and he used that momentary advantage to cut one down. Then the other two attacked. He fended a clumsy axe blow to one side and split the man's skull just as the other man thrust with his spear. In a desperate sideways lurch Kairn avoided getting the spear through his belly, but the edge of the spear burned against his side.

He hewed at the spearman's neck and saw the head fly free

Tor books by John Maddox Roberts

Cestus Dei
King of the Wood

THE CINGULUM

The Cingulum
Cloak of Illusion
The Sword, The Jewel, and The Mirror

THE ADVENTURES OF CONAN

Conan the Bold
Conan the Champion
Conan the Marauder
Conan the Valorous
Conan the Rogue

THE STORMLANDS

The Islander
The Black Shields
The Poisoned Lands
The Steel Kings

THE STEEL KINGS

JOHN MADDOX ROBERTS

TOR
fantasy

A TOM DOHERTY ASSOCIATES BOOK
NEW YORK

This is a work of fiction. All the characters and events portrayed in this book are fictitious, and any resemblance to real people or events is purely coincidental.

THE STEEL KINGS

Copyright © 1993 by John Maddox Roberts

Cover art by Ken Kelly

A Tor Book
Published by Tom Doherty Associates, Inc.
175 Fifth Avenue
New York, N.Y. 10010

Tor ® is a registered trademark of Tom Doherty Associates, Inc.

ISBN: 0-812-51831-4

First edition: March 1993

Printed in the United States of America

0 9 8 7 6 5 4 3 2 1

BOOK ONE
Deathmoon

ONE

He had no idea what the village's name might be, and at the moment he did not greatly care. He had been traveling a long time and he was weary. More importantly, his cabo was just as tired, and a plainsman always looked after his mount's needs before his own. He was impatient to push on, but he had to stop to rest himself and his animal. The village looked to be as good a place as any.

The rider was a young man with ice-blue eyes above broad cheekbones. His copper-colored hair was slashed off at shoulder length. He had discarded the heavy skin clothing of his native plains in favor of light garments made of thin, colorful cloth, for he had been traveling in warm lands for the last month.

The cabo stamped its small hoofs into the hard-packed dirt of the road, groaning and snorting as he patted its neck. There was a strong scent of water in the air and he knew they must be near a river. He sat in his saddle and looked down the slope to where the road ended at the village gate. The village was surrounded by a log palisade and he could see little more than that. It was still early morning and a dense fog lay over everything, obscuring his view beyond the palisade. The gate was open and someone stood beside it.

"I know, swift one," he said to the beast. "You would rather be out on the great grasslands, where you can run all day. But there is something important we must do, so you and I shall put up with these overgrown wetlands for a while longer. Come on, we'll go rest in that place." He nudged the cabo's ribs and it began to amble downhill toward the village.

At least the beast understood his native tongue. The people of the lands he had been traversing spoke a dialect of Northern that at first he could understand only if they spoke slowly and simply. He had grown used to its slurred vowels and leisurely cadences in time, but he was not comfortable speaking it.

A few peasants worked in the fields through which he rode, and as he passed they looked up from their hoeing and digging to blink at the handsome young mounted warrior who clearly was not from these parts. He carried a long lance before him and wore a sword at his belt. Tucked into the top of one high, soft boot was a knife, and a cased bow and arrows hung at his saddle. He rode with such easy grace that he seemed to be one with his mount.

The man who lounged by the gate studied the rider as he came closer; he wore a tunic, trousers and slippers, and a bronze medallion hung on a chain around his neck. He did not rise from his bench when the cabo stopped in front of him.

"You're a strange sight to see so early in the day," the man said. "Who are you?"

"My name is Kairn."

"Where are you from?"

The youth jerked a thumb back over his shoulder in a vaguely northwesterly direction. "Back there."

"That's a lot of territory."

Kairn nodded. "And I've ridden across most of it."

"You don't seem to have any pack animals. Are you selling anything?"

This seemed an odd question. "No. Why?"

"The government doesn't care about travelers, but it cares about taxes. If you're not bringing in anything to sell, you don't need to pay me anything."

"That suits me," Kairn said. "Who is the government you speak of? This is the first town I've seen in days and I don't even know what kingdom I'm in."

"This is the northwestern prefecture of Greater Mezpa."

"Where is Lesser Mezpa?" Kairn asked.

"There isn't any. There used to be many lands and little kingdoms here along the great river, but Mezpa absorbed them one by one over the centuries, and now there is nothing but Mezpa from here south to the Delta and east to the great sea."

"That sounds like a great deal of land. Who is the royal authority in this town?"

"Official power is spread thin this far from the great cities. I'm it here in Muddy Bottom."

Kairn knew a bit about this land, things his father had taught him, but he thought it best to act the ignorant bumpkin.

"Who is the king of Mezpa?"

"There is no king. Mezpa is a republic."

"How does that work?"

"There is an Assembly of Great Men. From their number they choose a Speaker, don't ask me how. The Speaker has something like royal power, until the Assembly decides to oust him. Last I heard, they were between Speakers. That might be changed, though. They don't tell us much up here."

"Is there a place here where I can find food and lodging for myself and my cabo?"

"There's an inn on the river. It caters mostly to the river trade, but has a stable. You'd better see to your mount personally, though. We don't see many cabos around here."

Kairn bade the man good day and rode through the gate. He hoped the inn might afford him better conversation as well. The gatekeeper was either very stupid or pretending to be so.

The streets of the village were muddy and narrow. The buildings flanking them were one- or two-story, with thatched roofs and walls made of upright timbers, the wattles between the timbers daubed with mud. He could see how the town had come by its name. The drab architecture was relieved by small gardens and flower boxes sporting a riot of blooms. He asked gaping villagers directions to the inn and followed their pointing fingers until he came to what at first seemed to be a hill, but which he soon saw was a long earthwork, twice the height of a mounted man, its top perfectly level.

A minute's ride brought him to the inn, a low, rambling structure as drab as the rest of the town. It had a rail-enclosed pen which held a few dwarf humpers. To one side of the pen was a shed with a thatched roof supported by poles. Kairn dismounted and tied his cabo to a gatepost.

He ducked through the low doorway and found himself in a sunken room with a bar along one end. Behind the bar, a man stood polishing horn cups. He looked up as the young man entered.

"What will it be, young sir? Food or lodging?"

"Both. For myself and for my cabo. We will rest here for a few days. Have you feed for a cabo?"

"The best, sir." The man came from behind the bar and looked Kairn over as they went back outside. "A warrior from the west, eh? We don't see many of those here."

"Have any like me been here in recent months? I am looking for a party of my countrymen." He feigned casualness.

The man shook his head. "No, not for two or three years. You come from the land of Hael, the Steel King?" This epithet referred not to the king's character, but to his nation's major export.

"I am," Kairn said, deeply disappointed. Where had his father gotten to? They discussed the cabo's feed and accommodation for a while, then Kairn looked around at the flat, muddy townscape. "The man at the gate said that the inn was on the river, but I see no river."

The innkeeper grinned. "You are not far from it. It is on the other side of that." He pointed to the great earthwork.

"Is this thing the work of men?" Kairn asked, surveying the seemingly endless wall of earth.

"So they say, although I can't see how anything so huge could be man's work. Go on up and have a look."

Using his lance as a walking stick, Kairn climbed the steep, grassy side of the earthwork. A few of his long strides took him to the level top, which was about ten steps in width. He crossed it and looked down the far slope, his mouth dropping open, his eyes widening in astonishment. People in these lands spoke of the river as if there were no other, and now he saw why. All the rivers of the west combined would not have matched this one. He had never dreamed that a river could be so huge.

His father had told him of the great sea: a body of water so vast that a man could not see across it, that you could travel upon it for days in a ship without coming to the end of it, but Kairn had not been able to visualize it. He could see across this river, but just barely. He could make out trees on the far shore, but they were smaller than blades of grass in the distance.

It was more water than he had dreamed could exist and it *moved*. The current was slow but he could see rivercraft moving to its surging power. The vast brown stream bore a dense, fecund odor, as if it were the place where life had originated.

So enthralled was he by the river itself that at first he took only scant note of its busy traffic. As the impact of the great water waned, he began to see that not only did it bear a good many craft, but that they were of numerous types, from log rafts to small, one-man boats to vessels for which he had no name. He did not think that any were as large as the seagoing ships his father had described to him, but he saw some larger than anything he had ever expected to see on a river.

Not far from where he stood, a rickety wharf thrust into the lazy, inshore current. Tied to it was a boat about ten paces long, with a stumpy mast and locks for six long oars. Though not large, it was fully decked and bore a small cabin in its center. Men lounged on its deck and several boys fished from the wharf with long poles. From the base of the wharf a muddy path wound over the earthwork, ending at a cluster of shabby buildings that looked like warehouses.

Having looked enough for the moment, Kairn descended the earthen bank and returned to the pen, where he unsaddled his cabo and turned it loose in the pen. It went to a pile of hay and began to eat, aloof from the squalid humpers sharing the accommodations.

He carried his saddle, his weapons and bags into the inn, where the owner showed him to a small room that seemed to be reasonably clean. He left his belongings there and returned to the common room.

"It's early for ale or wine," the innkeeper said, "but I have both."

Kairn shook his head. "No, but I am famished. What do you have?"

"My boy has not returned yet from the butcher's, but I have some fine fish."

"Fresh?"

"Caught not an hour ago and brought in still flopping. Is that fresh enough?"

Kairn took a seat and a few minutes later a serving girl set a platter of grilled fish before him. Kairn did not think highly of fish as food, but decided that this would hold him until he could set into some real fare. The rest of the meal was the usual for establishments of this sort: bread, fruit, cheese and a bowl of assorted nuts. Everything was fresh, to his great relief. He had spent too much time on preserved travel rations, and some people's methods of preserving food could be dangerous to strangers not used to it.

The serving girl stood shyly by his table as he ate and studied him through lowered lashes. Her brown hair formed a fringe that ended just above her eyebrows, the rest plaited into a score of thin braids with colored shells fastened to their ends. She appeared to be a little younger than he, perhaps about sixteen. Her skin was a pale shade of brown, her eyes darker brown. Everything and everyone in this village seemed to be brown, as if all had taken on the hue of the great river that flowed so near.

"Can I get you anything else, sir?" she asked.

"Just some information. First, what shall I call you?"

"My name is Yellow Bird."

"A pretty name." In his homeland and other places he had visited, names were just sounds. In these southeastern lands, though, people delighted in fanciful names. Some were taken from nature, others from myth, and yet others from no discernible source.

"What would you know?"

"For one thing, what is that great earthwork that lines the river?" He dislodged a sharp fish bone from between his teeth and looked at it with distaste.

"We call it the levee. It keeps the river out when the water rises."

The thought of that great river actually rising, becoming even more formidable, was unsettling. "How high does it rise?"

"In some years, it will come within a foot of the top of the levee. Then you can't see the far shore at all. It's as if the whole world had turned to water."

"You mean the whole town is below the level of the river?"

"Oh, certainly," she said. Despite her solemnity, he was sure that she exaggerated.

"I saw boats and rafts on the river. What sort of people work on the water? What do they carry or trade?"

"Most that you see are local. They fish or they ferry people and goods across the river, or back and forth to the nearest towns. Others carry cargo the length of the river. The southbound craft carry timber and grain and sometimes livestock. Those that come up from the south bear things like cloth and glass and wine. The rivermen are a rough lot, but there are family boats as well. Those people spend their whole lives on the river."

"Living on water. That is strange." He wondered whether this was another exaggeration.

"People say that your countrymen live all their lives on their cabos, that you even make love on them and your women give birth in the saddle."

He pondered this for a moment. "Making love that way is difficult," he said, "and as far as I know, giving birth while riding is impossible. Tales grow distorted with distance. It is true that we are fond of riding and dislike walking."

"It is also said that you are great warriors."

"We are the best warriors in the world," he said, with perfect sincerity. It did not bother him that so many other people made the same claim. They were simply wrong.

"Yellow Bird!" called the innkeeper. "Go help in the kitchen. The meat has arrived and you are not to flirt with the guests."

The girl grimaced, then smiled at Kairn. "If you want to know about the rivermen, they will begin arriving in the afternoon. This is their favorite gathering place in Muddy Bottom."

"Then I have come to the right place." He needed rest and soon he would need transportation, but just now he stood in greatest need of information. Asking people who traveled constantly upon the river might save him much time. Since he had lost his father's trail more than a month ago, he had been wandering from one settlement to the next, turning up nothing.

His mother had sent him in desperation, since his older brother was too exhausted by his recent adventures to undertake the task. She had wanted him to take along a strong escort, but he had rejected that as impractical. He had many borders to cross, and officials would ignore a lone rider where they might hold up a large, armed party for days while the diplomatic niceties were sorted out. When his brother had ridden in, half-dead and laden with the most terrible news possible, his mother had taken him aside.

"You must find your father and bring him home," she said, her face livid with fury and apprehension. "Tell him that he has no business wandering off to foreign lands when his people need him! It may well be his neglect that has brought this upon us."

"Now, Mother," he had said, "you know as well as I that no one, least of all his younger son, tells Father what to do."

"Just tell him what your brother has just told us. Believe me, he will come running." She stood, fuming, then said, "He has never taken his duties seriously enough. He acts as if he were still a young adventurer, free to go off whenever he likes, seeking who knows what. And in recent years he has grown even more erratic. This time he has gone off on a trade mission without even a warrior escort. Find him and bring him back, if you have to tie him across your saddle!"

Afterward, he had spoken with his brother. Ansa was thin and haggard from his long, solitary ride, but his voice was strong and his privations had not robbed him of his humor.

"Tell the old man that the people will need their leader, and now is his opportunity for a final showdown with his loving foster brother. Tell him that Larissa is even more dangerous, being the more intelligent of the two. I think Father knows that. And tell him that she is obsessed with restoring her youth. I think that may be important. I'm not sure what he knows about the Canyoners, he never spoke much about them, but they are truly . . . different."

Kairn sat on the pallet where his brother lay nursing a bowl of broth. "The stories of their magic are true?"

"Partly, I think. I saw things there that I still can't understand. They could be valuable allies or terrible enemies."

"Mother wasn't pleased to hear about this Canyon woman."

Ansa grinned crookedly. "I know. That's too bad. She'd rather we married women of our own people, but a man's heart is his own. Mine is, at any rate. Wait until you see her. She makes our women here look like second-rate cabos."

"Even a second-rate cabo is a beautiful creature," Kairn protested.

Ansa punched his shoulder. "Don't be so literal, little brother. Now, let's talk seriously. This will be your first solo venture as a warrior."

"And it's daunting, I won't deny that." Ansa had always been the more adventurous and daring of the two, headstrong and independent. It gave Kairn a secret thrill of pride to know that he would be venturing on a quest equal to his older brother's.

"Be prideful and arrogant," Ansa advised. "Humility gets you nothing among foreigners. You are a warrior of King Hael, and be sure that everyone knows it. We have a reputation throughout the world now, and it will ensure that you are respected. Let them once show you contempt, especially officials, and you will cease to exist for them. You will be just an alien savage. People who live in cities think we are uncultured, and that is annoying. But most of all they fear us, and that is far more important. Play up the importance of your birth and treat the highest nobles as your equals at best, but leave some doubt there, as if they are actually your inferiors."

Kairn smiled. "It sounds as if you got snubbed a few times."

"It is hard," Ansa admitted, "to be a king's son and unable to brag about it. But see that you keep that secret, too. When foreign kings get a prince in their clutches, the first thing they think is 'hostage!'."

"But we would be worthless as hostages," Kairn protested.

"They won't know that. Foreigners think we must have a royal family like their own, with succession through birth. If they ask your lineage, say you are the son of an important chief, a high member of Father's council. Your bearing and the excellence of your weapons should convince them."

"I may not get very far," Kairn said. "I could meet Father on his way back. Even if I cross borders, he should be easy to find. Father is not like ordinary men."

Ansa leaned back onto his pallet and studied the smoke-stained beams overhead. "Don't count on it. He's up to some game, sending his escort back without explanation. If he doesn't want to be found, he won't be. I just cannot imagine him staying away so long when he knows Gasam is expanding his power."

"Those two," Kairn said, "Gasam and Larissa. Are they as evil as he has said?"

Ansa closed his eyes. "They are worse than I could ever have imagined. Mother always says that he exaggerates when he talks about them, but now I know it is the truth. She cannot imagine anyone worse than that Amsi chief Father killed to win her."

"Impaba," Kairn supplied.

"Yes, Impaba. He was bad, but he was nothing, less than nothing, compared to Gasam, and Larissa is worse. It isn't just that they are evil, but that their capacity for further evil is bottomless. It's difficult to explain, but you will know what I mean if you ever see them. I hope you don't."

"And now they have our greatest secret," Kairn said, almost shuddering at the thought of delivering this piece of news.

Ansa gripped his wrist strongly. "I wish I could go with you, little brother, but I'd collapse before we went a hundred miles. But you can do it. You have the best blood in the world, the blood of Hael and Deena, the king and queen of the plains and the hill country! Find him, Kairn! Find him and bring him back!"

And so he had ridden forth with nothing but his cabo, his weapons, his clothing and this terrible knowledge. His first nights alone had been unsettling. All his life, he had been among tribesmen. His people traveled widely, but always in groups. To be alone was the ultimate horror to them. When he left his father's domains it was even worse. But he knew Ansa had done this, and the thought gave him courage.

Gradually, he had gained confidence. He had faced down would-be robbers more than once. They had studied this fierce-faced young rider, bristling with weapons, and had decided to seek picking elsewhere. He had found that, as Ansa had predicted, an arrogant assumption of superiority almost always secured cooperation from everyone he encountered. It was not natural with him, but he was quickly growing comfortable with his new manner.

So now he sat in a town called Muddy Bottom, his father's trail gone cold, and before him a river so vast that it numbed his imagination. Even so, it excited and drew him as few things had in his short life. He wanted to know more about it.

His breakfast finished, Kairn went outside to assure himself that all was well with his cabo. The beast stood headdown over the pile of fodder it had been munching, asleep. Satisfied with the animal's condition, he wandered through the town for a while, but the place seemed to be as dull as his first impression had suggested.

He climbed up the levee and was gratified to see that the late-morning sun had burned away the last remnants of fog, revealing the great river in glorious sunlight. From its pouch at his belt he took one of his most prized possessions: a telescope. It was a finely crafted instrument of wood, brass and glass, its lenses ground by the matchless craftsmen of Neva.

He extended the telescope and studied the craft on the river at leisure. The smallest craft were the most numerous: canoes of skin and bark, dugouts, and tiny rafts, each carrying one to three people. After these, there were larger boats such as the one he had seen tied to the wharf, some with as many as a dozen men on their decks. Some of these bore a mixed crew of men, women and children, and he assumed these were the family boats Yellow Bird had spoken of.

Once he saw a huge timber raft, easily a hundred paces long. He tried to calculate how many logs it must contain, but he quickly exhausted his mathematical talent, since the logs were of many sizes and were not lashed together in neat, even rows as were those of the smaller rafts.

Most fascinating of all were the really large boats he saw toiling their way upstream or drifting lazily downstream. Those going upstream were rowed by crowds of shavenheaded men standing at the long oars which were ranged fifteen or sometimes even twenty to a side. They also had sails to aid in propulsion when the wind was right, but these hung slack in the still air. Those bound downstream rode low in the water, as if they were heavy-laden, but with no more than a dozen men on their decks. He wondered where the rowers went when the boats turned around.

Each of these larger boats was twenty to fifty paces long, with a veritable house standing amidships, some of them two-storied. They were painted in bright colors and fancifully decorated, many with animal horns and antlers. One had a huge, long-beaked bird tethered to its roof, presumably some sort of pet or mascot. Others had painted statues at bow and stern. He felt a powerful urge to know what it was like to live on such craft, on such a river.

He felt a hollowness in his stomach when he thought of stepping onto a wooden construction, nothing below it but water. Nevertheless, it was a fascinating idea, to cast loose from the bonds of land and allow a river to carry him where it would.

He spent much of the day atop the levee, sitting upon its grassy crest, studying the river and its traffic with telescope and unaided eye. Almost as fascinating as the human activities was the river's abundant wildlife. He was accustomed to the vast herds of his native plains, herds that could stretch for miles and raised clouds of dust that were visible for hours before a rider came in sight of the beasts themselves. The life of the river was different, but just as impressive in its way.

Once a flock of thousands of birds flew in and came to rest on the water. They had red feathers and broad, flat beaks and they paddled about on webbed feet, occasionally diving below the water as they fed. They continued to feed for an hour or more and then, as if on a signal, they all took to the air in a thunderous flapping of massed wings, leaving only a few scarlet feathers on the water to mark their passing. Within minutes those, too, were gone. Something like a monstrous snake appeared close inshore. It raised a wedge-shaped head and blew spray from round nostrils set atop its snout, then it scanned its surroundings with globelike black eyes. Apparently it saw nothing of interest, for it soon dove beneath the surface, its fin-crested back seeming to arch and plunge forever.

A great white bird, its body almost as large as his cabo, swooped low on wings that must have spanned ten paces from tip to tip. Its neck snaked out and its long, narrow beak snapped below the water, emerging with a large fish wriggling in its grasp. It flapped away regally, and Kairn wondered what sort of tree could possibly support the nest of a bird that large.

In the late afternoon, a small herd of strange beasts came wading along the shallows nearest the riverbank. At first he had only an impression of bulky, wet, brown backs and lumpy heads. The things waddled ashore and he was moved to laugh at their ungainly round bodies, short, stumpy legs and comically wide heads. Thick tusks curved downward from their lower jaws and with these they rooted in the growth of the riverbank, tearing up vegetation and devouring it with ecstatic grunts, wiggling their small, round ears and blinking their long eyelashes. Their forelegs bore long, sharp claws and he sensed that these could be formidable creatures despite their laughable aspect.

He walked for a mile or more along the top of the levee, upstream. Soon he was beyond the town and in a thickly forested area. Inshore, the trees grew to within twenty paces of the levee. He guessed that the river dwellers kept the vegetation cut back lest the burrowing roots of the trees destroy the levee. On the other side of the levee, a spit of land, similarly forested, thrust into the river. He descended the bank and went out onto the spit, gripping his spear lest there be unfriendly inhabitants.

He heard a commotion in the branches overhead and looked up. Little creatures he recognized as man-of-the-trees clustered along the branches, looking down and scolding him. Unlike those described to him by well-traveled tribesmen, these had long, glossy pelts of gray, black and red fur. Their long tails, tipped with puffs of white fur, twitched rhythmically as they hung below the branches. Their almost hairless faces were miniature caricatures of human visages, with bright button eyes and twitching noses. Other small animals fled into the underbrush at his approach.

Flowering vines climbed the trees and the air buzzed with insect life. He identified at least three different plants with leaves designed to trap insects. One captured them with sticky, sweet-smelling pads, another had tubular leaves filled with water containing a poison that stunned the insects so that they could be digested. The third and most startling had leaves with toothed jaws that snapped close-flying insects out of the air. Winged lizards preyed on the insects as well.

It was all quite alien to Kairn. Over everything hung the dense smell of the river, so that he was never unconscious of its nearness. He reached the river and saw a crowd of fuzzy black lumps floating on the surface of an inshore pool overhung by drooping trees. At his approach they burst into the air amid a flapping of leathery wings. Swimming bats! He had never heard of such a thing. Was there no end to the strangeness of this place?

He began to feel uncomfortable on the landspit with its dense vegetation, its swarming life, its surrounding river. He missed the quiet of his native plains, the solitude of his land's hills, where the trees grew a reasonable distance apart and its wildlife was not greater than a man could keep his eyes on.

He turned and hastened back to the levee, then to the village. By now, he thought, the rivermen should be congregating in the tavern. Behind him, the forest buzzed and clicked with its multitudinous life.

TWO

Faces turned toward the entrance when he walked into the common room of the inn. Most of the men who studied him wore tunics or vests of coarse cloth and knee-length trousers. Long knives hung in decorated sheaths from belts studded with bronze or silver. Some wore boots or sandals but most were barefoot. Remembering Ansa's advice, he scanned the room arrogantly, and when his eyes met another man's, his gaze did not drop until the other looked away.

He took a seat at a small table and Yellow Bird hurried over to him. He ordered ale to go with his dinner and she brought a wooden tankard of the dark foaming drink. It was bitter but bracing, and he drained half of it before the girl returned with a platter of sizzling meaty ribs.

"Real food at last!" he said with satisfaction, tearing a rib loose from the rack and setting his teeth to it. He worked his way steadily through the rack until nothing remained but a pile of white bones. He sat back, replete, and pared a yellow-skinned fruit with his knife.

He wanted to talk to some of these rivermen, but he was not sure how to start a conversation. He feared that if he sought them out he would lose dignity in their eyes. It was a trifling problem, but he could think of no good way to resolve it. He beckoned to Yellow Bird and she came to his table.

"Yes, my lord?" The respect seemed overdone but he did not try to correct her.

"Girl, I wish to talk to some of these men concerning travel on the river. How would I go about it?"

She shrugged. "Give any of them a mug of ale and they will talk as long as you keep it filled. Here, I'll take care of it." She went to a table and bent over it, talking while one of the men stroked her bottom. She slapped the hand away and a man stood and came to Kairn's table.

"You need to learn summat of the river, sir?" The man's dialect was even thicker than the townsmen's. His brown hair and beard were abundant and curly. At Kairn's gesture he sat. At another gesture, Yellow Bird brought a tankard of ale and set it before the riverman. Kairn saw that his skin was deeply burned and weathered, his hands large, with cracked, blackened nails. His clothing was strictly utilitarian, but he had a gold bracelet and a ring of the same metal in his ear. His was a scarred, brawler's face but his eyes were a mild, clear blue.

"I am looking for a countryman of mine, a kinsman who is needed at home. Have you encountered any such?"

The man shook his head. "You plainsmen are the rarest sort of foreigners, and we see few. I remember a trading party that came through the northern prefectures three years ago. They were trading steel, and I got a good knife for ferrying them and their animals across the river." He tapped the weapon at his belt. Its handle was of bone, riveted with copper.

"The man I seek will be traveling alone, and he would have arrived here a few months ago."

"I haven't seen him, but it's a big river and a man can travel far in a few months. Where are you bound?"

He had not yet decided that himself. He asked himself

where Hael would be most likely to go, on his own in a strange land on a mission of . . . what? Spying?

"What large cities lie along the river?" Kairn asked.

"Three really large ones," the man said, "all of them south of here. Redrock lies where another river joins the great river. That is about ten easy days' travel south of here. Another ten days beyond that is Firetown, where they make the ceramics. Where the river joins the sea is Delta."

None of these sounded very promising. "Which of these is the capital city of this land?"

"None of them. The land is ruled from Crag. It's more a fort than a city. It's power they deal in there, not commerce."

This sounded more like it. "Where is Crag located?"

"A few days rowing up the Tensa. That's the river that comes in at Redrock. It's easy rowing. The river is wide but shallow and the current is slow most of the year. It flows through a flat plain so there are some sandbars, but few rocks or snags."

Kairn had no idea why the terrain should determine the nature of the river. He assumed that these were mysteries of the riverman's trade. The riverman gave his mug a meaningful look and Kairn gestured for Yellow Bird to come over and refill it.

"Is Crag where the Assembly of Great Men meets?"

The riverman downed half of his ale and set the mug back on the table. "Most of the time. They have other meeting places, but Crag is the principal one."

"Does their Speaker have his palace there?"

The riverman shrugged. "He must live somewhere, but the Assembly is made up mainly of great landowners, and they all have splendid houses on their estates."

"You say most are landowners. Does that mean some are not? I know that in some lands the priests are rich and powerful."

"There are no priests of any power here in Mezpa. We are a sensible people. No, the other great men are mainly manufacturers. They grew rich making glass and ceramics and firepowder."

Kairn sensed something important here, but he did not wish to press it lest he be suspected of spying. "How odd. I never heard of such an arrangement. Tell me: Today I saw a number of great boats on the river. Some were rowed upstream by large numbers of men. Others came downstream with small crews but low in the water, carrying heavy cargo. What cargo did they carry upstream? And how do the rowers return?"

"You're observant for a drylander. Those were Delta trade boats. The rowers *were* the cargo, slaves captured in war or raised in the Delta slave pens. They power the boats upstream, where they're traded to the plantations for produce or to the mines for minerals. Once loaded, they float back downstream on the current. Then they only need crews sufficient to steer and pole away from the shallows. Efficient, no?"

"Very sensible. What sort of land is the Delta?"

"Rich," said the riverman, succinctly. "The black soil is the most productive in all Mezpa: rice, sugar, other things. The city of Delta is the country's greatest seaport. That's why it's the center of the slave trade. The slavers bring their wares there for sale. There are whole plantations devoted to raising cheap slave-fodder for the Delta slave pens."

"What sort of riverman are you?" Kairn asked.

"I'm a rafter," the man said proudly. "My name is Bat. I'm called that because I see well in the dark. I can spot a snag through heavy fog better than anyone else."

"Why are you here and where are you bound?" He signaled for another round of ale.

"We're here for a few days, until our cargo is loaded. We're bound south. That's the only direction rafts go, south."

"What sort of cargo? How far south?"

"Here at Muddy Bottom they grow mostly redroot and blueroot; dyestuffs that fetch a decent price downriver. As for how far, that depends on a number of things. We deliver the cargo to the dyeworks at Cave Ridge—that's the center of the weaving trade—and maybe we pick up another cargo there. Maybe not. Anyway, somewhere downriver someone will offer to buy our raft for the timber. If the price is right, we sell it, then we hitch back upstream on a slaveboat or a barge. When we get back up to the timber country, we put together another raft and start over again.''

"Since I came to river country," Kairn said, "I've seen nothing but trees. I am surprised that there is a market for timber."

"There are long stretches of river where timber is scarce," Bat told him. "Especially around the older towns. And different sorts of timber are not all good for the same things. And you can't move sizable logs by road. If you need a roof-beam, and a perfect tree for it grows ten miles inland, that tree might as well be growing on the moon. But stand by the river and another such log will soon come floating by as part of a raft, still cheap after floating a thousand miles.''

Kairn was fascinated by this account from a man who knew his business well. Now he came to the meat of the matter.

"I have a desire to visit Crag. If I were to be ferried across the river and travel there overland, how long would it take me to reach the place?"

"Months. The roads are little better than mud tracks until you are near the capital. The land is full of hills and ridges, and the land is cut up with many streams and small rivers. Bridges are always chancy and the streams will be swelling soon.''

"But it is only a few days' journey by river?"

"The number of days is uncertain, naturally, but it would be a far quicker way to travel."

"Like all of my people, I ride a cabo."

"I saw the beast outside. A beautiful thing, although you will never catch me climbing up on one."

"If I were to take passage on your raft, could you carry my cabo as well?"

Bat nodded. "We carry livestock sometimes. We'd have to construct a pen, then floor it with brush topped with dirt so the animal won't step between the logs and break a leg. That will cost extra, you understand. And caring for the beast and cleaning up after it will be your responsibility."

"Understood."

Bat studied him. "If you plan to hire somebody to care for the cabo, his passage will be extra."

"I'll see to it myself," Kairn said.

"I just thought—you act like some sort of nobleman—"

"In my land," Kairn explained, "everything having to do with cabos is proper work for the highest-born. You've spoken of the business of the river. What of its dangers?"

Bat grinned. "Where do you want me to start? The river itself kills many each year. High water can catch you unawares. When there's snags—"

"You've used the word before. What are they?"

"Dead trees that've got buried in the mud. They can sit there just below the surface, waiting to catch you. Usually you just get hung up, but catch one too fast in a swift current and they can overturn a raft. They're more dangerous to boats and rip their bottoms out. There's collisions in the dark with other craft, too, and no telling what you might run into in a heavy fog."

"Today I saw some animals in the river as big as anything I've ever seen on land. Are they dangerous?"

"There's things in the river you want nothing to do with," Bat affirmed. "The great river snakes never bother a raft or boat, but they'll come for you if you fall in the water. Down near the Delta there's fangfish that school up in the thousands and they're mad with hunger most of the time. They'll strip a big humper to bare bones in minutes."

Kairn described the fat, wading animals he had seen.

"Those are riverwumps. Mostly they don't bother you, but if you plow into a herd of them unexpectedly, they'll turn vicious. And the males get to fighting each other at mating time, and then you want to avoid them. They come ashore to graze at night, so you needn't worry about them after dark."

"What about human dangers?"

"Sometimes the River Patrol can get it into their heads that you're smuggling and then you can have problems. And there are river pirates. They'll come down on a craft and kill everyone on board, make away with craft and cargo both. Some stretches of river are thick with them."

"This River Patrol," Kairn said, "do they do nothing about the pirates?"

Bat made a gesture new to Kairn but eloquently contemptuous. "They stick mostly to the lower river. They're more interested in collecting tariffs than in keeping the river safe."

This seemed strange to Kairn. Once, the plains had swarmed with outlaws of all the tribes, but when his father had come to power, his first order of business was to rid his kingdom of them. Patrols of picked warriors scoured the vast grasslands endlessly to prevent any resurgence. Hael said that a king who did not protect his people from the predations of lawless men did not deserve the kingship and should be deposed or killed by his own subjects. Apparently, the Assembly of Great Men and their Speaker did not feel that way.

"Do you travel well armed, then?"

"If you would live, you don't travel unarmed on the river." He thought a moment. "Or anywhere else, for that matter."

"That's wisest," Kairn agreed. They discussed price for a while. He had come well supplied with money, but knew better than to make a show of it. He haggled over the rate for the cabo pen and said that he would arrange for the fodder they would carry. Bat said that they would set off in three or four days, perhaps five. That suited Kairn. Despite the urgency of his mission, he wanted to put some flesh on the animal's lean ribs before subjecting it to the rigors of an alien environment.

As the evening wore on and the ale flowed freely, the rivermen's boasts grew louder, and they began to challenge one another to contests of strength and skill. There was much arm wrestling and head-butting, and then they went outside to wrestle in the mud. By the light of torches Kairn watched their strugglings and saw that they prized strength over skill. He had been taught wrestling as an art form and this was crude by comparison.

Men frequently lost their tempers and struck with their fists or feet, occasionally seeking to chew ears and noses from their opponents' heads. Twice, men drew knives, inflicting cuts that were bloody but not serious. Kairn noted that the knives were of bronze, with thin steel edges set into the softer metal. His father had been trading steel here in large quantities. He wondered where it was going, if it was still so rare on this stretch of river. Surely, men who had to defend themselves from pirates as a daily task would make sure to provide themselves with the best weapons they could procure.

In time the torches were extinguished and the rivermen wandered off to their rafts and boats or else slept on the ground where they threw themselves in a stupor. Kairn sought his own pallet and lay back, well satisfied with an eventful day. His spine tingled at the thought of setting out upon the river, but he was excited by the prospect. This was something none of his fellow tribesmen could boast of. He would have some good stories when he got back home. *If* he got back home.

The next day, he walked along the levee until he came to the place where Bat's raft was tied. A small island paralleled the riverbank, and the craft was tied up in the still water between island and bank. A small, rickety wharf reached from the land to the side of the raft.

The raft itself was more than thirty paces long, made of huge rough-barked logs. Part of it was decked with rough-hewn planks. On this part was stacked the growing cargo: two piles of what looked like dried brown snakes. More of this substance arrived throughout the day, carried on the backs of men or humpers. On closer inspection, he saw that these were fibrous roots. Those that oozed red sap went into one pile, blue-oozing ones into the other.

Trying to conceal his nervousness, Kairn went out along the swaying wharf and stepped onto the raft. He was surprised at its solidity in the midst of the fluid medium. It was almost like stepping onto an island. As men moved around on it, there was no sense of movement from it. He wondered if it might be resting on the muddy bottom.

As he watched, some of the men constructed a livestock

pen, going ashore to cut limber saplings which they wedged between the logs to the rear of the decked area. These they bent over into a series of loops, among which they wove vines and thin branches to form a light but sturdy fence. They tossed a heavy layer of brush into the pen and trampled it down, then threw basketfuls of earth atop the brush. In an amazingly short time, they had constructed a serviceable pen. Getting his cabo into it, Kairn thought, might prove a different matter entirely.

While the raft lay at rest in its quiet water, he continued to question travelers about his father, but with no luck. It was as if he had disappeared into the earth itself.

The morning of their departure, he led his cabo down to the little wharf. The animal was happy to leave the pen, where it had disliked the company of the humpers. It tossed its fine head, its four gilded horns flashing in the early sunlight. When he led it to the wharf it balked, not liking the look of the flimsy structure. But it was an obedient animal, and it followed him without undue fuss.

From the end of the wharf it leapt readily onto the raft, apparently thinking that it was solid ground. Kairn led it to the pen and closed a section of the fence behind it. The animal snorted, as if indignant that it was merely changing one pen for another. But at least it had this one to itself, and it soon settled down to munching fodder contentedly.

The rivermen watched suspiciously as Kairn brought his personal belongings aboard. His saddle and bags were hardly exotic, but his longsword and steel-tipped spear were unusual. Oddest of all to them was his great, recurved, compound bow, made of wood, horn and sinew bonded together. It was cased with its arrows, their bright-feathered ends protruding from the top of the decorated case.

There were bows among the rivermen's effects: crude weapons made from a single billet of tough wood. A glance told Kairn that his own bow had three times the range of these. Otherwise, the rivermen were armed with their knives and an assortment of small axes, stone-headed maces and short spears with bronze points. In the tent that was their common quarters were some shields of wicker and hide. It was crude armament, but Kairn presumed that the river pirates had nothing better.

When all was secure, they cast off. When the mooring lines were released and gathered onto the raft, Kairn expected some sort of movement to commence, but there was none. He watched with interest as the men took long poles and began to push them against the river bottom, leaning their shoulders into the poles and pushing with their feet. So slowly that at first he was not certain that the ponderous raft was moving at all, it began to inch its way along the still water between the island and the riverbank. As it got under way, the men leaned into their poles and began to walk along the length of the raft. Kairn found it a surpassingly strange sight, as the men stood in one place and literally walked the raft out from under them. When they came to the end of the raft, they picked up their poles, ran to the front, and began again.

A few minutes of this toil pushed the raft from the shelter of the island and into the slow, inshore current. Soon the poles would no longer touch bottom and the men stacked them near the decked area. Now they took long oars and set them into crude tholes made from forked limbs. The sweeps were merely poles fifteen feet long with broad planks lashed to their ends. With the oars set in their tholes, two or three men stood at each and rowed the raft into a swifter current a hundred paces offshore. A shorter, broader oar was set into a thole at the rear of the raft and used for steering. As soon as the raft was satisfactorily positioned, all the oars except the one used for steering were shipped and the sweating rivermen went to relax on the deck.

Kairn could see that the crudity of everything on the raft had a reason. The raft was on a one-way trip and everything on it was disposable. Here was none of the pride and fine craftsmanship he had seen on the riverboats, small and large. Soon fishing lines went out and a fire was kindled in a box of earth and stones.

He went to the pen to see how his cabo was taking this new experience. It snorted and walked to him and he stroked its head. It seemed completely unaware that it was afloat on a huge river. Kairn was relieved, but a bit disappointed. He had always thought cabos were more intelligent than that.

For a while he walked about on the raft, getting used to his new environment. It did not take long to exhaust the possibilities of a raft, he found. The river itself was as fascinating as ever, though. Late in the morning a sleek, black animal surfaced near the raft and swam alongside it for a while. It looked almost like a land animal, but it had broad paddles instead of legs. It was larger than his cabo, but had no visible teeth or other natural weapons. From a few feet away it studied Kairn with mild brown eyes while he studied it back.

"What is it?" he asked the steersman, a buck-toothed man whose hair was cropped close and dyed blue.

"A fresh-water sleen. The river's full of them. They're harmless and not much good to eat. Hides make good leather. The saltwater breed's twice as big."

Rafting, he found, was the most leisurely of all ways to travel. It was a good way to see the river, but lacking in excitement. He knew that his father would enjoy the tranquility. Besides being king and warrior, his father was a mystic who liked to meditate. Meditation was not greatly to Kairn's taste, so he took the opportunity to see how the rivermen passed the time.

Some practiced at crafts such as wood carving or leather work, but most just sat or lay about during the long, uneventful stretches. They were not totally inert, but seemed to be waiting, ready to spring to action at need. Their manner reminded him of the way herdsmen could remain still for hours, always aware of their surroundings, of the number, position and condition of their livestock.

He tried to engage some of them in conversation but the men, so frenetic and loud ashore, were taciturn and monosyllabic on the river, as if they begrudged the very energy required for speech. They were not snubbing him, for they did not even speak much among themselves.

Their interest was piqued when he took out his telescope and unfolded it. Bat asked if he could try it and Kairn handed it over. The man tried it and examined it for a long time before handing it back.

"A fine instrument," the riverman said. "Much better than the Mezpan lensmakers produce. Where was it made?"

"It comes from Neva. They have master glassworkers there. They've been trading their wares in my land as long as King Hael has reigned."

The riverman shook his head in wonderment. "Neva. It's a name out of stories. I've never met a man who's been there, and I think this is the first thing I've ever seen from that land. Have you been there?"

"No, but I have talked to men who have been there. We've sent them warriors to help in their wars."

"You are a far-traveled people," Bat commented.

The levee, Kairn discovered, was not continuous. In some stretches, hills came right to the river, often forming high bluffs, often pierced with the mouths of caves. Some of these were inhabited, for he saw the smoke of cooking fires rising into the still air. The levee resumed where the land dipped low.

He tried to calculate the time and toil that must have been expended in raising the levee, but the task defeated his imagination. He assumed that it must have been done in a richer, more populous, better organized time. He saw stretches where the levee had been neglected, and the signs of devastating flood were plain, where water had flowed unimpeded through the breached earthwork and left debris high in the branches of the trees.

"Look there," said Bat, pointing to one such gap in the levee. Kairn trained his telescope on the spot and gasped. A large riverboat rested atop some high trees, their upper branches piercing its hull.

"A flood five years ago did that," Bat explained. "The river can kill you fast if you let it."

Kairn nodded wordlessly.

* * *

The first night, the raft tied up at an island. As the craft drifted in the slow, shallow water near the island one man jumped into the water and waded ashore with a stern line which he made fast to a stout tree trunk. Others lowered the sweeps into the water, holding them there. Between the rope and the oars the massive raft lost way and came to a halt. At the end of the rope, it began to swing closer to the island and when it grounded in the shallows, other men went ashore and made bow lines fast to another tree. Once the raft was secured, the men picked up their weapons and went ashore.

"Can I take my cabo ashore and give him some exercise?" Kairn asked.

Bat shook his head. "We'll sweep the island first. Pirates sometimes hide on the islands."

"I'll come with you," Kairn said. He did not think his bow or lance would be of much use in the dense growth of the island, but he had his sword and knife.

"If you wish," Bat said. The riverman had a short axe of bronze with a steel edge. He picked up a shield and went ashore.

The sweep was conducted quickly and efficiently. They began at the upstream end of the island, where they were tied up. Here the island tapered to a wedge-shaped point and the men lined up almost shoulder-to-shoulder. As they began walking toward the other end they began to spread, but never got very far apart. The island was covered with brush and trees, their upper branches littered with flood debris. The land rose gently to a central ridge.

As they made their slow traverse of the island, small animals fled from before their feet. Kairn wondered how these managed to survive when the waters rose. Either they could swim, he decided, or else they could climb into the highest branches of the trees.

They discovered no other human inhabitants on the island and returned to the raft to prepare their evening meal. While there was still light, Kairn took his cabo from its pen and walked it around the island. The beast seemed to be grateful for the diversion.

When they returned he led the cabo back onto the raft and it did not object. He fastened the pen behind it and joined the rivermen at their fire, where they shared their dinner with him. It was the plainest sort of food, but he was used to far worse.

"Do you usually spend the nights on islands?" he asked.

Bat nodded. "When we're not staying at a town. It's easier to know who and what's near you on an island. On a stretch of unpopulated riverbank, you never know what might be lurking near, especially where there are caves in the bluffs above the river. Now this cargo we're carrying," he gestured toward the heaps of roots aboard the raft, "isn't very tempting. Not like slaves or wine or manufactured goods. Those mostly come upriver anyway. But it pays to be careful. Men who're desperate, who've come out second best in a fight with the local authorities or rival gangs, can be desperate. Then they'll attack a crew and slit throats for a few bags of provisions."

"We've passed a number of towns today," Kairn said. "Can't they band together to clean out the robbers?"

"They should," Bat admitted. "But the government doesn't like to see people taking the law into their own hands, even this far from the centers of authority."

"I'd never obey a government that was so lax in its duties," Kairn said. "That seems a very poor-spirited sort of behavior."

"True," Bat said. "That's why you only find people of spirit working on the river."

The next day passed uneventfully. When other craft passed near, they traded upriver and downriver news without stopping. The leisurely pace of river travel permitted fairly lengthy communication this way. The big rowed boats did not seem to participate in this camaraderie, and Kairn asked why.

"Too lordly," Bat grunted. "They're owned by big companies. The crews think they're too good for the likes of us common rivermen."

"So even on the river there are lords and underlings?"

"They only think so," Bat snorted.

* * *

For three more days they rafted thus, uneventfully. On the evening of the fourth day, they tied up in the slow water on the southern side of a mudbank. They were on a stretch of river that offered no islands for many miles, and Bat chose the east bank as the most favorable spot.

"It's not much of a choice," he elucidated as they moved ashore. "The other bank's too marshy for camping. There's no dry wood and the insects will carry you off, they're so thick."

Kairn scanned the bluffs that rose a few hundred yards inland. He saw no fires and smelled no smoke, but he knew that predators would not advertise their presence.

"I think I'll leave my cabo aboard the raft tonight," he said. "A night in the pen will do it no harm."

Bat nodded. "That may be wise. Keep your weapons handy."

"I always do."

The men were subdued at their evening meal and they paid more attention than usual to the scrubby woods around them. As soon as the meal was over they turned into their bedrolls with their hands on their weapons and fell into a nervous, fitful sleep.

Kairn had first watch. He went onto the raft and brushed his cabo, speaking to it in low tones. The beast snorted and groaned uneasily, tossing its four-horned head in an unusual display of nerves. Kairn attributed this to its disappointment at not being given its evening exercise. On a sudden impulse, Kairn stacked his saddle and bags within the pen, then added his bows and arrows. They would be all but useless in the dark, and his lance would not be much more use.

When the stars told him that his time was up, Kairn woke his relief and waited until the man was fully awake before turning in himself. He thought of going onto the raft to sleep, but he did not want to appear timid before these men, so he settled for a place near the low-burning fire. With a hand on his sword hilt, he fell into a restless slumber.

He did not know what woke him. He knew instantly that

two hours had passed since he had gone to sleep. Some change in the air, some difference in the sounds of the night had roused him. There was a faint, smoky glow from the embers of the fire. Most of the men were snoring regularly.

Without raising his head, Kairn slowly turned it to scan the campsite. He saw no one up and moving, and he could spot no sentry. The man might have gone a few paces into the woods to answer a call of nature, but no sound confirmed this. Then he did hear something: a faint rustling from several points around the camp. Simultaneously, his nose detected a familiar scent—the smell of fresh-spilled blood. His sword hissed from its sheath as he sprang to his feet.

"Wake up!" he bellowed. "Bandits!"

The rivermen scrambled to their feet, shouting and striking out blindly. "Backs to the fire!" Bat shouted. "Where's the sentry?"

"Dead!" Kairn yelled, the word almost drowned out by the shrieks of the attackers. He had no way of guessing their numbers, for they came from all directions save that of the river, whooping and capering to add to the confusion. There were sounds of strugglings and the thumps of blows striking home.

A vague shape bore in on Kairn, eyes and teeth reflecting the coals of the fire. He could not see the man's weapon but he struck a few inches below the eyes and felt his blade bite into flesh and bone. The man screamed as he fell. Kairn braced a foot against the body as he wrenched his sword free, then he jammed it through the torso just to make sure.

Crouching, he whirled to see what was going on. Someone had thrown some brush on the fire and the sudden flare revealed that the rivermen were getting the worst of it. Lean, ragged men who reminded Kairn of scavenging stripers darted among their prey, knives flashing. Even as he watched, one leapt upon Bat's back, pinioning his arms as another thrust a short spear into his belly.

Then three men attacked Kairn and he had no attention to spare. They hesitated at sight of his longsword, and he used that momentary advantage to cut one down. Then the other two attacked. He fended a clumsy axe blow to one side and split the man's skull just as the other man thrust with his spear. In a desperate sideways lurch Kairn avoided getting the spear through his belly, but the edge of the spear burned against his side. He hewed at the spearman's neck and saw the head fly free, then he whirled to find himself in the only relatively peaceful part of the camp. In his fighting he had worked himself away from the fire and by its light he saw that all the rivermen were down. The robbers were hacking and carving at the bodies, shrieking like demented spirits.

His arm clamped against the burn in his side, Kairn stumbled toward the raft. At the sound of his splashing through the shallows, some of the bandits shouted and pointed. They began running toward the raft as Kairn hauled himself aboard, cutting the stern line through with a slash of his sword. As he dashed forward, a javelin thunked into a log before his feet. He was almost to the bow line when a second javelin plunged into his right thigh.

Grimacing, he hewed through the line as his first order of business, then he wrenched the javelin from his thigh with a groan. He seized a pole, letting his sword fall, dangling by its wrist-cord. A bandit, his eyes wild in a mask of face-paint, tried to scramble onto the raft and Kairn brained him with the pole. He wedged its tip against the river bottom and pushed with all his strength, ignoring the pain in his side and thigh.

Slowly, the massive raft began to move out as more bandits splashed toward it. Kairn braced the pole against his chest and pushed as he regained his grip on his sword and carved clumsily at the first new arrival. The blow was weak and off-target, but the man fell back with a gashed scalp. He thrust at the next man, catching him just below the cheekbone and the bandit screamed as the point grated against teeth.

The remaining bandits might have forced their way aboard, but they had had enough. They stood in water to their knees, shaking fists and hurling curses but nothing more threatening. With a final shove, Kairn was free of the shallows and the current began to bear the raft southward. He limped to

the pen where his cabo was stamping and snorting in alarm.
Ignoring the beast, he snatched his bow from its case and
braced the curve of its lower limb against his left ankle. He
bit back cries of pain as he bent the powerful weapon around
the back of his wounded thigh, then he had the string loop
notched to the upper limb.

He stepped out of the now-strung bow and took an arrow
from his quiver. He chose his target carefully, knowing that
he would only have one shot and that he would not be able
to recover the arrow. Pain lanced through his side as he drew
back on the string, stopping only when the fletching touched
the corner of his mouth.

"One more for Bat and his men," Kairn muttered. Then
he released the string. The man he had picked was silhouetted against the fire, feathers nodding from his floppy hat as
he pranced and shouted curses. His shouts ended abruptly as
the arrow pierced his throat and he fell back into the fire,
sending up a high fountain of blood that fell back to hiss on
the coals. The others stopped just as abruptly; then there was
a mad scrambling as they sought the shore and the cover of
the nearest bushes.

With a sigh, Kairn unbraced his bow and went to sit on a
straw-stuffed cushion in the middle of the deck. He could not
see to tend his wounds, so he lay back to wait out the night
that was once again peaceful.

THREE

Hael got his first look at Crag as he rounded the shoulder of a hill. He was riding a cabo and leading one of this land's dwarf humpers, the ugly beast's back loaded with bales. The road beneath them was exceptionally fine. Hael had seen paved roads in the south and far west, but those had been paved with cut stone. This one was topped with an amalgam of tiny stones in a blackish matrix. It drained well and the animals never slipped on the rough surface.

He was forty years old, but few would have guessed him to be past his late twenties. His hair was long, the color of polished bronze. His skin was a paler bronze, and above his prominent cheekbones his eyes were startlingly blue. His striking appearance drew attention wherever he passed, for the people of this land were mostly dark, with hair and skin in every shade of brown, some of them nearly black. Brown eyes predominated, although he saw blue eyes here and there.

He was dressed in the style of a traveling merchant, with soft boots, baggy trousers, high-collared tunic and vest. A three-foot-long leather case slanted across his back. It contained his distinctive spear, taken down into its three component pieces. His great bow and its arrows were likewise concealed among his baggage. He did not wish to appear too much the warrior. The longsword at his belt was only what any traveling man might bear, although it was far more ornate than most and, had he drawn it, the locals might have been amazed to see that the blade was made entirely of steel.

For some time now he had been exploring a land unlike any other he had visited. It was as populous as Neva, and even more devoted to manufacture, but its cities had none of Neva's beauty. Where the smoke that hung over Nevan cities was that of incense and cooking fires, in this land it came from the belching chimneys of factories.

More peculiarly, he saw few small farms as he traversed the land. In other agricultural nations, small farms worked by free peasants or serfs were the rule. Here the land was instead divided into huge plantations, each devoted to a single crop and worked by slaves or else by persons condemned to some sort of temporary bondage. Even in the nations of the tropical south he had never seen slavery practiced on such a scale.

He viewed the phenomenon with distaste, but without horror. He came from a warrior people and felt that anyone who would not fight for his freedom, and would not die rather than be a slave, probably did not deserve freedom. If these people would not revolt against their masters, then it was probably best that they were put to some gainful employment. No man of his native tribe would have tolerated the slave's yoke for a moment.

Thinking of his former people depressed him. In recent years they had been transformed from warlike pastoralists into a conquering army. Their refusal to be slaves did not prevent them from enslaving other people. He shook off the mood. That was a distant threat, one to the far west. He had more immediate goals here.

The city of Crag was as forbidding as its name. The Tensa River flowed in a great loop around a massive wall of rock that thrust up at least two hundred feet from river to crest, and atop it was built a fortification of massive stone, its battlements and turrets as jagged as broken teeth. From its sheer river face, the upthrusting of stone slanted southward like an immense ramp to meet the forest far below.

It was a sight to dampen a man's spirits, but Hael shrugged it off. He enjoyed few things more than traveling by himself, and it was a pleasure he seldom got to enjoy. It was not easy for a man to go off on his own when he was a king. His wife frequently told him that he did not take his kingship seriously enough, and he did not doubt she was right.

His early years as king of the plains had been enthralling and exhilarating, but now he felt that his people could get along well enough without him, most of the time. With no war in the immediate offing, he had decided that it was time to take a tour of the southeastern lands. He had used the excuse that as king, he needed to know about the lands bordering his, and further, that it was essential he learn all he could of their revolutionary new weaponry. He had not fooled his queen.

"Nonsense!" she had said. "You just want an excuse to get away and be a free warrior again. You see our sons romping about as new-made warriors without thought or care, and it makes you long for the days when you had nothing but a spear and the world to wander in." He had winced at the accuracy of her assessment, but he had gone anyway. The one good thing about being king was that nobody could forbid you to do anything.

His followers on the trading expedition had been aghast when he had dismissed them to return home while he went on alone.

"The queen will have our hides!" protested the caravan master.

"Nonsense," he had replied. "She will do no worse than curse you for several hours. That never killed me, and it should not harm you either. Now go, and tell the queen that I will return when I have learned all that I require." He had ridden on with a single pack animal and several bales of

Nevan luxury goods. He had chosen these with care. He had no real need to sell anything, but some of these goods would guarantee him entry into almost any aristocratic house.

The cliff upon which sat the fortress of Crag was clearly unscalable, so he assumed that a road must lead to the foot of the "ramp," from whence one could ascend the great outcropping along its spine.

As he descended the hill, the road entered a broad stretch of flatland near the river. He passed through perfectly tended fields where gangs of slaves toiled beneath the eyes of mounted overseers. Wherever terrain allowed, the fields were laid out in perfect rectangles. Hael found the sight jarring. He was accustomed to the more irregular forms of nature. He was greatly suspicious of people who were enamored of straight lines and right angles. It suggested to him a spiritual deficiency.

When he was near the base of the immense outcropping, he saw that a village clustered in its shadow. This was Crag's riverport, where boats and barges did their loading and unloading. It looked like a good place to rest and pick up information before taking on the capital itself. As he rode toward it, his attention was drawn to activity in a nearby field.

This was another of the perfectly square enclosures, surrounded by a low wall of rough stone. It was not a cultivated field, however, and despite its grassy cover it was not a meadow for grazing livestock. It was a drill field, and it was in use. Hael drew rein and watched, for this was one of his prime reasons for coming to this land.

The soldiers who marched in precise lines were like none he had seen in other lands. Not one of them wore armor, nor was there a shield anywhere in sight. Instead each man bore a wooden-stocked firetube over his shoulder. Slung from their belts were shooting pouches containing projectiles and primer pellets. Just above these each man carried a powder flask. The hard ceramic of the firetubes shone white in the late afternoon sun. Hael had a number of such weapons in his possession, but they were militarily useless to him in small numbers, and even more so since he had never been able to discover the proper composition of the firepowder or the secret of making the incredibly durable ceramic of the tubes.

As he watched, the soldiers went through their evolutions. They changed face, wheeled, expanded and closed their lines with mechanical regularity. The men wore red tunics and green trousers and were shod with sandals. Their officers wore gaudier uniforms, gold circlets on their brows and low boots on their feet. The officers barked commands and the soldiers responded instantly, moving as one man.

Hael appreciated the value of discipline on the battlefield, but there was something repellent in this sort of maneuvering. It made the warrior's trade seem little more than a step removed from slavery.

The men began to practice their shooting drill. They pantomimed the actions of loading, ramming, priming, aiming and firing, in both standing and kneeling postures. Not once was powder burned. This told Hael that, even here, powder was too valuable to use in casual drill. He was fascinated by the spectacle, but he made himself turn away and ride toward the town, lest he be suspected of spying.

Unlike the other towns he had entered in this land, this one had no wall, no gate guarded by a petty official. He guessed that the riverside town was a mere petty adjunct of Crag, not worth defending. Anyone worthy of attention would have to ascend the ridge of the crag from which the fortress got its name, and he did not doubt that way would be heavily defended.

The road took him into a town with few solidly built structures and many tumbledown shanties. Here the streets were not paved, but were mere mud tracks, swarming with small livestock. Many tiny, fat, tuskless toonoo scavenged amid the garbage and little flocks of plump domestic lizards ran about, preying on the abundant insect life.

Constrained by the river on one side and the cliff on the other, the town was narrow and the buildings perforce multi-storied, with laundry-draped balconies much in evidence. Here and there he saw little shrines where incense burned before images of the local gods, but there were no great temples.

This was a thing he had noted everywhere in the southeast. Here there were no temples and no evident priesthood. It was unlike anything he had seen before. Elsewhere, primitive peoples were without temples, but they had a rich spiritual life and all had spirit-speakers to form a bridge between the spirit world and man. In the civilized world there were great gods, whose priests acted as intermediaries, relieving most people of spiritual duties, and performing their stylized rituals in temples.

Here there was neither system. The whole land seemed to suffer from extreme spiritual impoverishment. More than any other aspect of the strangeness of the place, this upset Hael. He was unique in the world: a warrior–spirit-speaker–king, and accustomed to spending much of his time in the company of the spirits of the land. Here he could make contact with the spirit world only in the deepest forest. Here it was as if something had driven the spirits from their usual haunts, leaving behind only the empty shell of human activity.

People stared at him as he passed, but he was accustomed to that. In this land, his appearance was exotic. People scurried swiftly from his path and he knew that this was not wholly attributable to his regal bearing. Here, a man on a cabo meant one thing: *nobleman*. Showing deference to a mounted man was all but instinctive with these people.

He continued along the flank of the sheer stone cliff until he neared the river docks. In this place the people were not so anxious to get out of his way. By their dress he recognized them as rivermen. They were more independent than most, and in this land they passed for free men. That was why he had chosen this district in which to spend the night. He wanted to be among people who would talk freely and he could not abide the company of slaves or cringing serfs.

He halted and dismounted before a four-storied wooden building with a bundle of mistletoe tied to its doorpost—the local sign for an inn. He arranged for his animals' stabling and went inside. The inn was filling with its evening crowd and he took a seat on a bench near the end of one of the long tables. He unslung the cased spear and propped it carefully beside him. The spear was his most precious possession, the final reminder of his days as a young warrior on an island far, far to the west, in an ocean most people in this land had never heard of.

The food was served in platters which were set on the table and the diners helped themselves. Hael had long since overcome his people's taboo against eating fish, and he found the fresh-caught river fish excellent, although he fastidiously passed up a platter of multitentacled freshwater molluscs that looked like something out of a nightmare.

The rivermen were used to encountering odd foreigners, and he did not need to work hard to overcome their reticence. The gossip of the rivers flowed as freely as the rivers themselves, and there was much trading of news and rumors of the doings in neighboring lands. He even heard a few stories about himself, much distorted by time and distance. His was the most distant kingdom that this land had regular dealings with, and the only thing that distinguished it from a place of myth was the undeniable solidity of the steel he exported hither.

But whenever he tried to steer the conversation in the direction of the fortress-city looming above them, the talk tapered away and everyone looked uncomfortable. Either they knew nothing of the place, or they were fearful of being overheard. He suspected the latter. At his least mention of the subject, men glanced furtively about them, as if looking for spies.

If Crag intimidated even these tough, brawling men, he thought, what must it be like? There was only one way to find out and he would essay that way the next morning.

When the last of the platters were cleared away, the last tankards drained, and the greater part of the company snoring on the straw, Hael rose from his bench and went outside. The smell of the river was strong in the air, and he followed it to the nearest docks. These seemed to offer solitude, so he walked along a pier to its end.

The night was moonless, so he did not perform his accustomed chant of apology to the wounded Moon. The stars glittered brightly in the tropical sky, and he picked out the familiar constellations and counted the odd stars that wandered independently of the others.

He could feel things moving in the river. As with the animals of the land, he could sense the faintly flickering spirits of the river creatures. The multitudinous fish and molluscs had so little awareness that their spirits were less than the glimmerings of the faintest stars. The massive river lizards had a steadier glow, and the great river mammals were like moons gliding beneath the placid surface of the river.

When he cast his thoughts inland, though, it was as if the land was lifeless, despite the abundance of animals everywhere. Crag was like a parasite that sucked the life from everything in its vicinity. This, more than anything else, filled Hael with foreboding.

The next morning, Hael took special care in grooming himself. He brushed his hair until it fell in long metallic waves over his shoulders. The passage of years had not dulled its gleam in the slightest. He unpacked his finest clothing and donned an assortment of fine ornaments. He was about to seek entry into the finest houses and he would never succeed if he was not presentable.

He paid his score, mounted and rode along the upthrust flank of the massive outcropping. The tight-packed multistoried buildings gave way to smaller structures, then to ramshackle sheds with spaces between them, then to open fields. The slaves were out in the fields, busy with spade and grub hoe. They looked up dully as he passed, losing interest quickly when they saw that he bore no whip.

He was on paved road again, this one built up on an earthen embankment topped with a layer of cut stone covered with the usual black amalgam. He guessed that this was to preserve the roadway in flood times. By the time he had ridden a little less than a mile, the great natural ramp was level with the surrounding ground. The road looped and he began to ascend.

The road up the stony spine was perfectly straight, with scrubby growth flanking it in narrow strips to the precipitous edge of the outcropping. As he climbed, the ground widened into something resembling a conventional hilltop, but there were no buildings between him and the tower-flanked gates ahead.

He was not alone on the road. Lines of slaves carrying loads upon their heads and backs ascended and descended the hill. People of importance rode cabos and twice he saw persons lofty enough to be borne in palanquins.

True to its forbidding aspect, the gate was heavily defended, with men holding firetubes at the ready ranged along the walkway between the flanking towers, above the gate itself. In the gateway were more guards and an official armed with pen, ink, parchment and a formidable timepiece, which was hung around his neck on an elaborate golden chain. Hael joined the line of travelers seeking entry into Crag. When he reached the head of the line, the official looked him over carefully.

"Name and business?" he demanded.

"Alsa, purveyor of fine luxury goods from the far west."

The official studied him dubiously. "Why do you come here, merchant?"

"Few people in any district can afford my wares. I understand that the wealthiest persons concentrate here in Crag, so I thought to save myself some travel time by setting up here."

"That good? Let's have a look at these wares."

"I can give you a glimpse," Hael said, dismounting, "enough to show that I carry nothing threatening. But these items may be fully displayed only to the most discerning of patrons."

The nonsensical qualification seemed to satisfy the official. "That will be sufficient."

Hael opened his bags and the official stifled a gasp at the jewels and fine metals glittering within. "Did you bring any timepieces?'' he half-whispered. ''Mine is very old and grows inaccurate.''

Hael shook his head. ''Alas, no. The Nevans make wonderful devices for telling time, but their mechanisms are too delicate to travel far.''

''Pity. Very well, you may enter.'' He scribbled on his parchment. ''Alsa, merchant, arrived during the sixth hour of the morning. When you have established lodging within the city, you are to report your location to the police station in the quadrangle. You will report there each morning before noon. If you fail to do so, they will come looking for you and you do not want that to happen.''

Hael remounted and rode inside. This place was already living up to his worst expectations. Immediately within the gate was a sort of tunnel formed by stone buildings with balconies that nearly met overhead. This gave onto a small plaza which he crossed to a continuation of the street. Here it ascended steeply, in some places becoming a stair that his cabo did not like but climbed without complaint.

At the top of the steep street the ground leveled and he found himself in what had to be the quadrangle the gate-keeper had mentioned. It was at least two hundred paces long and half as wide, perfectly rectangular and paved with square-cut stone. Its periphery was lined with great houses and what appeared to be government buildings. There were no smoke-stacks or other evidence of heavy manufacturing. The quad-rangle ended at a massive fortress set somewhat higher than the rest of the city. From its turrets hung banners that waved lazily in the breeze. Guards in ornate uniforms patrolled be-fore its gates, but these carried swords and poleaxes that flashed in the sunlight. By this Hael knew that they were ceremonial guards. The real guards would be in the towers, armed with firetubes.

He was puzzled to note that there was not a single mer-chant's stall in the entire plaza. In other cities he had visited, such public areas served multiple purposes: ceremonial, rec-reational and commercial. That did not seem to be the case with this one.

A few questions led him to a cul-de-sac a few streets from the quadrangle. At the end of the blind alley was a sizable inn where the rates were high, but where he quickly learned that there was nothing cheap in Crag. As a prosperous merchant of the highest standing, he did not quibble, but he insisted on examining his animals' accommodations minutely.

He demanded a spacious room with a balcony and was informed this would be even more expensive, but that meant nothing to Hael. He already felt the city squeezing the breath from him and he intended to sleep on the balcony any night there was no rain. Once established, he went to the police station to report. This proved to be a discreet building situated in an alcove facing one of the longer sides of the square.

As he climbed the steps to the entrance, people came from the building looking thoroughly subdued, even cowed. Puzzled, he entered. He found himself in a long waiting room of stone and dark wood. A number of policemen lounged about and he did not like their look. They wore black tunics and trousers, and their wrists were banded with black leather. All had short truncheons thonged to their belts along with shortswords. Close-fitting helmets of hardened leather framed faces that were uniform in their brutishness.

A man seated behind a desk beckoned and Hael approached. This one wore the black uniform, but his face was more refined and he wore no helmet. Tucked into his sash was a pair of unusual weapons—firetubes no more than a foot long, their stocks made of finely oiled dark wood.

"And who might you be, newcomer?" the man asked.

Hael gave his assumed name, his business and his place of lodging.

"I don't think that I have ever seen one like you before. Where is your homeland?"

"The wide plains beyond the great river, far to the north and west. But I travel even beyond, to Chiwa and Neva and the far ocean."

The man sat back in his richly carved chair. "Then you

travel far. Strange that a man would travel such great distances alone, bearing goods so valuable and so tempting.''

Hael knew the sound of a man who was suspicious for a living. ''I rarely travel alone, sir, but the caravan I was with turned back some time ago, whereas I was determined to see the capital of this land and display my wares before its wealthiest and noblest personages. The country is so well policed that a few days of solitary travel did not seem daunting.'' Hael had dealt with a great many merchants, and he knew how they spoke.

The man nodded and withdrew a folded parchment from a drawer. ''Here is your license to trade within the city. Since you will seek custom only among the highest-born, I will not require a licensing fee or set a time limit upon your stay.'' This was as Hael had expected. In an oppressive land, those who catered to the highest suffered less oppression than others. The man eyed the sword that hung at his side.

''You may not go armed within the city. Leave that in your lodgings. Anyone going armed is subject to arrest.''

Hael bristled at that. He had not gone unarmed since being made a warrior, twenty-five years before. But he saw no way to resist without arousing suspicion.

''As you wish, sir.'' He removed the sheathed sword and wrapped its belt around it.

''You may go, then,'' said the official. The policemen glowered after him as he left.

Hael returned to his lodging to leave his sword, but he slung his disassembled spear across his back as compensation. It did not look like a weapon and it made him feel less undressed. By asking directions he made his way to a small market where luxury goods were traded. Here he saw finely dressed people walking among tiny shops furnished with strong shutters.

He wandered among the establishments, seeking one that was suitable for his purposes. A number of them dealt in jewelry, but he rejected these. Likewise with the scent shops and the purveyors of fine cloth. Between a drug and cosmetic shop and one selling rare spices, he found just what he needed. Behind its large front window, on a bed of artfully rumpled crimson cloth, reposed an exquisite statue of a dancing goddess. Her pose was complicated yet graceful, her serene eyes made of gold, set into the red stone of her face and body. Hael knew that no such goddess was worshipped in this land. Anyone who bought such a statue must do so for its artistic value alone. He strode inside.

The interior was cool and dim, but a skylight and an arrangement of carefully angled mirrors illuminated the wares for display. He saw a miniature painting from Chiwa, a tapestry of splendid workmanship depicting geometric designs in blazing colors, a relief carved in polished jasper with concentric circles of erotic couplings. Other wares were as artistic and costly.

"May I be of service?" Hael turned to see a man of middle years who studied him closely. Hael knew what he was thinking: The newcomer was not dressed richly enough to be a patron, nor poorly enough to be someone who had wandered in by mistake.

"I hope so. My name is Alsa, a purveyor of works of finest craftsmanship to persons of discrimination. I've just arrived in your city and I require a venue for the display of my wares. Do you undertake such commissions?"

"I have been known to do so," the man said judiciously, "for a percentage of the sale, and always providing that the rarity and aesthetic value of the objects meets the standards of my establishment. You understand that my patrons are of the very highest levels of society, persons of the most exacting taste."

"Only such persons could afford, much less appreciate, the articles in which I deal," Hael said.

"Did you bring an example?"

Hael withdrew a flat, wooden box from his pouch. Carefully, he laid it upon a table beneath the skylight, unlatched it and raised the lid. Inside, nestled within a plush lining, was an instrument of bronze. It consisted of two eccentric rings with a pivoted pointer slanted across both. All the metal surfaces were wonderfully carved, etched and inlaid. Various points around the peripheries of the rings were distinguished by tiny, inset jewels. The merchant studied it for a long time.

"It is exquisite," he said at last. "It is an astrolabe, is it not?"

"It is," Hael concurred. "You have seen its like?"

"Infrequently. I know that it is an instrument of navigation. The mariners upon the seas far to the east and to the south of here use them for finding the angles of certain stars for means of determining location. But those I have seen are poor things, made of plain bronze or even wood."

"And do you think I might find buyers for such items here?"

"You have others like this?"

"This is the only astrolabe, but the rest are items of this sort—all are instruments of utility, but they are made and decorated by the finest craftsmen and artists of Neva and other western lands. I do not deal in objects of pure art, such as your vases and sculptures and carpets."

The merchant nodded. "Yes, I think I know a number of collectors who might be very interested. Here are my terms: Bring the rest of your wares and I will display them here. I will pass the word that these extraordinary objects are to be seen in my shop. Whatever you sell here in Crag, I will receive a commission of ten percent."

"That seems fair. Do these collectors come here regularly?"

"By no means. I do not know how such things are done in your homeland, but here the highest persons do not go about in markets and shops. They will send servants versed in their tastes. If the servant judges the wares worthy of the master's attention, the vendor will be summoned to the great house. I will, of course, be more than happy to—"

"Not at all," Hael interrupted. "I would greatly prefer to go to these houses to praise my wares personally."

"As you will," the merchant said, slightly disgruntled. "But the ten-percent commission stands."

"That is understood. You are, after all, providing the display facilities and the local contacts. That is well worth the ten-percent commission."

"Excellent. Then by all means bring the rest of your goods. I am anxious to see them."

This was working out more smoothly than Hael had dared hope. He returned to his inn and separated from his bags a number of items he judged most attractive to the people whose company he sought. Not wishing to lead his humper through the streets of the city, he hired two boys from the inn to help him carry the goods to the shop.

As they unpacked the works for display, the merchant, whose name was Beak Nose, sighed with appreciation.

"We so seldom see work of this quality. I am sorry to say that the great people of this land do not often take an interest in artistic things. And those that do are mostly collectors, not patrons of the arts. What lands Neva and Chiwa must be, where even utilitarian objects are lavished with such richness." He admired a complex lamp, its windows made of faceted, multicolored crystal set in a fretwork of gold and silver.

"I questioned a good many travelers and merchants before coming here," Hael said. "I decided that while there might be few aesthetes in this land, even very practical people might take an interest in instruments which were also works of art. Even a blunt warrior can appreciate a finely ornamented sword."

"That was very shrewd," Beak Nose said. "My few collectors of fine art are mostly great ladies, and these seldom control the household coffers and must indulge their tastes on sufferance from their husbands. Now what might this be?" He took up a flat rectangle of bronze. Across its longer axis was slotted a sliding silver bar. Bronze and silver were minutely inscribed with lines and symbols.

"It is a mathematician's instrument," Hael said. "By sliding that center piece and lining up the lines and symbols they determine—" he shrugged "—something or other. I learned to add and subtract, and a bit of division, but anything more complicated is beyond me."

"No matter. It's beautiful." He placed the instrument on a tabletop and turned to a boy who fiddled with the complex of mirrors below the skylight. "Let's have some light on this." When the reflected light was to his satisfaction he turned to Hael. "The mirrors are troublesome. They must be continually adjusted as the sun moves across the sky, but it is by far the most effective way to display fine goods. Otherwise they must be taken outside."

By the time they had the last of his goods displayed the sun was too low for the mirrors to do any good. Well-satisfied with the day's work, Hael bade the merchant good evening as the shop was locked up. He walked back through the darkening streets to his inn, wondering if others carried out espionage in such an indirect fashion, and if other kings did their own spying.

FOUR

Kairn woke with a raging thirst. The sun burned down upon him, and the air was stifling, but he shook with chills. He knew he must be sick, but he could not remember contracting any illness. He tried to sit up and call to the rivermen, but when he did, a blinding pain engulfed him. Then he began to remember.

Slowly, gritting his teeth against the pain, he worked himself up to a sitting position. His leg throbbed from hip to toes in rhythmic waves and he gasped to see how swollen his thigh was. His trouser leg was stretched tight as a sausage skin and soaked with blackened blood. He tried to pull up his shirt to examine the cut on his side, but the garment was so glued down by dried blood that he gave it up until he would be able to soak the shirt off.

Next he investigated his situation. Sometime during his unconsciousness, the raft had nosed into a sandbar, drifted sideways, and was now set solidly against the obstruction. A glance at the direction of the current told him that he was on the east bank. How long he had been out, how far he had drifted, he had no way of knowing. He had a powerful urge to plunge his head into the river and drink, but he knew that to be dangerous. He dragged himself to a keg the rivermen had filled from a clear-flowing stream. First he drank a gourdful of water, then he sluiced water all over himself. That made him feel marginally better, and he drank another gourdful, stopping only when his stomach began to cramp.

He crawled to the pen and used the bars to draw himself upright. His cabo came to him looking none the worse for the recent events. It groaned and nuzzled his palm. He saw that it still had plentiful feed but its water bucket was dry. He grabbed his lance to lean on and let the animal out. With a hand on its halter, he led it to the edge of the raft and let it drink from the river. When it was done he led it back to the pen and saddled it. The exertion made his wounds bleed afresh, but by this time bleeding was the last thing he worried about.

When all was done he led the beast ashore. With a hand on the saddle, he let the beast half-pull him up the bank of the levee. At its crest he surveyed his surroundings. He was in a flat, floodplain area, densely forested. A narrow, dirt-surfaced road paralleled the earthwork. Gritting his teeth, unable to put it off any longer, he mounted.

Swinging his wounded leg across the saddle was perhaps the most agonizing experience of his young life, and it left him pale and sweating despite his chills. He sat still for a full five minutes, recovering. He had never felt so sick. Before nudging the cabo down the other side of the levee, he tied the halter to his wrist. He knew that he might well fall off and he did not want his cabo to wander away should that happen.

He descended to the path and headed south, reflecting that there was more to the warrior's life than strutting about in weapons and finery. The realities could be as miserable as the meanest peasant's existence, and his misery was compounded by his utter aloneness. To distract himself he thought of other warrior matters. How many men had he struck down in the fight by the raft, and on the raft itself? It seemed to him that there had been six or seven, but the fighting had been so hectic that he was not sure.

He wondered whether it would be proper to brag about it when he got home. Six men was a very creditable score, but these had been inferior people, mere bandits. It was not as if they had been honorable warriors. On the other hand he had been severely, perhaps fatally wounded, and it would be embarrassing to admit that he had been injured by inferiors. He would have to stress the numbers of the attackers, he decided.

Somewhere, he did not notice when, the road veered from the levee and entered the forest. It was a depressing place, full of insect buzzings and clickings. Furry things scurried around in the trees or scampered from beneath his cabo's hoofs. He saw something that looked like a man-of-the-trees, but it was man-sized, with a long snout. So swiftly did it fade into the bush that he thought it might be a creation of his fevered mind.

He knew that he had to find a settlement where he could rest and have his wounds cared for. Already he feared for his leg. He did not yet smell gangrene, but he knew that it was inevitable without doctoring. Still, there was nothing he could do save ride, so he rode.

The world around him faded in and out, as in a dream. One moment he would be riding as through a tunnel, with trees arching overhead to interlace their branches into a roof that all but excluded light, and such light as made its way through dappled the leafy floor with glimmers like flickering insects. Next he would be riding through an open meadow, with great beasts cropping the grass, and no sense of when he had passed from one to the other.

Once, he rode among colossal ruins. Crumbled remains of great walls and pillars lay shattered, overgrown by vines and bushes. One tower rose three stories, clearly a fraction of its original height. Frowning faces stared down from some of the ruined walls. He wondered what people had risen here and reared such structures, only to disappear. Later, he wondered whether he had seen the ruins at all. Perhaps he had fever-dreamed them.

The sun was almost down when he tumbled from his saddle. He seemed to be drifting, floating as the world whirled around him. Then he landed with shattering reality. The pain shot through his entire body with blazing force and he screamed. He had lost all sense of warriorlike fortitude. He felt no shame when he screamed. There seemed to be absolutely nothing else to do. After what seemed an eternity the pain receded and localized itself in his leg and his side. His cabo looked at him curiously, then began to munch grass.

Kairn decided that he was going to die, and that did not seem such a bad prospect, if it meant an end to this suffering. He thought of his cabo. How would it fare, tethered to his corpse? Would it be able to gnaw through the halter? A predator might attack, and encumbered with his corpse the cabo would not be able to escape. He dragged his bound wrist across his body and fumbled at the loop with his other hand. Both hands had gone numb. He tried to loosen the noose until even this effort was too much; then he gave up and passed out.

He woke to dimness and the smell of smoke. He lay on a bed of coarse material stuffed with fragrant plant fibers. An orange glow told him there was a fire nearby, but he was afraid to turn his head, lest the pain come back. Overhead he could see a series of poles, smoke-stained and still covered with bark. A broad-headed bird sat on one and looked at him, huge eyes flanking a short, curving beak.

He tried to take stock of his injuries. He was aware of a deep, throbbing pain in his thigh, a lesser pain in his side. Neither seemed as overwhelming as they had been, but it was when he moved that they had tortured him, so perhaps it was only because he lay still that he was not in agony. He sensed no human presence in the room. He slipped back into sleep.

A change awakened him. A door had opened, flooding the room with light. The light faded and he heard someone moving near him. He felt a rustling sensation, then cool air moving across his body. Someone had drawn a coverlet away from him. He opened his eyes.

"They breed tough men where you come from." The speaker was a woman. She had a round, small-chinned face and wide-set brown eyes. Black hair tumbled to her shoulders and formed a fringe above her brows.

"So I have been told," Kairn said, amazed at the weakness of his voice.

"Either of these wounds should have killed you. The blood loss alone was enough. The infection was more than enough. Well, you pulled through the blood loss and my doctoring brought the infection under control, though I thought you were lost a number of times. Do you believe in gods, stranger?"

"We have spirits," Kairn said. "Gods are for foreigners."

"I think there must be gods, because one of them was surely watching over you. Aside from your wounds and the infection, exposure and deprivation would surely have finished you had you fallen off your animal anywhere but where you did. Mine is the only habitation for more than a day's travel."

"My cabo," he said, "where is it?"

"You must be a plainsman," she said, "to ask after your animal first rather than about your own condition."

"I will live or die," he said. "Either way, I don't want to walk."

"It is penned outside and has plenty of forage and water. You, on the other hand, are in terrible shape. You've just come out of a raging delirium, you haven't had real food for days and you haven't even been able to keep down water. If I sit you up, will you try to drink?"

Suddenly he was aware of a terrible thirst. "Please."

With an arm beneath his shoulders she raised him to a sitting position, stuffing heavy pillows behind his back. The pain was bearable, and he noticed that he wore only two huge bandages.

"Your clothes were a total loss, I'm afraid. They were completely soaked with blood and I'm amazed that the smell didn't draw every predator and scavenger in these hills. There are carrion bats in these parts big enough to dismember you and carry away the pieces." She helped him raise a dipper to his lips and he felt the delicious coolness of water slide down his throat. So parched was he that he felt the fluid soak into his tissues as soon as it reached his stomach. "More," he said when the dipper was empty.

"Later. More will make you sick just now. We have to get water into you, then we can try some food, but we can't rush things. It would be a shame to lose you to overindulgence after you survived so much."

With his thirst partially satisfied, he rested back against the cushions and studied his surroundings. He was in what seemed to be a small, single-room house, not much more than a hut, but clean and tidy in a way the peasant huts he had seen never were. From the overhead beams hung bunches of fresh and dried herbs. Flasks of varying designs lined the shelves of one wall. More of them stood atop a wide table along with pots and a mortar.

"Who are you?" he asked, then: "Forgive me, I forget my manners. My name is Kairn, and I come from the plains to the northwest, the kingdom of King Hael."

"I guessed as much. My name is Star Eye."

"You are a healer? A physician?" He managed a weak gesture toward the surrounding paraphernalia.

"To your great good fortune." She leaned back, arms folded. She wore a tight-laced dress, closely fitted to her upper body. She had a slender but full-breasted build that gave an impression of limber, wiry strength. She looked as if she felt more at home outdoors than inside.

"Why does a healer live so far from other people?"

She countered with another question. "Why does a plainsman travel alone in an alien land? I know that your people are tribal, and tribesmen rarely leave their own people."

"I seek someone," he said, "a man of my own race who disappeared into this land some time ago. I must find him."

"You'll not be looking for anyone anytime soon," she said. "You need time to recover from your injuries."

He let his head fall back, aware of his weakness. "It seems I must."

She drew the coverlet back over him. "Try to sleep, then you'll have more water and perhaps some food. Your wounds are healing well."

He lay back and watched as she went about her activities. Her movements were graceful and clean, without wasted motion. After a while she left the house and he slept—a deep, restful sleep without sweatings and ravings.

He awoke thirsty and famished. He smelled something cooking on the fire and his stomach growled. The woman was crouched by the fire. She looked up and smiled when she heard him move.

"Awake again? Let's see what you can keep down." Once again she raised him to a sitting position and brought a dipper of water. He drained it gratefully, and this time she refilled it. "Sip at this one. I'll bring you some food, and you are to drink the water as you eat." She went to the fire and ladled something from the pot into a bowl.

He studied the bowl as it warmed his shaky fingers. The smell was strange, but the food was mouth-watering. It was a stew of meat and wild vegetables swimming in a rich broth. The odd smell came from the many different herbs chopped up into the broth. He took a horn spoon and began to eat, forcing himself to do it slowly. The herbs made the taste pungent, but not disagreeable.

"Those are not all seasonings, but medicines," she informed him. "Some are for the infection, others relieve pain or provide things your body needs."

When the bowl and the dipper were empty, he set them aside. "You aren't just some peasant herb-woman," he said. "You speak like an educated person."

"And you don't speak like some barbaric tribesman," she countered.

"Among my own people I'm accounted well-taught."

"And highborn," she said.

"After a fashion. We don't have nobles and commoners and slaves like other people."

"That does not mean that all are the same level," she pronounced. She rose from her seat. "I must go now. A woman is about to give birth and the family wants my help."

"How long will you be away?" he asked. "You said that no one lives within a day's travel."

"Don't worry, I am not deserting you. These are traveling people, entertainers and small traders. Their camp is only an hour from here. If there are no complications, I should be back by morning. I'm leaving a pitcher of water here by you. Don't drink too much at one time, but drink it all by morning."

She took up a large basket and slung it over her shoulder by a cloth strap. She took a staff from beside the door and went outside. There was a flash of wings overhead and Kairn saw the broad-headed bird fly from a beam out through the door in an eerie silence. Its wings made no sound at all. Then the door closed and she was gone.

It had not occurred to him to ask her if she felt safe going abroad alone after dark. Then he chided himself for foolishness. The woman lived here alone, she must be accustomed to looking out for herself. She had been distinctly disinclined to giving any information about herself. Any time his questions had turned that way, she had replied with a question of her own. She was a mystery, and one he intended to probe further before he left this place.

The next day he felt immeasurably better. His wounds were reduced to a dull aching and he found that he could sit up in bed without help. He decided to test his newfound strength and swiveled to sit on the edge of the bed so that his feet touched the hard-packed earth floor. Cautiously, he tried to stand, but his legs were too shaky and there was a sudden stab of pain from his wounded thigh.

"What are you doing? I didn't say you were ready to walk on your own! If you fell, how would you get up again? Lie back down this instant!"

Kairn recognized the tone of physicians everywhere and complied. She fussed over him for a few minutes, feeling his forehead, peeling his eyelids back to examine his eyes more closely. Then she began to unwind his bandages. The cut on his side was healing cleanly, the edges of the wound already bound together by healthy new flesh. She washed the wound and rebound it with a fresh bandage.

The wound in his thigh was far uglier, a star-shaped rip in the flesh where he had torn the javelin-head free, rending skin and muscle alike. This was still in the process of closing, raw, and seeping a clear fluid, but there was no blood and the inflammation was confined to the edges of the wound.

"If there were red and black streaks radiating from the injury," she explained, "then you would be in trouble. Once the poison is in the blood, there is little I can do about it. As it was, I feared that you would get the convulsive sickness, where the body goes rigid and the jaws lock tight. You seem to have escaped that."

"You are a wonderful doctor," he said.

"I am that. You are better than most patients, although I sometimes wonder why I bother."

"Why is that?"

"Because you are a warrior. That is not difficult to guess because you're a mounted plainsman and half your possessions seem to be weapons. Warriors do nothing but make work for me. When I patch them up they go out and make more work for me yet. I've brought you back from the brink of death, but for you these scars will be something to show off and brag of around the campfires. I might have done the world a favor by allowing you to die, but that is not my way."

Kairn was unsure how to respond. He had never encountered someone who did not pay respect to warriors. "I will be most happy to reward your services."

She glared at him. "You miss the point. You would reward me best by letting your fellow men live in peace. But this is an evil world and I suppose I should not blame you for living by its rules. Speaking of reward, you travel well supplied with money. And all your weapons are of steel. That is a great rarity here and I'll wager it isn't exactly common even in the realm of Hael the Steel King.''

"You are nosy," he said, disgruntled.

She shrugged. "A few days ago I was ready to give you up for dead so I thought it would do no harm to look through your things. I would not have done it otherwise."

He wanted to say something biting, but he knew that his possessions must represent great wealth to this woman, yet she had exerted herself to save him. His sword alone would be worth a fortune in this land, his cabo worth even more. She could have let him die.

"My father says that each of us has a purpose in life, and there are some things only a warrior can do."

"Your father is a philosopher," she said.

"I don't know that word. He is a spirit-speaker." This was not untrue.

"A spirit-speaker," she said. "I would like to meet one of those. We have none here. The authorities discourage any trafficking with the supernatural."

"These authorities of yours must try to control every aspect of people's lives," he noted.

"Much of the time they succeed."

"Why do they care whether people believe in spirits or gods or whatever?"

"Rivalry. They want the people to have no loyalty save to their superiors. Even the soldiers are taken as children to be raised in military camps. That way they have no family loyalty to interfere with their devotion to the Assembly of Great Men." There was real bitterness in her voice. "They are levied on the districts, as a sort of tax—so many male children per hundred acres of land."

"Why do people tolerate it?" he asked.

"People will tolerate anything once they're used to it. They fear change and uncertainty more than the evil they know."

Two days later, she allowed him to rise from the bed and stagger a few steps around the hut. After that, his recovery was rapid. In this time he saw little of Star Eye. During the days she was outdoors gathering the herbs she needed for her practice. He wondered how she could carry out her work while living such an isolated existence. She explained that once each month she traveled to the nearby villages, treated the sick and injured, sold her herbs, then returned home.

"When you are a healer," she said, "people will seek you out at all hours of the day and night. That is a good reason to live away from people."

He explained a little of his mission, but not that the man he sought was the king and his father.

"I hesitate to say it, but the most likely place to look for your errant friend is Crag," she said.

"That was where I was headed when the bandits attacked. Why do you not like the idea of me going there?"

"Because it is an awful place. It is the seat of government, where the Assembly meets. There is nothing there but corruption and brutality."

"And wealth?" he said.

"That, too. All the great, rich people are there, much of the time. If he trades luxury goods, that is the place to go."

"What makes it so bad?"

"The great ones spy on each other and plot against one another. The members of the Assembly intrigue ceaselessly to form new alliances and destroy one another. The police watch everybody. It is better to be dead than to be in that place."

"You seem to know a great deal about it," Kairn observed. She said nothing to that.

It was as always with this woman. She would speak endlessly of her work. She knew the animals and plant life of these woods better than he knew those of his native plains. Every last plant seemed to have some useful property and she knew how to extract and apply it. She spoke of her "neighbors," none of them dwelling very close, some of them seminomadic, passing through her territory several times each year.

But whenever he tried to question her about her past she turned him away. What had brought her here, who she had been before, these were closed subjects. He could only judge and guess from what he observed and the crumbs of information she inadvertently dropped.

He was certain that she was well-born. She had the poise and address that come only from an upbringing in a great household. She was educated. She could read and write, and had scattered about the hut parchments covered with notes about her researches into the medicinal properties of plants, complete with careful renderings worthy of a professional artist.

She had a wide breadth of knowledge about distant lands. When he spoke of the plains, of the Canyon, of Chiwa to the far south and Neva to the west, she was aware of all these places, and of many others. Most peasants never strayed five miles from their places of birth, and any place beyond their cramped boundaries constituted an impenetrable mystery.

Once, he had spoken admiringly of her careful, methodical researches and the wonderfully helpful way she interpolated her drawings with her text. He could not read the characters she used in writing, but he knew a finely illustrated text when he saw one.

"Each people has its own genius," she said. "Your plainsmen are known for warrior passion wedded to a close relationship with the spirits of your land. The Nevans, I understand, are energetic and adventurous, but also highly artistic and they revel in far travelings and things of beauty. My own people, far back in our history, delved into the material nature of things. We tore the earth open for minerals and worked endlessly to learn their properties and devise ways to use them.

"This way, we learned many wonderful things, and we became preeminent in manufacture, but our minds were bent in the direction of pure utilitarianism. My people see no value in things that are not useful. Nothing to them has spirit, only useful properties. They do not care for beauty. Without these things, I do not believe that they value even themselves as highly as other peoples do."

This did seem truly alien. His own people were not highly cultured by the standards of the great, civilized nations, but they had a rich spiritual life and their arts were crude but vigorous. Even the warrior life was as much a matter of spirit as of strength and skill. And his father had insisted that his boys study the ways and knowledge of other lands. He had brought tutors from far away to teach them.

As a child Kairn had bitterly resented these lessons, longing only to be free, out on the broad plains with his bow and a good cabo, hunting or riding patrol with the grown warriors. To live a life such as Star Eye described seemed to him like being half-dead.

"Why are you different?" he had asked.

"Who says I am different?" she had answered.

Once he commented that his cabo was probably suffering for lack of exercise. Later that day he woke from an herb-induced sleep to the sound of familiar hoofbeats outside. He rose and lurched to one of the small windows. Outside, he saw Star Eye riding his cabo across a clearing. She had discarded her skirt and rode clad only in her tight-fitting bodice. She rode without a saddle, her shapely legs gripping the flanks of the cabo with assured firmness. The sight was both stirring and illuminating. He was recovered enough to be excited by her beauty thus revealed. Her mastery of the animal confirmed what he had long suspected. He knew of no land save his own where riding was not restricted to the highest nobility. He went back to his bed and lay down. When she came back in he made no mention of having seen her.

As she had noted from the first, his constitution was extraordinary. Once the recovery process was under way, he healed with amazing swiftness. One day he was able to walk freely around the hut. The next he was outside and ambling around the clearing and even a little way into the woods. By the next, he was able to mount and ride a little.

Star Eye was pleased with his progress, but saddened by it as well.

"I've grown used to having you to doctor," she said as he began riding. "I shall be sorry to see you leave."

"If my mission were not so important," he told her solemnly, "I would not leave."

She smiled at him. "Yes, you would. You might want to
tarry a while with an interesting woman, but you could never
stay off that beast for long, and once mounted, you would be
off on the road, bound for far places."

He flushed, knowing that she spoke the truth. He dismounted, turned the cabo into the little pen which it shared
with several odd beasts.

Inside Kairn and Star Eye shared a meal as the light of day
faded to blackness and the stars came out. He felt that he
owed her more than his thanks, that she should have some
explanation. He was not certain why this should be. He had
been injured, near death, and good luck had allowed him to
avail himself of a service she was accustomed to giving others. His thanks and a simple payment should be enough. But
he knew they would not be.

"The man I seek," he began, lamely and haltingly, "he
is not just any man. For one thing, he is my father."

"Surely only one man can lay claim to that title," she said.
"That alone makes him unique."

"Are you mocking me?" He tried to read her face.

"Not at all. Please continue." If she was amused, she hid
it well.

"Well, he is a most important man among my people, and
something terrible has happened back in his . . . back home,
and I have to find him and tell him."

"He must be very important indeed to require such a summoning," she said.

"Ah, well . . . yes, he is, in fact, the king. King Hael."
Why, he thought, was he telling her this?

"And you, by logical extension, are the son of King Hael,
and therefore a prince."

"After a fashion. I mean, I am his son, but we don't have
royalty and princes and so forth as you would understand
them. I am just a warrior."

"I see. I must admit that your errand sounds urgent."

"You don't seem very surprised," he said, disappointed.

"I appreciate your candor. I know that you are saying this
as some sort of explanation for leaving so soon. But I guessed

some of this. You raved a great deal when I first brought you here.''

His face burned. ''What did I say?''

''You were delirious, so it was somewhat disjointed. And you were speaking in your native dialect, which I had a hard time following. But I could tell that 'Hael' and 'Father' referred to the same man. You babbled of a steel mine. And you went on about some truly frightening ogres named Gasam and Larissa.''

''They are not ogres. They are—''

''I know who they are. The news of the far west takes time to reach here, but it makes the trip eventually. Gasam the Conqueror is well known here by reputation, and Larissa, his queen. The hatred between Gasam and Hael the Steel King has become a byword for mutual antagonism. You were naive to think this nation would be completely ignorant of these things.''

Kairn was a bit crestfallen. ''I suppose I was. I am used to the slow pace of communication by the caravans that cross our country.''

''They reach here in time. But more important, we are a maritime people as well. Our ships trade into the southern ports even as far as Chiwa. News travels swiftly by sea.''

''I should have thought of it. My father did some seafaring in his youth. But I've never seen an ocean. I thought the great river was impressive enough.''

''This is wandering far afield. Be satisfied that I understand how urgent is your mission. I know that I could not keep you here, even if I wanted to.'' He was not quite sure what she meant by that last part. ''But I do wish you would stay a few days more. I know you feel you are fully recovered, but you aren't.''

He was torn between his need to find his father and his desire to stay with Star Eye. ''Well, perhaps a day or two would do no harm. The more fully I am recovered, the faster I'll be able to ride.''

She smiled as she cleared away the dinner things. Before she went outside to tend to her animals, she ordered him to go back to bed. He did so, but this time he did not fall into an exhausted sleep and he knew that his healing was almost complete.

She was gone for a long time. When she returned her hair was wet, and her clothing clung to her damp body. She said nothing to him, but she sat before the fire, brushing her hair until it lay dry and glossy over her shoulders. He watched her perform the simple, sensual act with great pleasure. She set the brush aside and rose. Unlike the other nights, she did not go to her own bed, but instead came to stand by his. He heard a rustle of cloth and the dress slid down her body. He smelled one of the scents she made from flower petals, mixed with the aroma of her own body.

"You understand," she said as she slid into the bed beside him, "that this is only fleeting. You have already said you must go."

He could think of absolutely nothing to say. In the dying light from the fire her body was pale except for her dark nipples and the black triangle between her thighs. He took her in his arms, ignoring the mild pain from his wounds, drowning them in the richness of these new sensations. She was unbelievably soft except when her nipples turned shockingly hard. She drew his tongue into her mouth and his hand slid down her back to the cleft of her buttocks, kneading.

Her breath quickened. A hand cupped his scrotum, then gripped the hard stem of flesh, stroking up to the broad, soft tip. He slid his hand between her legs and there was a wet sound as she parted her thighs. He felt the richness of her black-curled mound, parted the tender, damp flesh.

Gently, careful of his wounded thigh, she rolled him on top of her. "You rode your cabo today," she gasped. "Are you ready for another kind of mounted activity?" Then she cried out joyously as he slid into her.

FIVE

ael waited until late afternoon to go to the shop of Beak Nose. He spent the rest of his time exploring the strange, disturbing city. In his experience, cities were raucous, crowded places where people spent much of their time scrambling for a livelihood, usually trying to dominate the competition by outshouting all rivals. This place was quiet.

Other cities delighted in revelry and pompous public ceremony. There was no such thing in Crag. Instead, all was subdued. People worked with feverish industry, and seldom seemed to take time off. This was not a manufacturing center, but people busied themselves at necessary trades. He got the impression that slaves were used in great gangs primarily for agriculture. The rest of the population were of the artisan or tradesman classes. Otherwise, he saw a great many soldiers drilling in the streets, marching in lockstep from one place to another. Most carried the firetubes that so fascinated him. Even the soldiers marched to the rattling of a small drum, instead of to the blaring horns and squealing pipes that delighted the soldiery of other nations. There was a furtiveness about everyone here, as if their industriousness masked a great and pervasive fear.

From a parapet, he enjoyed a spectacular view of the river and its traffic. Boats and rafts made their way along the great stream in the shadow of the frowning fortress. He knew it was his imagination, but it seemed to him that they crept furtively downstream until they were safely past Crag, then sped on in great relief.

He could not put his finger on what it was about the place that so repelled him. He had been in cities where cruelty was rampant, where masters publicly flogged their erring slaves, where bloody human sacrifice was carried out in smoky temples. He had seen poor people sell their children out of hunger and desperation. This was different. The evil was not readily apparent, but he had never been in a city that he was so anxious to be away from. But, he had business of great importance and his personal, possibly irrational feelings were not of importance.

At the shop of Beak Nose, a finely dressed man turned to study Hael when he entered. The man was tall, with a shaven head such as Hael had noticed on a number of men in this city, all of them dressed too well to be ordinary artisans, but not splendidly enough to identify them as nobility.

"Merchant Alsa," Beak Nose said, coming forward, "a number of highly placed servants of the great houses have come by to view your unique items. This man, Dragon House Steward, has done you the honor of greatest persistence. He has patiently awaited your arrival, which I expected somewhat sooner."

"Other matters detained me," said Hael without apology.

"My mistress, Lady Morning Bird," said the bald man, "is a connoisseur of fine arts and workmanship. I saw these things this morning and informed her of them. She has sent me back to wait upon you. This is a measure of her interest, for it deprives her of my services, but she would entrust this task to no one else."

"I appreciate the compliment," Hael said, drily.

"My mistress has directed me to summon you—"

"Summon?" Hael interrupted sharply. Beak Nose made alarmed, calming gestures.

"To invite you, then, if you find the word more pleasing, to her house this evening for a personal presentation. I suggest that you bring one or perhaps two of your best wares. If my lady thinks them sufficiently interesting, she may send servants to fetch the rest for her viewing."

Hael was not much encouraged. He doubted that in this land even the highest women had great power or influence. Still, he had to start somewhere. "I shall be most happy to do this. Does she wish to receive me this evening?"

"She would prefer that you return with me," said the steward.

"Then allow me a few minutes to prepare some of my wares and we shall be off." Beak Nose helped him pack the chosen items and as he did, he hissed advice: "The Lady Morning Bird is probably the richest woman in the nation! She is somewhat eccentric, but on no account should you behave insolently with her, or any other noble. She is extremely generous when a thing takes her fancy, so be humble and persuasive, and we may both do well out of this."

"What is her political position?" Hael asked.

"Political position? Whatever can you be talking about? She is rich! Just keep that in mind." The wrapping finished, Beak Nose patted Hael on the shoulder and smiled. "Remember: ten percent."

"Ten percent," Hael acknowledged.

With the bundles strapped over his shoulders, Hael walked out into the late sunlight with the shaven-headed man. Without a word, the man began walking uphill and Hael fell in beside him.

"Dragon House Steward has a most impressive sound, but do I understand correctly that it is a title rather than a name?"

The man looked at him as if he had spoken the most egregious nonsense. "I am a Steward, therefore my name is Steward. As steward of Dragon House, I am Dragon House Steward. It seems simple enough."

"And so it is," Hael said. It seemed to be of a piece with what he had seen in this place so far. They climbed almost to the level of the upper citadel, then they turned into a street of high-towering town houses. The steward led them to a doorway above which was a stone plaque carved with a snarling, bat-winged, reptilian monster. They passed beneath the creature and into a dark hallway. They passed entrances to several small cramped rooms. Through the open doorways Hael could just make out heaps of dusty bales and what appeared to be cloth-draped furniture. Apparently, the ground floor was devoted to storage.

They climbed a stairway and emerged into a spacious room with tapestried walls and a floor of polished stone. In its center was a massive wooden table.

"Wait here," said the steward, and he was gone.

Hael fumed. He did not enjoy being treated the way nobles and their flunkies customarily treated tradesmen, but it was the pose he had chosen to adopt for his own purposes, so he resigned himself to living with the consequences. To distract himself during what would no doubt be a lengthy wait, he studied his surroundings.

The room was illuminated by tall window-doors at one end. The doors consisted of a wooden framework holding large panes of glass. This nation produced a great deal of glass, and they employed it in greater abundance than other lands. The doors opened onto a balcony overlooking a courtyard and garden. In the relatively abundant light, he was able to examine the room's odd furnishings.

The table held a collection of figurines depicting humans and animals. He picked up one and held it to the light. It was a cat of a breed he had never seen, beautifully carved from what appeared to be red coral. He set it down and picked up another. This was a male nude, crafted in a realistic style unfamiliar to him. The body was vigorously muscular, but the man was in a recumbent position, as if he had just collapsed to the ground. He seemed to be dying with a sort of voluptuous surrender. Hael found it vaguely repellent and put it down.

There were paintings hanging on the walls. He had seen many fine paintings in Neva and in Chiwa, but in those lands the paintings had been applied directly to the walls, forming an integral part of the decoration of the rooms. These were separate paintings, made with glossy pigments laid on a background medium of what appeared to be wood or tight-stretched cloth. They were confined within frames of carved wood. Some were portraits, darkened with the smoke and grime of centuries. One very large painting depicted a celebration or ball at which people wearing incredibly elaborate costumes struck unnatural poses, the significance of which were utterly lost on him.

He turned away from the paintings. In a corner stood a statue of a man on a pedestal. His head came just to Hael's chest, but his massiveness made him appear larger. He wore a long robe that just revealed his broad feet and the calves of thick, stumpy legs. He stood stiffly, one foot in front of the other, one arm straight down, the other bent at the elbow, the sleeve revealing a heavily muscled forearm and a clenched, knotty fist. His hair and beard were in stylized curls and his eyes stared straight ahead past a curved, razor-like nose. Despite its crudity and its static pose, it contained a coiled, forceful power. The pedestal was covered with row upon row of strange, sticklike writing. He had seen its like before. It was much like the Guardian, a colossal statue that stood in the mountain pass that led from his own land to the southern desert, thence to the steel mine that was the source of his power. He had seen no other artifact of that long-vanished civilization.

The room held other objects of interest. In the center of the table stood a candlestick of colorful ceramic, molded in the likeness of twining, flowering vines, the pigments of the blossoms startlingly bright. He recognized it as a product of the workshops of Floria, a city of northern Neva, largely destroyed by the invasion of Gasam and his islanders years before. He wondered how the delicate thing had made the long journey intact.

"You appreciate my things?" He turned to see a woman

dressed in an elaborate gown, her brown hair piled atop her head in a complicated coiffure. He gave her the formal bow he had learned many years before in Neva.

"I am Alsa, traveler in fine works, at your service, my lady."

"So I was led to expect. I have been watching you from the gallery." She gestured with a folded fan toward a curtained balcony of stone that jutted from the wall at one end of the room. "You show excellent taste. You spent the most time with my very best pieces." Her gown had long sleeves but it left her shoulders and the upper surfaces of her breasts bare almost to the nipples. These, along with her face, were powdered a startling shade of magenta. Her overlarge eyes were heavily outlined in black, her lips a deeper purple. She had once been a great beauty. Much of the beauty remained, but the years and overindulgence had rendered it haggard and half-demented. Her eyes were too wide, as was her smile, which revealed teeth all of which were sheathed in gold.

"But of course," Hael said. "Works of art are my life and livelihood. Your collection is wonderful for . . . for . . ."

"For a hideous city like Crag where the highest standard of beauty is a smoking, foul-smelling object like the firetube? You need not fear to express yourself. I am the first to admit that my people are famed for their lack of taste."

"Then I rejoice that I have found the one exception."

Her smile went even wider. "I am not the only exception, but I am surely the best you could have encountered."

"Perhaps not." Her smile faded fractionally and he went on: "For this journey I chose beautifully crafted objects of utility, thinking I might find here such as appreciated them. Yet here," he gestured toward his surroundings, "I find a connoisseur of beauty for its own sake."

Her smile regained its former, gilded splendor. "In that I am truly unique. But I appreciate wares like yours as well."

"Then may I be permitted to display them to you?"

"By all means."

He placed a box on the table and opened it. Within a padded lining reposed an object of bronze, shaped somewhat like a pair of shears. At one end were oval loops for the hands, at the other were oddly shaped hooks. Between the loops was an arrangement of ratcheted bars designed to keep the hooked ends rigidly separated when opened. Every surface, save the hooks and ratchets, was covered with a design of leaves, each tiny leaf overlaid with silver or gold, wonderfully detailed down to the last stem and vein.

"It's marvelous," Lady Morning Bird proclaimed. "I can tell it is a tool, but what sort? No common workman's tool merits such exquisite decoration."

"It is from Chiwa, and it is a surgeon's instrument. When a major incision must be made, the hooks grasp the edges of the wound and hold them open so that the surgeon may work inside. It is also used in their religious sacrifices, when the priests remove the organs from a living victim."

"Human sacrifice?" she all but whispered.

"Oh, yes. They deem it the only sacrifice worthy of some of their gods. You can tell which god by the nature of the decoration. These leaves are sacred to the Earth-god Ichotli."

"Grotesque," she said, "but stimulating." The fingertips of one hand rested lightly atop a powdered breast. "We lack even the tamest religious ceremonies, and the few I have seen practiced by subject peoples have been dull. I would like to see such a sacrifice. How I have come to long for stirring sensations."

He had not misjudged these people, it seemed. "Now this," he went on, "is quite different." From another padded case he took a foot-tall figurine mounted on a swiveling pedestal. It was in the form of a slender, nude woman. She stood arched on tiptoes, her arms stretched overhead at full length. Between her palms was a lens two inches in diameter.

"Lovely," Lady Morning Bird said, running a hand slowly down the tiny, gilded body, pausing over the swells of breast and hip, sliding down the slender legs. "But what does it do?"

"For this, we must step out onto the balcony. I think there is enough light remaining."

They went outside and he set the pedestal on the banister of the stone balcony. The sun was lowering in the west, but he thought it was still high enough for his demonstration. A tiny knob protruded from the pedestal and he pulled it out. A small, rectangular dish on a pivoting rod slid forth. From his belt pouch he took a small cone of incense, put it in the dish and arranged the dish to his liking, then slanted the lens to the proper angle, until the focus point was a fraction of an inch from the cone.

"Now watch." Within a minute or two, the focus point crept to an edge of the cone, touched it, and a plume of fragrant smoke wafted upward.

"How clever," Lady Morning Bird said. "And where does this come from?"

"Neva. The little lady is a sky goddess, part of the cult of the Sun-god. With these little idols, the worshippers can arrange things so that incense is burned to their deity at all the proper hours with little effort."

"It's enchanting," she said. He had thought it would have a special appeal for these people. The beautiful little thing was trifling, but at least it *did* something. "I must see the rest of your wares."

"Of course, my lady. Tomorrow I can bring—"

"Nonsense. My servants will go to the shop of Beak Nose and fetch them at once."

"Undoubtedly he has closed for the evening," Hael protested.

"That is of no consequence. He will reopen." It was the childish willfulness of the aristocrat that he knew all too well. "You must be my guest."

"You flatter me beyond all expectation," he said. "I will have to go to my inn—"

"My servants will fetch your things," she smiled again and took his arm. "Come with me. I will show you to my guest rooms. You are *quite* sure that no one else has seen your display?"

He knew what she meant. "No one of importance. Just Beak Nose and the servants who came to his shop today."

"Excellent. I will not make you show me the other items tonight. I want good light to appreciate them. Tomorrow I shall have a banquet and invite friends who share my tastes for a showing of your artworks. I will ask one favor of you. Please allow me first bid. I assure you I will not try to buy everything you have at my own price."

"How could I refuse such an offer?" he said. He was not sure that he liked the idea. This meant that he was a guest in a great house on his second night in the city, but he did not want to be stuck here. At least her proposed banquet would give him introduction to a number of other aristocrats. He hoped they would not prove to be effete nonentities.

"I must say," she went on as they climbed a curving flight of stairs, "that you are yourself more than easy to look upon, to one who adores comeliness as I do."

"You are more than kind, my lady." He had feared this, but his mission was too important to compromise with squeamishness.

"Oh, yes, in this land you are a rare creature, Merchant Alsa. And I use that title with all due respect. Be assured that I would never rate a man of your caliber as I would a common tradesman. You are a man of artistic vision, and one of adventurous spirit, who has traveled widely, among many peoples. I do not doubt that among your own people you are wellborn?" The sentence was phrased as both statement and question.

"I would not stress my birth," he said, "but among my people it is as high as any."

"Well said." She tapped his shoulder with her folded fan. "Yes, you speak as a merchant must, but your bearing and, how shall I say, your intonation, are those of a nobleman. Do not be embarrassed, Alsa, this is not unknown among us. A younger son, unable to inherit, must make his own fortune. I think it splendid that you have chosen to make your own way as a dealer in fine artworks. So many choose obscurity and an early death in the military. Here we are!"

They had come to a door carved with another of the dragons. She pushed it open, revealing a spacious room with a broad bed and excellent furnishings. At a snap of the woman's fingers servants appeared as from nowhere and busied themselves about the room, plumping pillows, throwing back shutters to admit fresh air, dusting furniture.

"Make yourself comfortable here. Dinner shall be served within the hour, and there we shall speak much more of things of beauty."

Perhaps it was the gold in her mouth, he thought, that made her look more than ordinarily carnivorous.

To distract her he pointed to the door and said, "I have seen the beast of your house a number of times here. Is it a creature native to this land or is it mythical?"

"No one has seen a real dragon, but there are many historical references to it. Who knows? Among us it represents power and wealth, and a certain relentlessness in pursuing one's own desires." She stroked a hand down his arm, oblivious of the servants who swarmed about the room. Some straightened curtains, others placed flowers in vases, yet others laid out a sideboard of refreshments—small appetizers and delicate glasses of wine. None looked at their mistress and her guest.

"A fitting symbol for a ruling people," Hael said.

"Is it not? Until dinner, then." With a slight bow and a meaningful widening of her oversized eyes, she withdrew. Hael let out a pent-up breath. This was a more than commonly delicate situation. He was among people of unknown mores and customs, unaware how he might mortally offend them. He shrugged off the problem. He would just have to trust his instincts. He had traveled more widely than anyone he knew, and there was no one better qualified to make his way among these strangers.

Within an hour, servants arrived with his belongings. He tried to speak to them, but they only replied in monosyllables, clearly uneasy at being expected to speak with a master. This told him much about the local social order.

A servant opened an adjoining door, revealing a bath and demonstrating ingenious taps for hot and cold water. Hael examined them with interest. The pipes and taps were made of a hard ceramic, their design far more sophisticated than the primitive plumbing he had encountered elsewhere. Once again, these people astonished him with their mastery of utilitarian things. He luxuriated in the hot water. It would never replace a plunge into a clear lake, but it was more than acceptable within walls.

He declined the offer of scent, using instead the fine fistnut oil to which he was accustomed. Its natural smell always reminded him of his home island where, at least, life had been simple. Among his own people, the Shasinn, the very idea of posing as a member of another people and class would have seemed insane. To be a Shasinn warrior was the most glorious thing in the world. Why, therefore, aspire to something else? How he longed for that elemental simplicity, knowing all the while the stupidity of such thoughts. Life had not been simple then. *He* had been simple, an unthinking boy who believed his island to be the world. The life of his tribe was complex and even sinister, as he would have found out had he been among them long enough to become a senior warrior and then an elder. Exile had taken care of that, preserving his brief warrior time like one of his exquisite artifacts—a thing of beauty to be contemplated in repose, but never roughly handled, even in thought.

He shrugged off the momentary reverie brought on by the delicate scent of the oil. There were plenty of matters to concern him in the here and now, without borrowing unchangeable events from the past. For the first time since embarking upon this expedition, he had no idea what he was going to do next. His next moves would depend upon what he learned here.

He still had no idea of what these people were, their aspirations, their vision of themselves. In the past there had been very little contact between his kingdom and this one. There had been minor trading, usually through intermediaries. When he had become king there had been no acknowledgement of the fact from Mezpa. As far as he knew, they had no diplomatic relations with anyone. They traded here and there, but otherwise had closed themselves off from the rest of the world; not by shutting their borders, but through a seeming lack of interest.

One thing he knew: Such military power as he had seen in this place was intended for more than keeping the local population in check. Everywhere, he had seen troops drilling, and the majority of them were armed with the bizarre firetubes, weapons that launched small, dense pellets at invisible speed. They had no accuracy beyond a score of paces, but armor was useless against them and a projectile one could not see, one could not dodge. To one accustomed to the superb accuracy of his archers, the smoke-belching tubes seemed like innocuous weapons at first, little more than noisemakers. But massed fire made up for poor accuracy, and to wield the weapons required little in the way of warrior qualities. Great strength, swift reflexes and good eyesight were irrelevant. The ability to maneuver in formation and the fortitude to stand fast before enemy weapons were all that were required. With the firetubes, farm boys with a few weeks' drill could be the equal of seasoned warriors. And the rulers of Mezpa were drafting enormous numbers of men to carry the things.

What were their plans? That was what he was here to find out. To the west and south of Hael's kingdom, Gasam's power was expanding every day. A sudden thrust from the east could destroy Hael's people. He had to learn the Mezpans' intentions, and he had to analyze their military powers. No military system was without its weaknesses, and he had to know the weakness of this one. He could trust no one else to carry out the task. He had long since learned as much as he could through intermediaries. There was no substitute for first-hand observation.

A servant appeared to lead him to dinner, and he followed the man through gloomy halls hung with old tapestries to a room with a small table set for two. In its center was an elaborate candelabrum in the shape of a multiheaded dragon. Around the walls were oil lamps with wicks burning inside globes of delicate blown glass.

He bowed as Lady Morning Bird entered. She was dressed

in a different gown. To his surprise, this one was somewhat more modest. He waited for her to be seated, then did likewise.

"We are to dine alone?" he asked.

"My husband is away at our estate in the south, and there are no other persons of quality in the house at the moment."

"Please don't think that I pry," Hael said, "but this city seems like an odd place to stay when one could be in a fine country house."

"Oh, I'm not here because I want to be. I'm a hostage." At his look she smiled. "Nothing as serious as all that. One of our rules is, that when a great lord is away from the capital, his wife or a child or other close family member must remain here as guarantee of his good behavior. We are not so far from our old feudal ways. Since both of our sons are with the army, it is my turn to inhabit this gloomy pile of stone."

"I see. You must find that irksome."

"One gets used to it. One finds activities to compensate." Upon that enigmatic pronouncement the servants brought in the first course. "If you see anything that disagrees with you, please don't worry about offending me by refusing it."

"That is unusually cosmopolitan, even among civilized people," Hael said approvingly. "Most people fancy their own dietary customs to be the sole acceptable ones and anyone else's to be in need of correcting. I've long since learned to eat whatever was put in front of me." He lifted a glass goblet and admired the play of light through the rose-colored wine. All the tableware was of glass or colored ceramic. To his relief, there was no eating implement more challenging than a spoon to master. At least he would be spared that source of embarrassment.

"I cannot promise that my compatriots are all as understanding as I am," she said, "but I find people from other lands far more interesting in their natural state than when pretending to be just like ourselves. After all, I find most of my countrymen boring, why should I wish for more of the same?"

"An excellent point," Hael said. The soft lighting flattered the lady, reducing the marks of age and debauchery, rendering her cosmetic adornment mysterious rather than garish. But as conversation and the wine caused him to relax in her presence, from time to time she would smile and the metallic glint of gold from her teeth restored his unease, reminding him that he was among an alien people.

"Have you a wife and children in your own land?" she asked. He had been waiting for that one.

"Yes, I have a wife, two sons and a daughter," Hael admitted. He could not tell whether this news pleased her or not. She had been open enough about her own familial entanglements and for all he knew she had not the least physical interest in him. Her earlier coquettishness might have been pure habit.

"And the ages of your children?"

Hael hesitated. He had never grown accustomed to thinking in such terms. "Let me see . . . the eldest has seen about twenty-two summers, my younger son about nineteen. Our daughter is sixteen. I am sure of that because she was born in the terrible winter when we lost so many of our cabos."

The lady regarded him skeptically. "Surely you cannot have children of such an age!"

"My lady flatters me."

"Not at all, I but speak the truth. I had thought you a man of no more than thirty years."

"My people are not in the habit of counting birthdays, but I must be over forty by now," Hael said.

"How wonderful it must be to hold one's age so well," she said wistfully. "Is it true of all your people?"

"Of some," he said evasively. In fact, the Shasinn were noted for this quality, but he wanted her to think that the plains was his native land. It could prove difficult just keeping his persona straight.

"You will find that we are forced to employ artificial means to achieve the same thing, with mixed results."

This was an obvious ploy, to which Hael rose gamely.

"I am sure that it will be a long time before you are forced to employ any such subterfuge."

She smiled her gold-flashing smile. "It is good to hear such words, however insincere."

The servants cleared away the plates and serving platters and brought in a long-necked bottle and two tiny conical glasses. Evidently, the succession of courses and beverages was rigidly formalized. Lady Morning Bird raised her glass.

"To your great success." Hael was not sure how to respond, but he raised his own glass and she clinked the two rims together, making a musical sound. The drink was highly aromatic, and so rich that it could only be taken in tiny sips.

"This is a thrice-distilled brandy, more than a hundred years old," she informed him. "It is a traditional way to cap a pleasant evening."

"You do me honor," Hael said. "I wish I could repay your hospitality as it deserves."

"You have, by relieving my boredom. Now, we have spoken a great deal of pleasant inconsequentialities. I suspect that you are bursting with questions you have been too polite to ask."

Once again, she surprised him with her perception. Was this urbanity or a calculated means of setting him at ease before grilling him?

"I did not wish to bore you, for I fear my questions are of the most tedious sort. You people are a great mystery to me, as to the rest of the world, but those things that intrigue me are no doubt the dullest mundanities to you."

Another lurid gold smile. "Please feel free. I am skilled at changing the subject when it bores me."

"Well, then. I've traveled more than widely, and I've seen a number of political systems. Generally, they fall into two categories. Primitive people usually favor a loose rule by a council of elders, although there may be a putative monarch. Civilized lands usually have a powerful monarch who rules from a central capital, although he may be strongly influenced or even dominated by a council of advisers. One encounters the occasional republic, but those are mostly very small states, under the thumb of some great kingdom. But I confess that your system here in Mezpa defeats me. Power seems to emanate from Crag, but who is in charge and how he or they hold power escapes me.''

"I can see that one who travels in many lands must become adept at learning where lies power and how it is wielded.''

"Safety and prosperity both depend upon it,'' he affirmed.

"Then here is what I can tell you: The Assembly of Great Men is made up of the major landholders. Membership is largely hereditary, but every ten years an assessment is held of each one's property, and if a man has somehow lost too much of either land or wealth, he is expelled. Likewise, if someone has acquired enough property—a very difficult task, I might add—then he may apply for enrollment on the Assembly. From among their number, by secret vote, the members elect a Speaker. As you might imagine, there is a great deal of intriguing and infighting to win the post, and many power blocs form within the Assembly. When none can muster sufficient votes to force an issue, there can be long periods when there is no Speaker.''

"Does that not make for a certain instability?''

"Not really. Most of the landholders would rather have no Speaker at all. Then they can be little kings on their own property. The common people are scarcely aware that the Speaker exists. The only authority that matters to them is the local authority and the local military commander. These are the officials with the power to affect their lives directly. I daresay that there are many who are unaware that we have had a Speaker for the last year, after a lengthy period of rule by the consensus of the Assembly.''

This was something new. "And who is the current Speaker?''

Her look grew evasive. "Why . . . a Lord Deathmoon.''

"That's an ominous name.''

"Isn't it? He is one of those I mentioned, the ones who gained a seat on the Assembly through property assessment.''

"And how many Assembly members are there?" Hael asked.

"Usually about three hundred, I think. But these are largely dominated by a core of twenty to thirty really great landowners."

"And among so many jealous rivals this Lord Deathmoon not only gained a place, but got himself elected Speaker? How could he do that?"

She was distinctly uneasy. "I really know very little about him. These are men's things and Mezpan men are not in the custom of speaking of political matters to women."

He knew she was lying. Hael had been in many lands and moved among the highest, and he knew for a fact that men of power told *everything* to women. It was as much a law of nature as the way things fell to the ground when they were unsupported. Something told him this was not the time to press.

"Well, I doubt that I will be having any dealings with the man, but it's always good to know how these things work."

She seemed to be relieved. "I hope I've been of some aid. And now," she rose from her seat, "I see that the hour has grown late." She nodded toward a timepiece he had not noticed previously. It had a circular dial and its pointer touched what appeared to be a numeral in the Mezpan writing system.

"It is near midnight," she said, "and I know you have had a tiring journey from which to recover. I want you well rested for my banquet tomorrow. My motives are not solely hospitable, you see. I intend to show you off as a major catch."

He rose likewise and bowed. "I shall strive not to disappoint you, my lady."

"Until tomorrow, then." She favored him with her golden smile and swept from the room in a rustle of skirts.

As he followed the servant back to his room, Hael pondered the unexpected turn of events. Earlier in the evening, he would have sworn that the woman intended to seduce him. He had too many years behind him to be flattering himself about it.

He felt both relief and alarm. What had changed her mind? Had it been his questions about the ominously-named Death-moon? That had certainly frightened her. Or had she made her decision previously? She had received him dressed in a gown that would have done credit to a Nevan prostitute, but for dinner she had changed to far more seemly garments. That might be explained by local custom. But then she had made a point of asking him about wife and children, not a subject usually brought up by a woman with seduction on her mind. She had mentioned her own husband and grown sons.

Some new factor had entered the equation, and his situation now looked far more dangerous than before. On the other hand, it looked as if opportunities were opening up.

SIX

Kairn wondered if the life of a lone warrior was always like this: travel, battle, narrow escape, recovery from wounds, love and eventual desertion. Leaving Star Eye had been wrenching, and he wondered whether it was something he would have to do often. He suspected that a woman like Star Eye did not fall into a warrior's life very often. Their parting had not been tearful, but he could read the resentment in every line of her.

"I know you must be off," she had said, "and I won't demean myself by begging you to come back."

"Star Eye," he had said, half-choking, "I cannot say how grateful—"

"Oh, shut up! Be off with you, then."

Puzzled and feeling very unheroic, he had wheeled his cabo to leave.

"One more thing." He turned back. She stood in the doorway of her hut. "In Crag there is a man. His name is Death-moon."

"Yes?"

"Avoid him." She went inside and closed the door.

He rode off remembering his father's saying that women always got in the last word. What these words meant was unclear, but they definitely had been the last. Perhaps that was all she had wanted to do. He was scarcely likely to seek out a man with a name like Deathmoon.

Two days of riding along narrow, winding country roads brought him to a highway. This one was raised above the surrounding land and had a paved surface, gently arched and well maintained. It carried a busy traffic, including coffles of slaves connected by odd-looking chains running through rings fastened around their necks.

Four-wheeled wagons rumbled along, laden with cargo and drawn by complaining, foul-smelling humpers. Two-wheeled carts similarly laden were hauled by yoked slaves. Once again, Kairn felt repugnance at the lavish use made of slaves in this land. He had difficulty feeling much sympathy for slaves, but this seemed excessive.

Occasionally there were mysterious litters, borne on the shoulders of matched slave teams. The open litters always contained men, so he guessed that the curtained ones bore women. Once, as one passed him, he saw a dainty hand adorned with multiple rings push aside a curtain, and for a few seconds he was studied by a huge, brown eye, heavily made up with black cosmetic. It was intriguing, but Star Eye had temporarily drained him of interest in women. Besides, she was going in the opposite direction.

He also saw files of soldiers, firetubes slanted over their shoulders, marching in the lockstep that seemed proper and soldierly to civilized people and seemed comical to all the rest. There was nothing comical about the soldiers themselves, though. They looked grim and competent, but it still seemed strange to see warriors who bore no bladed weapons save knives or small hatchets.

He noticed that the soldiers differed somewhat as to uniforms. One group he passed wore white tunics and black trousers. Another group he saw later in the day, camped by the road, were clad all in red. He guessed that these meant

different regiments, but they might equally be the troops of
different landholders, wearing their masters' livery; if the
landholders were allowed private armies. They usually were,
in his experience.

What was strangest was the extreme uniformity of their
equipment. Every man, regardless of uniform, seemed to
carry exactly the same weapons and gear. They were not
differentiated into light and heavy infantry, scouts, mounted
troops, regulars and local auxiliaries, and so forth. This
hinted of a formidable centralized organization that con-
trolled all aspects of the soldiers' lives. This was an ominous
thought. Not even his father's old enemy, Gasam, wielded
such control.

When the light began to dim he rode away from the road,
into the forest. He had had enough of walls for a while. He
longed to sleep beneath the stars once more, even if the stars
around here were barely visible through the tree branches.
He did not go far. All he wanted was solitude, he did not
want to get lost.

He watered his cabo at a small stream, then picketed the
beast in a tiny clearing where grass grew abundantly. He did
not plan to do any cooking, but he built a small fire for its
cheering light and in hopes that the smoke would hold the
insects at bay. Before the light was gone entirely, he scouted
around his campsite, looking for signs of dangerous animals.
The area was fairly densely populated, and he knew that big
predators rarely were found where man was much in evidence. Still, it paid to be careful.

He found the tracks of a great many small beasts, but none
that could harm him. There were other marks as well, human
marks. These gave him pause, and he wondered whether it
would be such a good idea sleeping out here instead of finding the nearest village.

The marks were those of sandaled feet. Whoever they were,
they were armed, for he could see the impressions of some
sort of pole weapon where men had leaned on them. Local
farmers looking for strayed livestock? He did not think so.
He had yet to see a farmer here who carried so much as a

staff. Beside one footprint he saw a strange, rounded impression that had him puzzled until he realized that it was made by the butt of a firetube. Its owner had grounded the weapon and probably leaned upon it, making the mark. Did soldiers patrol these woods? But he had seen no soldiers carrying polearms. That left hunters and outlaws.

He decided to hope that it was hunters. He was too tired to go on after dark. His wounds still ached and his energy was not yet all it should be. Whoever they were, there were only five or six of them, and by now his self-confidence was high enough to think that he was equal to handling that many outlaws.

He ate from his store of travel rations, then rolled into his blankets to sleep. It felt good to be outdoors again, although he missed having Star Eye nearby. Amid the buzzing of insects, he slept.

When he woke he knew that he was not alone. He sat up, reaching for his weapons. They were not where he had left them. Too proud to jump up and make an outcry, he waited for his visitors to make themselves known.

"Greetings, plainsman." The voice came from a point opposite him, across the pile of still-smoking wood where his fire had been. He could make out a seated form, but little else. He sensed others nearby.

"Who are you?" he asked. "And why did you not make yourselves known like honest men?" It was a foolish question, but a little dignity never came amiss.

"We are always cautious with intruders," the man said.

"Intruders? I was unaware that I was intruding anywhere. I was traveling on the road and did not wish to spend another night in a settlement, so I camped here."

"But then, you are a stranger. Plainsman, in this land any man who seeks to be where he may not be observed is automatically suspect. Would you have come here if you knew there were men in these woods?"

"I knew you were here. I saw the marks all around this spot. Are you the one with the firetube? And you have four or maybe five others with you, at least if you are part of the same band.''

There was a pause and he knew he had impressed the man.

"You read all that from the marks we left? You are a skilled tracker then?''

"No more than most of my people. We learn to notice such things. So who are you? Outlaws?''

He heard several men chuckling. "Only in the freest sense.''

"Well, I am no threat to you, so let me have my weapons back.''

"They are just out of your reach. I just didn't want you to do anything rash before you were fully awake. Build up the fire.'' This last was spoken to somebody else and a man came forward with an armload of dry brush. In moments the fire flared up and Kairn could see who sat across from him.

It was a man a little older than himself, dressed in simple clothing of good quality. The firelight made it hard to discern color, but it seemed to be in the subdued tones of the forest, the sort of clothing hunters might wear. Now he could see the other men and they were dressed much alike. Their clothes were not as fine as the speaker's, but the men were clean and neatly barbered. These were no bandits. Two leaned on straight wooden bows. The other two had short spears.

"So what brings you to our forest?'' asked the speaker. He sat cross-legged, a firetube slanted over his shoulder. Something seemed odd about it and Kairn realized that its tube was dark. The others he had seen had been white. This one would be hard to see in the deep woods.

"By what right do you ask?'' Kairn demanded. "Are you officials?'' At this the men laughed heartily.

"No, but these woods are mine, and I make it my business to know who is abroad in them.''

"Your woods? Is that stretch of highway yours also?''

The man smiled. "The road I generously allow the government and travelers to use. By ancient law the high roads belong to the state.''

To Kairn the man spoke very oddly, as if he were an outlaw

but at the same time had respect for the law. Although their meaning was strange, his words sounded well and carefully chosen. Like Star Eye, this was an educated person, whatever his circumstances. This country was full of unexpected people. From his next question, the man thought the same thing.

"What sort of man is armed and mounted like a plainsman but speaks as formally as a prince?"

This was uncomfortably close to the truth. "Even a wild nomad can acquire a bit of learning, and good manners are the birthright of a warrior people."

"To be sure," said the man, smiling as if the two of them shared a secret. "You intrigue me, outlander. Come, be my guest for a while. Dawn is almost upon us and it's time for some breakfast."

"I thank you for the offer, but I must be on my way. I have a rather urgent mission that will brook no delay."

"Then there is no problem. Spend but a while with me, and I will give you a guide who can save you more than a day's travel by the high road."

Kairn noted that he still did not have his weapons back. "Then I accept."

A man fetched Kairn's cabo and his few belongings were bundled onto it. They set out, the men moving assuredly in the dark forest. Kairn led the animal by its reins. It was grumpy, groaning as if to say that any fool could see the sun wasn't up yet.

"We've yet to exchange names," the man noted.

"As stranger in the land I suppose I should identify myself. I am Kairn, from the land of Hael the Steel King."

"Just the name, no title?"

"We are a free people. We feel no need of titles."

"Well, we are most assuredly not a free people, and are very fond of titles. I am Noble Stone, Lord of the Black Wood."

Surely, Kairn thought, he must have made that up. Even in a land of ringing, resounding names, it sounded like a poet's fancy.

They walked for no more than an hour and the sky shone

lead-gray through the trees when one of the men gave a low-pitched whistle. The sound was answered from high in a tree ahead. Looking up against the lightening sky Kairn could just make out the shape of a man stationed on a tiny observation platform among the branches.

Another hundred paces past the sentry's tree, they entered a broad clearing and Kairn blinked as if at an illusion. In the center of the clearing was a great log hall, two-storied with a steeply pitched roof. High wooden blockhouses stood at either end and it was surrounded by outbuildings.

"Welcome to Woodhouse, Kairn," said his host. "Turn the cabo over to one of my men and let's go inside."

The ground floor was higher within than Kairn had expected. Heavy crossbeams high above were draped with ceramic chains supporting candelabras. These were extinguished, for by now light streamed through the front door, which was wide enough to admit a large wagon. Windows overhead admitted more light through glass panes.

At a long table, women were setting out food. Apparently the return of the patrol had been anticipated. Noble Stone seated himself at the head of the table and gestured for Kairn to take the seat next to him. Trying not to appear too hasty, Kairn began to eat. He was not especially hungry, but he knew that most people had taboos against attacking a man who had eaten with them. If his host noticed, he was too polite to remark on it.

"This is the first great house of this land I have entered," Kairn said. "I admit, it is not what I expected."

"Nor should you have, for you'll find few others like it. The Mezpans do not favor anything so rustic."

"You speak of the Mezpans as if they were not your own people," Kairn noted.

"They are not. Black Wood is a part of North Riveria, which was once an independent kingdom. Oh, we acknowledged the sovereignty of Mezpa, but that was really an alliance. Then the Mezpans advanced north and made it a sovereignty in fact. Our throne was abolished, and a traitor lord was given a seat on the Assembly as a sop to our autonomy, not that anyone takes it seriously.''

"You have little love for Mezpa," Kairn said, "and less fear of expressing it.''

"I am a lord and I'll speak as I like in my own home.'' For the first time the man showed anger.

"If they could conquer your country," Kairn said bluntly, "why do they tolerate you?''

"I keep them away from me by being obscure. A petty lord in the path of an expanding power is well advised to remain obscure." He sat back, his tone softening. "Your plains kingdom is such an expanding power.''

Kairn shook his head. "My king has subdued the plains and hill country, united them and made all the peoples keep peace with one another. He seeks no more territory.''

"They all say that. No king ever took land without wanting to take more.''

"King Hael is not like other kings," Kairn insisted.

"So I have heard. Some sort of mystic holy man, is he?''

Kairn laughed. "Something like that, but it is very difficult to explain. There is no hereditary king. He is a chief above chiefs, a spirit-speaker, but he is also the greatest warrior of the age.''

"A potent combination. But it does not mean that he lacks a hunger for more territory.''

"Our population is small, our horizons are wide. There is little to attract us or our king in far lands, save what can be got by trade. He has made us strong to keep us safe. We, too, have enemies who would expand into our land. King Hael has caused them to reconsider such plans.

"And now," he leaned forward on his elbows, "it strikes me that for a self-described petty lord who wishes to escape the notice of his sovereigns, you take a great interest in the expansionist ambitions of a king far from you.''

At this Noble Stone leaned back and laughed. "Wild nomad indeed! No need of titles, eh? What are you, Kairn? A chief? A prince out of favor? Ordinary warriors do not think politically. They praise their king or curse him but they seldom notice his relations with the rest of the world unless it means war. Yes, I am very much interested in King Hael. I've hosted a great many travelers and traders in this crude hall, seeking to learn about him. But you are the first native of his land I've spoken to except for a few warriors who escorted trade caravans, and they were men of narrow vision. To them Hael was a holy king, and the rest of the world just bewildering foreigners. But you are a man of the world.''

Kairn cautioned himself against the implied flattery. He was better taught than the ordinary tribesman, but none knew better than he the limits of his experience.

''Why this interest in King Hael?'' Kairn asked.

''Understand that what I am about to say could be construed as treason by some, and should you run to Crag with it, I will deny it with my last breath.''

Kairn shrugged. ''Your internal politics are nothing to me.''

''Very well. I've heard how King Hael has forged a matchless army out on the plains. They are all mounted and armed with great bows like yours, and with this army he swept all before him even before he came to possess his legendary steel mine.''

''That is so,'' Kairn agreed.

''Then in all the world his is the only army with a chance of defeating Mezpa's!'' This last was said with vehemence.

''The capability may be there, but the desire? Why should he want war with a nation that has never threatened or harmed him?''

''Mezpa is bounded on the south and east by the sea. It has expanded as far north as is profitable. A generation ago, Mezpa crossed the river and now controls all the old states of the western bank as part of Greater Mezpa. The far west beckons.''

''Why?'' Kairn demanded. ''Does Mezpa covet grass? Furs?''

''The Assembly of Great Men is now headed by Lord Deathmoon, and Deathmoon would like very much to own a steel mine.''

Kairn hoped that his expression revealed nothing of his own desperate mission. "Tell me more."

"What could be more logical? The Mezpans do wonderful things with glass and ceramics and such metal as they can lay hands on, gold and bronze and such. But steel is the most precious stuff in the world, and they could do far more with it than anyone else! To the rest of the world steel means weapons and tools. To Mezpa it means machines, things most people could never imagine!"

"But the location of the mine is a closely-guarded secret," Kairn said uncomfortably.

"It will be found," Noble Stone insisted. "There are always traitors in every land. And there is more."

"What?"

"I try to keep abreast of happenings in the world, remote as I am from the center of power. The Assembly is far better able to do so. Like all rulers, they have spies in every land. They are aware that there is a new king in the far west, a ruthless conqueror."

"Yes. Gasam. We've met him before and defeated him."

"Temporary setbacks, as I've heard it. Gasam wants that steel mine too. It comes to a question of who Deathmoon would rather fight for its possession: Hael the mystic or Gasam the conqueror."

"Gasam is not half the warrior my . . . king is! Deathmoon is a fool if he thinks Hael would be an easier opponent than Gasam. Our arrows have laid Gasam's spearmen down in rows."

"That may be, but Deathmoon is a man who believes in force and force alone. Such a man will always fear a conqueror, and hold a peaceful king in contempt. I think he will attack Hael before he has to fight Gasam. Hael would be well advised to attack first."

"My king would need far more than your speculations to go to war. Even if he were not a man of peace, it would be foolish to do so, and he is no fool. You have heard how he fought his battles in the west?"

Noble Stone nodded. "They say his cabo-mounted archers went through the western armies like wind through grass."

"Exactly. Most importantly, he was able to take advantage of the rigid military thinking of his enemies, their inexperience with mounted archers. They thought our small numbers meant weakness. He would not make the same mistake."

"How do you mean?"

"Mezpan armies are armed with the firetubes. King Hael will never assume that these weapons are contemptible because he is unfamiliar with them. On the contrary, he will never offer battle to such an army unless he knows its capabilities precisely."

His host regarded him for a long time without speaking. "You know your king well." It was not a question.

"As much perhaps as any man."

"What, think you, might it be worth to him to be taught the secrets of such an army?"

Kairn thought hard and chose his words carefully. "I think he would value even more the secret of how to make the firetubes, and the fire powder."

Noble Stone shook his head. "Useless to him. The powder is amazingly simple, anyone could make it. But the tubes are made of a super-hard ceramic. The clay for it is found only in a single pit, as carefully guarded as your king's steel mine, and its manufacture is a complex process requiring industries no land save Mezpa possesses. That is another reason why— Well, never mind."

Kairn wondered what the man had been about to say when he had caught himself.

"The Mezpans have been experimenting with bigger fire weapons," Noble Stone went on, "tubes the size of small trees, firing projectiles than can knock down walls. Not very successfully thus far, though. The ceramic isn't strong enough and it takes an extravagant amount of bronze to make one, but they'll be terrible weapons when they're perfected."

"What do they use for projectiles?"

"Stone balls in a ceramic sheath. Metal would be better but it's too valuable."

"It sounds frightening, but I can't imagine that such weapons would be of much use against us. We don't have castles or fortified cities."

"I think King Hael had better be the judge of that," his host cautioned.

"And so he shall, when I tell him."

"You have not answered my question, you know. What might my instruction be worth to your king?"

"If we were already in a hostile state with Mezpa, I am sure it would be invaluable, but we are not. Whatever your wants in the matter, you are in vassalage to Mezpa. I take it you want your independence, and I know you will have his sympathy, but what you propose it not an alliance, it is an intrigue. It is not King Hael's style to conspire against rulers with whom he is not at war."

The man looked as if he were restraining himself, not wishing to speak in anger. "Just tell King Hael what I have said. He will make his own decision."

"I shall. As soon as I return to my homeland."

"You need not go that far. I know that he is within Mezpan borders, on what mad errand I cannot guess, but he is said to be an eccentric king."

Kairn was stunned. "How do you know this?"

"I am not alone in wanting to see an end to the Mezpan hegemony. We have our own networks of spies, our own ways of trading information among ourselves. Some of our people have been on trade missions to Hael's court and have seen him. He was seen entering Mezpa with a caravan. The caravan left without him."

"Nonsense," Kairn said. "Just some warrior who decided to stay behind and see the sights."

"I've never seen him myself, but I've heard him described. He is a very striking man and not likely to be misidentified. He looks a bit like you, from what I've heard."

Kairn felt a chill of fear. "You have that wrong. I look like all the rest of my tribe. The plainsmen you've met were probably Amsi, the darker people from the south."

"Perhaps you're right. In any case, when you find your

king—you are here looking for him, are you not?—tell him what I have said. I think he may want to pay me a visit before he quits Mezpan territory for good.''

Then, with a mock-rueful look: ''But, what a terrible host I am! You must be starving, and I've kept you talking and not allowed you to eat. Please forgive me. I so seldom waylay interesting strangers to talk to.'' He turned to one of the serving women. ''Cloud, bring our guest hot food. His breakfast has grown cold.''

For the rest of the morning his host prompted Kairn to speak only of his travels. No more words were exchanged concerning power or political matters. He did want to know about the latest doings of Gasam and his islanders, and Kairn saw no harm in telling him what was common knowledge over most of the western world. He withheld the crowning catastrophe which was the burden of his mission.

Before the sun reached zenith, Noble Stone sped him on his way with a store of fresh provisions and a guide to show him the promised shortcut.

''The last word I had said your king was seen on a road that leads to Crag. Since I can hardly imagine him desiring to go anywhere else, Crag would be a good place to look. Remember what I said.''

''I will tell him,'' Kairn said, noncommittally. ''I will not presume to advise.''

Noble Stone laughed. ''You're as cautious as a diplomat, but at least you don't make empty promises. Farewell, then, and good fortune. And remember this: Mezpans are never your friends, no matter how courteously they act. They are enemies to the whole world.''

Kairn thanked his host and rode from the clearing, following his guide. By evening, he was back on the high road to Crag.

SEVEN

Hael laid out his best clothes for the banquet. In anticipation of meeting high personages he had brought
along court garments. They were simple, for he knew
that his own striking appearance was his best ornament. He
was not vain, but too many people had assured him of the
fact for him to doubt it.

He donned trousers and shirt of a shiny black Chiwan fabric,
woven from the silk of giant spiders. The fabric would never
wrinkle and was light as air. He drew on knee-length Amsi
boots with soft soles, the even softer uppers beautifully embroidered with colored thread in floral designs. Over all he threw
a short mantle of spider silk heavily woven with gold thread. It
was a bit heavy for the climate, but persons of high rank always
valued appearance far higher than comfort.

After some thought he added several rings and a large ruby
on a neck chain. These were gifts from other monarchs, and
he never wore them at home. Satisfied that he was presentable, he awaited the arrival of a servant to inform him that it
was time to join the company.

But when the knock came it was not a servant, but Lady Morning Bird herself.

"Our guests have arrived. If you will come with me, I will tell you a little about them as we go."

Hael rose, gave his clothes a final adjustment, and took her arm.

"You look wonderful, my dear," she said.

"As do you, my lady," he replied. She was dressed much as he had first seen her, but with more jewelry and heavier powdering over her abundantly exposed flesh.

"Dawnlight is here. She's a slut and she will be all over you, but she has excellent taste. Valley House is probably the richest. That's his title, by the way. He never uses his name and I don't even know it. Dreadful snob. Oh, and there's Lord Broadfield. He hasn't arrived yet, but I know he'll be here. He's a little eccentric, but just wonderfully knowledgeable about everything. Be sure to talk with him a lot. I've seated him across from you for that purpose." She went on about other personages, giving each a concise, usually unflattering, characterization.

At their entrance the guests turned to view the new curiosity. The banquet room was dazzlingly illuminated and the guests were extravagantly clothed. Their masklike makeup gave them a rather ghastly appearance to Hael's eyes. They did not exactly line up, but Lady Morning Bird made introductions in what seemed to be strict order of precedence. Lord Valley House was tall and fat, dressed in clothing much too tight for him. He gave his hand as if bestowing a royal favor. Lady Dawnlight wore a gown that left her breasts fully exposed. Her nipples were rouged with bright red, in odd contrast to the blue powder that covered the rest of her skin. She studied him with wanton eyes and smiled with silversheathed teeth.

Hael had been in some strange places in his life, but never had he encountered such fanciful names coupled with such bizarre appearance. They were utterly unlike the other Mezpans he had seen, causing him to wonder if the nobility were totally divorced from the common people, or might it be just this small, decadent group? He despaired of keeping all the names straight, knowing he would have to get by with "my lord" and "my lady" most of the time.

His unique wares formed the centerpiece down the long banquet table. He received many questions, but their hostess did not want him to make his presentation until their last guest arrived.

At a sudden silence in the room Hael turned to see that a man had entered and Morning Bird was hurrying toward him. She took the newcomer's hand and drew him toward Hael.

"Merchant Alsa, may I present Lord Broadfield."

Hael took Broadfield's hand. He was a small man, dressed simply in silvery gray clothing, with a lace ruff around his neck. His skin was very pale and he wore no powder. His beard was neatly trimmed to a point, his mustache curled at the ends. His midnight-black hair came to a sharp peak low on his forehead and his eyes were as black.

"Thrice welcome, Merchant Alsa." His voice was surprisingly deep from so small a man. "It is good to have a man of such discernment among us. And one who brings such marvelous things!" He scanned the table, black eyes blazing.

"Then perhaps it is time for me to explain them, if our hostess thinks it best."

"By all means," she said.

"Then, with your permission, we shall begin at the head of the table." With that, he went into his well-rehearsed program. His audience was rapt, their eyes blazing with an almost childlike greed as each new toy was displayed and explained. He hoped he was not wasting his time on a pack of moneyed nobodies.

As he spoke, he noticed that Broadfield, who stayed close to his elbow, was shown a special deference by the others. When he spoke, the others remained silent. None stood too close to him. This, coupled with his unapologized late entrance, spelled a rank far higher than the others.

Near the foot of the table he took up the smallest of his displays, an exquisitely ornamented instrument of gold and bronze with numerous oddly shaped holes and clamps and an oblique, razorlike blade working across an oval aperture. He allowed them to pass it around, and they admired its workmanship while trying to guess its function.

"I confess myself mystified," Broadfield said, handing it back to him. "What is the beautiful thing?"

"It is a very specialized surgical instrument from Chiwa. It is a slave castrator."

"Oh, I must have it!" said Dawnlight, her face unsettlingly eager. Hael wondered whether he had done the right thing by bringing it. He had thought they might be interested in it as a ghastly curiosity, but these people might well want to use it.

"Dinner is ready," Morning Bird announced. "We can all argue and make bids and plague our guest while we eat." Everyone agreed that this was an excellent idea and they took their seats and soon platter after lavish platter made its way to the long table. Hael studied the others as they dined. Valley House ate gluttonously, with the true aristocrat's indifference to the impression he made. Dawnlight ate more daintily and never took her hot eyes from Hael.

Broadfield seemed uninterested in food, taking only a few tiny bites and sipping at a glass of sparkling water. After a token bite from a new course he addressed Hael.

"I notice that there is no steel to be found in your goods."

Hael shrugged. "I've never seen a work of art made of steel. Steel is for tools and weapons, valuable as it is. I never took much interest in it. It is hard but not very durable, unlike gold or silver or bronze. Who would waste artistic merit on a metal that rusts?"

"I had not thought of it that way, but what you say makes sense. I hear that you are widely traveled. Have you actually seen Neva with your own eyes? And Chiwa and the other southwestern states as well?"

"I have been to them all, although Chiwa is not a good place to be since the islanders invaded. A trip there can be profitable if one wants to take the risk. The islanders are savages and do not know the value of what they have won."

"Ah, the islanders! I would like to hear of them. They are said to be unbeatable."

"That is said of all conquerors until they meet a reverse. In fact, the islanders were driven out of Neva several years ago."

"From the news that reached here," Broadfield said, "it took a combined army of King Pashir and King Hael to do it. It is also said that Gasam merely withdrew to find richer pickings in the south, which by all accounts he found in abundance. He has been snapping up the southern kingdoms one after another. How do these islanders fight?" For a connoisseur, the man seemed to have very little interest in art.

"The great bulk of Gasam's army is levied from the subject peoples. The elite are the warriors from the Storm Islands, and of these the supreme elite are his native tribe, the Shasinn. They are all spearmen of great skill and bravery."

"And has he some tactic that has made him so formidable?"

Hael shook his head. "Courage and fanaticism. That is all he needs or values. With those and with his carefully nurtured reputation, the enemy is half beaten before battle is joined. Otherwise, they fight as all western armies do, with sword and spear, axe and mace. They make little use of missile weapons except for javelins and Gasam has only a minuscule mounted force."

"He likes to get close, eh? Does he find that more effective?"

"I think he just enjoys it. He and his queen revel in bloodshed."

"Oh," said Dawnlight, "the terrible Queen Larissa! We have heard of her. Is she as beautiful and cruel as men say? Have you seen her personally?"

"I am not the sort of man to interest such people," he said. "They are warriors interested only in slaughter. They have nothing but contempt for one whose business is trading works of art."

"But surely," said Morning Bird, "the nature of your travel requires an adventurer as bold as any warrior."

"That is how it seems to me," said Broadfield. "No mere money-grubber blithely crosses a continent pursuing the subject he loves."

"You are too kind," Hael protested.

"I think not," Broadfield said. "Now, let's to business! As the lucky one who discovered you, Lady Morning Bird gets to choose the two works she fancies. For the rest, we shall hold open auction. How does that strike you?"

"Eminently fair," Hael said, wondering if they would lose interest in him as soon as his wares were auctioned off.

Broadfield took the role of auctioneer, and all the others bid frantically, amid tipsy hilarity. Dawnlight, Hael noted, got her castrator. This boded ill for some unfortunate slave. Within an hour the entire lot was sold and Hael was the owner of a massively weighty sack of gold.

"Are you satisfied with your takings?" Broadfield asked.

"Most satisfied, although it pains me to part with these lovely things. But I notice you sought nothing for yourself, my lord."

"Oh, I have the finest prize of all," Broadfield insisted.

"How so?"

Broadfield smiled, a narrow display of predatory teeth. "Why, I have you." He snapped his fingers and a file of guards came into the room. They were armed with short firetubes that had exceptionally wide mouths. Quickly, they formed a circle around the dumbfounded Hael.

"Take him to the prison beneath my palace. Do not harm him so long as he doesn't resist, but take no chances. He is a Shasinn warrior and they are said to be great fighters. If he tries to escape, blow a leg off him and apply a tourniquet. I want him in condition to talk."

"As you command, Lord Deathmoon," said the leader of the guards.

Hael's erstwhile companions smiled and tittered as he was led from the room. At least, he thought, he had accomplished his main purpose here: He had made contact with the very highest circles.

* * *

The dungeon turned out to be less objectionable than he had expected. The stone walls had only a single door of thick timber and a small, barred window, but it was furnished much like a room in a modest inn. He suspected that there were far worse accommodations for recalcitrant prisoners.

He felt alarm and disgust, but most of all he felt shame. What disaster might he have brought upon his people by his rash and foolhardy actions? He had always stressed to them that he was not essential to them, that he had to die someday. It made no difference. If they found out that he was held prisoner here, they would undoubtedly mount a grandiose military expedition against Mezpa, and would probably be slaughtered by the massed firetubes.

He would kill himself before he would allow that. But perhaps it would not come to such a strait. Deathmoon knew who he was. Perhaps he could make some sort of deal with the man. Perhaps he could arrange a ransom to be paid in steel.

He wondered who had spotted him. Probably some trader who had seen him at a fair. He should have taken some precaution, he realized belatedly, perhaps cut his hair and dyed it a darker color. Too late now.

He rose from his leather-covered chair when he heard the bolts being drawn from the other side of the door. Deathmoon came in, accompanied by two of the hulking guards, each armed with one of the stubby firetubes. Hael had been informed that these special weapons were charged with a handful of soft lead pellets and meant certain death at close range.

"I trust you find the accommodations to your liking?" Deathmoon said.

"I know they could be far worse."

"And shall be, should you prove uncooperative. I am sure you understand my vexation with you. It was not your presence here, but the manner of your coming, under an assumed identity instead of openly." His words and tone were mild, but Hael was not gulled. There was a mad gleam in the man's eyes that Hael had seen before in men of great cruelty and insane ambition.

"I wished to know more of this place before revealing myself," Hael prevaricated.

"Good spy's reasoning," said Deathmoon. "But it was foolish to try this without altering your appearance. Your people are remote to us, but I am careful to keep myself informed. I, too, have spies, as do all rulers. The Shasinn physiognomy is far too distinctive to mistake, even if one has seen it only in artist's drawings and written descriptions." Here was one, Hael knew, who hid his madness behind a facade of prosaic routine.

"I misjudged your alacrity," Hael confessed.

"You are a unique, and uniquely valuable prisoner."

"Now it is you who misjudge. I am worth very little to you."

"Come now, no hedging," Deathmoon snapped, allowing a bit of his malignancy to show. Then, in a milder tone: "You see, all is not lost. It is my usual practice to have spies put to death very slowly. But you are not an ordinary spy, are you? No, indeed you are not, so what are we to do with you?" He paused, undoubtedly to let the awful implications sink in. "But, after all, I am not entirely displeased by your arrival here."

"I am happy to hear it," Hael said.

"Yes, I would have preferred a diplomatic mission, but now that you are here, something more clandestine may be preferable after all."

Hael was mystified, but wanted to hear more. "Please continue."

Deathmoon paced, speaking on as if to himself. "Yes, I think you can be of real help to me if you cooperate. After all, I think that your master and I have much in common."

"Master?" Hael said before he could stop himself or think it through.

"Well, mistress, then," Deathmoon said testily. "Queen Larissa is in charge of the spy corps, is she not?"

A wave of relief surged over Hael. The man thought he

was one of Larissa's spies! Of course, it never occurred to him that a king would enter his country incognito, but a spy for Gasam would make perfect sense. Apparently he did not know that Larissa never used Shasinn as spies, only mainlanders.

"It was foolish of me to think I could deceive you," Hael said, scarcely able to believe his luck. He might have given himself away at any time since his arrest.

"Your pose strained credulity. Quite aside from your looks, you tried to tell Morning Bird that you were forty years old or more! Any fool can see you cannot be more than thirty, if that. Your past is quite plain to me. King Gasam and his queen have been on the mainland for how long? About fifteen years?"

"About that."

"Plenty of time to take a bright boy and train him as a spy, teach him languages, send him to established houses and schools to give him a little polish. I'll admit you learned well. You could almost pass for nobility."

"In the islands, there is no higher birth than that of a warrior," Hael said, playing his new role to the hilt.

"Yes, you savages have your arrogance, don't you?" He turned to his guards. "Leave us."

"My lord, he—"

"Out!" Deathmoon snarled. "He and I have an understanding now." When they were gone and well out of earshot he turned back to Hael. "Now, is Alsa your true name?"

"It is, I saw no reason to change it."

"Then tell me, Alsa, what information your queen instructed you to seek out."

"I suppose the same things you want from your own spies, which means anything that may be of aid in judging a foreign leader and his land. Much of it is the most ordinary things: the extent of the land, the sorts of commerce, the number of great cities, the condition of the roads, the climate—"

"Yes, yes, I know all that. As you say, it's what I want to hear from my spies. But it is the military and the government that concern them most, is it not?"

"Yes. And I do not lie when I confess that I have so far found little of interest to report. Your armies are like none I have ever seen, and your government mystifies me! When my queen sent me, we had no idea whether you were governed by a king, a priest or a council of elders. We have never encountered anything like you before."

Deathmoon seated himself on the bed, cross his legs and laced his fingers over one knee. "Governments differ only at the top. You were instructed, were you not, to seek out corrupt ministers, officials who could be subverted by your king and queen for their own purposes?"

Hael shrugged. "All kings take advantage of such people."

"They do indeed. You were not here long enough to contact any such, as it fell out. Unfortunate, in a way. I have some truly imaginative ways to dispose of traitors."

"Perhaps all your ministers are loyal," Hael said.

Deathmoon smiled dementedly. "Do not be naive. Tell me, Alsa, does King Gasam plot war against me?"

Hael kept his face straight. "I assure you, my king's intentions toward you are only the most peaceful and brotherly."

Deathmoon slapped his knee and laughed aloud. "You should have been in the diplomatic corps rather than the spy service. Let's not speak like children. Your king will attack me when his borders abut mine, if he thinks I am weaker. That is what conquerors do and I would expect nothing else. But a war between us would be wasteful. An alliance, however, could be immensely profitable to us both."

"How so?" It occurred to Hael that, by an amazing stroke of fortune, he might learn from Deathmoon himself all he had come here to discover—assuming that he would get away alive.

"Gasam, the last I heard, is secure in the south. He has a few more petty kingdoms to gobble up, then he will be on my doorstep. Should we engage in war, two things will happen: I, with my new model army, will decimate his forces. I do not boast; warrior skill and courage have nothing to do with my sort of warfare. The other thing that will happen is that Gasam will leave an immense northern flank utterly exposed. King Hael will fall upon that flank and destroy him.''

"Do not expect my king to believe that you can beat him. His armies have swept all before him.''

"Nonsense. Neva and Hael combined forces to expel him from the north. The fat, decadent lands of the south were easy meat for him. I shall not be.'' Deathmoon got up and paced again. "But, there is no need for this. It would be far more sensible for us to combine forces against Hael.''

Hael pretended to be thinking this over. "Hael and my king have been enemies since childhood,'' he said.

Deathmoon dismissed his words with a wave of a beautifully manicured hand. "Your king's personal feuds are of no interest to me. Gasam has an expanding empire. Mezpa has an expanding empire. I want to expand my borders to the west, as is my right. It offends me that so vast and potentially rich a land should be inhabited only by a handful of nomads ruled by a primitive king. Your Gasam is also a savage, but he is a man of vision and ambition. I think he is much like myself. Hael is some sort of shaman who talked a lot of dreamy nonsense and caught the fancy of those unspeakable aborigines. He is unfit to hold land that I can make good use of.''

Deathmoon began pacing again, caught up in his own harangue. Hael guessed that the man was frustrated with Mezpa's political secretiveness. He would have been much happier speaking to huge crowds, whipping them into an imperialistic frenzy.

"The west is rich! It has great rivers and fertile land that has never been tilled. There are minerals to be found there, and peoples to enslave to work the land. There is plenty of room for both our empires to expand. Oh, I know that your king has little interest in the potential wealth of such a place. He prefers to conquer those who have already amassed the plunder he craves. But we Mezpans *create* wealth; we *develop* wealth. Well, that is of little matter. The fact is, Gasam cannot conquer me. But, together, we can destroy Hael.''

Not a word, Hael noted, about the steel mine. "You understand, my lord, that I am not empowered to act for my king."

"Nor should you. What I want of you is your continued presence here. You shall dwell here in the palace, and I shall acquaint you with certain realities of Mezpan life and Mezpan might. Thus you shall be able to make a wholly authoritative report to your queen and perhaps convince your king of the folly of any action he may contemplate against me. Is that agreeable?"

"I will report what I see," Hael said, "and pass on what you tell me."

Deathmoon grinned. "Well put. You know your work well, spy. Now, come with me. We have far better rooms than this for our honored guests."

Hael followed him from the cell and they walked down a long, cell-lined corridor to a guardroom where the thuggish men gaped at them.

"Bring his belongings," Deathmoon snapped. They climbed two flights of stairs and crossed a dining hall to a wing of guest quarters. The room they entered was sparsely furnished, but spacious, with a large balcony overhanging the dizzy drop from the top of the crag to the river.

"I think you will be comfortable here. None of the decadent luxury Lady Morning Bird and her degenerate companions favor, but then you Shasinn favor far rougher living than this, do you not?"

"This is more than satisfactory, my lord, especially after your dungeon."

Guards entered with Hael's belongings. One of them carried his spear, now reassembled. Deathmoon took it.

"The Shasinn spear is quite distinctive. I have had it described in many reports. My agents discovered this in your room on your first day in Crag. You should have left it behind."

"A Shasinn warrior is never without his spear," Hael protested.

"Your sentimental attachment to this token could easily destroy your value as a spy. Did that occur to you?"

Hael smiled. "But I am a dealer in rare artworks, and is it not beautiful and unique?"

Deathmoon tossed the spear and Hael caught it. "So it is. You might have gotten away with that explanation, had you been dealing with someone less thorough than I. You may keep your weapons here, but do not carry them away from here. My laws against bearing arms within the city are strictly enforced."

An elderly, silent serving man brought wine and glasses on a tray, and Deathmoon directed him to a table on the balcony. When the man was gone, he gestured for Hael to join him at the table. Each took a sip. The last thing Hael worried about was poison.

"Enough of policy," Deathmoon said. "Satisfy my curiosity. Is Queen Larissa as beautiful as everyone claims? Such tales grow with distance."

"She is the most beautiful woman in the world," Hael said, quite truthfully. "I cannot describe her in any words that would mean anything. You would have to see her."

"I hope to, sometime soon. She is said to be immodest even by the standards of those ladies you saw at Morning Bird's banquet, showing herself all but naked before the common crowd."

"Our standards of modesty are different in the islands. My queen judges her beauty to be clothing enough, and in any case our king and queen are not to be judged as ordinary people."

"I see." He sounded doubtful. "And she is the one who sees to the administration of the conquered lands and international affairs, while the king does rather less?"

Hael knew that the man was probing him. Was this spy loyal to the king or to the queen? There were several ways to play this, but the man was a born conspirator and wanted leverage against Gasam.

"The queen has charge of those affairs that suit her. Our

king is a warrior and spends much of his time occupied with military matters.'' The idea, Hael decided, was to sound less than supportive of the king without obvious disloyalty. Death-moon would suspect anything too blatant.

"And yet the queen is, shall we say, somewhat the more capable?''

"All the islanders worship her,'' Hael said, "and the subject peoples fear her as they do the king.''

"Then perhaps I should address myself to her, as director of foreign affairs, after sending my salutations to King Gasam as fellow sovereign.''

Hael nodded his head judiciously. "This is not my field, but I think that would be wise.''

"Excellent. Then, having taken care of the amenities, I think I shall propose a meeting, somewhere on neutral ground. One can accomplish only so much at a distance, through intermediaries. In order for sovereigns to come to a true understanding, there must be face-to-face consultation. How fortunate that your king and queen enjoy what is in effect a joint reign, and Gasam may send his queen on such a mission with full powers to act in his behalf.''

Again the judicious nod. "Queen Larissa has done so in the past. She usually chooses an island in a river that forms the border between our land and another's.''

"Well, we share no common border as yet, but an accommodation of some sort may be made. Does Queen Larissa travel in great state?''

"She usually rides only with an escort of Shasinn junior warriors. They are a sight more impressive than the pomp of the southern kings.''

"I daresay. Then I shall be equally unpretentious. If you only knew how bored I get with the tedious struttings of my fellow monarchs.''

"I have noticed that you Mezpans set little store by display.''

"Very true. What we value are efficiency and results. That is how your rulers impress me—efficient.''

"They are that. And they get results. Many thrones lie beneath my king's feet. He has a footstool made of surrendered crowns."

"A formidable monarch, indeed. And there is bad blood between him and King Hael? I mean, other than the usual rivalry between kings. It is known that Hael is an islander himself."

"You said that their feud was of no interest to you," Hael pointed out.

"Even so, I wish to know my brother ruler better." Being caught in the contradiction did not embarrass him in the least.

"I cannot tell you much. Hael and my king were of the same village, and are said to have been foster brothers. Gasam despised Hael as a fool and coward from the time they were children. Anyway, Hael was exiled for something, but nobody speaks of it, and it is unwise even to speak that man's name where my king and queen can hear it."

"Well, they must hear that name from me, whatever their feelings in the matter."

"Since you propose an alliance against Hael, I am sure they will not object."

Abruptly, Deathmoon stood. "Very good. Now I have matters to attend to. Make yourself comfortable here. We shall confer often in the next few days. Should you wish to leave the palace, you shall have an escort. I now regard you as an honored guest and unofficial emissary. Therefore you must have an escort. You understand?"

"Perfectly."

"Good day to you, then." Deathmoon whirled and left.

Hael sighed and poured himself another glass of wine. He could remember very few times in his life when his fortunes had taken so many startling turns in so short a space, although these things happened to him more often than to most men. He knew himself to be a man of destiny, and destiny played many strange tricks.

From a condition of utter despair, he was elevated to perhaps the best position he could have hoped for. Now he could learn many of Deathmoon's secrets while poisoning relations between him and Gasam. This was not merely valuable, it could even prove enjoyable.

Then he saw the guards watching him from a higher balcony and reminded himself that he was still a prisoner.

EIGHT

His first sight of Crag was daunting. Viewed from across the river, wreathed in early-morning mist, it was as ugly and evil-looking a place as Kairn had ever seen. There seemed to him something unnatural about it, as if it had been imposed upon its environment by some alien and malignant being. *It looks*, he thought, *like a creature that sucks blood*. He knew he was being fanciful, but the place imposed an inescapable mood. It struck him that that might be its purpose. He had never before heard of a work of man erected solely to intimidate, but all he had learned of the Mezpans suggested that they might do just such a thing.

He nudged his cabo down the muddy bank toward the bridge spanning the river. He had ridden most of the way on the ground alongside the road, for the hard surface hurt the cabo's hoofs. The travelers who used the road seemed to be as oppressed as he by the proximity of the fortress. They spoke in low tones or not at all. Beasts of burden drew wagons loaded with produce and other necessities toward the fort, while traffic in the other direction carried little or nothing, reinforcing his impression that Crag was parasitic, draining the region and giving back nothing.

The bridge across the river was an ingenious structure, made of cut stone supported by arches, with a central span of heavy timber that could be raised to allow the larger rivercraft to pass through. Kairn stopped by the central span to admire its construction, the movable roadbed balanced by counterweights so delicately that little effort was needed to raise and lower it; a task accomplished by a mere half-dozen slaves working in a pair of large wooden treadmills.

Once across the river he found himself in the disorderly town that crowded the base of the great outcropping. Almost at once he felt better. Whatever the nature of the ruling elite atop the crag, the inhabitants of the lower town were the same brawling, independent rivermen he had grown to know well. Within a few minutes of riding through the town, he saw drunks being thrown out of taverns, prostitutes displaying their wares, and two serious fights. It was rough, but he found it infinitely preferable to the regimentation preferred by most Mezpans.

His dread returned as soon as he left the river settlement. When he saw the soldiers on the drill field, his mood increased. Everything they did seemed utterly unwarriorlike to him, but their machinelike regularity was ominous and he knew well the capabilities of the firetubes. The Mezpans had devised a way to make the noisy but innocuous weapons into decisive implements of war, despite their slow rate of fire and indifferent accuracy.

The long climb up the ramplike highway leading to the squat, brutal-looking main gate was intimidating in the extreme. Absurdly, he felt as if the fortress was watching him, and he felt utterly exposed on the wide stone road. It occurred to him that his appearance, mounted and armed as a plainsman, might make him too conspicuous. He decided that, surely, in such a town, a mere foreigner would pass unnoticed.

The official at the gate allowed him to enter without undue

difficulty, and assured him that no person of his father's description had entered the city recently. The same question got him the same answer from the police he was sent to. He was greatly puzzled by this, and indignant at the order that he must go unarmed within the city. He knew better than to dispute the matter. The last thing he wanted was trouble with the authorities.

As he went to look for lodgings he wondered what might have become of Hael. If he was not here, where could he be? With all his delays, how could Kairn have arrived ahead of his father? He decided to wait in Crag for a while, to see whether his father would turn up. Could Hael be dead? He refused even to think about.

Once he had arranged for quarters and stabling, he had nothing to do save familiarize himself with the city. The place was grimly busy, something he found repellent. He was accustomed to the silence of the wild places, and he had been in uproarious towns. A heavily populated city that was also quiet seemed to him unnatural.

Once in a while he saw people who were oddly different from the others, people dressed richly and idiosyncratically, as if the dull conformity he saw at every hand was for the masses only. More than one of these colorful people seemed to look at him longer than was necessary. *Don't often get a chance to look at a foreigner,* he thought.

Nearly everyone in Crag seemed to have a standardized dress according to their status and occupation: shopkeepers in long, dark gowns; workmen in jerkins and tight trousers; slaves in drab tunics. Household servants wore livery, soldiers and police were in uniforms.

The town had the usual markets and noisy workshops, but no temples or other places of worship. It was scrupulously clean, but no more welcoming for all that. Nothing, he thought, save so desperate a mission would make him spend so much as a day in such a place.

In the course of his explorations he came to an alley with stairs leading down to a walk carved into the side of the crag, just below its crest. The path had been crudely hacked out of the rock and afforded a splendid view of the river below and the land beyond. He gazed out over the forested hills and wished he were out there instead of here. He walked along the narrow ledge, which seemed to encircle the crag just below the inner citadel. Perhaps, he thought, it had been carved there to support scaffolding when the structure above had been built. As he walked, he studied the multistoried fortress that hulked above him.

He noted that it was not a fortified wall overhanging the outcropping. Instead it was studded with windows and balconies. Apparently, the inhabitants did not fear attack from this side of the city and regarded the sheer face of the cliff defense enough. Sentries patrolled the crest of the wall, and there were guards standing on some of the balconies. On others, parties of fancifully dressed people seemed to be entertaining each other. These colorful touches did not make the place seem any less grim.

High above him, he saw two men come out onto one of the balconies. One was a small, bearded man dressed in gray. The other caught Kairn's eye instantly and he almost cried out unthinkingly. He caught himself and backed up against the rough stone of the crag, hiding himself in the deep shadows of late afternoon.

He watched the small, distant figures for several minutes, trying to convince himself that he could be wrong. But he knew he was not. He knew every stance and gesture of that figure far better than he knew himself. It was his father, King Hael, in close conversation with somebody.

His breathing quickened and the sweat sprang out on his scalp. Something was terribly wrong here! The gatekeeper and the police had denied seeing any such man! Could he have arrived here secretly, or was his presence deliberately kept secret? Was he conferring with a fellow monarch, or was he a prisoner? Suddenly, Kairn's mission was far more complicated.

He studied the wall for a way to climb to that balcony. If he could find a way, perhaps he could come back after dark.

This presumed that his father would be in a room behind that balcony, a proposition that was by no means certain. Still, he had no better plan. He certainly could not pound on the fortress gate and demand to be taken to King Hael.

No amount of study revealed a plausible climbing route. The wall seemed to be smoothly finished and the only protrusions were the balconies. He considered climbing from balcony to balcony by means of his rope, but he saw no posts or other protrusions he might rope for purchase. This, plainly, would bear some thinking.

He hurried back to his inn where he ate a hurried supper and tried to formulate a plan. He saw his cased bow and arrows hanging from a wall peg and thought of the ledge upon which he had been standing and the doorway behind the balcony. Might he be able to send a message by arrow? It was an intriguing possibility, but he was unsure of the range and angle, and there was still the uncertainty of whether the room behind the balcony was Hael's. There was also the possibility that his shaft might skewer some unsuspecting person, but that was remote. If the shot could be made at all, it would most likely strike the ceiling.

He took his writing implements from his saddlebags, wetted an ink block, and tried to compose a message. Even as he thought about it, unpleasant complications reared themselves. He could write in Nevan script, using his native dialect. Both were foreign here, but this was a capital, and there were probably scribes in this place versed in many scripts and languages. And any message delivered in such a fashion might compromise whatever game his father was playing, should the missive be found by someone else.

The more he thought about it, the more foolish the plan seemed to him. He crumpled the note before he had it fairly begun, then set fire to it with a candle to make a thorough job of it. With a frustrated sigh he tumbled onto his narrow bed, laced his fingers behind his head, and stared at the ceiling, where a tiny spider was weaving a complicated web.

For years he had fretted under authority: that of his parents, of his older brother, of the warriors and elders of his people. He had longed to be on his own, an adventurer with none to answer to save himself. Now he was experiencing the pitfalls of such an estate; it would have been convenient to have an older, wiser, more experienced person to ask for advice.

Already, he could see that he had made mistakes. He should never have come here so openly, asking everyone he met if they had seen a man answering to his father's description. He should have guessed that his father would be up to something surreptitious, might even be a prisoner. Now Kairn had drawn attention to himself and might have endangered his father as well. He wondered how one survived long enough to gain experience at this sort of activity.

He was sure that he would have done better if this whole city were not so strange. He had been prepared to deal with the sort of town he was familiar with, or even with the great, magnificent but chaotic cities he had heard traveled people describe. But this was something else. Police, for instance. Cities were often guarded by soldiers who manned the walls and who sometimes patrolled the streets to guard against riot and insurrection. But what were police? They were too lightly armed to be warriors, and too few in number to be a credible fighting force, but they appeared singly or in twos on every street. In fact, now that he thought of it, there had been men in ominous black uniforms everywhere he had been since reaching the city. There had even been a brute-faced policeman seated in a corner of the common room where he had eaten supper. It was all very strange. With his stomach full and his mind perplexed, he drifted off to sleep.

Something gripped his shoulder and shook him. Kairn tried to snap out of sleep, but his mind was too sleep-fuddled to function properly. Then hands went under his arms and he was hauled to a standing position.

"What? What is this?" Something clicked around both wrists and he saw that two light bands of hard ceramic, connected by a short chain, now encircled them. A man he recognized from the common room stood before him while others gathered up his belongings.

"Foreigner, you are under arrest," the brute-faced man announced. He was squat and muscular, and he held a short wooden truncheon as if he were anxious to use it.

"For what reason? I have done nothing!"

"For spying on behalf of the enemies of Mezpa. You were seen going about your mission today, so don't bother to deny it."

"It is untrue! I—"

Almost lazily, the man swung the truncheon alongside Kairn's jaw. Shattering pain shot through his whole skull.

"Save it, boy. There are others who want to hear all you have to say. Our job is to take you to a place where they can question you in comfort. Their comfort, not yours. So don't trouble us with your story. Guilty or innocent, alive or dead, it's all one to us." He turned to the others. "Take him to the station. Lord Deathmoon will interview him in the morning."

At least, Kairn thought as he was half-dragged from the room, *now I know what police are for*.

Once in the station lockup, the police took no further interest in him and Kairn was able to finish his night's sleep, which he needed. Even as he was dragged there, he understood that they had waited until he was asleep at least three hours, as deep under as he would go, before rushing in to overpower him. It was the same tactic as that used by warriors on a nighttime raid. The victim was groggy, unable to collect his wits, and demoralized by his sudden arousal from deep unconsciousness. Kairn's jaw ached, but he was satisfied that it was not broken and the back teeth seemed to be only slightly loosened. Since he could do nothing to affect his fate, he decided he might as well sleep.

The sky was still dark outside his barred window when his captors returned and ordered him to get up and come with them. Lacking any credible alternative, he complied. The walk through the cool, early-morning darkness of the city streets was not a long one. It ended at the massive gate of the great keep, where he was handed over to uniformed guards and the police in return were given a receipt acknowledging delivery. Kairn had often seen merchants do this, but never warriors. Well, these were not true warriors, he reminded himself.

The guards took him to another cell, this one below ground level. It was bare and dank, and the walls were draped with ceramic chains and neckrings. In a greater room just outside the cell were whips, chains, frames and wheels suggestive of elaborate torture. Bronze tools lay beside a gently burning brazier. The sight was meant to intimidate, and in this it was entirely successful.

Kairn's viscera spasmed with despair. It was not just that he would have to endure torture, but that any endurance he could summon would be futile. These people would have no respect for his warrior courage. That was the worst prospect—to die under hideous torture at the hands of people who were entirely indifferent to how well he bore his suffering. It would mean a death utterly devoid of dignity. No one would know how he had died. He would just be one of those who rode away from home and never returned. He would be forgotten, and that was a bitter thought.

It never occurred to him that he might not die in the coming ordeal. The thought of torture was just marginally bearable. Death was quite acceptable, although he would have preferred a later date and a more seemly fashion of it. But to survive as a helpless cripple was unthinkable.

The guards clamped a neckring around his throat and left him in the cell. He looked around for other prisoners but there were none. The chain was long enough to allow him to sit with his back against the wall and, after a few minutes of futile tugging, he did so. He still wore his wrist bonds and he twisted at them. The ceramic looked fragile, but it was incredibly strong.

He wondered whether it would be possible to commit suicide. With the ring around his neck he might contrive to hang himself. It was repugnant, but preferable to death by torture.

Then he remembered his mission and cursed his selfishness in wishing for a swift death. Of what importance was his own agony when he had so important a message to deliver?

But, if his difficulty in contacting his father had been great before, now it seemed insurmountable. How could he get word to Hael? Then he remembered that Hael had to be someplace within this very building. Knowing that he had already surmounted one obstacle made him feel better, and he began to think that he might get out of this after all. He would just have to begin using his brains and such education as he had absorbed at his father's insistence. One thing was abundantly clear: Warrior skills were of no use to a man in chains.

About midday he heard someone open the door at the top of the stairs leading to the torture room. He had not been fed since his arrival and he hoped it was someone with food. All thought of hunger fled when he saw that it was the small, bearded man he had seen on the balcony with Hael.

The man was accompanied by servants and guards. One of the servants carried a folding chair and he set it up in the cell. Then the small man came in and seated himself. Kairn knew that the man would be just out of reach of an attacking prisoner. With his delicate hands braced against his wide-spread knees, the man leaned forward and studied his prisoner. His eyes were like cold black stones in a face that might as well have been a mask for all the feeling it displayed.

"Young man," he began, his voice as cold as his eyes, "before we begin, I want you to understand your precise situation. I know you are a foreigner with some knowledge of our language. Can you understand my words?"

"I can," Kairn said, proud that his voice was steady. Then he remembered that nothing really bad had happened yet.

"Excellent. My name is Deathmoon, and I am lord of this land, of Mezpa and its empire. I am unthinkably powerful and you are my prisoner. You are to abandon all thoughts of escape, for that is impossible. You must not lie to me, for I will know it when you do and my officers are extremely skilled at inflicting pain and dismemberment without bringing about death. Do you understand all this?''

"I do." Kairn answered.

"Very well. First, to avoid needless redundancies in your confession, I shall tell you what I already know about you. Do not bother to deny any of these things, they are a matter of record." He held up a hand and a servant placed a leather folder in it. He opened the folder on his lap and another servant came forward with a lamp to supplement the light streaming through the small window.

"You arrived at the main gate of Crag yesterday, mounted on a fine cabo, and identified yourself as one *Kairn*. You said that you are searching for a man whom you described in some detail: tall and powerfully built, with long hair of a peculiar bronze color, and a complexion of the same hue but paler, with broad cheekbones and eyes a brilliant blue. Quite a striking fellow, I must say; we shall get to your reasons for seeking him in a moment.

"To continue, after registering with the police, once again asking after this odd-looking person, you prowled all over the city, spending a suspicious amount of time examining its walls and battlements, at one point disappearing for nearly an hour. While you were thus engaged your belongings were searched. Your arms are those of a northwestern plainsman, and they are of princely quality, the sword and lance-point made entirely of steel. Tell me, how does a lone vagabond come by such arms?"

"I am just an ordinary warrior," Kairn said. "These last years, steel has become common in King Hael's realm. You seldom see the old stone and bronze weapons anymore."

"We shall let that pass for now. Soon enough I'll know if you are telling the truth."

"I am telling the truth and I am not a spy!"

"Just because you are a fool is no reason to assume that I am one as well. You have come here alone, for no good reason. You have no goods to sell, and you do not seek employment. Your sole activity here has been to examine our defenses. Not only are you a spy, young man, but you are a most clumsily obvious one. A skilled spy would have provided himself with some plausible excuse for visiting Crag. Nobody comes here just to see the sights.''

Kairn's mind worked feverishly. Apparently, the man didn't know that he had been on the ledge below the palace and had seen him with Hael. He, too, was trying to act as if he had never seen such a man. What did this signify?

"The only question," Deathmoon went on, "is on behalf of which of my fellow rulers are you spying? You seem to be a plainsman, but that means little. Spies will work for anyone. I doubt that you work for King Gasam. The spy corps organized by his queen is said to be of high quality, and I can scarcely imagine the lady employing such a bumbling amateur as you. The few southern lands left unconquered by Gasam are far too worried about him to be plotting anything against me. There is always the Canyon, but that place is so mysterious that I am not at all sure that it exists." He leaned forward, his eyes colder than ever.

"This leaves King Hael. All others are too far away to bother with espionage. Hael has good reason to sound out my defenses. I have grounds for expecting him to invade my country within the near future."

"That is nonsense! King Hael—" He did not see the guard's hand move but he felt the slap along his jaw, the pain magnified a hundredfold by the truncheon-blow it had already absorbed. Dazzling light flashed behind his eyelids and he could not have spoken, but he could hear.

"You will speak only when I indicate I wish you to, and you would be well advised never to contradict me. Now, we have established certain unquestionable facts: You are a spy, sent hither to fathom the defenses of Crag. You are a spy sent by my would-be enemy, King Hael. These things are not to be questioned, denied or contradicted. They must, however, be elaborated upon."

Kairn looked into the cold, mad eyes and he knew that all protest was futile. The man could not be swayed from his monomaniacal fixation. Not by words, at any rate. Kairn's only hope was to manipulate what the man already believed and hopefully gain some advantage thereby.

"Will you cooperate?"

Dumbly, unable to trust the functioning of his jaw and tongue, Kairn nodded.

"Good. You display sound judgment. You shall answer all my questions, fully and without stint. I will not apply torment unless I see that you are lying. Are you able to speak now?"

Kairn moved his jaw a bit and said, hesitantly, "Yes."

"When did King Hael send you here?" The voice was dry and clipped, like that of a merchant hearing the report of a field agent, precise and very aware that his time was too valuable to waste.

"Last dry season, after the assembly of the army was dismissed." His mind worked feverishly, seeking to build a credible story.

"And did he tell you why he chose you for this duty?"

"I have traveled more than most warriors my age. I am able to read and write."

"That is an unusual accomplishment among the nomads," Deathmoon interjected.

"Not so rare as it used to be. The king established a school where the sons of chiefs were taught along with his own."

"Then you are a chief's son?"

"My father is a village leader, and any such may send their sons to the new school."

"And what is your tribe? I understand there are many in King Hael's domain."

"I am of the Matwa hill people." He was glad now that he favored his mother's people. His elder brother Ansa shared more of their father's Shasinn look.

"And what intelligence did your king instruct you to collect?"

"Anything that might be of aid to him."

"Of aid in the event of an invasion?" Deathmoon demanded.

"Of *any* aid," Kairn retorted. "He said nothing to me about war!"

Deathmoon studied him for a long moment. "Yes, that makes sense. Kings do not confide policy decisions to boys. And what specific information did he seek?"

"Distances, rivers to be crossed, location of bridges, towns, populations, livestock."

"All of which he could have had from his trade missions," Deathmoon said, showing impatience for the first time. "What else?"

Kairn hesitated and swallowed, as if only now realizing how incriminating his instructions had been.

"Well . . . he wanted to know about fortifications, and how well the land favored the maneuver of large bodies of mounted men. And he is very curious about your firetube weapons and how your soldiers use them."

Deathmoon smiled and nodded, as if all his suspicions were confirmed. "Just so. And what did you conclude about those weapons and those soldiers?"

"My king did not ask for my opinions, only that I should observe and report back to him what I saw."

"A wise king. Many people confuse useless opinion with useful intelligence." Kairn decided that the man was in love with his own voice, especially when bestowing gems of pragmatic wisdom. "But, surely you have come to some conclusions? I am interested to know how a plains warrior views my army. Speak freely and do not fear that you will offend me. This is for my own edification, and not a part of your interrogation for unlawful espionage activities."

"Well, sir, I have seen those arms demonstrated. Frankly, they make a fearsome noise and flame, but that is about all. They can inflict a terrible wound, but they have little accuracy. You can rarely hit a man beyond thirty paces with one, while with our bows we plainsmen readily hit small game at a hundred. In the time it takes to recharge one of your firetubes we can discharge ten arrows."

Deathmoon nodded. "Go on."

"In several places I've watched your troops training, and I cannot see how marching and maneuvering in lines improves the effectiveness of those weapons any. It looks to me as if an army equipped only with firetubes would be slaughtered by mounted bowmen.''

Once again, Deathmoon smiled and nodded. ''I will not bore you with a lecture on the proper way to apply my new model army, especially against mounted men. Your opinion is exactly what I would have expected from a mounted warrior who values only courage, mobility and marksmanship. I will not be displeased if your king thinks exactly as you do. Now, to serious business: How many others came here with you?''

''None. I came alone.''

Deathmoon nodded to a guard and the man clamped something around Kairn's upper arm. It was like the collar that encircled his neck, but there were protrusions and screws. One of the screws was tightened and a stud was forced against the bone of his upper arm, at a point where the biceps and triceps did not sheath it. Excruciating agony shot through him. He clamped his already painful jaw against the scream, and his body was instantly inundated with sweat.

''Feel free to scream. No one will hear you but those of us here in this cell, and we care nothing for your warrior stoicism.''

''I will hear,'' Kairn said, his voice a shocking croak.

''Truly, warriors are children, but you have a certain style, and I like that. You may not credit it, but we value style. Now, once again, how many came with you?''

''I came alone, I swear it!''

Deathmoon nodded, and again the clamp was tightened. He repeated the question a third time and received the same answer.

''Very well, I believe you.'' His voice was as dispassionate as always. ''Actually, I believed you the first time.''

''Then why . . .'' Kairn was barely able to speak past his clamped jaw. Tears streamed down his face and he was unable to stop them. He felt deeply shamed.

''Because it is imperative that you understand now, at the outset, the deep seriousness of your situation. The humerus clamp—that is what that bone in your upper arm is called, by the way, the humerus—is very painful, is it not? It achieves its effect by bringing pressure against the bone and its sheathing at a point where nothing intervenes except skin. Yet, painful as it is, at the pressure just applied to you it is quite harmless and will result in nothing more than a bruise.''

He leaned forward and spoke very earnestly. ''You must understand that this is the very mildest torture that we employ. From now on, everything else will be far, far worse, both in terms of pain and irreparable damage inflicted. Is that clear to you?''

''Yes,'' Kairn choked out.

Deathmoon smiled. ''Good. You are an intelligent young man, and I think your king chose well, except that he sent you out with far too little experience. Had your king been more expert in the practice of espionage, he would first have sent you on far safer missions under the tutelage of more experienced men. Well, we can do nothing about that, can we?''

Of all the horrifying aspects of Kairn's situation, he thought that the sheer *reasonableness* of the man was the worst. It had never occurred to him that a man could be so mad and so utterly in control of himself at the same time. In all his inner bleakness, Kairn could find one source of pride: whatever else, he was not telling Deathmoon the truth.

Kairn slumped in his chains, hoping he gave the impression of utter defeat and dejection. It was certainly close enough to what he actually felt.

''Tell me what you want to know,'' he mumbled.

''Now you understand. That is excellent. Now we can begin a serious discussion.''

The session dragged on and on. Deathmoon's questions were prosaic for the most part: His route into the kingdom, how he had sent messages back to King Hael, whether he knew of other spies sent into Mezpa. Kairn answered as he hoped would best please Deathmoon, which meant what would best feed his suspicions. By now Kairn was certain that the man planned to invade his father's kingdom and probably others. The form of Deathmoon's madness began to take shape. He wanted to believe that everyone else was plotting against him to do what in reality he was planning to do to them.

At last Deathmoon rose from his chair.

"Well, this has been a most productive session. I have been very favorably impressed by you, young man. If you continue to cooperate, you just may live through this ordeal. Oh, there is one last thing." He turned to face the stairway without.

Kairn's mind spun. Fear, degradation, pain, despair, now hope. Deathmoon considered him to be fully softened up and was about to spring his final, devastating blow. Kairn steeled himself. What would it be? A shadow appeared at the bottom of the stair and Kairn knew instantly who it was.

"You came here looking for this gentleman," Deathmoon said. "Why?"

Kairn tried to keep his face slack and defeated. All would depend upon what Hael did when he recognized his son. The familiar figure stepped into the light. Hael's face was set and stern. It displayed nothing but an amused contempt.

Then Kairn knew. Hael had seen him on the ledge the day before! If his father would take the lead swiftly enough, they might both be saved.

"I'll tell you why he's looking for me,' Hael said, ignoring Deathmoon's gesture to be silent. "He came here to kill me! Hael knows that I am one of Queen Larissa's spies. He must have got word that I was sent to Mezpa and thought to eliminate me as a threat."

"I would rather have heard it from him," Deathmoon said through gritted teeth. He turned to Kairn. "You neglected to tell me of this."

"You did not ask me, lord. I was afraid to volunteer any information."

To his horrified surprise, he heard Deathmoon laugh for the first time. It was a strangled, snorting sound, as if the man laughed seldom.

"Oh, this has been an enjoyable day. The two of you provide me no end of amusement. Tell me, boy, is it as he says?''

Kairn nodded. "Yes. The king told me that there might be a Shasinn spy or envoy lurking about your nation, and the most likely place to encounter such would be the capital.''

"Did your king mention this one by name?''

Kairn had no idea what name his father might be using. He shook his head. "No. I think he may not know himself. He said that any Shasinn here would be up to no good. I was to kill any such, if it could be done discreetly.'' Deathmoon looked doubtful, but Hael distracted him with a snort of contempt.

"Sending an untried boy to kill a Shasinn warrior! Hael has gone as soft in the head as King Gasam says. What are you going to do with this little fool, lord?''

"Oh, I shall keep him for a while. No telling what useful information he may have. You don't throw a book away just because you've read it once.''

They walked out of the cell, speaking in low tones. Kairn slumped back against the wall, racked with pain but awash in relief. He was almost certain that they had succeeded in fooling Deathmoon. If his father had not seen him the day before, if he had betrayed by his expression what he must have felt upon finding his son in such a condition—it did not bear thinking about. He was filled with admiration for Hael's quick recovery, concocting a story that would explain both of them to the satisfaction of a man like Deathmoon.

What now? He rattled his ceramic chains idly. Now, obviously, the next move would have to be up to Hael. With that thought, he made himself as comfortable as possible and fell into a fitful sleep.

He woke to a rustling sound. His surroundings, the chains that bound him, were so bizarre that he did not at first know where he was. The last days rolled back in an instant and he knew all too well. Slowly, trying not to make a sound, he worked himself to a sitting position. The little rectangle of sky gave him no indication of the time, but he knew it was well past midnight.

The glowing brazier and a single candle gave him a dim view into the room beyond. A single guard dozed there. The sound that had awakened Kairn did not disturb the man's slumber. The sound came again, louder. This time the guard roused. Kairn saw a shape at the bottom of the stair. The guard began to turn.

"Guard," Kairn said in a low voice. The man turned his way and a large shape loomed behind him. There was a muffled thump and the man collapsed with a long sigh. Then Hael was fumbling at the cell door. It opened with a mechanical clack and his father's arms were around him.

"My son! How did you get here, you young fool?" He released Kairn and went to work on his bonds with a ring of oddly shaped keys.

"Father, I have a message—"

"Later, when we're away from here. Your message will do me no good unless we are free." The last of the bonds fell away. "Are your limbs sound?" Kairn stood stiffly and worked his arms and legs.

"I'm whole."

"Good, because they'll have a strenuous workout before we're safe."

"Actually," Kairn said as they left the cell, "it's my head that hurts the worst."

"Strange. That's the part you've been using the least."

"What's happened to the guards?"

"What usually happens to enemy sentries when they get careless. Quiet, now." They went up the steps and emerged into a guardroom. Two guards lay inert upon the floor. Hael pointed to a heap in one corner and Kairn suppressed a growl of triumph as he picked up his belongings.

"Just your weapons and such things as you can climb with. You can't carry a saddle and bags where we're going. Leave the lance."

Regretfully, but glad to have a whole hide, Kairn obeyed. He could always get another spear and saddle. The bow and its arrows made an awkward burden across his back, but it was light. He belted on sword and knife, stuffed a few items into his belt pouch, and was ready.

Moving silently as wildland hunters, they entered the main part of the fortress, a combination of castle and palace with narrow halls and relatively spacious rooms. As they traversed the halls, Kairn saw a number of recumbent forms, guards his father had encountered on his way to the dungeon.

Then they were in a room illuminated by a number of candles. Hael gathered a few things, among them a three-foot-long bundle which he slung over his back. Kairn saw that a balcony opened onto one side of the room. This must be the balcony where he had seen his father and Deathmoon. He began to walk toward it, but Hael grasped his shoulder.

"Not until I blow out the lights," he said in a low voice. "We don't want the guards above to see us. We're going out that way."

Kairn's stomach lurched when he understood what that meant. At the same time his heart thrilled. *This* would be something worth boasting about when he got home. Assuming he lived, of course.

Hael went about the room, extinguishing the lights. Then he took Kairn by the arm and led him onto the balcony. When he spoke, it was in a whisper.

"If I hadn't seen you down there yesterday I would never have noticed that ledge. It took all my control not to let Deathmoon see how upset I was, but that man sees little when he is talking."

"I noticed," Kairn whispered.

"Anyway, I had to wait till dark to tear up enough cloth to make this rope." Kairn caught a glimpse of teeth bared in a smile. "Let's hope it's long enough." He stooped to gather up a bundle of something and heaved it over the edge of the balcony. Both of them looked up to see if any guards above had noticed anything. There was no sign, but that meant little in the gloom.

"I'll go first," Hael said.

"No, I should—"

"If your arm gives way as you're coming down, I can catch—"

"Father, don't be ridiculous, nobody is going to catch anybody on that ledge."

"Why do my sons never obey me?"

"Because we are your sons. Now, I am going first. Keep a hand on the rope. When it goes slack, I'll be on the ledge and you can follow." *Or I'll have fallen*, he thought. With his heart in his throat, Kairn scrambled over the balcony rail, gripped the knotted cloth rope and began to descend.

Immediately, he knew that his ordeal had weakened him far more than he had thought. The arm that had endured the clamp was weaker, the grasp of that hand constantly slipping. He found that the slackness of the rope reduced the effectiveness of his legs in descending. Even gritting his teeth didn't help, because his jaw hurt too much. He vowed to himself that, should he fall, he would not scream. His father's escape depended upon Kairn's silence. Above all, King Hael had to get back home.

Just as he was sure that his arms could stand no more strain, Kairn's questing toes felt the edge of the ledge, but only its very rim. He would have to swing inward to get enough purchase to stand. Pleading with his arms to hold on a little longer, he worked his body like a pendulum until he felt more of the ledge beneath his feet. Holding his breath, he took a last swing and let go. He was standing securely on the ledge, half-fainting, and with a thundering in his ears, but safe.

He looked up and saw Hael descending, coming down swiftly, hand under hand, making it look easy. Kairn gripped the rope to guide his father down to the ledge and realized that he shouldn't be able to see him. The sky was growing lighter. It was later than he had thought. Hael stood on the ledge and clapped him around the shoulders.

"When the rope went slack I didn't know whether you were here or I'd lost you."

"You came down easily enough," Kairn said.

"I hadn't undergone your ordeal. Now let's stop talking

and go find our cabos. I think there's a stable near the castle gate. They don't keep animals in the fortress.''

They hurried along the ledge until Kairn found the stairway that led to the alley above. They had to double-back toward the fortress when what Kairn wanted most was to be away from it, but there was no other way. The streets were deserted, and they encountered no patrols. Soon the main gate of the fortress hulked before them as they kept to the deepest shadows of the square fronting it.

''Somewhere around here,'' Hael whispered. ''I can smell it and I can feel them.''

This, Kairn knew, was his father's mystical ability to feel the spirits of animals. He could spear a threatening predator in the blackest night by sensing its location. Kairn could see nothing, for the shadows were deep and the sky was no more than a deep blueness above them, but Hael led them unerringly to the stable gate. They went inside and found an attendant sound asleep next to a dimly glowing lantern. Hael picked up the lantern.

''These are ingenious lamps,'' he said. ''They burn a sort of oil, and if you turn this little knob the wick comes up and increases the flame.'' As promised, the light grew brighter. The attendant continued to snore unabated.

''Just the sort of thing Mezpans would make,'' Kairn commented as they went back among the pens. There were at least fifty cabos, snorting softly at this unexpected intrusion.

''Find yours,'' Hael said. ''We'll take some others as remounts.''

They located a pair of bridles and a lead rope and prepared to mount, first picking out several of the soundest-looking animals. Kairn knew his own cabo by the distinctive pattern painted on its horns. It seemed happy to see him and anxious to be away from this place. Swiftly, they made their preparations. Almost as an afterthought, they bound and gagged the attendant.

''With luck,'' Hael said as they mounted, ''the guards on the fortress will think we're a party of aristocratic hunters going out early.''

"Does anyone here hunt?" Kairn asked. "I've seen no sign of it."

Hael shrugged. "It's the best we can hope. Come on." Keeping the animals to a slow walk so as to make as little sound as possible, they rode out into the little square and turned down the first street that led in the right direction. Kairn's back tensed in anticipation of an alarm from the fortress, but their luck seemed to be holding.

"What do we do when we reach the city gate?" Kairn asked.

"We'll decide that when we get there," Hael said. The small hoofs of the cabos rang softly on the pavement as they approached the gate. To their great delight, it was already open, admitting carts and slave gangs bearing produce for the hungry city. An official came toward them as they approached.

"Leaving? Your documents, please."

Hael pointed to Kairn. "He has them." The man turned his head and Hael struck him sharply behind the ear with the base of his fist. As the man crumpled, the two urged their animals forward, scattering slaves and guards alike. They broke through the gate and sped down the long ramp. Behind them they heard loud cracks and whizzing noises as bullets flew past them. They laughed with excitement as people leapt from their path or ducked to avoid the flying projectiles.

"The bridge!" Kairn cried. "We have to get across it before someone thinks to signal the bridgekeepers to raise the center span!" They redoubled their efforts and within a very few minutes they were at the base of the ramp, wheeling to take the road back along the length of Crag's base until they came to the town that was just waking to the early morning. They slowed to a trot to pass through the narrow street, not wishing to raise alarm.

They halted at the edge of the town, where the road led to the bridge. Hael unslung the bundle from across his back and took out the three sections of his spear, which he quickly assembled. From ahead of them they heard shouting and saw someone pointing up at the fortress. They looked up and saw that a huge red banner had been unfurled. Then they heard a mechanical clatter.

"Look!" Kairn shouted, pointing. Slowly, the central span of the bridge was coming up.

"We'll have to jump for it. The remounts should make it, but if you feel them starting to fall, let the rope go. No sense all of us going into the river." Hael loosed a wild Shasinn war cry and sped ahead. Kairn rode behind, leading the remounts.

Two men rushed forward to block them but Hael swung his spear in a wide figure eight, slashing with the weapon's sharp edges. The men fell back bleeding. Somebody ahead of them raised a firetube. There was a bang and a flash but the shot flew wide. *Two good bowmen*, Kairn thought, *could have skewered both of them in an instant*. Then they were on the bridge, speeding toward the rising span. The sound of the beating hoofs changed as they rode up the inclining wooden span, then Kairn saw the rear hoofs of his father's mount as it leapt off the lip of the span. Then he was there and his cabo was sailing into empty air, the beast trusting that its rider knew what he was doing. Then he landed on the stone of the far span. Kairn looked behind him and saw that the remounts were making the same leap, jumping easily because they were unburdened, but constrained by the length of the rope that connected them. In a graceful flurry of horns and hoofs they sailed across the gap and Kairn allowed himself to breathe again as the last one landed with no more than two inches of stone behind its rear hoofs.

Laughing and whooping, the two sped off the bridge and past a few gaping travelers. As soon as they were out of sight of the fortress, they got off the road and ran on the dirt to spare the animals' hoofs. For half an hour they rode, then halted to let the animals rest and transfer to fresh mounts.

"As long as we keep changing cabos," Hael said, "we should stay ahead of pursuit. The few mounted Mezpans I saw were wretched riders." He jammed his spear into the ground by its butt-spike and Kairn pointed at it.

"You came here with *that* and you accuse *me* of acting foolishly?"

Hael smiled ruefully. "Yes, it turned out to be an error in judgment. Luckily, when Deathmoon jumps to a conclusion he maintains it against all evidence. He decided that I was a Shasinn spy working for Larissa and he wasn't going to be persuaded otherwise." He stroked his cabo's soft nose and said bitterly, "But I didn't get what I came here for. I still don't know how they make the firetubes or the powder, or how they use the clumsy, inaccurate things in battle."

"There's a rebellious nobleman to the north of here who wants to talk to you about exactly that subject. He claims to know all that, and says he's part of a consortium of nobles who'd like to see an end to rule from Crag."

Hael beamed. "You've done better work here than I have! Well, lead me to this fount of information and possible ally."

"Ally?" Kairn said.

"Yes. Deathmoon thought he had caught a Shasinn spy and wanted to use me as an envoy to Gasam. He wants to ally with Gasam to crush me and divide the plains between them. Soon I may need all the allies I can get."

Kairn's heart sank. "Then I'm afraid I must bring you even worse news."

Hael's face darkened. "What is it? What is this message you came here to bring me? Is it the family? Is your mother all right?"

"Nothing like that," Kairn assured him, "but worse in its way. Ansa returned from his wandering in the south, and he discovered something so awful that he nearly killed himself getting home to tell you, only to find you gone. Mother sent me to bring you back."

Hale mounted a fresh cabo. "Out with it! What's happened?"

Kairn remounted as well. There was no way to make this easy.

"Father, Larissa's spies found out where the steel mine is and Gasam immediately began mounting an expedition to seize it. Gasam has your steel mine!"

BOOK TWO
The Steel Kings

NINE

King Gasam rode at the head of his personal guard of veteran warriors. Most of them were islanders and half were Shasinn senior warriors. All were veterans of innumerable battles and raids. There were a hundred of them. He felt no need of so large a guard and would have been content with a score of Shasinn, but his wife insisted that he travel in considerable state and he always deferred to her in these small matters.

He was not fond of riding, but traveling in this wretched land on foot was unthinkable. With her usual foresight, his queen had established water and forage stations along the route, so that they did not need to be slowed by a train of pack animals. Since leaving the River Kol behind, they had gone into land that grew more barren with each mile, until it seemed to be as lifeless as the scarred face of the Moon.

"My King," said a hard-faced Shasinn warrior who rode nearby, "we have fought for you in the islands, we have campaigned on the mainland, we have gone on shipborne raids into the jungles of the south. I have wielded my spear in your service from the coast to the top of mountain chains. I thought the stinking jungles and the freezing mountains were the worst the world had to offer, but I have *never* seen anything as awful as this place!''

The guard erupted with laughter and the king joined in. He allowed these men a familiarity denied to all save his queen. Death was the mildest penalty for any others who might speak insolently to the king.

''If I am to be king of the whole world,'' Gasam said, ''then I have to be king of this part as well. Believe me, nothing would make me come here if it weren't the only place to find the most precious metal in the world. Look, here comes some of my new wealth now!'' He pointed ahead of them, where a double column of slaves hauled a wagon that creaked loudly in the silent desert air.

As they neared, an overseer barked a command and popped his whip. The slaves, small brown men in white kilts, fell to their faces. The overseer recoiled his whip and knelt, lowering his head. Gasam ignored this human cattle and rode to the wagon. ''Look at this!'' he said, throwing back a cover of heavy cloth. His guard gasped with admiration at the sight. The bed was covered with glittering silvery bricks.

''Once,'' Gasam proclaimed, ''even a king could never hope to see so much steel in one place. Now I have it by the ton!'' He threw the cloth back over the load. ''Come. The queen awaits!''

They rode off and behind them the slaves rose to continue dragging their weighty, fabulously valuable burden.

The ride to the crater was dusty and brutally hot, the bleak landscape livened only by shimmering mirages and occasional dust devils. The men, ordinarily cheerful amid the harshest and most dangerous conditions, were depressed, speaking in low, ill-tempered mutters.

They were right to feel so, Gasam thought as he rode. This was not natural for warriors such as his. They needed war and raiding and plunder. They should be out campaigning, or else living at ease amid the wealth they had conquered with their spears. This was slave's work, and taking any part in it was degrading to warriors. Only his urgent need to best Hael and conquer the world forced Gasam to put his warriors to such a task.

In time, the long ride came to an end. They caught sight of the crater rim beneath its pall of smoke. A huge camp surrounded the raised rim and they saw sunlight twinkling from bared weapons. They broke into a brisk canter for the last half-mile, eager to reach something that approximated an encampment of their own kind.

To one side Gasam saw a dark patch of ground. It seemed that the desert was not truly lifeless, for scavengers tore at something. On impulse, he rode over to see what it was. He found the ground carpeted with dead slaves, worked to death under inhuman conditions, their corpses dragged here to be rent by the stunted, toothy stripers, the carrion bats and a breed of huge, dust-colored lizards Gasam did not recognize. The stench was appalling. He reined aside and continued his ride toward the crater.

When he was close enough to be recognized, a huge cheer went up from the camp and it continued while weapons were waved and brutalized slaves looked on dumbly to see what new terror had come to further blight their lives. A small figure draped in white came to the fore and Gasam urged his mount toward it.

"My queen!" Gasam cried, lifting the small form of Larissa into the saddle before him. Her arms went around his neck and they embraced amid the plaudits of their subjects. After a fevered hug, Gasam held her at arm's length, his massive arms and shoulders taking the weight with no appreciable strain. Larissa was swathed in flimsy white cloth with only her hands and feet showing. Her incredibly lovely face was shaded by a wide hat of plaited straw.

"What is this, little queen? Have you decided to be civilized and wear clothes like the mainlanders?"

She swatted at him. "Have you any idea what the sun here does to my skin? I would look like a ration of dried meat if I went about here in my usual fashion. You had better do the same." He brought her back to the saddle and they rode toward her great tent. ''I've tried to get my boys to cover themselves, but they think it unmanly.''

''It is,'' said Gasam.

''Look at them!'' she said.

Gasam did so. A crowd of Larissa's personal bodyguards stood around the tent, smiling at the royal couple. They were all Shasinn junior warriors, their junior status proclaimed by their hairstyle, consisting of hundreds of thin plaits gathered behind the neck which hung down the back. Their hair could not be unplaited or cut until they were made senior warriors when they reached their mid-twenties. He could see the change the desert sun had wrought. Dressed only in their brief loincloths, their naturally bronze-colored skin had turned a deep brown and the hair of some of them had bleached nearly white.

Gasam laughed. ''They'll lighten when they go back to more reasonable climates.'' He pointed to one, a boy of about sixteen. ''You, come here.''

The boy ran up. Like all Shasinn he was sleek and graceful. The Shasinn were so similar in look that he and the others in his age group might as well have been brothers. ''Yes, my king?''

''Have you cared well for your queen?'' he said, feigning sternness.

''We guard her well for what that is worth. There is no one here worth guarding her *against*. She could handle all these slaves by herself with no more than a small whip.''

Gasam laughed again. ''Well, you never know what might come down from the north. What do you and your brethren think of this place?''

''We hate it,'' the boy said frankly. ''It stinks, there are no animals save scavengers, there's no fighting and the sun is so bad that you can burn yourself by just touching the bare metal of your spear.''

''Don't despair. There will be better times ahead. But this duty must be done just now, and I trust no one else to do it. My queen must direct this operation, and the only warriors I want here are my islanders, and only Shasinn may guard the queen. Go rejoin your brethren.'' The boy returned to the sun-scorched crowd and Gasam could see the pride spreading through them as he repeated the king's words to them.

''Nobody handles warriors like you, my love,'' Larissa said. ''Come, rest in the tent a while. Then I want to show you this operation. You will not believe what you see.''

''Excellent!'' He slid from the saddle with Larissa still in his arms. A guard took his reins and he addressed the rest. ''Go find what comfort you may. I shall not require you for a while.'' As they rode off, Gasam and Larissa entered the tent.

Once under cover the queen sailed her hat to a slave girl and another pulled the flimsy gown over her head. Wearing only a flimsy cloth wound her around her hips, the queen might have been a girl of twenty instead of a woman more than twice that age. Only one who had known her all her life, as Gasam had, could see the near-invisible wrinkles at the corners of mouth and eyes, the occasional dull gray hair among the mass of hair so light that it was almost silver. Even so, the queen fretted obsessively at even these tiny signs of age. For the rest, her strenuous life in the desert kept her as taut and lithe as any young warrior.

Gasam embraced her and their hands roamed over one another's bodies as passionately as when they had been adolescents together, primitive tribal children on an obscure island. Now they were monarchs of a great part of the world, but this was unchanged between them. They tore away their brief garments and toppled onto a couch, oblivious of the queen's slave women, one of whom discreetly closed the tent flap, not that the royal couple cared who saw them.

Gasam and Larissa had many strange and sometimes brutal games to add spice to their lovemaking, but this time they had been separated too long for any such refinements. They grappled and touched, stroking with a sureness that came from long familiarity with each other's bodies. Gasam lay back and Larissa writhed down his belly, grasping him and taking him into her mouth for a few long, exquisite moments. Then he could wait no longer.

He took her beneath her arms and raised her over him, lowering her to straddle his hips. Her eyes rolled back and she groaned as he slid into her. Her hands braced on his shoulders, her slender hips began to churn. They ground together violently, making wordless animal sounds until, at the same moment, they achieved explosive relief.

Afterward they sipped wine together while the slave women plied their sponges and cloths. Sweat streamed down their bodies from the heat and their exertions, to be blotted up even as it ran. When their breathing returned to normal, they spoke.

"The operation has been going far better than I had even dared to hope," Larissa said. "We must have taken out five or six times as much steel as Hael got in a single season. And we aren't constrained by his time limit, since the mine is so close to our borders now."

"Why did he get so little steel?" Gasam asked.

Larissa laughed. "Because he was unwilling to waste slaves! In fact, you may not believe this, but he did not use slaves at all. He hired peasants from south of here to come up and work for a season at a time. Actually *paid* them! That meant blindfolding the whole lot for much of the march each way, to keep the location secret, and providing them with an escort, and seeing to it that they had sufficient supplies to keep them healthy coming, working and going back."

Gasam shook his head in wonderment. "How did such a fool ever become a king?"

"And on top of that," Larissa continued, "he could not carry out more than they could take on the entire long trek back to his grassy kingdom. But there is virtually no limit to the amount we can take out."

Gasam turned somber. "But how much is that? Surely this steel must play out in time. In the past, finding a few hundred pounds of steel was the stuff of legends. Tons have been taken from this place! How can it last?"

"Wait until you see, my love," she said, her face glowing.

"I must see this wonder now," he said, setting down his cup. "Show me."

The two resumed their clothing and went outside. As they walked toward the crater the queen's bodyguard fell in behind them. The climb up the side of the crater was not steep. At its crest they paused and Gasam looked across the crater. At first he was disappointed. He had expected a bowl gouged tremendously deep, but this was shallow. It was huge in extent, at least half a mile, but the bottom of the crater was only a few yards lower than the surrounding desert. Everywhere he saw huge slabs and chunks of grayish, stonelike material and from the crater came a continuous ringing clamor of hammers working against stone that yielded only grudgingly.

"Brace yourself," Larissa said, and they began to descend.

He understood the warning instantly. Awful as the desert outside was, the heat that concentrated within the crater was like a physical blow. It made the brain reel and dried the membranes inside the nostrils.

"There are desert nomads who pass by here," Larissa said. "Strange folk who ride big, flightless birds, like the killer birds back in the islands. They know of this place but they never come into the crater. They believe it is cursed."

"I can understand that," Gasam gasped. "I think it's cursed myself."

"Whatever the curse is, it's kept prying eyes from this place since the time of the ancients. Come, look at this." She led him to a mammoth lump of whitish stone where slaves toiled, smashing away at the stubborn material with big, heavy hammers. The tools were grounded and work ceased as the sovereigns approached. The slaves had been engaged in reducing the mass to rubble, which other slaves were carting away. From the mass protruded three long bars of steel, I-shaped and extending an unknown distance into the gray matrix. Gasam ran a hand over one of the bars, ignoring its burning temperature. The surface was rough but not pitted by rust. It was still dusty from its centuries embedded in the matrix, but where tools had scratched it the steel shone bright silver. He picked up a chunk of the gray stuff.

"It's concrete," Larissa said. "Some say the ancients used it for building material. The Nevans still use it so, but that is soft compared to this."

"I've seen bits of it, here and there," Gasam said. "But never this much. Over the years, people must have broken it all up to get at the steel. Why did the ancients bury so much steel in it?"

She shrugged. "That is one of the mysteries. Steel is valuable, and it rusts when exposed to wet air. Perhaps they thought to keep it safe this way. This may be the last great deposit."

He picked up one of the hammers. Its massive head was a solid block of steel. He shook his head in wonderment.

"Tools of steel. Steel has always been for weapons. Who would think of such a thing?"

"Hael," she said. "Convenient for us that he did. All the tools were stored right here. This stuff," she patted the artificial boulder, "is as hard as any natural stone. He saw that he would need hard tools to break it up and what is harder than steel? He must have used the first batch of steel to make these hammers and picks and wedges. After that, the work must have gone much faster."

"Hael was always clever in his way," Gasam said, "but they were not ways worthy of a warrior."

Larissa smiled indulgently. She loved him even for his limitations. Her own intelligence and talents made up for his deficiencies. He was a warrior, a conqueror with the rare ability to inspire men to die for him and enjoy doing so. She was the planner, the organizer, the consolidator. Gasam led his armies to conquer new lands, she administered the new populations, turning them into docile, obedient and productive subjects. His armies supplied the intimidation, she conducted the diplomacy that kept foreign lands unsuspecting until they were ready for conquest. She had created a corps of spies that furnished them with detailed information about the enemy's weaknesses. The bribes she sent out subverted foreign officials, further weakening prospective conquests. One of her spy teams had found this steel mine.

They continued their tour of the crater. Everywhere were gigantic masses of the concrete, most of them untouched. Scabby clusters of rust on the surface revealed where the steel had rusted back flush with gray matrix.

"How much do you think there is?" Gasam asked.

"Enough to bring out many tons each year for the . . ." Gasam knew that she had been about to say, "for the rest of our lives," but she never liked even to think of their mortality. She searched endlessly for a way to restore their youth and convey longevity, perhaps immortality. "For many, many years anyway," she finished.

"Think of it," he exulted. "Steel weapons for every soldier in my army! Even the inferior troops will be more effective than any foreign power."

"And you will have stockpiles to make you by far the richest king in the world," she pointed out patiently. "All the other kings will come begging to you, offering everything they have in trade for steel."

"That is for merchants," he said. "I intend to conquer them all. Why bother to trade with them?"

She sighed. "Because it makes you richer and them poorer. First make them dependent upon you, my king, then conquer them. That way you gain their wealth to make you stronger, and in the end you will have back the steel they bought from you."

He grinned and draped an arm around her. "How fortunate I am to have you to think these things out for me! Come, little queen, let's get out of this hole. I've seen enough here."

As they left the crater the drop in temperature was refreshing. "One good thing about it," Gasam said. "At least it makes the rest of this desert feel cool."

"There is more to see," she said. "Come." She led him to a line of trenches where gigantic bellows raised charcoal fires to white heat, and masses of steel melted in great crucibles.

"It takes a tremendous amount of charcoal to get the temperature we need to melt this steel," Larissa said. "All of it has to be hauled up from the south. Hael set up this system, because he had to haul his steel all the way home on the backs of humpers. When my new road is finished, we can stop all this and just haul out the steel in rough form. The smelting can be done in places where it is more efficient. Unlike Hael, we have plenty of slaves and animals to do the hauling."

They watched as a team of sweating slaves toiled at long bars to lift a glowing crucible from the coals. Puffing and heaving, they carried it to a long stone mold where they carefully tipped it and the fiery flood spilled along a channel and into side-molds to form the steel bricks.

"Sometimes the bars give way," Larissa said, "or a crucible breaks. We recover the steel, but we lose a lot of slaves that way. Another reason to move everything but the mining away from here. If nothing else, it just makes it hotter."

"Everything shall be as you desire, little queen," Gasam promised. They began to walk back to the great tent.

"Is everything else to your satisfaction?" the king asked. "Do you need more slaves?"

"The attrition in slaves is bad, but of all our livestock the two-legged sort are the most plentiful. I've sent word to my suppliers to send only the darker ones. Fair people don't last long here. Rations are no great problem. Most of them lived on little even before they were slaves."

"They were always slaves," Gasam said. "When we conquered them, we merely eliminated some nonsensical distinctions, like 'peasant' and 'farmer' and 'workman'. There are only warriors and slaves. Even the soldiers are slaves, although they are useful in battle. I will see to it that you have all the slaves you need. I plan to eliminate many of the farms and plantations in my new southern lands. There is too much land under cultivation. I want more pasture."

Larissa closed her eyes. In so many ways her husband was still the primitive, island tribesman he had always been. Farming was beneath notice to him. What he loved was great herds of livestock, especially kagga. Given his will, he would turn the whole world into pasture.

"But surely, my lord, your empire must be fed. Farmers are contemptible, but they raise food for the rest to eat."

"Most of it just goes to feed the farmers themselves. Then they breed more children and have to bring more land under cultivation, ruining it for anything worthwhile. Have no fear, my subjects of real value will not go hungry. The excess farmers I move off the land can be used up on projects like this."

She knew better than to argue. She would just have to correct whatever damage he accomplished when she had the opportunity. He needed a new war to keep him occupied. They went into the tent and made themselves comfortable; as comfortable as anyone could be under the circumstances, at any rate. They undressed and lay on cushions while the slaves fanned them. The sun was almost down, and the evening air would cool quickly.

"Until this operation should be firmly established," Larissa said, "I've been reluctant to work on future plans. Now it is going well and is efficiently guarded. Nobody can bring a large enough force across that desert to threaten us now. The time has come to consider the near future. What is our military situation?"

"The new southern territories are well into consolidation," Gasam told her. "The new military levies are still raw, but they will be ready for their first taste of battle soon. To the east are just three petty southern kingdoms. I could take them without too much trouble, but for now I prefer to leave them as a buffer zone. Beyond them is the great river and then Mezpa. We know too little about that place."

Larissa nodded. It had taken her a long time, but at last Gasam had learned the value of good intelligence.

"It galls me to leave Neva unconquered to our north," he continued. "That female longneck who runs the place has to fail soon. No nation of farmers and merchants and sailors should be able to stand against us."

"Nor should she," Larissa answered, "were it not for

Hael. Invade her from the south, and his mounted army will pour across her northern border to her aid.''

"Hael—'' Gasam all but spat. "It's enough to make me believe that gods really exist, because one of them seems to have raised him up to plague me.''

The one military obstacle they had never been able to overcome was the bizarre army of cabo-riding plainsmen created by Hael. They rode like a river in spate and shot multitudes of arrows that fell like sleet upon footmen who could do nothing in return, with little to protect themselves save huddling under their shields, something proud warriors hated to do. In battle the riders seemed to be everywhere and were effective far beyond their actual numbers.

"The last time I fought the Nevans,'' Gasam said, "my army was far smaller. If we were to mass on their southern border secretly, and attack in full force at highest speed, we could sweep the entire country from south to north before Hael even knew there was a war.''

She shook her head. "My lord, your greatest strength has always been your magnificent warriors—the islanders and especially the Shasinn—and there have never been enough of them. They can fight at a run, sweeping all before them. But the rest are all simple foot-sloggers, just like Shazad's. Your warriors can defeat her armies, although she has built a formidable land force in the years since our last war. But the best warriors cannot take her fortified places by storm. That would call for your slow infantry and the engineers. Before you had half the country conquered, Hael would be there.''

She saw how his face clouded, so she took a less galling line: "How go your efforts to build a force of mounted archers like his?''

"Slowly, and I doubt that we shall ever have anything like his army, unless we take a subject people who have the ability. I think those plainsmen are born riders and archers the way the Shasinn are born runners and spearmen. It is not something that can simply be learned. And we have not yet been able to copy the bows, although some of the bowyers have come close. The cabos are a problem; they breed slowly.

Hael must have come upon a great herd of wild stock to work with.''

''If we cannot copy his army, his weapons or his tactics,'' she said, ''then we must come up with something better.''

''What might that be? I can see that you have something in mind. Have your spies been reporting to you here?''

The queen smiled and nodded. Above all things, Gasam and Larissa loved power and the instruments of power. They spoke of these things with the passion and intimacy that other couples reserved for matters of love.

''First of all, those petty southern kingdoms you spoke of are truly ripe to fall into your hands. When you plan that campaign, use your raw troops. I say this for several reasons: One, it will give them needed experience. But more importantly, that war will be observed. There are nations across the great river, and the greatest of these is Mezpa. I now know more of it than before, but it remains largely an enigma. Their weapons are like nothing we have encountered before.''

''The firetubes,'' Gasam snorted. ''You forget I was there when those merchants brought us the smuggled examples and demonstrated them. A great flash and noise and little else.''

''I have not forgotten, but I know that they have conquered many neighboring lands in recent years with these things. Until we know how they have accomplished this, we should avoid hostilities. That is why I say use your lesser troops when you conquer their neighbors across the river. They will be watching, and the less they know about us, the more we know about them, the better.''

''That is wise,'' he admitted. ''What do we know thus far?''

''My spies have reported much that is familiar, and some things that make little sense. Mezpa is a maritime nation like Neva, and does a great deal of manufacturing. The ruling and laboring classes are supported by farming, mostly large plantations using many slaves. That may be a reason why they are expanding—they need a constant supply of slaves. But how they are governed I cannot find out. They have an

Assembly that is something like our Council of Elders in the islands, but these are chosen on the basis of land and wealth. One of them lords it over the others, but how he is chosen I do not know. My spies say the latest of these rulers is a man named Deathmoon, and that is all I know about him. I would like to know more.''

"And this is something your slaves are not likely to learn?''

"I am afraid not. But I might learn much, personally.''

He looked at her in surprise. "Surely you do not plan to go there yourself?''

"And why not? I have gone on embassies before. What could be more natural than the powerful but peaceful ruler of the west sending an embassy to his brother ruler of the east? And what greater sign of his purely peaceful intentions than sending his own queen to bear pledges of eternal brotherhood? Of course, he will be most anxious to entertain me royally. Should I request it, he could hardly refuse to stage a large-scale demonstration by his famous army.''

"This man seems to have gone to some trouble to keep his tactics secret,'' Gasam said doubtfully.

"Men have done foolish things to impress me before now,'' she pointed out, complacently.

"Very clever,'' Gasam said, nodding. "This will bear some thinking. We need not be hasty. Above all, I want you kept safe.''

"We can work something out,'' she said. "I needn't place myself within his borders. That river must have some large islands where we can meet. I'll take a strong escort of Shasinn. He will be amused by the primitive tribesmen, which is all to the good. Civilized men always think tribal people are a sort of man-shaped animal, like the man-of-the-trees. That sort of thinking has provided us with many of our victories.''

"Indeed,'' said Gasam. "What have your spies told you of Hael's latest doings?''

"It is a long trek from here to his heartland. My last news is several months old. At that time he was away. It seems he went with a trade mission to the east. Perhaps he wants to learn about Mezpa as well. He must be back by now. He takes no precautions against espionage, and why should he? What is there to learn, save the location of his steel mine, which we now have.

"For the rest, everyone knows where his strength lies, with his hard-riding people and their hard-shooting bows. He rules a great deal of grass. He roams off into the hills to speak with the spirits and experience visions. All this is common knowledge. He has one problem: His young warriors grow restive. They want him to lead them against an enemy and they are not particular who it might be."

"What a fool," Gasam said. "He was a simpleton as a child and he has grown no wiser. To have such an instrument under his control and not use it! I would turn those young warriors loose against my enemies. He could own much of the world were it not for his ridiculous reluctance to crush his weaker neighbors. He had a chance to take over Neva when he was there as an ally, and what did he do? He rode away, leaving Shazad in power!"

Larissa had been pondering while Gasam delivered this opinion, sipping idly at her wine. "My husband, I've been considering a new source of intelligence, one just suited to this evaluation of Mezpa, and it may be especially useful in the eventual invasion itself."

"Tell me, my queen."

"We now have complete control of the southern coast, do we not—almost to the delta of the great river?"

"All but perhaps a hundred miles," he agreed.

"That river might prove a terrible obstacle to our invasion. We may have to consider an amphibious operation, as we did when we conquered Chiwa."

"I've already considered that," Gasam said. "Our transports are in dry dock, as well maintained as our warships."

"That being the case, it would be well to know about their harbors and coastal defenses. Some probing raids along their southern coast might be in order."

Gasam grinned. "While we are pledging eternal friendship?"

"We won't need our naval forces. Our harbors are alive

with pirates who have been out of work for some time. Get a few of your coastal defense skippers together. Half of them were pirates in the old days. Give them ships and tell them to raid along the coast as far as practicable. Nothing military, just ordinary pirate raids for loot and slaves. Then they are to report back to me about everything they have seen and learned.''

"And if this Deathmoon protests anyway? He will be sure they are coming from my domains.''

"I'll assure him that these pirates have strongholds in some unsubdued islands off the Chiwan coast. For all he knows, there might be such. We certainly used those islands for the same purpose.''

He smiled once more. "I shall do exactly as you desire. The sailing season will begin soon. We should know something in less than six months.''

"Good. That leaves one place still undealt with. The Canyon.''

"A needless distraction,'' the king said. "An obscure place where we can lose many soldiers from accident alone, and accomplish nothing of worth.''

"They have the secret, I know it!'' the queen insisted. "The Canyoners are sorcerers and they never grow old or die!''

"My love,'' he said, "I do not believe in gods or spirits, magic or sorcerers. If people believe these things about the Canyon and its people, that is because the Canyoners have spread these tales about themselves. And it works. It has kept them secure in their worthless corner of the world for a long, long time.''

"How can you say that?'' Larissa demanded. "You saw Lady Fyana. She was a powerful sorceress and she looked to be no more than a girl.''

"Lady Fyana looked that way because she was a young woman. She only *claimed* to be a sorceress. Rather, she did not contradict you when you insisted that she was one. Besides, she was in love with a son of Hael. Does that speak highly of her wisdom?'' Idly, he fingered the thin scar that ran down one side of his face, the mark left by that surprisingly capable young man's sword.

"Your armies virtually surround their land now," Larissa insisted. "Send a token force under a flag of truce and demand their cooperation! What use are all our conquests if we merely grow old and die like other men?"

This was an old contention between them. *Why this?* he thought, wryly. His queen, who was in all other things so levelheaded, was quite insane on this one obsessive matter.

"Very well," he agreed. "An envoy with an escort, and no more! I will demand that they send a mission to acknowledge my overlordship and pledge fealty to me. You may then question these supposed sorcerers to your heart's content. I think you will be disappointed, though. Time is the one enemy whose power over me I freely acknowledge."

"Then the rest of your conquests must be swift, my love," Larissa said. "Your warriors follow you fanatically, because you have proven many times that you are the greatest warrior in the world. Will they so willingly follow a failing old man?"

TEN

"It is true, then?" said the woman in the thronelike chair at the head of the long table.

"Indisputably, Your Majesty," said the councilor who was also Lord of the Southern March, a title the queen had created when she completely overhauled Neva's defenses. "King Gasam is in possession of the steel mine. Even now, tons of the metal flow like water into the forges of the south. Queen Larissa has ordered the complete rebuilding of the old metal founding center of Gwato. The furnaces and foundries are being restored and the land is being scoured for skilled metal workers to learn the arts of working steel. The impudent woman is even offering bonuses for skilled Nevans to come over to her."

Queen Shazad felt like burying her face in her hands, but she knew better than to show weakness before her councilors. *Hael, Hael,* she thought, *how did you let this happen?*

"I must confer with King Hael on this matter," she said, with little conviction. For months there had been no word from Hael, despite the splendid relay system they had established between their nations. Their hard-riding couriers could traverse the hundreds of miles in a few days, weather permitting. But Hael had disappeared. He might be dead. She could scarcely bear the thought. It had been decades since they were lovers, but his archers were her nation's security, the only true check on Gasam's mad, expanding power.

"What indications have you seen of his priorities?" she asked the southern lord.

"Weapons, Your Majesty. Spears, swords, axes and maces, perhaps even body armor of steel."

At this, the military men around the table, who made up most of the Council these days, laughed.

"Come now," said the prince consort, a scarred old campaigner himself. "Gasam's elite are island barbarians, and they despise armor. He would never waste steel on his foot soldiers!"

From a belt pouch the southern lord took a small object. "A few days ago, a deserter came across the border. He went straight to the nearest tavern and began to trade these for drink. One of my soldiers was in the place, sober enough to arrest the man and bring him and his trade goods to me." He passed the little object up the table and as it rested in each palm in turn, each face clouded with horror. When it reached the prince consort and he looked similarly dismayed, the queen snatched it impatiently from his hand.

It was an arrowhead, like thousands of others she had seen, except that most were made of stone, the finer ones of bronze. This one was a dingy silver color, apparently made of steel.

"Is this terribly significant?" she asked the prince consort.

"Your Majesty," said her husband of fifteen years, who in this assembly was required to address her formally, "among Gasam's troops, the archers are by far the most despised. Hand-to-hand combat is the only sort the islanders deem honorable. They even consider their javelin-hurling to be more of a sporting prelude to battle than serious weapon-play. The lowest slave-spearman ranks higher than a bowman. If Gasam is issuing steel arrowheads to the archers, then he must be confident that he has more steel than he can possibly use."

"How long has he had control of the steel mine?" she asked.

"Somewhat less than a year, we think," said Bardas, her senior councilor.

She felt a wave of relief. "Than he cannot have fully equipped his army with steel weapons!"

"Certainly not," assured the southern lord. "I brought the arrowhead to demonstrate to Your Majesty the man's confidence in his abundance. As soon as I saw these I summoned some master smiths and questioned them. They told me that the working properties of steel are quite different from those of silver, gold, copper and bronze. In any place, there are few men skilled in the forging of steel, and a great many of these have emigrated to King Hael's land, since he has enjoyed a near-monopoly for years."

"Then why does Gasam not arm his elite warriors with steel weapons before the despised archers?" she asked.

"The smiths told me that these small, simple objects would be ideal for training new apprentices in working the metal. As they gain competence and confidence, they will essay more complex tasks. Soon we should see javelin-heads, then spear-points. Only then, after a year or two of working steel, will they be able to turn out swords and the sort of all-metal spears favored by the Shasinn."

"He will not try to move against us until he is fully armed with steel weapons," she said.

"So it is to be hoped," said Bardas, judiciously.

She dismissed the Council, including her consort, and bade Bardas attend her in her adjoining private chambers. The men bowed their way out and the queen retired to the palace suite adjoining the council room. Her ladies and well-trained staff of servants had the terrace prepared for her, knowing, in the ineffable fashion of courtiers and domestics, that she would have had a disagreeable council session. As she collapsed into a chair with perfectly arranged cushions, a cup of iced wine appeared in her hand as if by magic. A lady discreetly loosened the lacings of her dress, which she insisted be laced overtightly to combat the inexorable thickening of her waist.

Queen Shazad of Neva was a handsome woman in her forties, her once-black hair now shot with gray. Her face retained much of its youthful beauty, but the cares and burdens of office had etched deep lines in her face, lending it a strength that in her younger days had been apparent only in her spine.

"Have your councilors been insolent again, Majesty?" asked Lady Zina, her closest companion.

"No, but they were full of doom. Justified this time, I think. And it's not over yet. I have Bardas outside cooling his heels and I'm going to have to confer with him before I can relax for the evening."

"You allow your councilors too much license, Majesty," said Gulda, a sharp-faced woman who brought her all the court gossip.

"They are no good to me if they are obedient pets," Shazad said. "These times call for strong men. I learned years ago what disasters befall one when weaklings and toadies occupy places of power. I must have men of spirit and if they sometimes speak to me oversharply, well, I've grown a thick skin over the years. Better a bad taste in my mouth than Shasinn in my territory."

"Of course you are right," said Zina, who thought no such thing. She would have been happier, Shazad thought, if all men, including the consort, approached her queen on their knees, or better yet, crawling on their bellies.

"Summon Bardas and leave us," Shazad said. Silently the others withdrew. Moments later, the senior councilor appeared. He was a tall, portly man, once a soldier but now well past his military years.

"Sit, Bardas," she gestured to a chair facing hers. "Have some wine and let's talk about danger."

"Then we have much to speak of, Majesty." Bardas settled his bulk into the chair and took a cup which he held without drinking.

"I don't consider myself obtuse," Shazad said.

"By no means, Majesty," Bardas hastily put in.

"But somebody is going to have to explain to me just why this change of metals so seriously upsets the balance. Oh, I know perfectly well that steel is far harder than bronze, but it is a harder sword enough to guarantee military superiority?''

"I fear, in this case, it is," Bardas said, his face woeful.

"But we have quite a bit of it ourselves," she protested. "I've been buying it from King Hael for years. All of our officers have steel swords now."

"Not nearly enough," Bardas said. "If all of Gasam's soldiers have steel weapons, their advantage will be terrible. A steel sword will shear through our hide and wicker and light wood shields as if they were made of paper. Our armor, even the bronze armor worn by officers, will not keep out their spears and arrows. And there is more. Consider, Majesty, that most of our soldiers have seen very little steel in their lives. The metal is almost legendary, a symbol of invincibility. Not so many years ago King Gasam's spear of steel was considered not only a great extravagance, but a sign from the gods that he was destined to rule the world.

"What will be the effect, my queen, when our soldiers face Gasam's hordes, and they see the sunlight flash from spearpoints of steel, and the steel swords are unsheathed, and the Shasinn appear, not with their great bronze spears but with spears all of steel, like Gasam's? I will tell you what will happen, my queen: Your soldiers will drop their weapons and run."

"Never!" Shazad shouted, wine splashing from her cup. "I did not build the finest military machine in Nevan history to have it run before island savages without striking a blow!"

"Your Majesty," the man said hastily, "I did not mean to infer—" She silenced him with a gesture.

"I do not believe the problem is as serious as you suggest," she said, her calm returning. "The problems may be addressed." That was always her style, never to dither in the face of obstacles. She believed that all such problems could be overcome, and that it was foolish to delay action when action was called for.

"You say that Gasam will need at least one year, and perhaps two, to fully arm his men with steel. We shall take steps in the meantime. First, I shall buy all the steel I can from King Hael. We may not be able to fully, or even partially, arm our soldiers with steel, but I want there to be enough in every unit that the men grow used to the sight of it."

"An excellent idea, Majesty," Bardas murmured.

"Second, I want a summoning of all our arsenal masters and the heads of the armorer's guild. This is to be done as soon as possible. I want better armor designed and manufactured for our men; armor that is more resistant to steel. The men will grouse because their armor and shields are heavier, but let them. Above all, they must be made to believe that their new equipment will protect them from Gasam's new steel weapons."

"An excellent course of action, Majesty."

"Bardas, I've lived long enough to see a good deal of war and it has taught me a few things. Most of all it has taught me this: There are no magic weapons and there are no invincible warriors. Those things exist only in the minds of men. Most of what happens in war takes place in men's minds. On the battlefield, ideas are more important than weapons and numbers and tactics. More generals are defeated by their own delusions than by the enemy, with delusions of their own superiority or delusions of enemy strength."

"Most sagacious, Majesty."

"Don't patronize me! I can see that you're bursting to say something. Out with it." She took a drink of her wine and was annoyed to see that her hand trembled slightly.

"Ah, Your Majesty, we seem to find ourselves in one of those times when all the world changes, as we did years ago when the islanders first came to plague our shores. Your idea to buy steel is excellent, but it suffers from some problems: First, it is expensive—"

"What of it? I'll strip the treasury and the temples if need be. They're no use to us if Gasam comes and takes everything."

"But second, consider this: King Hael has been cut off from his source of the metal. He may not be willing to part with it."

This was true, and it gave her pause. "I will stress to King Hael the urgency of the situation. Gasam was his enemy long before he was ours."

"Yes, that may be of some help. Now, my queen, I know that for many years you have exchanged royal correspondence with Queen Larissa?"

"Certainly. She is a most amusing correspondent and we always stay on friendly terms even though we hate each other."

"It is good that you have chosen to maintain a friendly tone, Your Majesty, very good. Perhaps, now, it would be advisable to adopt an even warmer attitude."

"What do you mean?" she demanded coldly.

"Do not misunderstand me, my queen, but we must re-examine old ideas and old certainties. In the past King Hael has been our stout friend and Gasam has been our deadly enemy, but the world changes. Soon, it may be time to reach a new accommodation with both of them."

She glared at him. "Arrange the summoning of the armorers. You may go." The councilor bowed his way out.

At last she allowed herself to slump forward and she rested her face in her palms. She had trusted Bardas for many years. Now she would have to watch him. He was thinking defeatist thoughts and it was only a short step from that to plotting with the enemy. She would have to instruct her agents to be on the alert for secret contact between him and Gasam. Between any of the councilors and Gasam. Now she could trust no one. She sat back up and called for more wine, cursing herself for a weakling. A monarch had no business trusting anyone.

By tradition in Neva, the great councilors and generals were high noblemen. By definition, noblemen were men with much land and property. Therefore, they were men with much to lose, and were very reluctant to lose it. They spoke much of honor, but it had been her experience that honor never got in the way of self-interest. It was a simple enough equation. If they thought her policies threatened their holdings, they would treat with her enemies.

Her ladies and servants reappeared. "Get me out of this court gown," she ordered.

While she stood, she was expertly stripped of the complicated heavy garments and draped in a simple lounging robe. Her cosmetician removed the heavy formal makeup from her face and her hairdresser took her hair down, unwinding the innumerable strings of tiny pearls and golden beads that decorated her long tresses. The woman began gently stroking her hair with a brush.

"Your Majesty," the hairdresser said, "you should allow me to apply some tint. Your hair is so beautiful, and there is no need for it to lose its luster while you are so young."

"No," Shazad said with finality. "That was what my father did, to make people think he was still young. I will allow myself no such delusion. Everyone has to tell me I'm young and beautiful, even if I'm not, that's the important thing." She held out her cup and it was instantly refilled. "As long as no one will tell me to my face that I'm getting older, it means they still fear me."

She called for food and it was brought. While her ladies fussed over her, she ate honeyed wildfowl, seed cakes and glazed fruit. Her wine cup was refilled frequently.

"Ah . . . Your Majesty . . ." Lady Zina began, hesitantly.

"I know, I know. I'm upset, and when I'm upset I eat too much and drink far too much. I'm upset a great deal these days and that is why you have to keep letting out the waistline on my gowns without telling me. Well, it could be worse. It wasn't so long ago that I would have called in half a dozen guardsmen to help me wile away the time."

There was a scandalized twittering from her ladies. Most of them were too young to remember when the name of Princess Shazad was a byword for depravity throughout Neva. She was rumored to have poisoned her first husband, to practice forbidden religions with orgiastic rites, to be fond of strange drugs and stranger amatory practices. Some of it was true, much of it was exaggerated.

More to the point, she was believed to have gradually seized power when her father was in his dotage, to have killed most of his traitorous advisers, generals and admirals, to have executed many nobles whose loyalty was suspect. All of that was true, and very few of her subjects complained. She had forged a military machine from a degenerate shambles, restored Neva's naval might, and raised the land to a level of prosperity it had not known in centuries. Whatever the doubts of her advisers, she had the unstinting loyalty of her subjects.

Not, she was beginning to think, that the loyalty of her subjects was likely to prove crucial in the looming crisis. *Where was Hael?*

ELEVEN

"**A**re you sure this is the right way?" Hael demanded. He and Kairn had been trudging all morning along a barely marked path, leading their cabos for much of it because the constant downpour made the track slippery. Above all just now, they could not afford a lamed beast.

"Of course it is!" Kairn insisted, shaking a curtain of water from his face. He was almost certain that he was on the same shortcut path he had been shown days before, but it was hard to tell in the rain and murk and general gloom. Both of them had been raised outdoors and were used to being caught in the open by the great storms that swept their world, but there was something especially miserable about rain that filtered down through the leaves of trees.

"If nothing else," Hael said, "they'll never be able to track us through this."

Kairn knew that his father was right about that. They had been off the main road since the night before, and the downpour had been continuous since that time, obliterating every trace of their passage. Behind them, their remounts snorted and groaned unhappily. The instinct of cabos was to stand still while a rainstorm passed and they resented being made to walk. Abruptly Hael stopped and held up his hand. Kairn did likewise and the animals stopped instantly, grateful for this uncharacteristically sensible behavior on their masters' part.

"What is it?" Kairn whispered.

"Something ahead. People, I think." Kairn knew the look. When his father stood in that attitude, he was casting his unique senses in all directions, feeling the spirits of all the nearby animals. He also knew that the closeness of the cabos would confuse things. Their proximity acted much like a mass of steel had when near one of the Nevan compasses he had seen, throwing the needle off its mark.

"You want me to lead the cabos back a ways?" Kairn whispered.

Hael shook his head. "They're too close already. Come on. If we're where you think we are, they may be friends."

They went on. Kairn was not at all sure, but he said nothing. There was nothing they could do about it anyway, so why cast doubts?

"Stop." The word was spoken from nearby, but was barely audible, like the challenge a sentry gives when the enemy might overhear.

"Show yourselves," Hael said as quietly. Five men stood, two of them holding bows at full draw.

"Who are you?" said the challenging voice. The speaker himself remained invisible.

Kairn stepped forward. "I am Kairn of the plains. I was through here just a few days ago. Are you Noble Stone's men?"

"How many more of you are there?" the man asked.

"None," Hael said. "Check our back trail if you don't believe me."

"Why should I believe you?" the man said. "Rock, Riverwind, go scout the way they've come."

The plainsmen heard the two dash off through the woods, but they, too, were unseen.

"You are woodsmen of more than ordinary skill," Hael complimented.

"It never hurts to be cautious," said the speaker. "When you don't know the other man's number, why reveal your own? We won't get any wetter than we are while we wait for them to report back."

"There are twelve of you," Hael said. "The five we can see, the two who went to check out our back trail, you who are doing the talking, two men up in a tree ahead of me to my left, another in a tree to the right." There was silence for a few seconds.

"It's him," said a new voice.

"Must be," said another.

"You shut your mouths!" said the original speaker. "Even if it's them, there could be half of Deathmoon's army right behind them. We wait."

Apparently these people did nothing by half-measures, for it was a full hour before the two scouts reported back.

"Nothing," said one of them. "We went back as far as Black Rock Fork and there's no sign of pursuit. Even we couldn't track them through this."

Now the speaker came forward. Kairn didn't recognize him from his earlier visit, but he had the same look as the others: rough, bearded and shaggy, dressed in forest-colored clothing.

"Come along then. It's time for you to talk to our lord."

By mid-afternoon they were in the clearing and the familiar hall was ahead of them. A runner had gone forward to bring word of the impending visit and Noble Stone was there to greet them, grinning broadly.

"Welcome, doubly welcome, to my house. Come in and dry yourselves."

A serving woman handed them cups of warmed wine and they drank gratefully. A great fire had been built up in the hearth, and drying poles erected. Hael and Kairn were given dry clothes to wear while their own garments dried by the fire.

"We don't get to entertain a king very often," Noble Stone said, "but we will do our best. Come, sit and eat. You look as if you've had a rough few days."

"I thank you," Hael said graciously, "but I am afraid we cannot linger. I must get back to my homeland and there is a manhunt of great proportions out looking for us."

Noble Stone's look sharpened. "We've not heard of it."

"That is because we're still ahead of pursuit," Hael said. "We left Crag in haste, and have been changing mounts frequently ever since."

"Truly?" Noble Stone's smile grew even wider. "Anyone who can annoy Deathmoon like that must be our friend. Does he know who you are?"

"He didn't when we left," Hael said. "He may be suspecting by now."

Noble Stone laughed heartily. "Eat, rest and get dry, then we shall speak of some serious things."

The two needed little encouragement. Both they and their cabos were in need of some restoration. The food was the simplest sort: wild game, fruit, cheese and bread. Besides wine there was a heady beer brewed from local grain. It was food for men who had run a long way, and had a much longer run ahead of them. When they were replete, the platters were cleared away, the table taken down, and they sat in a wide semicircle before the fire, Noble Stone in the center and Hael next to him.

"I wish you could remain with me for a while," Noble Stone said by way of opening. "There are others like me, nobles who want to see Mezpan power curbed. There is a powerful alliance here, and with your help we could hold a decisive edge against Deathmoon."

"Urgent matters call me home," Hael said. "But I believe what you say. I now know from his own lips that Deathmoon plans an invasion of my land very soon."

"This brought about consternation. "He told you so himself?" Noble Stone said, incredulous.

Hael gave them an abbreviated version of his adventures in Crag.

"Believing me to be a spy for Larissa," he said, "Deathmoon thought to use me as an emissary. Now I know two things that are of immense importance: Not only does Deathmoon plan an invasion of my territory, which I might be able to deal with, but he wants an alliance with Gasam, the object being to destroy my kingdom and divide the plains between them."

"With such an alliance," Noble Stone said as the hubbub died down, "you cold be crushed like a nut between stones."

"I am not so easily crushed," Hael maintained, "but it is a distressing prospect. They force my hand. I must destroy one or the other of them first."

"I admit to a certain bias," Noble Stone said. "I hope you decide to eliminate Deathmoon first."

"I am still uncertain about his military capabilities," Hael said. "I will not commit my army to war until I know what I can accomplish. I know Gasam, I have fought him and his army before. I can defeat them in the open field handily. I've seen Deathmoon's troops, but I don't know how they fight."

"Then we must enlighten you," Noble Stone said. "What would you know?"

"I own several of the firetubes," Hael said. "I know now that I cannot hope to duplicate them; the materials and skill are not to be had in my land. I can see their great usefulness in defending a fortified position or city, where soldiers have protection and anyone can be pressed into service. A boy or an old woman can operate one of the things. But they have the accuracy of a thrown rock. I cannot see how they can be effective in the field. Once, I thought that if a great enough mass of men used them, they would be decisive. But then I considered how many that would mean. Such an army would have to be difficult if not impossible to supply, and still would not be all that effective. My warriors could circle around the flanks of such an army, pouring arrows into them. They would not be able to keep up sufficient fire to do us any harm."

"As for the accuracy of the weapons, they need none," Noble Stone said. "For it, they substitute sheer volume of fire. You have seen how they maneuver in lines? Standing shoulder-to-shoulder, the whole line fires as one man. They don't have to pick individual targets, just the mass of the enemy army. With that many balls discharged at once, a lot of people on the other end are going to get hurt."

"But you can't hit a man with one of those at fifty paces!" Kairn protested.

Noble Stone addressed his answer to Hael. "In your case, they won't be shooting at men. They'll be shooting at cabos. A cabo presents five or six times the target area a man does, and that goes for unaimed mass fire as well as for the aimed sort. How effective will your archers be, King Hael, with their cabos shot from under them, advancing against Deathmoon's army on foot?"

"But the weapons are so slow to load," Hael pointed out. "They could get off only one such mass firing, and they could not wipe out my whole army with it. Most of their balls would plow into the dirt or fly toward the clouds or pass between the riders. We stay in open order when we fight."

"They don't *all* fire at once," Noble Stone said. "They fire by lines. I will explain: Picture them as you have seen them on the drill field, standing in lines. That is how they face the enemy, drawn up in ranks, five or six lines deep. As the enemy approaches, the first line takes aim. As soon as the enemy are in range, upon command, the first line fires all at once. Immediately, the first rank kneels and begins to reload. The second rank takes aim and fires *over the heads* of the first rank. Then they kneel likewise and the third rank aims and fires. By the time the last rank has fired, the first rank is ready to stand and fire again.

"The concentration of fire is terrible. Only one-fifth or one-sixth of the army fires at each volley, but the fire is continuous. And they can keep it up all day. It takes no great physical exertion."

Hael and Kairn thought over these implications for a while.

"Much becomes clear now," Hael admitted. "Still, I cannot believe that this method is without weaknesses. Standing in long battle lines like that, they must be very vulnerable to flank attack."

"They have means of dealing with it," Noble Stone retorted. "That is why they maneuver endlessly, why they drill hour after hour, day after day. They can change fronts faster than you would credit, wheeling by lines to transform a flank into a front. If they are attacked from all sides, they can form squares that can shoot in all directions."

"Are you a military man, Lord Noble Stone?" Hael asked.

"I've done a bit of fighting," the rebel said.

"Then you know that tactics and maneuvers are only a part of winning battles. Picking the place to fight and the time to fight is usually the most decisive factor."

Noble Stone nodded. "That is true."

"And you did not want me to come here so that you could tell me my enemy is invincible, did you?"

Noble Stone laughed. "That I did not! No, I wanted to let you know how your enemy will fight, and that you had better not try to engage him on the open plains as I understand you have done in your previous victories."

"Broken, hilly country would be better," Hael said. "We could maneuver closer to them before coming in range and retreat behind high ground and in gullies after pouring in our arrows. Their formations will not be so cohesive on uneven ground."

Noble Stone gestured around him. "Forest is good, also. In forest you can catch such an army in marching order, pour in some fire, then fade back into the trees to hit them again somewhere else."

"My riders are not much good in forest," Hael said. "Mobility and long-range archery are everything in the way we fight."

Noble Stone grinned. "Just to the north of here, just across the Gray River, there is a stretch of hilly country that might be ideal. An army that has just marched through this forest, taking casualties with every mile, would be nicely softened up were they to encounter your riders in the broken land. In fact, the river crossing itself might be a good spot.''

"It might at that," Hael said. "But, as I have said, I have problems at home. This will bear some thinking about. We shall keep in contact. In the morning, before we leave, we shall arrange some signals, signs and passwords, so that you will know that the messengers I send are genuine.''

"Excellent," Noble Stone said. "And, King Hael, if you want my further advice?''

"Yes?''

"Don't spend too much time getting your problems sorted out at home. I don't think Deathmoon will wait too long to come for you.''

The next morning, after making the necessary arrangements, Hael and Kairn continued their flight. The rain had lessened, and they now had guides to take them swiftly through the forest to the nearest river crossing. Hael had quietly told Kairn that they were not to speak of anything consequential while the guides might overhear. Thus, the younger man was much in the company of his own thoughts.

He had hoped to visit Star Eye once again before they left, but now that looked as if it were not to be. He had spoken of the woman to his father, and Hael had been impressed but cautious: "A remarkable young woman, but be careful. From your description, she's a noblewoman and probably has good reason to hide herself away in the forest. She may have fallen afoul of Deathmoon and his group. She could even be a member of his family who has fallen from favor.''

"Surely not!" Kairn had protested.

"Why not?" his father had retorted. "Gasam was my foster brother once. It can happen in the best of families.''

Now it occurred to Kairn if there were to be a war, it would probably take place very near Star Eye's abode, and he might seek her out at that time. Of one thing he was certain: After his recent deeds, his father no longer had any excuse to forbid Kairn to ride with the army as a warrior.

At last, their guide, the man who had challenged them in

the forest, led them over the levee and down a muddy path to a ferry landing. A narrow road ended at the landing, and it did not look as if it had seen much recent traffic.

"This is the last place that'll get the word you two are fugitives," the man assured them. "The way you were traveling, you're probably still a good day ahead of any pursuit. Well, I'll leave you here and good luck to you." The man went back over the levee and into the forest beyond.

An old man looked up in surprise as they approached, leading their string of animals.

"Cabo traders, is it?"

"That is so," said Hael. "We are headed to a trade fair on the other side of the river, and we're likely to miss it if we don't get across soon."

"Well, you've come to the right place. This is the fastest ferryboat on the river. Get your animals aboard and we'll be off."

The two travelers eyed the rickety, leaking barge dubiously, but they went aboard. The cabos did not like the idea and protested, but Hael exercised his legendary control of animals and calmed them. The ferryman began to tug on the endless rope that spanned the river and slowly, sluggishly, the barge began to inch its way across.

"If one of you will help pull," the old man said, "and the other one bail, we'll go even faster." Hael began to heave on the rope, immediately tripling their rate of travel. Kairn found a wooden bucket and began bailing. He found that by working very fast, he could get rid of the water almost as fast as it was coming in.

"You're a pair of strong ones," said the garrulous old ferryman. "That's right, keep bailing, lad. It's the weight of all this livestock, you see. They make the boat sink lower in the water, and that makes the water come in faster than usual. Livestock's a burden. They're hard on the craft and you have to clean up after them later."

"I shall pay you extra for the trouble," Hael said. With a powerful surge of muscle he hauled the little craft another three feet. By this time the old man was doing little more than pantomiming the action of hauling on the rope.

Near the center of the river the rope was raised on high pilings to allow riverboats to pass. They had to draw the boat from one piling to the next by means of long, hook-tipped poles until they could again lay hold of the rope on the far side. An exhausting hour of pulling and bailing finally got them to the western bank.

"There," said the ferryman, giving them a toothless grin. "Didn't I say this was the fastest boat on the river?"

"I'll- wager no one ever survived the slowest," Kairn groused. He was cheerful anyway. He knew he was still in Mezpan territory, but just crossing the river made him feel as if he were almost on the plains already. Hael paid the exorbitant fare without argument.

"Now we must ride hard and be careful," he said as they rode from the river. "It's possible that Deathmoon sent word this way by fast boats and couriers. We run when we can, fight if we have to. Let's go!" They set off at a swift canter. It was tempting to go at a gallop, but even with changing mounts that would exhaust their cabos swiftly. Galloping was an emergency measure, to be resorted to only in headlong flight from a mounted enemy.

Even at this reduced speed, the roads and villages seemed to fly past them.

"What did you think?" Kairn asked as they rode.

"Think of what?" his father asked.

"Of Noble Stone, and of his words? What of his proposed alliance?"

"The man seems decent and honorable. Many men can fake that, but I was impressed by the way his people acted. He has their loyalty and trust. He spoke freely before them and it would be easy for any of them to betray him."

"That struck me as well. And it would have been even easier for him to betray you to Deathmoon."

"His explanation of the battlefield use of the firetubes made a great deal of sense. I will know some things to avoid should it come to open battle with Mezpa. I must give it a lot of thought. I'll have to work out new tactics to face this threat, then drill my army in them.''

"Will you accept Noble Stone's offer, then?"

"That I will have to ponder at length before committing myself. We saw only Noble Stone, none of the others he claims are his fellow rebels. What if he is alone? He urges a battle near his own territory. I can understand that his main wish is for the liberation of his country, but I must think of the welfare of mine. I wonder, would he be so anxious to send all his men to reinforce me, were I to decide to march south against Gasam?"

"I had not thought of that," Kairn admitted.

"A king must consider such things. It is all too easy to be led into an unfavorable alliance, especially if your ally is a good man with a just cause. I wish Noble Stone well, but I must know much more about him and about his friends before I will send my army to sacrifice their lives on his behalf.''

"But Deathmoon may march against you first," Kairn pointed out.

"That will change things, but not urgently. Whatever else his army is, it is not fast, and mine is very swift indeed. I am far more concerned about his proposed alliance with Gasam.''

"Will he go through with it now, do you think? He knows that he betrayed his plans to you."

"It is a complicated problem," Hael said, rising in his stirrups to look behind them for any sign of pursuit. "He does not really know who he admitted those things to. I'll wager he doesn't yet know it was to King Hael. He may still believe me to be working for Larissa, although how he will square that with my freeing you, I don't know. He may decide I am a free agent, selling my knowledge to the highest bidder. From what I saw of him, he will come to a decision and stick by it even if it is foolish. Men like Deathmoon have a great facility for believing that which they most want to believe.''

"What will you do about him and Gasam?"

"Somehow, I must find out when and where he will meet with Larissa. I must know what transpires at that meeting."

Kairn thought about it for a while, and an idea occurred to him. The more he thought about it, the more excited he grew.

"Father, if we learn where and when the meeting is to occur, why shouldn't we raid it? We could take both of them prisoner."

"It's a tempting thought, but, technically, I am at war with neither of them for the moment. This is a trivial point when speaking of Gasam, since he's at war with the whole world at all times, but so far there has been no warlike action between my kingdom and Mezpa."

"But you know they'll be plotting against you!" Kairn protested.

"What of that? Kings plot with one another all the time. Plotting is just talk. It's action that justifies action. And if I kidnapped or even killed Deathmoon, that would solve little. The Assembly of Great Men would just choose another Speaker and that one might be just as hostile and ambitious as Deathmoon."

"With Larissa in your hands, you could dictate terms to Gasam. He would return the steel mine to get her back."

Hael looked pained. "That may well be true. But it would not be honorable."

Kairn considered this for a while. "As a warrior I am bound to respect and obey the tenets of honor, but when we consider the stakes, I think you may be overvaluing the importance of rectitude."

At this Hael laughed. "You're learning statecraft, my son. Yes, a king must be flexible and have the interests of his subjects at heart, not nurse his own honor. That is foolish vanity. Still, this trafficking in the persons of sovereigns is something that must be handled with extreme caution. Let me think about it. There may be other ways to make this proposed meeting work to our advantage."

They rode on, day and night, avoiding settlements wherever possible. When they were compelled to stop at a village for provisions, they saw no indication that any alarm had reached the place. They were in an area remote from the capital, where contact with the government was rare at any time.

The land ascended gradually as they rode. before long they were out of the heavily forested lowlands and riding through the gently rolling hills that rimmed the edge of the great plains country. Here the game was abundant and they had no further need to stop at settlements for food. The grass was rich enough to keep their cabos healthy, although the animals were losing flesh from the long, hard ride. Each night they slept beneath the stars, extinguishing their fires as soon as their evening meal was cooked. They had no shelter and the heavy seasonal rains kept them drenched much of the time, but this was the sort of thing plainsmen endured without complaint.

The situation for themselves was dangerous and their nation was at a moment of crisis, but it seemed to Kairn that he had never been happier. He had never spent so much time alone with his father, and as they rode they spoke of many things besides war and statecraft. When Kairn told Hael of his adventures on the river, and of his encounter with Star Eye, the king was intrigued.

"Does it not occur to you," Hael said, "that, wounded as you were, you would have died almost anywhere else? Yet your cabo took you near her and you fell practically on her doorstep? The only true healer for leagues around, and you found her!"

"I've thought of it many times," Kairn said.

"You know that I do not believe in gods," Hael said, "and that I do not believe that the spirits have much interest in the affairs of men. Yet I know that there is a working of destiny that catches us up in its plans like leaves in a stream, and takes us where it will. Some of us share more in this power of destiny. Me, for instance, and Gasam. I think you may also be part of this special singling-out by destiny."

"I have no wish to be touched by destiny as you have been."

"What man does? I was happiest as a warrior-herdsman back in the islands. The fact is, our own wishes don't matter."

Kairn twisted uneasily in his saddle. "I don't like to think that some unseen hand controls me. What is destiny anyway, if there are no gods?"

"That I cannot say. I think it may be a sort of collection of all the spirit-force in the world, a thing that the individual spirits themselves are not aware of. Spirits don't actually have minds, you know."

"As a matter of fact, I didn't know," said Kairn, nettled. "I've never spoken with a spirit in my life. We always speak about them, but only you spirit-speakers talk to them."

"You don't actually talk to spirits," Hael maintained. "A creature without a mind can't hold a conversation, after all. No, you commune with spirits."

"Father," Kairn said impatiently, "you are not as other men. When you speak to me of communing with spirits, you might as well try to describe color to a blind man. You are at home with spirits, but they make me uneasy. I like to deal with things I can feel and see."

"I had hoped that one of my boys would have the spirit-power," Hael said sadly, "but it was not to be. Your sister is different. Already, I detect in her the ability to commune with spirits." His voice took on the slightly foolish complacency fathers have when speaking of beloved daughters.

"Kalima is barely fourteen years old," Kairn said.

"I was far younger when I knew I was different from all others," Hail maintained. "I was barely eight when our old spirit-speaker, Tata Mal, took me aside and began to teach me his arts, even though he knew I could never follow him as apprentice."

Kairn sighed. He had heard this story many, many times before. Then he saw something far ahead. They were on a rise of ground and could see to a horizon many miles away.

Along that horizon, Kairn could just descry a line of tiny dots, silhouetted against the sunset.

"Riders!" Kairn said.

Hael saw them instantly. His eyes were as keen as ever. "Keep riding as we are. I cannot believe that Deathmoon could throw out a search so far ahead of us, traveling as we have been. All the mounted Mezpans I saw rode wretchedly."

"Who, then?"

"Plainsmen, most likely, and there are few left who don't acknowledge their allegiance to me. We'll know when they come closer. Be prepared to run, though. I can't be sure I've cleaned out all the bandits."

They continued to ride cautiously. In less than an hour, they could see clearly that these were plainsmen, a strong band of thirty well-mounted warriors. They caught sight of the two riders, paused, then rode forward, whooping. Hael and Kairn did not slow down or run. By now they could see that these were a mixed band of Matwa and Amsi, tribes from the heartland of Hael's far-flung kingdom.

The newcomers rode in a circle around the two, then came up to flank them, forming an escort. Hael took hands all around while the riders shouted joyfully. He let them celebrate for a while, then asked the leader: "How do you come to be here?"

"The queen has bands all over the eastern borders, looking for you and for your son. We are to bring you to her as soon as possible." The man was a Matwa, with brown hair, wearing a colorful tunic of woven cloth.

"Well, I would have got home just as soon without you," Hael said.

"You can tell the queen that when you get there," said an Amsi warrior, attired in embroidered skins. "None of us were going to argue with her." Amid much laughter they rode on.

The leader explained how distraught the queen had been at their king's long absence. The Matwa among the escort seemed faintly censorious. They were a stolid, realistic peo-

ple and thought Hael had been neglecting his responsibilities.
The Amsi maintained that the king had a perfect right to do
as he pleased. They were firm in their belief that he was
insane, a quality much admired among the plains nomads.

"I can see," Hael said ruefully, "that I will have a lot of
explaining to do when we get home."

TWELVE

It had been many years since Queen Larissa had had so much to keep her busy. There was the processing and distribution of the steel they now had, the training of the steelworkers and the complicated support organization entailed by that project. There was the pirate expedition, which had to be organized and carried out in near-secrecy, so that the Deathmoon would not know what they were up to.

There was her longed-for penetration of the Canyon, a project that all but obsessed her. For many years she had been sending her spies into that land. Some died, some disappeared. A few came back claiming that they had found nothing out of the ordinary, but her rigorous questioning had revealed large gaps in their memories. This had frightened her as few things had in her life. Still, she would not give up. If the Canyoners had terrifying powers, there was all the more reason to believe that they truly held the secret of eternal youth and life.

More accessible was the formulation of another project: the proposed conference with Mezpa and its ruler, the oddly named Deathmoon.

The queen lounged in her temporary palace erected outside the former Granian territorial capital of Pamia. Neither Larissa nor her husband had any taste for the Granian's overbuilt, rockpile cities, and so she had ordered this permanent camp built away from the city proper. Her palace was a spacious villa of stone and wood decorated to her own taste, which was luxurious but relatively spare. She preferred wide windows and fresh air to any amount of wall decoration, and she liked to have only a few items of furniture, mostly couches, richly draped with precious cloths and covered with fragrant cushions. Her domestic slaves were mostly women handpicked for their beauty, and her guards were young Shasinn warriors who were handsome by definition. Thus, Queen Larissa's palace resembled a series of open, roofed verandas through which moved creatures of great comeliness and grace.

Foreign envoys to King Gasam's court arrived terrified and expecting the worst. The terrible conqueror's reputation caused them to expect a blood-drenched camp full of hideous sights. They were invariably stunned to find a scene of such beauty, with the incomparably lovely queen as its centerpiece. No one could be there very long, though, without sensing the horror that lay beneath it all. Here, they knew, were people to whom they could never be more than a passing convenience, who would exterminate them the moment they became inconvenient, and who would instantly forget they had ever existed. That was perhaps the most terrifying thing about Gasam and his queen: They were people for whom other human beings existed only as tools for their own purposes, as enhancements for their own glory. Otherwise, people had no more value to them than insects. This was not an utterly unknown attitude among monarchs, but no one else had ever taken this idea of natural superiority to its extreme limit. These two conquered and slew with an almost sublime joy, and their dedication to slaughter was infectious, so that their soldiers derived a perverse joy in dying, exalting the two most bloodstained sovereigns in history.

These thoughts did occur to Lord Threetowers, who had come to deliver a letter from Deathmoon to this formidable queen. As she read the letter, which Deathmoon had thought-fully set down in Nevan script, the envoy studied her. It seemed incredible that this rare creature, who looked little older than his twenty-year-old daughter, could be the fearsome queen. As she lounged on her divan, dressed in little more than some jewelry and a tiny scrap of silk, she looked like no more than an exceptionally expensive whore.

And her guard, those slender, golden young men who lounged about the palace, looked like so many dancers. It was hard to believe that these were the fearsome Shasinn, even if they were warriors of the junior grade. He had begun to feel that the reputation of these people had been grossly exaggerated. Then, but an hour ago, there had occurred an incident which stripped the veil from his eyes and exposed the true nature of the queen and her followers.

He had been conducted into her presence, and the queen had graciously greeted him, seating him at a table and insisting that he take some refreshment before speaking of serious matters. He had presented his credentials and the letter, which she had set to one side until later. They had conversed for a few minutes on matters of little import when the ugly scene took place.

The room opened to a terrace, where a team of workmen cut flat stones to build a pavement around a newly installed fountain. The workmen were natives, newly conquered and of the usual Granian type: short, squat men with broad, dark faces. Without warning, one of the men raised his mallet and ran toward the queen, screaming words in a language Threetowers did not understand. The broad face was twisted with rage and foam flecked the screaming mouth. It had happened so swiftly, so unexpectedly, that Threetowers knew the queen was doomed.

Larissa barely glanced at the man but the young guardsmen moved so quickly that Threetowers thought his eyes deceived him. The lounging, idling, chattering boys were transformed in an instant into bronze machines. A dozen arms rose and flew forward at once. The long spears transfixed the mad workman from a dozen directions. The spears stuck out of him from so many angles that he did not truly fall, but rather slumped forward, supported by a number of spears. At the instant the spears flew, Threetowers felt a pressure upon his shoulders and saw that two of the long spear-blades had been crossed beneath his chin, their razor edges just touching the sides of his neck.

The queen looked crossly at the two guards behind him. "*He* hasn't threatened me, you silly boys! Take those things away!" The guards complied instantly and, after a few seconds, his heart recommenced its beating. She had then ordered that the foreman and the other workers be impaled on stakes in the courtyard, and that slaves wash the blood from the floor before the flies began swarming.

Then she turned to Threetowers. "I am sorry about all this. Our rule is still a little new to some of the local people." Throughout the incident she had maintained the cheerful demeanor of a housewife entertaining a neighbor for a morning's gossip.

Now he watched as she read her letter, and he knew that he could report truthfully that what they had heard about these people did not come close to describing how fearsome they were. If this was the queen and her guard of boys, what must King Gasam and his veteran warriors be like?

Larissa had forgotten the envoy's presence as she read the letter from Lord Deathmoon.

My dear Queen Larissa, it read, *I have read with great pleasure the letter that you have sent me, as it mirrors so closely my own desire for a meeting between us. We have many matters of importance to discuss, including a treaty of friendship, which I ardently desire.*

At least, she thought, he dispensed with the flowery salutations most monarchs delighted in.

I understand, from one who need not be named but whom we both know, she had no idea what he meant by this, *that you have in the past found neutral islands most*

congenial to meetings of this sort. I think this is an ex-
cellent idea, and I take the liberty of suggesting such a
site. In the Gulf of Imisia, just off the coast of my prov-
ince of Delta, is an island named Xata. It is claimed by
several nations and occupied by none. It is no more than
an hour from shore by rowed barge, and it has abundant
fresh water and wild game. On the north shore, in the
center of the island, is a broad meadow ideal for the
accommodation of pavilions and the grazing of any ca-
bos you may wish to bring.

He closed with felicitations and instructions that his trusted
aide, Lord Threetowers, was fully empowered to make arrangements concerning the meeting. She set the letter aside.

"Lord Deathmoon is most accommodating," she said.

"He desires nothing so much as a peaceful agreement between our nations," Threetowers assured her. "Of course,
he would have liked to meet with King Gasam as well, but
he understands that the great conqueror must be preoccupied
with the continuing siege of Great City." The unimagina-
tively named capital of Gran had been under siege for months
and that was likely to continue for another year or more. The
former rulers of the land refused to recognize Gasam's right
to rule their former nation. In truth, it was the sort of grind-
ing, boring work for which Gasam had no taste, and he was
nowhere near the siege, which was being prosecuted by his
more than competent engineers and infantry drawn from the
subject peoples. Gasam was busy with other preparations.
Larissa saw no need to enlighten the emissary concerning
these things.

"Oh, the siege! It is terribly dull, but it must be done. It
is our firm policy to crush all resistance to our rightful conquest. The rulers of Great City and its people will be destroyed, and the city itself torn down."

"You are very . . . thorough people, Your Majesty," the
Mezpan said.

"We are. Besides, I do not like the architecture of this
land. It is too cluttered and it is oppressively massive. I may

have all the cities torn down and rebuilt according to my liking.''

"Would that all of us could indulge our whims so confidently.'' Threetowers had regained his aplomb and reminded himself that these were, after all, mere savages. He had great confidence in the Mezpan military machine. These people may have overrun other primitive people by their sheer vigor and old-fashioned warrior skills, but these would little avail them against the overwhelming fire of massed firetubes. And soon the big, city-smashing tubes would be in service. On the battlefield, these would cut huge, bloody swaths through the charging wild men.

"This island—'' Larissa said, getting directly to business "—does Mezpa claim it?''

"We do, but we make no serious effort to press the claim, any more than the other nearby kingdoms. It is not an important place. It isn't suited to agriculture, it has no harbor and no defensive qualities. Ships sometimes put in there to take on water or to hunt for fresh meat. In the past, pirates have made it a base and we have had to send ships to clean it out, but that is all. For a long time it was claimed by Imisia, a nation that became a province of Mezpa a few years ago. It is an excellent site and you will find none better, I think. In truth, there is little left in this part of the world save what belongs to you, what belongs to us, and what belongs to our mutual enemies.''

"Mutual enemies,'' she mused. "That is something yet to be decided.''

"All the more reason for you to speak with Lord Deathmoon. There are too many expanding powers these last few years. It would not be good if all were to lurch blindly into one another. These things must be orderly, or all will suffer.''

She was aware that he spoke condescendingly, but she feigned not to notice. All people were her prisoners and slaves though they might not yet know it. All slights would be repaid in time.

"We certainly would not want a misunderstanding,'' she assured him. "These insolent southern nations have offended us, and we had no natural barriers to protect us from them. But we have no quarrel with Mezpa, and the great river serves admirably as a natural frontier.''

"Actually," Threetowers said judiciously, "a good deal of territory on the western side of the river is Mezpan.''

She waved a hand airily. "Details we can work out at the conference. I doubt that Lord Deathmoon would object to transferring a little of his less productive territory to us in order to establish amicable relations, and to gain our aid in projects I am sure he has in mind.''

"Ah, exactly so, Majesty. Is the island agreeable to you, then? Lord Deathmoon was most specific that all should be to your liking. If you would prefer another site, you need merely say so. My lord would be most happy to entertain you in the capital.''

"I am most grateful for the honor he does me by this offer. However, I cannot travel so far and stay away for so long. My husband depends on me for so many things. The island will be satisfactory.''

"How large an escort will you wish to bring?''

"Just my bodyguard, about a hundred men.''

"So few?" the emissary said.

"We do not like to travel in great state," Larissa said. "I will bring along a few slaves to erect and staff my pavilion, but that is all. If Lord Deathmoon wishes to bring a large retinue, I will be perfectly content. I know that other people have customs that differ from my own.''

"Very well. If you wish, the Speaker will provide all banqueting supplies, entertainment and so forth. He has a lesser distance to travel and the island lies so near our wealthy province of Delta that it would be unseemly to do otherwise.''

"As you wish," Larissa said.

"It is agreed, then. I believe this shall be the beginning of a most friendly and mutually beneficial relationship between the Hegemony of Mezpa and the Empire of the Islands.''

"I think the Empire of Gasam is a better title," she said. "We have not returned to the islands since our invasion of Chiwa some years ago, and we do not expect to go back.''

"I shall so inform my government. In the future, all formal correspondence shall be addressed thus."

Threetowers took his leave and returned to his quarters. His honor guard fell in beside him. The firetube-armed Mezpan troopers feigned not to notice the contemptuous looks they got from the island warriors. On their return trip they passed the unfortunate foreman and workmen, who groaned, screamed and wept atop wooden stakes thrust into their rectums, the weight of their bodies driving them inexorably down onto the sharp points. They might spend a day and a night of hideous agony before shock, blood loss or the piercing of a vital organ released them. The object lesson was not wasted upon the Granian slaves who hurried by, trying not to look.

In his quarters, a spacious room with a good view in all directions, Threetowers prepared to write his first letter to Lord Deathmoon. First he posted his guards to assure that no one could approach near enough to spy. This was the habit of many years of service, for it was not truly necessary in this instance. He would use a simple but utterly reliable code and the islanders could have no excuse for molesting an official messenger. If they tried, it would be a virtual declaration of war. He readied his writing implements and paper and began.

> *My Lord Deathmoon,*
> *Speaker of the Assembly of Great Men:*
> *I have met with Queen Larissa of the islands this day. She is indeed as beautiful and as shameless as rumor has it. She is also a woman of quick wit and intelligence, although she, like all her people, is an abysmal savage. These creatures delight in bloodshed and cruelty, not as a matter of state security, which would be proper, but rather for its own sake, a proof of their primitive nature.*
> *The queen agrees to all your terms for the meeting on the island of Xata. She shows no slightest trace of suspicion, which I attribute to her arrogance rather than to a trusting nature. She proposes to bring only a bodyguard of a hundred of the rather picturesque island war-*

riors. *You must bring Lord Baldmount to the meeting.
He has a taste for handsome young men and I have never
seen comelier youths than these warriors.*

Queen Larissa let slip that she expects territorial concessions in return for an alliance, these territories to
consist of our holdings on the western bank of the great
river. Although the name of Hael was never mentioned,
I must assume from this that she fully realizes that we
seek an alliance against the Steel King. Nothing else
would justify the slightest territorial concession. Yet it is
the nature of these savages to make importunate demands, and they perceive it as their right to invade and
enslave all other people.

Until now, they have met with great success, crushing
all before them save the civilized and powerful kingdom
of Neva and the fluidly mobile army of King Hael, if a
pack of mounted barbarians can be styled a true army.
As I can see with my own eyes, the crescent of southern
kingdoms has fallen to the savages through their own
bloated decadence. The lands are huge but weak, their
armies and officials corrupt, their kings little better than
degenerate imbeciles. If they lack all other redeeming
qualities, these primitives at least have a manly vigor
that slices through these moribund nations like a spear
through cheese.

I believe that you have been most perspicacious in
seeking an alliance with the savages against Hael's barbarians. Neither would have the slightest chance against
our disciplined regiments armed with modern fire weapons, but it will be far better policy to allow them to waste
themselves fighting each other. After that, we should be
able to mop up the survivors handily, thus assuring the
preeminence of the Hegemony for many generations to
come.

I have not as yet seen King Gasam. He seems to be
occupied with the lengthy siege of the capital city of
Gran, where the King of Gran and the rest of the royal
family carry on a stubborn but forlorn resistance to the

islanders. Here, again, it seems that Gasam met a weak army led by incompetent royal relatives who could not divest themselves of tactics practiced many generations ago. The open-field battles he won handily. Laying siege to fortified positions is more difficult, but Gasam has impressed into his army a huge number of men from the lands he has conquered, including skilled sappers and engineers. His second-rate infantry, which means all who are not islanders, do the filthy drudgery of siege-soldiering while the elite warriors lounge about enjoying the spoils of war like the lazy primitives they are.

This, I think, is the defining quality of these islanders. They have conquered half the world, but they retain the instincts of the herdsmen they once were. They are energetic only in the making of war. In all else they are supremely lazy. After the battle is won, they are content to let their new-made slaves do everything that has the slightest resemblance to work. Gasam is just a typical island warrior on a great scale. Larissa is unusual in possessing a certain capacity for the labor of government, but no one who spends her days sprawling naked on a couch need be taken seriously as a hardworking monarch.

In conclusion, my lord, I repeat that the work here is well begun. I would not wish to underestimate the cleverness and cunning of these two, especially the queen. At the same time I think you have found in them a most useful tool for the furtherance of our ambitions to keep our beloved Mezpa safe, powerful and, as always, the greatest among nations. I sign this, your most loyal aide,

Lord Threetowers

When the ink was dry, Threetowers rolled up the sheets and thrust them into an official message tube, the end of which he then sealed with hot wax, impressing it with his personal seal while it was still soft. At his summons a man in the livery of the Assembly's messenger service came in. Threetowers handed him the tube and the man thrust it into a pouch at his belt.

"Ride like the wind. This is for the hands of Lord Deathmoon alone." The man bowed and ran for his saddled cabo.

When the sound of galloping hoofs faded, Lord Threetowers called for wine and relaxed with a sense of a task well accomplished. Surely, he thought, the civilized lords of Mezpa would have no difficulty dominating these primitive savages and bending them to the greater will.

In her own chambers, Queen Larissa was equally well satisfied. If this Lord Threetowers was typical of the Mezpans, they would prove to be a most interesting conquest, requiring caution and careful handling. His contempt and belief in Mezpan superiority were perfectly plain to her. She was used to being underestimated, and always used it to her own advantage.

As he spoke, she had made a reading of the man, analyzing all his tones, his looks and his gestures. If she was correct, these Mezpans were something new. They were city-dwelling people with a highly developed, hierarchical class structure and an army composed of professional soldiers. That much was common. Unlike the others, however, they did not seem to be afflicted with the debilitating decadence that elsewhere seemed to be the natural consequence of a slave-based society with a hereditary ruling class. They were manufacturers, very concerned with making things, and they expected even the wealthy upper classes to work. She was sure, for instance, that if she were to look in on Lord Threetowers, she would find him busily at work, in all likelihood writing out a report, and that he would not allow himself to rest until his full day's work was done.

She thought this a tiresome way to live, but it constituted a strength they had not previously encountered in an inferior people. This was a great nation that had arisen from a population of plodding workmen. They had become slave-owners not from a will to dominate, as had the islanders, but rather as a more efficient way to organize their agriculture. They were not naturally warlike, so they had developed a means of defeating their enemies that was mechanical and required no warrior qualities. She was not certain what that was, but she was certain that when she found out, it would be a triumph of organization rather than an innate capacity for waging victorious war.

Apparently these people had found an effective way to expand and bring other nations beneath their hegemony. But to Larissa it seemed such a dismal, bloodless, desultory method that she wondered why they bothered. To the islanders, the imperial dream was a thing of blood and passion. They followed their invincible leader from conquest to conquest, reveling in the excitement and blood of battle, glorying in the headiest of sensations: the sight of inferior peoples acknowledging their mastery, grovelling before the conquerors. To the islanders, slaves were not work units. They were incontrovertible proof that the lordship of the warrior peoples was the law of the whole world.

This, to Larissa, was what made life worth living. Of what use was a worldwide empire if the conquering people could not enjoy it? Her warriors were treated with an awe bordering upon worship. They could do as they wished with the conquered, forcing the men to act as beasts of burden, using the women at will, killing any who showed the slightest defiance. This was the ultimate mastery, to know oneself to be a member of the conquering race and by natural right the master of all other, lesser people.

Why should they not revel in this, taking whatever pleasure attracted them at any expense to the defeated? She could not understand how a people like the Mezpans could do so many of the same things and remain a race of plodding merchants and accountants. They had power, but they had no sense of their own heroism.

Even as she mused upon these things, a small group of Gasam's women warriors entered the room. These were her husband's pets, the only mainlanders he allowed among his elite warriors. They were natives of the southern jungles and, before his war of conquest, had owed their allegiance to the king of Chiwa. Unlike most others, he had made great efforts to cultivate these women and convince them to transfer their allegiance from Chiwa to himself. In this he had been entirely successful and now his most loyal followers were these terribly strange women.

Larissa admired the newcomers, for in their grotesque way they had beauty in her eyes. In their natural state all of them would have been handsome women, with tawny skin, abundant brown hair and pale eyes, but they had left no aspect of their appearance unaltered in their pursuit of the warrior mystique and aesthetic: Their glossy skins were carved with complicated patterns of scars, the flint-cut incisions rubbed with fat and soot to form raised blue welts. Their teeth were filed to points and capped with bronze. Ornamental plugs of jade or gold distended their pierced lower lips, drawing them downward to reveal the bronze teeth. Other ornaments dangled from their pierced nipples and their constant exercise with weapons left their bodies lean and ropy with muscle.

Even the Shasinn were made uneasy when these women appeared, and the terror struck by their very appearance made their battle effectiveness far greater than even their number and ferocity justified. There was also their reputation, for they were known to delight in torture and to celebrate victories with ghastly cannibalistic feasts. Larissa had attended a number of these celebrations and had found them to be stirring in the extreme, touching something in the most primitive portion of her soul. That Gasam not only used but honored such creatures made his name that much more feared.

One of the women came forward and bowed slightly, the only act of obeisance these women practiced. She was covered with scars of battle as well as the ornamental ones carved in whorls all over her skin. All she wore was a belt in which was thrust a dagger and a steel-headed axe. In her hand was a short, stabbing spear.

"What is it, Cutter?" the queen asked.

"The king our god wishes you to join him as soon as possible, Majesty," the woman said.

Larissa lay on her back, and now she reached up and took between thumb and forefinger the blood-red ruby that dangled from Cutter's left nipple. She began to tug, first slowly and then forcefully. Reluctantly but without protest, the woman went down on one knee next to the queen's couch. Now Larissa pulled the ruby toward herself, until the woman's face was within three inches of her own.

"And what is the occasion of this summons, Cutter?" she all but whispered.

"There has been a victory, Majesty," Cutter said, her face showing none of the pain Larissa knew she must be feeling. "The last border fort has fallen."

"Ah. And is there to be a victory feast?" Now she began to twist the jewel. Cutter's face paled slightly, but she smiled, an expression rendered frightening by her pointed bronze teeth and distorting lip plug.

"Yes, my queen," Cutter said, her voice husky with pain or lust. The two were much the same to the fighting women.

"Wonderful. You know, Cutter, I find your insolence all but intolerable." She gave the jewel a sharp yank and was rewarded with a slight wince. "If you women were not so loyal to my husband, I would have you all impaled like those slaves outside. You know that, don't you?"

"Yes, my queen," the woman whispered.

"Then learn to kneel without this encouragement. And guard my husband well, or you too will ride the stake one day." She took the other ruby and pulled the woman even closer, glared into her eyes for a few seconds, then kissed her, the lip plug and metal teeth providing a unique sensation.

Then with a push of both hands she sent the other

woman sprawling on the polished floor and rose from the couch.

"Come, the king awaits. You'll have a good hard ride to work up your appetites." Her guards and the women followed her from the chamber. Cutter's eyes were bright with a new worship, the sort she had heretofore bestowed only upon her king.

THIRTEEN

After the first joyful, tearful spasm was over, Kairn left his parents to explore the great encampment. His mother, a willful woman, had ordered that the tribes establish the semiannual fair far to the east this time, so that they would be close to the place where Hael had disappeared. She had wept over his haggard appearance, and fumed that her husband, whom she had feared dead, was as handsome, healthy and youthful-looking as ever.

Kairn had slipped away at the first opportunity. Now he wandered among the tents and traders' stalls, looking for familiar faces. He found one quickly, a tall young man who was admiring the wares of a harness merchant.

"Ansa!" Kairn cried. The man turned and whooped.

"Little brother!" He wrapped the younger man in a fierce embrace, whirling him off his feet. Then he set him down and held him at arm's length.

"I sent you away as a boy, but this is a grown warrior I see before me! What befell you? How is Father? I heard that he had ridden back in, but I'm not going near that tent until

Mother has vented the worst of her wrath and regained her good humor.''

"It won't take long," Kairn said, grinning.

Ansa threw an arm around his shoulder. "Come, let's find something to wash the dust from your throat so you can tell me everything that's happened.''

They walked through the rough lanes of stalls and tents, crowded with people wearing the garb of a score of tribes: plains wanderers, hillmen, village farmers and traders from every nation that bordered Hael's far-flung kingdom. There was a great trade in weapons of steel. Kairn wondered how long that would last. He jerked his head toward one such stall.

"Do they know yet?" he asked.

"Yes, but they are merchants. They assume that they will be able to buy from Gasam. It didn't take long for the word to spread.''

They found a long tent, its walls pulled up to let the fine air circulate freely. Under the shelter, men sat on the ground drinking and talking, while behind a crude bar a fat, shaven-headed man dispensed drink from a number of casks. Behind him, outside the tent, was a two-wheeled cart bearing more casks, its team of nusks picketed nearby, cropping the grass and swatting at flies with their long, spatulate tails.

"Just what we were looking for," Ansa said. They went up to the bar. "Two bowls of ale for a pair of upstanding warriors.''

The barkeep delivered the bowls, beaming. His long mustache was looped at the ends and dyed a vivid pink.

Ansa took his bowl and sipped a little of the foam off the top. "Let's take these outside. It's too crowded here." They walked out from under the tent. Here and there on the ground sat little clots of men, drinking and talking, some of them engaged in the games of chance that were a passion with the nomads. The two brothers found a spot in the shade of a wagon and sat, leaning against its huge wheels.

"You seem to be fully recovered," Kairn said.

"I was just worn out, not wounded. A little rest, some

decent food, that was all I needed, although Mother came near killing me with her family remedies. As soon as I was strong enough I got away from her and was as good as new in a few days. Now, tell me what has happened to you. Start at the beginning and take your time, we have all night.''

Kairn took a drink of the foamy amber liquid. It cut through the dust wonderfully. He stretched and sat back against the massive wheel. Then he began to talk. When he told of the fight on the riverbank, his brother interrupted.

"You cut down how many?" His eyes and mouth were wide.

"Six, I think. Maybe seven. I wasn't sure whether I should talk about it. They were only bandits and I let scum like that wound me badly.''

Ansa wrapped his arms around his brother. ''You're a warrior in truth now, not just by custom! And brag all you like. That modesty business is just a pose old warriors affect, mostly to hide the fact that they never performed any worthy deeds. Six, maybe seven! Show me your scars.''

Perforce, Kairn stripped off his shirt and leggings to display the new scars, still an angry pink color. Ansa whistled in admiration. Other idling warriors wandered over and offered their compliments.

Kairn resumed both clothing and story. With some bemusement, he told of his interlude with Star Eye.

''Strange,'' Ansa commented, ''how both of us ended up meeting healing women, your Star Eye and my Lady Fyana. Do you think there is some power at work, leading us to such women?''

''Now you're talking like Father,'' Kairn said. ''He spoke of destiny, and tried to rope me into it. It scares me, and I want no part of it. The difficulties ordinary life throws me are quite enough, without getting tangled up in a higher purpose.''

Ansa rose and went to get them fresh bowls. He returned with a larger bowl full of fruit, flat bread and roasted meat. They ate and traded stories between mouthfuls of food, Kairn finishing his own story and Ansa fleshing out the tale of his wanderings, a story Kairn had only heard in barest outline, so precipitous had been his leaving to search for their father.

The stars twinkled in the cool night air and both brothers had donned cloaks by the time their tales were finished. Men formed snoring heaps on the ground and the sounds of revelry had long since faded to silence. Here and there, a few sleepless ones sat around fires, conversing in low voices.

"The world is changing again," said Ansa when they were done. "As it did when Father left the islands and came to the mainland. And when Gasam came to stir things up all over the west and south."

"I think it's all of a piece," Kairn said, remembering the things taught him by his childhood tutors. "For hundreds of years things went along with little change. Nations fought each other over small matters, and nothing really happened. All the nations stayed the same, borders moved around a bit but remained as always, for all practical purposes. The same dynasties ruled as they always had.

"Then Father showed up. Before you knew it, there was a new kingdom where none had been before. Not just a little, inconsequential state, either, but a powerful force that could tip every balance at will." He was not accustomed to this sort of thought, but the ale he had drunk lent him insight and eloquence, or so it seemed to him.

"Then came Gasam, and everything collapsed into chaos. Everything that is happening now came about because Father and Gasam hated each other since childhood. No, that's not just. Father has always done what he thought best for his people. He'd have forgotten Gasam in time, if the monster hadn't followed him to the mainland."

"And now Mezpa wants to found a world empire as well," Ansa said.

"Mezpa was not created yesterday," Kairn said. "It's been there a long time, expanding, growing by eating up weaker states. It only seems new because it has been remote from us, far away and existing for us only as stories told by travelers. Now they've hopped the big river and the only direction for them to expand is into our kingdom or Gasam's. It looks as if Deathmoon wants an alliance with Gasam against us.''

"He sounds like a strange person," Ansa mused. "Gasam I can understand in a way. He's a warrior, and in most ways he's just a child grown powerful, a willful infant who gets whole nations of people to kill for him and do his will. Larissa is the brains of the pair, and I don't think either would amount to much without the other.

"But this Deathmoon, what are we to make of him? He sounds in some matters a genius, and in others a fool. His people don't worship him as Gasam's do, or revere him as our people do our father. Instead there is what you describe as a sort of—of quiet fear. What sort of leader is that?''

"I don't know," Kairn said. "Even when he was torturing me it was like being in the power of a merchant's clerk. I'm not at all sure that Deathmoon himself is the real leader, the way Father and Gasam and Queen Shazad are leaders. It may be the Assembly itself that is the evil power behind this expansion of Mezpan power.''

It occurred to Kairn that he and his brother had never spoken like this before, seriously, on matters of state and of destiny. It was a sign of their new maturity, but it was also a frightening and humbling sign that the two of them, who had never aspired to be anything other than warriors of their people, had at a very early age found their lives entangled with the most powerful people in the world. Between them they had been held captive by Deathmoon and Gasam, had had dealings with the sorcerous Canyoners, had ridden over much of the world to bear news of danger and catastrophe, and had experienced more adventure than most warriors saw in a lifetime.

"The steel mine," Ansa said eventually. He drained his last bowl. "Everything hinges on that steel mine. Well, little brother, we've done all the damage we're going to do tonight. Let's get some sleep. In the morning, we'll undoubtedly hear all about Father's big plan to solve everything. He always has one.''

The two rolled into their cloaks and lay quietly, waiting

for sleep to come. Kairn was not at all sure that his father had a plan. Perhaps he would make one of his trips to the hills, to commune with the spirits. Kairn doubted that the spirits would have any helpful suggestions. This disaster was man-made from beginning to end.

Elsewhere in the camp, King Hael rose from the side of his sleeping wife and left his tent. He wore only the breech-clout of plain cloth that he favored as closest to the garb of his younger days in the islands. He took his famous spear from its place, jammed into the ground on the right side of the tent door, where it was convenient to his right hand as he left. Many years before, as junior warriors, he and his hut-mate, Danats, had cast lots for this position. Danats had lost and had to spike his spear into the ground on the left side, thus having to reach across his body to retrieve his spear in an emergency. Danats had been dead for many years, but Hael still kept his spear in the same place.

No man saw the king as he walked through the camp. He moved silently as a ghost and when he did not wish to be seen, he might as well have been invisible. When he was at the outer edge of the camp he began to run toward the north, his senses feeling out ahead of him, steering him around packs of lurking predators, letting him know where the larger her-bivores dozed. Only the tiniest nocturnal creatures ever no-ticed his passing, and they were the quiet ones, who would not betray him by raising a noise.

He had seen a flat-topped hill to the north, and he wanted to go there. He had many decisions to make, and he did not want to be distracted by the presence of other people. He did not think well in the presence of a great crowd. Other peo-ple's spirits disturbed his own.

His queen had been furious with him, but he had expected that and knew that it would not last. She would be further upset to learn that there was to be war, but she would under-stand that, this time, he truly had no choice in the matter. This time, his enemies were closing in on him.

When he reached the hill, he trotted up the long bluff,

feeling the hard soil flex beneath his feet. The dirt was held in place only by the tough, springy plains grass. Thousands of years of its growth had created a turf composed of a dense layer of grassroot, resistant to the growth of trees as it was to the plow. As he ascended it occurred to Hael that a plow of steel could break the tough plains turf. This was not a happy thought. He did not want to see farmers moving into his limitless grasslands, which were the natural abode of nomads and their livestock.

Gasam would never think of steel plows. For him, steel was a material for weapons, to further his conquests. But the Mezpans were different. Their weapons required little metal. They wanted the steel for other purposes, and they were fond of huge, slave-worked farms. He could almost regret having ever found the crater with its ruins and its steel. But it was never Hael's way to rue the past, which could not be changed. Nor did he believe that his discovery had been accidental. He knew that he was a man of extraordinary destiny, and that the steel mine was somehow tied up in that destiny.

For now, his needs were more immediate. At the crest of the hill he faced east, planted his spear in the ground and stood on one leg, with the foot of the other braced against the opposite knee, his hand resting lightly on the spear. It was the stance of his native tribesmen when in repose, watching over their herds. They would choose such a high point from which to oversee their animals. They could stand thus, still as statues, for hours. A viewer would think them to be in a sort of trance, but they were alert to the slightest change in the herd and could spring instantly to action.

Relaxed, in his customary pose of meditation, Hael let his mind roam, not seeking to direct his thoughts, opening himself to the spirits of the land, as he had when he was a boy. In those days it had been a near-ecstatic indulgence, without purpose save the sheer not-quite-sensual pleasure of it. But the facility had matured as Hael had, and now he used it to help him solve the seemingly insurmountable problems of kingship.

As he stood, barely breathing, his heartbeat slowed to a

handful of beats each minute, a vision of his world formed in his mind. Once, to him, the mainland had been something like a big island, just out of sight. He had learned of its vastness, its many kingdoms, each a thousand times the size of his home island. He now knew how those kingdoms abutted one another, how they interlocked to form their friendships and their rivalries. He saw the world before him now, like a great hide upon which a scribe had painted the nations. To the west, south and east, great oceans. To the far north, a great unknown, cold and forbidding.

On the northwest, just offshore, were the Storm Islands, where he had been born. On the west coast was primitive Orekah; in the north, huge, weak Omia; and south of them, the rich, powerful and advanced Neva. These comprised the Stormlands. South of Neva were Chiwa, Sono and Gran along the southern rim of the continent, together with a few small kingdoms of little account. Then the great river, bisecting the continent from north to south. To the east of the river had been a number of older kingdoms: Delta, Imisia and others. And Mezpa. In the north, stretching across the vast belt of grasslands was Hael's Kingdom of the Plains. Between his kingdom and the southern nations were the Poisoned Lands: the Zone, the Canyon, the wilderness of the great desert—unpopulated save for peculiar nomadic peoples who were seldom seen by outsiders.

Now the Empire of Gasam spread like a great stain across the south, and Mezpa was absorbing the southeast, the two forming the jaws of a huge trap ready to snap shut on the plains, taking his kingdom in one bite. There was no help for it, he would have to fight. But how? His choices were few. He could fight both nations at once, or he could take them on one at a time. To fight both was folly. Therefore the choice was: Which should he fight first? He reviewed the enemy he knew—Gasam.

As he thought, the face of Gasam swam before him. He tried to put from his mind the old hatred that lay between them, all the hurtful snubs and slights, the sadistic jokes he had endured all through childhood. That was Gasam the boy.

The man he faced was different. He tried to suppress thoughts of Larissa, the beautiful young girl he had loved, who had betrayed him for Gasam. What was Gasam? He was the heartless, bold monster who had swept from one island to another, conquering and uniting their peoples, welding them into a piratical army, swooping down upon the mainland, plundering and sailing home; until Gasam decided that he needed a base on the mainland and had taken the Nevan port of Floria. He brought his warriors over from the islands over the space of a year, building a powerful navy in the meantime, annihilating a Nevan land army and a naval expedition led by Shazad's father. Then Hael had arrived and his new, mounted army had seen their first real battles, combining with the Nevan army to drive Gasam from Floria and from Neva.

Gasam had taken his ships and gone south. He formed an alliance with the king of Chiwa, helping him subdue petty rulers in the southern islands and mainland, always growing in strength, until he attacked his former ally without warning, taking Chiwa as a prize. Then he had taken Sono in a lightning campaign. They had had no warning that Gasam was on the way until refugees began pouring into the capital. He had attacked Gran while in the midst of peace negotiations and now had it all but subdued.

That was Gasam: a rapacious predator, always hungry, always jealous of another's wealth and strength. He plotted and fought, capable of fair words to another monarch, but never meaning them, always playing on the other's fears and hopes for peace. Always, he attacked when there was no legitimate cause for aggression.

Hael felt a tingling in his spine, knowing that he had found the key. It was folly to fight Gasam on his own terms. Why had Gasam never seriously mounted an expedition against his hated enemy, Hael? Because Hael was ready for him. Instead, he fell upon unsuspecting victims. And this, Hael knew, was the key to Gasam's character and to his weakness: Gasam had never been attacked!

Abruptly, Hael realized that the sun was rising. He had

missed the dawn entirely, so absorbed had he been in his spirit trance. And the spirits had given him the answer. He now knew how he would defeat both his enemies. With a whoop, he tossed his spear high into the air, the light from the rising sun glittering along its spinning length. He caught it before it could touch the ground and began to run down the hill.

Sleepy tribesmen, just risen to the new day, blinked in astonishment as they saw the near-naked king running through the encampment, frisky as a boy and grinning like a man who has just been told that his wife has borne twin sons. When he got to the royal tent Hael saw one of his sub-chiefs, an Amsi, loitering with a group of his young warriors. They saluted at his approach.

"Amata, how many of the chiefs are here?"

"More than half, Spirit-King," the chief said.

"That will be enough. Round them up. I will hold a war council at noon." The young warriors whooped and ran. Within seconds, there was whooping all over the camp. Hael went inside the tent and found his wife sitting up in their bed, rubbing the sleep from her eyes. When she looked at him her stare was bleak.

"I know that sound," she said. "It's war." She took in his appearance. "You've been in the hills again. Have the spirits told you you must be off to war again?"

"I needed no spirits to tell me that. I told you last night what I learned in Mezpa. I have two choices: I can fight a war and win, or I can fight a war and lose. I would prefer to win." He began to pull on his clothing.

"Did I get you back only to lose you again? Will we never have peace?"

"What I learned out there this night is how to defeat Gasam, and in doing so, to neutralize Mezpa, before they can combine forces against us. If all goes as I foresee, we will have peace, perhaps for the rest of our lives."

"That will happen only if Gasam is dead."

"I see no reason why he should not die along with his warriors."

"Do you really think you can do this thing?" she said, aghast.

"It can be done. It must be done. Rather than let Gasam conquer the whole world, it is better that the world should die. Gasam and the Mezpans both want to make slaves of everyone else. I will not allow it to happen. I have transformed these plains into a training ground for an army such as the world has never seen and now I am going to use it. No one can say that the war will be unjust."

"But it will take you away from me again!" she cried. "And our sons! They will demand to go and I cannot stop them."

"Nor should you," he said, sitting by her side. "How could I demand that my young warriors, who are as dear to their families as are our sons to us, to risk their lives in my service if I spare my sons the same risk?"

"You can't," she said. "But is there no way out of this without war?"

"If there were I would take it without hesitation, you know that. But the world will not know peace while Gasam lives. Now I know that the Mezpans form the same threat. They are merely not so colorful."

There were more tears, but she could not sway him from his path. It grieved Hael that his queen had to suffer so, but these matters were no more within his control than they were in hers. He had no choice, except the choice to fail, which he would not consider.

At noon Hael took his spear and walked through the encampment. The only people to be seen were women, children and the merchants and travelers who looked about themselves wide-eyed, wondering where all the men had gone. At the edge of the camp he found his two sons and he embraced Ansa.

"You avoided me yesterday," he chided.

"No, I avoided Mother. Is she resigned yet?"

"It will take a few days, but she will recover. As soon as

the council is over, I want to hear all that happened to you in the south.''

''Yes, you must hear. I learned some things that are very important, and we may have an ally in the Canyon.'' Then he smiled boyishly. ''I told Little Brother last night that you would have the answer to everything by today. Are we to hear it at the council?''

''It may not be the answer to everything, but it's a plan to pull us out of our present predicament.''

''Wonderful!'' said Ansa. ''What is it? A raid to kidnap Gasam and Larissa?''

''An assault against the Mezpan city where they make the firetubes?'' Kairn suggested.

''When faced by problems such as these, one cannot think on a small scale,'' Hael told them. ''What I have in mind is the biggest war in history.'' That kept his sons silent until they reached the council site.

Beyond the encampment a huge tent had been erected. Around it sat the massed warriors who had come at the queen's behest, a sizable fraction of Hael's military might. When the king and his sons came in sight, the thousands of warriors got to their feet and chanted his name, waving spears, bows and swords in the air. They were men from a score of tribes, united in their loyalty to their spirit-king.

The men made a lane for him to pass through and Hael walked to the huge tent with his sons behind him. Inside the light was dimmer and the air was close, but this council had to be held in private, and the warriors outside ensured that no foreigner could eavesdrop. The assembled chiefs stood respectfully as Hael entered and walked to his seat, a folding chair set upon a low dais. When he sat, the others did likewise.

''My sons are not chiefs,'' Hael began, ''but I want them to attend this council.''

''That is your right, my king,'' said Jochim, his Matwa war leader.

''For the last year and more,'' Hael said, ''My sons and I have been traveling among our enemies. Many of you have heard from my son Ansa about his adventures in the south, and how he was held captive by King Gasam during the conquest of Sono. We shall hear more of that presently. Yesterday, my son Kairn and I returned from a sojourn among the Mezpans, where I learned that even now they plot war against us, and an alliance with Gasam to accomplish it!''

The tent erupted in exclamations and Hael waited for it to die down; then he began to describe his adventures in the land beyond the river, and what he had learned there. When he described the army of firetube soldiers, there were cries of derision. Most of the chiefs had seen the newfangled weapons demonstrated, and they had not been impressed. He tried to explain how the orderly tactics and massed fire of the Mezpans could be devastating to a mounted army, but his words were received with some doubt. He decided to let the implications sink in slowly and went on to describe Gasam's latest moves. Gasam was understood and was universally hated.

''We cannot allow ourselves to be caught between the two expanding powers and I would rather not fight both at once. I have decided that we shall fight one of them!''

These words were greeted with cheers.

''The Mezpans!'' shouted one. ''They should be easy!''

There was approval for this.

''No!'' Hael said. ''We will go after Gasam!''

''My king,'' said Jochim, springing to his feet. ''The great desert separates us from Gasam. It is hard, slow traveling, and when we arrive in his territory he will be ready for us, his fresh warriors against our tired men and half-starved and thirsty cabos. Our army is the greatest in the world but under those circumstances it would be no contest.'' This was greeted with boos and the Amsi said that the Matwa, as usual, were too cautious. Hael waved for silence.

''My chief Jochim is right. I do not propose to cross the desert.'' There was a puzzled silence which Hael filled with a question. ''My chiefs, what has made Gasam so great? How has he come by his conquests?''

There was further silence, then a grizzled old Ramdi chief

stood. "Gasam strikes like the longneck, my king. His enemies do not even know he is there. Then, in a flash, the monster is upon them."

"Exactly," Hael said. "He attacks when his prey are half-asleep. Only we, and the Nevans, with our aid, have been able to push him out of territory he had taken, and it was like scaring a longneck off a carcass. He roared defiance, then slunk off to search for easier pickings. He speaks friendly words to unoffending nations and then attacks without warning. Always, he attacks. My chiefs, *no one has ever attacked Gasam!*" There was much muttering and nodding of heads.

"Well, my chiefs, I propose we remedy this. We will attack Gasam, suddenly and without warning! We will be upon him before he knows we are there!"

Men shouted enthusiastically. They were catching the fever now. They had been too long without a war and they were ready for it. And their revered king, to whom they attributed mystical powers, was proposing something extraordinary.

"My king," said Jochim, "how are we to do this?"

"Gasam expects to attack us, or to get Mezpa to attack us, just as Deathmoon wants to persuade Gasam to do the same thing. Even if Gasam believed that I would go on the attack, he would expect me to come down from the north and be easy meat, as Jochim has said. But we will not hit him from the north. We will come in from the west!"

Amid the puzzlement, it was Jochim who first caught the implications. "Through Neva?" he said. Hael reached into his belt pouch and drew out a number of bronze tubes and held them high.

"These were waiting for me when I returned yesterday. They are letters from Queen Shazad of Neva. She has been alarmed by my long absence, by Gasam's latest conquests, especially by the word that Gasam has taken over the steel mine. In her most recent letter, she said that Gasam is even issuing steel arrow heads to his warriors. She knows that it cannot be long before he has another try at conquering Neva.

"Today I will send her a letter of my own. I will tell her to mobilize her forces quietly, and that I am coming with my whole army. We will ride through the passes into Omia, and thence to Neva. We'll pass through Neva without stopping, and pick up their army as we go. We'll fall upon Gasam's forces at the Chiwan border and drive on through that country, snapping up his garrisons piecemeal. We riders will be the shock force, destroying his armies in the field. The Nevans can have the plodding work of besieging and reducing his fortresses. Remember, the Shasinn and other warrior peoples are the spearhead of Gasam's conquest. They will be with him in the east. What he has left behind are native levies, second-rate troops who will fall before us like grass! We will ride on into Sono and take that from him as well, and then ride into Gran. We will roll up his empire behind him like a man rolling up a hide! Before he knows he is in danger, Gasam will have his empire stripped from him and he will see us riding down upon him! He has never been surprised before. He will be this time.''

Now the chiefs were growling their enthusiasm, their eyes bright with this heroic new prospect. A single campaign that would take them in a great crescent across half the world!

''We will smash him with his back to the southern sea!'' cried a chief who knew a little geography.

''That will be good,'' Hael said. ''But the alternative could be even better.'' Once more he had puzzled them.

''What do you mean, my king?'' asked one.

''What did Gasam do last time he met someone he couldn't smash with surprise and ferocity?''

''He ran from us!'' shouted Chief Amata.

Hael smiled. ''I am willing to bet that he will run again. Where is the only place he can run?'' He waited while they figured it out.

''Into Mezpa!'' Kairn shouted.

''And that should take care of this proposed alliance,'' Hael said. The glee was general now, the chiefs, never needing much persuasion to take part in a war, wholly with him. Jochim stood and signaled for silence.

''What are your commands, my king?''

''First, no word is to be spoken of our plans until the host is together at the foot of the mountains. When this fair is over, those merchants out there will scatter all over the world. I've no doubt that Larissa has spies among them. They will know something is happening, but they won't know what. I want word to go out to the chiefs who are not here. I want you all to round up all your warriors and they are to meet me at the foot of the first pass with all their cabos and all their equipment, ready for the biggest, fastest war anyone has ever seen. Our tribes will sing about this one for a thousand years!''

At this, a ferocious cheer went up. When it died down Hael spoke again.

"We must be through the passes before they are snowed in. That means we have little more than a month. We cannot waste time."

The council broke up. There were no protests against the war, despite its epic scope. Rather there was a sense of exaltation, the warriors knowing that they would take part in an adventure like nothing ever mentioned even in the oldest legends. To them it was further proof that their king was touched by the spirits, and that they were uniquely fortunate to be living in his time.

When they left the tent, the chiefs went among their warriors, warning against any excited demonstrations before the foreigners. It was painful to the young warriors, but the young men managed to contain themselves.

Hael and his sons returned to the royal tent, where Queen Deena had dried her tears and determined to put the best face on matters. They ate together, and after the meal Ansa told his father about his time in the south the previous year.

"She is obsessed with restoring her youth, Father," Ansa said, "and she believes the Canyoners can do it. They are a very strange people, the Canyoners, and I was never able to determine whether they are truly sorcerers. But Fyana can do things that do not look natural. She brought King Ach'na of Gran back from the brink of death. She read what was going on in his body by touching his brow."

"Much good did it do him," Kairn said. "The city has

probably fallen by now, and no ruling family ever survives one of Gasam's conquests.''

Ansa shrugged. "I cannot say that I liked the Granians. They are too foreign. But anything is better than Gasam and his horde. Wait until you see his women warriors, little brother. They are like something from a nightmare. They are torturers and cannibals and the Shasinn are as bad, just better-looking.''

Hael shook his head. "Of all the things Gasam has done, I think the worst is the way he has perverted our people. The Shasinn were noble warrior-herdsmen, back in the home islands. Our customs were rigid, but they were good ones. To be a warrior of the Shasinn was to be the finest creature beneath the sky. Now they are mindless murderers, feeding Gasam's monstrous ego and ambition. How can self-respecting warriors surrender themselves to a single man?''

Deena snorted delicately. "About fifty thousand mounted young fools are about to do the same for you.''

"This is not for my greater glory," Hael said with unac-customed heat. "This is to save us as a people.''

"It's all the same to them," she said. "They are going because you will it, and for the sheer joy of the thing.''

Hael sighed. "That may be true. Gasam and I may be the greatest disaster that has ever befallen the world. We are two sides of the same coin.''

"You are nothing like him!" Ansa said. "I have met Gasam at last, to my own grief, and he is evil incarnate. You are the world's only hope, Father. Never doubt it.''

"And I've met Deathmoon," Kairn said. "Ansa is right.''

The queen smiled ruefully. "I can see that I am outnum-bered. Very well, go off and have your war. I will stay at home with my daughter and we will count the moons until you come back.''

"We have a while before the war host is gathered," Hael said. "I intend to return to the hills and get reacquainted with Kalima.''

"Excellent," Deena said. "From the sound of it, by the

time you finish with this war, she will be grown and married."

"You exaggerate. This war will be huge and we will cover great distances, but it will be swift. I plan to have it over with in a single season. We will be through the passes before the snows fall. Look to see us again before the next rainy season."

"Less than half a year to make a circuit of the world?" Ansa said.

"I must remind my daughter," Deena said, "never to marry a visionary spirit-warrior."

FOURTEEN

arissa did not like the low coastal country, but after the steel mine anything was an improvement. She had followed her husband through every sort of terrain in his career of conquest, and this hot, humid, insect-ridden coastal swamp was far from the worst.

Besides her personal guard, she now had an escort of local foot soldiers. This land was the small but defiant kingdom of Thezas, the last independent nation between Gasam's empire and the Mezpan province of Delta. He could have overrun Thezas easily, but for the moment, Gasam preferred to leave the buffer state between his lands and Mezpa. As always, he assured the king of Thezas of his peaceful intentions, claiming that he had made his last territorial gains and wanted only peace and brotherhood with his neighbors. Larissa doubted that the king was fool enough to believe it, but he had no choice but to put the best face on it. Before coming hither, Larissa had written to the man in the most flattering terms, begging the favor of a safe-conduct through his kingdom. He had agreed, insisting that she have an honor guard of his warriors.

Now she studied those warriors, and she liked what she saw. They were men of a different race from the Granians next door, taller, paler of skin, many with blue eyes. Their hair ranged from near-black to light brown and they had angular, hard-edged facial features. They eschewed the paint, feathers and colorful uniforms of their neighbors, wearing reptile-hide cuirasses buckled over short, mud-colored tunics. Each man had a tall shield of wicker and hide, a short-sword at his belt, and a thrusting spear in his hand. Their helmets were of hammered bronze, with pendant cheek plates and neck guards cut from what appeared to be a sort of tortoise shell. On their feet they wore stout, thick-soled sandals. They looked tough and competent, and her first glance told her why Thezas had remained an independent kingdom for so long, despite its small size and relative lack of wealth. These men would be first-rate heavy infantry, once they were broken to Gasam's yoke.

"How much farther?" she asked the Thezan officer who rode beside her. His cabo and his gold-hilted sword were the only things that distinguished him from the others.

"No more than an hour," he said. The Thezans spoke a dialect of Southern so heavily accented that she still had some difficulty making out the words. Her conversations with the man were restricted to short, simple sentences. He rode with his face turned straight ahead, which amused her, because she knew that he had to be curious about the legendary queen of the Island Empire. He would just have to remain in the dark concerning her appearance, she thought. The coastal sun and the clouds of stinging insects forced her to ride in her voluminous desert garb, with the addition of a fine-meshed net that fell from the brim of her hat to her shoulders. He could see only the vaguest hints of the famous beauty.

She sighed with relief when the coastal town came into view. It was a cluster of low-roofed buildings made of stone, the roofs made of what appeared to be heavy slate. Beyond it was an endless stretch of water, a welcome sight after the years she had spent inland.

"Those are strong buildings for so small a town," she said, speaking slowly and enunciating clearly.

"Big storms come in off the sea," the officer said. "They will blow away anything that is not strongly built. Sometimes, even stone is not strong enough."

She nodded. She came from another stormy land. As she looked about her, she saw the signs of great storms in the recent past: huge trees uprooted, great swaths of forest laid flat, new growth struggling riotously up through the tangled trunks, branches and roots. Flowing vines were everywhere and there was a pervasive stench of rotting vegetation.

They rode into the town. It had no wall, but merely began at the end of a stretch of cultivated fields. They were not extensive, and she assumed that the inhabitants lived mainly by fishing. Along the shore she could see upturned boats and nets stretched out for drying. She wrinkled her nose with disgust. Fish had been forbidden food to her people, and though Gasam had long since abolished the old taboos, she could not get used to the idea of fish as food.

The town had a single stone jetty, and moored to it they found a broad-beamed ship, almost an oversized barge. A richly dressed man came forward to greet her and, with the pop of a whip, at least a hundred slaves swarmed to help stow her baggage aboard the vessel.

"Welcome, Queen Larissa of the Islands. I am Lord Blackriver, and it is my mission to expedite your journey in every way possible." He reached up to help her from her mount but she ignored the offer, springing lightly to the ground where two of her guards immediately stepped forward to flank her.

"Your honor guard awaits your inspection, Queen Larissa," Blackriver said.

"Oh, yes, by all means," she said. "I am anxious to see these famous soldiers."

The guard was drawn up in two ranks, the men holding their firetubes slanting across their bodies. Larissa walked down the lines, trying not to laugh. They looked comical compared to the Thezans, less than comical when compared with her Shasinn.

And yet, somehow, the Mezpans had employed these non-warriors to accumulate a respectable empire. How had they done it?

Her Shasinn bodyguards did not bother to hide their contempt for the Mezpan soldiers. That was to be expected. But the Mezpan guards did not seem at all impressed by the Shasinn, and that was something entirely new in her experience.

"We will be ready to leave within the hour, Your Majesty," Blackriver said. "If you will come aboard, we have prepared some refreshment. I know you have had a long ride."

"You are too kind," she said. It had been a long time since she had felt a deck beneath her feet, since the days when Gasam was a pirating raider. The familiar feel and smell of tarred wood was reassuring. She noted that the ship was furnished with wide rowing benches, which accounted for the exceptional number of slaves. The Mezpan guard filed aboard and ranged themselves along the battlements of the fore and aft castles.

"So many guards?" Larissa said, settling herself onto a couch beneath an awning near the stern.

"It will make for a crowded voyage, but it is necessary, I am afraid," Blackriver said. At the snap of his finger slaves hastily set food and iced wine near Larissa. "There has been an inordinate amount of pirate activity lately. We had thought it a thing of the past."

"How unfortunate," Larissa said, blandly.

"Yes. We're not sure where they came from, but they seem to have rounded the southwestern cape some time ago. They may be from Sono, perhaps Chiwa." He said this in carefully neutral tones.

"My husband's navy has scoured out their old haunts in the islands and the coastal bays. Perhaps they have fled here for easier pickings. Has the damage been great?"

"Bad enough. They come ashore at some little harbor like this, sack it, then range inland. When they can find cabos, they use them for mobility. They slaughter livestock to provision their ships and carry away wealth and slaves."

"Have you captured any for questioning?" She selected a small fruit pastry and ate it delicately.

"None so far. We have concentrated on our land army in recent years to the neglect of the coast guard and navy. That is being rectified."

"An excellent idea." She held up her cup and admired the droplets of condensation. "Where do you get ice at this time of year?"

"In the winter the lakes freeze in our northernmost territories. It is sawed into great blocks which are packed in the holds of river barges and covered with sawdust. Thence it floats down the river to the major towns and is stored through the summer in ice houses. Lord Deathmoon knew that you would be uncomfortable in this climate and bade me bring a plentiful supply."

"Lord Deathmoon is most thoughtful." She took a lump of the ice and rubbed it on her face and neck, relishing the feel of a cold trickle that ran down between her breasts.

"My lord desires only that this historic meeting be as pleasant as possible for our distinguished guest." At his gesture, slaves took up fans and a cooling breeze swept over Larissa.

Sipping her wine and nibbling idly at her food, Larissa watched as sailing preparations were completed. The last of her belongings were stored in the shallow hold and the slaves filed aboard and sat at their benches, where an overseer fastened them by their ankle rings to a rod that ran the length of each bench.

The Shasinn came aboard and lounged on the deck, happy with this interruption of their long march. Larissa noticed that the ship had no mast or sail, and commented upon the fact.

"This is a rowed vessel," Blackriver said. "When there are plenty of slaves and the distances are not great, why depend upon the wind? This vessel is useful along the coast and for a day's travel offshore, and can be rowed the entire length of the great river.''

"Slave power is a wonderful thing," Larissa agreed, admiring the sheen of sunlight on the tanned skins of the rowers. They seemed to represent a score of races, some of which she had never seen before. "We have conquered so many lands, the glut of slaves is enormous. When you dispossess the old ruling classes you end up with many slaves and few owners.''

"We have found uses for great masses of them," Blackriver said. "Plantations are wonderful places to put huge numbers of them to work. Perhaps before you return you may wish to take a tour of some coastal plantations. It may give you some ideas for disposing of your surplus slaves.''

"That might be pleasant, if time permits." She did not bother to tell him how Gasam disliked farming. He would consider slaves better employed for spear practice.

At last, all preparations were complete and the ship cast off from the pier. The Thezan escort saluted, and Larissa inclined her head in response. A whistle shrilled and the oars backed water, moving the vessel away from the pier. At a more complicated series of trills, the oars on one side were pushed while those on the others were pulled, rotating the ship on its axis, until the bow was pointed out to sea. Then a naked brown man who stood beneath the aft castle began pounding a drum monotonously. In time to the beats of the drum, the oars began to rise and lower rhythmically, and the heavy-laden ship began to move out to sea.

Once they were past the sheltered waters the ship began the familiar, rolling motion. Larissa knew that it was good the voyage would be short. Most of her guard had not been at sea since coming over from the islands as children and they were sure to be sick after a few hours of this.

An hour out from land a lookout shouted something. Lord Blackriver strode to the fore castle to see. Then he came back to Larissa to report.

"Two strange ships coming toward us under sail," he said.

"They may be pirates. You are not to worry. They'll run when we show them our teeth."

"I fear nothing in the midst of my Shasinn," she said.

"Even so, Your Majesty, you may wish to go below. If they have bows, they may be able to get a few arrows as far as our deck before we drive them away."

"Nonsense. I have been present at more battles than any veteran of your army. I have never hidden myself from a foe."

Blackriver smiled. "I see that your reputation as a warrior queen is well merited. Very well, but you must have some men standing by you with shields."

"My guards are skilled at such work," she assured him.

"Then, I must go to supervise preparations." When he was gone she spoke to her guards in the island dialect.

"Stay sitting where you are. There won't be any real battle. I don't want those ships to see that there are Shasinn aboard, so don't show yourselves or your black shields. Two of you borrow shields from the sailors and come here to protect me from arrows. I want to see what is about to happen."

Disappointed that there would be no real fighting, her men complied. Two of them came back to stand beside her, carrying long shields painted in bright patterns. She rose from her couch and saw the two ships under sail, closing fast from the south. They were low, rakish craft, their slanting, triangular sails giving them a speed advantage over the rowed ship, which could achieve high speed only in spurts.

On board her host vessel there was some sort of activity going on at the fore. A hatch cover had been removed, and a group of soldiers and sailors were winching something weighty up to deck level. Gradually, an odd object came into sight.

It was a squat tube, at least eight feet long, made of the same white ceramic as the firetubes carried by the soldiers. Unlike those, this one was strapped with bands of thick bronze at intervals of a foot, and there was a bronze cap at one end. The strange thing was hoisted to the starboard side and laid into a massive wooden frame and pegged solidly in place. The front end of the thing was open and a team of soldiers busily crammed things into the open end, ramming them back with a long, padded pole.

Larissa had seen the firetubes demonstrated before, and she knew that she was seeing some sort of super-firetube being readied for action. Could such a thing destroy a ship? The others were closing in fast. She knew that she could make them run just by showing herself and having her guard stand. These were Gasam's pirates, after all. But she was curious to see how the ship would be fought, and she did not want to answer any questions about why these pirates were reluctant to attack her and the Shasinn.

There were no preliminaries. As soon as the pirate vessels were within range, their arrows began to arc toward the Mezpan ship. The first ones fell short, then they began to strike the sides.

"Fire!" Blackriver shouted. There was a multiple *crash* as a group of the Mezpan soldiers discharged their weapons as one. They stepped back from the rail and a new line took their places and fired likewise. The Shasinn whooped and grinned and covered their ears against the splitting clamor of the firetubes. As Larissa watched, she saw how there were always men in firing position at the rail, while others were reloading behind them. It seemed a clever way to manage the weapons. The soldiers went about it with machinelike regularity, their faces devoid of expression. No warrior passion here, just obedience to the will of their officers. She could not tell what effect, if any, the shooting was having on the other ships, which closed inexorably.

Men sprang back from the huge firetube as an officer took something from a pouch at his belt and placed it in a recess at the rear of the tube, atop the bronze cap. This she knew to be a priming pellet of the sort used in the firetubes she had seen. The officer stood back and pulled on a cord. A hammerlike striker fell upon the pellet. There was a thunderous bang, the loudest sound Larissa had ever heard, loud enough to make her senses reel. A number of the Shasinn sprawled to the deck, knocked from their sitting position by the concussion. Through her daze, she saw a fountain of water erupt just before the bow of the lead pirate ship.

Immediately, the strange weapon's crew readied it again. When it was charged, the officer worked for a few seconds at a wedge beneath the breech. This, apparently, raised or lowered the tube. Then they stood back again. This time, Larissa clamped her hands firmly over her ears. This marginally reduced the shock of the monster weapon's roar, and when it fired she kept her eyes on the other ship.

The pirate ship was much closer now, close enough to distinguish individual faces along its bow rail. They were bearded for the most part, shouting as they waved weapons. This time, an instant after the big tube's thunderous roar, she saw a section of the rail explode into a thousand splinters and she saw human limbs spring into the air amid a vapor of blood. Then a cloud of white smoke obscured the view. When it cleared she saw that a crescent of wood had disappeared from the ship's bow, as if some huge monster had taken a bite from it. The ship was sheering off. It had had enough. Behind it, the other pirate ship lowered its sail, allowing the Mezpan vessel to go on its way unmolested.

The Mezpan crew and soldiers raised a fierce cheer, making gestures of defiance. Some of the sailors went to the rail and exposed their backsides in derision. Larissa's men were somber and subdued. They did not like this sort of fighting. There was something unwarriorlike about it, yet the slaughter was the same. Blackriver came back, smiling and sweating.

"I trust Your Majesty is well? I am sorry, I should have warned you about the noise that thing makes. It can be distressing to one who is unused to it."

She smiled, knowing that he had not told her deliberately, wanting her to be overwhelmed by this mighty new Mezpan device.

"It is a most formidable weapon. It made an enthralling spectacle. Can it sink a ship?"

"That would take a larger ball than this one throws. But it is excellent for killing men on deck. The trick is to hit a rail or bulwark or a bit of superstructure and let the flying wood splinters do most of the destruction." She noticed that he did not say whether they actually had ship-killing weapons. "Please take your ease and enjoy the rest of the voyage. We will be at the island in no more than another hour. It may even be in sight by now." When he was gone she spoke to the Shasinn who stood near her.

"What did you think of all that?"

"It is not way to fight, my queen!" said one. "What sort of battle is it when you cannot see your enemy's blood on your spear? This is nothing but noise and smoke, but it seems to kill men just like real fighting."

"Well, don't let it bother you. Those pirates ran because they were not used to it, either. You saw how long it took to ready that smoky, noisy thing. They could have been alongside before it had a chance to fire again, but they ran because they didn't know that. We won't forget it."

"And those others," said the other Shasinn. "The way they operated the firetubes, it was not like fighting. It was like . . . like . . ." He waved his spear expressively, ". . . like a *job!*"

"Yes, I think we have little fear of such soldiers," she assured them. "Their weapons are only good for letting weak men feel a little stronger." Her words were confident, but inwardly she was not so sure. What she had seen frightened her. This was just a small honor guard aboard a barge with a single big firetube. A whole army of them might be a more stubborn enemy than they had faced before. Always, before, she had had perfect confidence in Gasam and his invincible warriors. Now she was shaken by doubts.

She put her doubts from her mind. This was not the time to have such thoughts. She was to meet with a potential enemy and she could afford no weakness. She sat on the couch, took a small looking glass from her saddlebag, and began to adjust her appearance.

The meadow was bright with pavilions when the ship came into the tiny bay. Three other ships were already there, moored in deeper water. The barge approached the beach at a slow walk, then the rowers plunged their oars and held them, slowing the vessel further, so that when its bottom touched sand, only the slightest shock was felt. The long gangplank came down and the Shasinn warriors ran ashore, forming a double file leading from the gangplank toward the meadow.

A regiment-sized honor guard formed up before the Shasinn, and in the middle of them stood a small group of men who were not in military clothes. Larissa, who now stood at the top of the gangplank, had no way of knowing which was Deathmoon. She would impress him, whoever he might be. She always did. She walked down the plank and passed between the files of her Shasinn. The eyes of the men ahead of her widened as she drew near. She had opened her traveling cloak so that it fell behind her shoulders like a cape. Around her narrow waist she had wound a three-inch-wide sash of scarlet silk, its tasseled ends reaching her knees before and behind. These and a great deal of jewelery formed her only garments. A man in rich gray clothing stepped a little in advance of the others.

"Mezpa greets you, Queen Larissa of the Islands. I am Lord Deathmoon, Speaker of the Assembly of Great Men."

She smiled and took his proffered hand. "On behalf of myself and my husband, the Emperor Gasam, I greet you." She saw him wince slightly at the title of emperor bestowed on the piratical barbarian Gasam, but she knew no one more deserving of it.

Deathmoon glanced along the double file of her warriors. "I see that the Shasinn are as handsome a people as I have always heard, but even they pale beside the beauty of their queen." He conducted her to a huge pavilion furnished with carpets, cushions and draperies.

"You may of course prefer your own tent, but this one is at your disposal should you find your own too cramped. Please make use of it."

"You are too generous. Rest assured that I shall." She wondered whether this tent provided him with facilities for spying, eavesdropping or assassination. Whatever it might be, it looked comfortable and she didn't plan to be doing anything that would be of advantage to him.

The Mezpan officials withdrew to give her time to get settled in before the banquet scheduled for that evening. She posted her guards and settled amid the cushions while her tent was set up. Low, round tables held flagons of iced wine and bowls of fruit and other light fare. She knew better than to befuddle herself before a momentous meeting, and she did not wish to insult her hosts by eating nothing at the banquet, so she ignored the temptations while she rested.

She closed her eyes and thought of the day's battle, or rather hostile encounter. She had seen things that made her uneasy, but she did not doubt that Gasam would quickly find a way to neutralize any threat it represented. She was happy that the Mezpans had brought so large an honor guard. A regiment ought to be able to put on a demonstration that would answer her questions.

And, if Deathmoon were to prove reluctant to provide such a demonstration, she would have to work a little. She had never met a man she could not seduce into anything she wanted.

When the exhausted royal messenger staggered into the royal chambers, Queen Shazad snatched the message-tube from his fingers before he could even stammer out a greeting. He stood for a few seconds and collapsed to the tiles. She ignored him as she tore away the seal and pulled the rolled-up letter from inside.

Her ladies waited tensely as the queen scanned the sheets, her face having gone pale. Two rushed forward with a chair and she collapsed into it as if her bones had turned to jelly.

"Is it bad news, Majesty?" whispered Lady Zina.

Shazad collected herself. "Zina, stay by me. The rest of you, leave us. Take him." She pointed to the collapsed messenger. Two servants dragged the man out between them as the remaining ladies bowed their way out and closed the door behind them.

"I am saved, Zina," Shazad said. "King Hael is coming!" Her nerves were so shattered that she could not even summon the smile she wanted to display. Inwardly she was elated beyond her power to express, but her body would just not respond. She had been living in terror, fearing that she would lose the nation she had built out of the wreckage her father had left, no longer able to trust her highest councilors, seeing evidence of treason everywhere. But now Hael was coming! And his entire army would be with him.

"That is wonderful news, Majesty," Zina said. Then, "Ah, Majesty, just what does King Hael have planned?"

"I don't know. He would not commit it to writing, but I know that he never takes action without knowing exactly what it is he plans to accomplish, and how to accomplish it."

"Then perhaps all will be well, Majesty."

"You don't sound terribly elated," Shazad said, offended that the woman was not as joyous as she felt.

"Well, Majesty, when a foreign ruler comes into one's country with an army, it is often for purposes of invasion."

"What! You know that King Hael has always been my friend!"

Zina smoothed the gown over her knees. "Of course, Majesty. But these things change."

Shazad glared at her. "If he wanted to invade my country, he surely would not send me a letter saying he was coming!"

"Of course, Your Majesty knows these things best."

"So I do. You may go, Zina. Pass the word that I will summon a council meeting this evening." The lady rose and bowed her way out. For a long time Shazad stared at the door in stony silence. Now she would have to watch Zina.

The councilors looked decidedly nonplussed. She did not read them the whole letter, but she told them some of its substance.

"We can expect King Hael to arrive in Nevan territory within a month," she said when she had finished.

"My queen, by what route does he plan to arrive?" Bardas asked.

"He does not say in the letter," she lied. "We'll have no trouble recognizing him when he gets here."

"The plainsmen have a distinctive appearance, to be sure," Bardas said. "But as to this mobilization of our forces, this is far too hasty—"

"No, it is far too slow. I want it to start immediately. King Hael is quite adamant on this point and I have never known him to fail in his military judgment. I so command it. It may be done quietly and discreetly, like ordinary maneuvers, so as not to raise a fuss, but it shall be done."

"As you say, Majesty," said Bardas, bowing.

She gave her orders, saw her reluctant councilors wilt before her will, and sent them out to do her bidding. Then she sat back and waited. She already had her own agents in place. That night they brought in three messengers; each had been sent to Gasam with the story of Hael's coming. Shazad quickly had the names of their masters out of them.

Before morning those who had sent the messengers had been arrested and executed. Two were councilors. One of these was Bardas. The third was Lady Zina. There would be no more betrayals.

FIFTEEN

The trek through the mountains was slow as always. It no longer featured the privations it once had, for Hael had in years past established fodder and water stations at intervals. The air was crisp, but as yet no snow had fallen. Hael sent the army through by regiments, with intervals between so that the narrow road would not become overcrowded. His chiefs knew the routine well and the chaos of earlier crossings was avoided.

The king himself rode with the lead regiment. It was his place as leader and he would have to soothe some ruffled feathers as they advanced. Knowing how undependable the rulers of Omia were, he had not told the king of that land he was coming.

At the western foot of the pass Hael waited while his regiment cleared the road behind him, then rode with them at his back, toward the nearest border station.

As they neared the roadblock by the little mud fort, a sentry gaped at them, then ran into the fort. Minutes later, a portly figure emerged from the fort, buckling on an ill-fitting cuirass, his gilded helmet winking in the morning light.

"Is it King Hael?" said the man as Hael rode up. "We are not prepared to receive royalty. We had no word that you were coming!" In his astonishment the official neglected to use titles.

"I was in a great hurry," Hael said soothingly. "I am afraid I neglected to inform my brother king of my arrival in his territory."

"This is improper, sir, most improper!"

"I know that, and I do apologize. By way of apology, I have brought rich gifts for your king, and, of course, a few presents for you, to make up for the inconvenience." He knew the Omians well.

"Ah, well, then, I am sure that His Majesty will not take it greatly amiss. He knows how it is when a brother monarch must deal with an emergency. It *is* an emergency is it not, sir? That is a rather large force of men behind you." He squinted down the long line of riders.

"There is a rather larger force of men behind them, some sixty-five regiments, in fact."

The man gaped. "That must be the greater part of your army! Is this an invasion?"

"Oh, by no means. We are going to hold joint maneuvers with the Nevans. My good friend, Queen Shazad, has agreed to a large training exercise, to ensure that our armies continue to work well together."

"Very wise, very wise," the official muttered, his face pale. Sweat ran from beneath his helmet. The last time Neva and the plains had joined forces, they had utterly smashed an Omian army that had unwisely sided with Gasam.

"I think my gifts will easily cover the cost of our foraging as we ride through. I shall inform King Umas—"

"Ah, it is King Luso now, Majesty," the official corrected.

"King Luso, then." Hael could never keep straight which of the brothers or cousins held the throne of Omia, and which were exiled or imprisoned. What made it more confusing was that they rarely killed each other, so the same man might wear the crown at several different times. "I shall inform him of my intentions along with my gifts. Of course, by the time he gets word we shall be out of Omia."

"He will appreciate the thought, I am sure," the official said.

Hael rode on with his regiment. He had designated an assembly area well inside Omian territory, near the border with Neva. It was on the land of a local lord who received a stipend from Hael to keep the place well stocked with wood and its broad acreage ungrazed against just such an occasion as this. It was a private arrangement, there being no real need to trouble the king of Omia with such trifles.

Ansa and Kairn rode behind their father. They had never ridden to war before, and they were impressed not only with the sheer size of the army but with the degree of organization and foresight Hael displayed with every action. Whatever his mystical tendencies, he was utterly realistic when it came to moving his army. He knew the names and personal characteristics of every feudal lord whose lands he would cross, and had brought appropriate bribes for each.

"You must never assume that all men are the same; friend, enemy or neutral," he explained to them. "Some are merely greedy. That is true of most of the Omian lords and it is simple to deal with: Give them money and jewels. Others have touchy honor and you have to learn what soothes them. It may be nothing more than compliments and a respectful attitude. The worst are the ones who are easily bought but then refuse to honor the deal."

"What do you do with them?" Kairn asked.

"Remind them that I will be marching back through their land. If they have betrayed me, they will regret it."

The ride through Omia was uneventful. The land was thinly populated and abundant with wild game. Hunters were out at all times to bring in fresh meat at the evening halt. It was a land of many small streams so water was adequate. When they reached the assembly area they pitched camp and waited.

Within two hours the next regiment rode in and they kept on coming, regiment after regiment, for five days.

Kairn and Ansa could not keep themselves from gaping at the sight of so many warriors in one place. Each man had brought as many remounts as he could. The poorest warrior had at least three cabos. Chiefs brought ten or more. The horde on the march resembled a vast cabo herd with men riding on its fringes. After two more days to rest and let the animals put on flesh, King Hael ordered the march to resume.

When they reached the Nevan border, Hael saw a familiar face at the head of the military delegation awaiting him. The scarred, grizzled veteran held out a knotty hand and Hael took it.

"Welcome, King Hael," the man said.

"You honor me. May I present my sons, Ansa and Kairn. Boys, this is His Highness, General Harakh, Prince-Consort of Neva."

"They favor you, Hael. I envy you. Shazad and I never had children."

"They're a mixed blessing," Hael assured him. He was introduced to the others in the military party and he studied them. They looked competent at least, although overdressed by his standards, with ornate uniforms and gilded weapons and armor. He knew that Shazad would keep no incompetents on and he did not plan to ask great things of them.

"How goes the mobilization?" Hael asked as they continued the march toward the capital.

"Well under way. The northern garrisons are already well ahead of us. We'll find them assembled at the capital with those from the west country. The southerly troops we'll pick up as we move south from Kasin and the whole force will be together by the time we reach the Chiwan border."

"Have you been able to keep word from reaching Gasam?"

"We've caught a number of spies and messengers in the act," Harakh said. "And we've caught the ones who sent them. I am confident that Gasam and Larissa have no inkling that we're coming."

"Good," Hael said. "All hinges on surprise."

"We'll have it on our side," Harakh assured him.

The ride was brisk but not breakneck. Hael saw no point in wearing men and animals down before the fighting could even begin. It would be grueling enough once they were engaged.

Their first sight of Kasin, the capital of Neva, was dramatic. The walls were illuminated by the setting sun, tall and majestic. The city was situated on a broad bay, and for many of Hael's men it was their first sight of an ocean. The fields encircling the landward side of the city had become a vast camp, white with tents and the smoke from a thousand campfires.

When they were a half-mile from the walls a gate opened and Queen Shazad rode from the city to greet them. Hael gave orders for the quartering of his men and animals and rode to meet her, his two sons riding close behind him.

The two sovereigns embraced formally while her citizens cheered, then rode side-by-side into the city.

"I've seldom been so happy to see thousands of barbarians descend upon my capital," Shazad said.

"Your subjects are cheering," Hael said, "but not as joyously as last time."

"Last time you came as a savior," she said. "This time, they aren't sure why you are here, or what is to happen."

"They will be glad to have the threat of Gasam removed."

"True, but best not to burden them with the knowledge beforehand."

"I understand there were others who lacked zeal," Hael said, "and you've thinned the ranks of your council and high command."

"There has been a housecleaning," she said grimly. "There is nothing like the prospect of a catastrophic war to let you know who is loyal and who is not. An occasional purge is good for the nation, although it is distressing at the time. I had to execute some friends."

"They were not your friends if they were disloyal," Hael said.

"No monarch has real friends," she said, "but I've come to cherish even my illusions."

They rode to the palace and dismounted to climb the long ceremonial stairway while the populace cheered lustily. Whatever her problems with her council and military command, Shazad was the most popular ruler Neva had ever known.

"Hael, you depress me," Shazad said as they entered the cool shade of the palace.

"Why is that?" he asked.

"You, Gasam, Larissa, all the Shasinn depress me. I am a middle-aged woman, and you look like the young warrior I met so many years ago. I hear that Larissa is as beautiful as always, and Gasam still leads his warriors into battle at a run, while my husband groans and winces just getting off his cabo."

Hael smiled. "Age comes to us all. Some of us put off its worst effects a little longer than others, and you are still renowned for your beauty."

"Thank you for saying so, even if you are lying. Well, we have more serious matters ahead of us. I'm afraid you'll have to endure a banquet, it's customary. After that we will have a council of war with all the senior commanders."

"Has the map been prepared?" Hael asked.

"As you requested. I had artists working day and night. It covers most of the council room floor."

"Good. Choula always stressed the importance of proper maps."

Shazad smiled. "Old Choula. He died a few years ago, you know. He taught three generations of Nevan sovereigns how to read."

"He taught me as well," Hael said. "I was sorry to learn of his death. He was a good friend."

While this conversation was going on, Ansa and Kairn paced a few steps behind their elders, studying the palace with interest. A couple of years earlier, they would have been wide-eyed at its magnificence, but both had traveled widely in the interim, and had seen what great cities were like. They had never been among people with such a highly developed sense of beauty, though. The paintings and mosaics were of the highest quality, splendid but with a restrained good taste.

"Will you and your sons accept quarters in the palace?" she asked.

"We thank you," Hael answered, "but among us, summoning the host means we are at war, and we must bivouac with the army."

"Very well, but I've had a suite of rooms set aside for your use while you are here in the palace to attend conferences." She showed them to a suite comprising a virtual wing of the palace and left them to bathe and change apparel before the banquet.

"The banquet will be magnificent but tedious," Hael told his sons as they luxuriated in a huge pool of hot water. "It is one of the burdens of kingship to attend these things. Don't drink too much and keep an eye on my officers. I don't want any unseemly incidents."

"How do we stop an Amsi chief from drinking as much as he wants to?" Ansa asked.

"Whisper my name in his ear. That's usually effective. If he starts to fight with a Nevan, throw a choke-hold on him and drag him out. I'll make up excuses."

"Why does Queen Shazad rule alone?" Kairn asked.

"Because she can trust no one," Hael said.

"From what she said, it is not a good idea to earn her distrust. Being queen does not seem to have made her happy."

"It is her sense of duty that keeps her on the throne, not any joy it brings her. She is a great woman."

The banquet was, indeed, long and tedious. The platters of food kept coming in long after everybody had had far too much to eat. There were tumblers, jugglers and dancers for entertainment, but with war on their minds few of the guests were of a mind to appreciate their skills.

At last, Queen Shazad dismissed the company and the council, along with the military officers, and went into the war chamber. This was a cavernous room with banks of seats around its periphery. On the sunken floor had been painted a huge map, detailing all the southern lands from the southern provinces of Neva all the way to the Gulf of Imisia and the Mezpan province of Delta. There were murmurs of appreciation from the assembled soldiers, who appreciated good maps. As they entered, each was handed a smaller version of the same map drawn on parchment. Shazad took her throne and Hael took another throne beside her. The throne provided for him was one inch shorter than hers.

"My officers," she began, "honored warrior chiefs of the army of King Hael, we gather here to plan the great campaign to come. Gasam's pirate empire has become an intolerable threat to the whole world, especially now that he has taken my brother king's steel mine. Gasam before was threat enough. Gasam with a limitless supply of steel is not to be tolerated. It shall be the purpose of this campaign to eliminate that threat forever!" There was subdued applause.

"I will now yield the floor to King Hael, who will explain to you his strategy for the destruction of Gasam's tyrannical and illegitimate empire."

There was applause as Hael rose from his chair and descended to the pitlike floor.

Gentlemen," he began without preamble, "I will not tire you with speeches. The requisite decisions have already been made at the highest levels. It only remains to explain the plan and carry it out. When I am finished, you may address any questions to me. Queen Shazad has given me fullest military authority for this joint campaign by our two armies." He walked to the part of the map depicting the southern border of Neva.

"This map depicts our theater of operation for this campaign." There were mutters of astonishment. "Yes, we will be fighting over *all* this territory."

"In a single campaign?" someone asked.

"King Hael will entertain questions *after* his presentation," Shazad snapped.

"The question is understandable," Hael said. "Yes, this will be the largest single campaign ever attempted, its scope far exceeding anything ever done by Gasam.'' The doubters wavered and the rest began to catch the enthusiasm. This promised to be an adventure where there was unrivaled honor and glory to be won.

"In a few days, the army will be massed here," he pointed toward his toe which almost touched the border with Gasam's empire; "the border of what used to be the kingdom of Chiwa. We will be encamped a few miles from the border, in the hills. The border guards' first sight of us will be my mounted regiments coming down upon them. This will be an invasion, pure and simple. Gasam has put himself beyond the pale of civilized behavior. There will be no negotiations, no warning, not even a letter of defiance. He has never bothered to tell his victims that he was coming. Neither shall we." At this a ferocious cheer went up from the assembled officers.

"I have divided my mounted regiments into six divisions under my most experienced chiefs. As we invade, these shall be the shock troops of the army, riding ahead to smash whatever smaller forces Gasam's slaves can muster into the field. They will form three corps of two divisions. One will go ahead of us along the northern border of Gasam's empire, one through the center, the third along the southern periphery." He held out his hand and an attendant gave him a brush tipped with powdered red chalk.

"The corps will head for each of these major camps, where Gasam is known to have field armies." He marked the areas on the map with a series of dots. "After each battle, each corps will split, one division circling to the north, the other to the south, encircling whatever fleeing forces remain at large, to converge at the next camp site." He drew curving lines on the map to illustrate. The divisions moved across the map in a series of gigantic pincers, taking in all the ground of the old kingdom of Chiwa suitable for mounted armies, ending at a mountain range.

"While these operations are in progress, a special unit will charge straight through old Chiwa to secure the passes so that none can flee into Sono to spread warning." He walked back to the Nevan border.

"As soon as the mounted forces are across the border, the infantry will cross immediately behind them. The siege train will follow behind them. As the mounted archers scatter terror and confusion, the bulk of Gasam's subject troops will retreat into their strong points, the old forts and walled cities where our archery is of relatively little use. Neva's matchless infantry and engineers will reduce these places and force them to surrender." He was careful to flatter the Nevans, because the description of the mounted campaign made it look as if the archers could win the war by themselves.

"Remember, defeating armies in the field means nothing if we leave the lands in the hands of his garrisons, safe behind walls. We must be prepared for anything, but I think we need not expect great slaughter in this stage of the campaign. Gasam keeps his island warriors with him, for his lightning campaigns of aggression. In Chiwa we will be facing armies of subject peoples left behind as occupiers. They will have no reason to fight stubbornly if they know we will give quarter and offer generous terms. We can afford to be generous.

"When the land army leaves Kasin for the border," he went on, "the navy will sail to blockade the Chiwan harbors. Their duty will be to keep any vessel from leaving to take word of the invasion to Gasam. They will not seek to assault the harbors unless one of these port cities is stubborn in resisting our land forces. Then a combined land-sea operation may be necessary."

The listeners sat enthralled at the astounding scope of the campaign. They maintained a respectful silence while a servant brought Hael a cup of iced wine. He sipped at it, then continued.

"So much for the first phase of the campaign. I have allotted thirty days for it, from the day we cross the border." He smiled at the amazed gasps. "Yes, gentlemen, we shall all have plenty of blisters before this is over. The next step is to take Sono. We shall cross the three major passes here, here and here." He marked the spots on the mountain range separating the two formerly independent nations. "This is the same route Gasam took, and we shall follow much of his strategy for that campaign, which was a good one.

"Once again, the mounted force will go first, one corps to each pass. Each will advance as far as the River Pata, which splits the land in two. The northern corps will then sweep south to link with the middle corps, smashing any armies between them. The combined corps will then move south to meet the third. Then all three will move south. Here is where we differ from Gasam's campaign: There are no strongly fortified cities or military bases west of the Pata. The land force will embark on naval vessels which will ferry them to the port of Vasa, located here." He marked an indentation on the coast of Sono. "It is not a great port, so it probably has little in the way of defenses. Prince Harakh will lead a flotilla that will land Nevan marines to seize the port. As soon as it is secured, the infantry will disembark and march north, up the eastern bank of the Pata. In the meantime, the flying squad of riders will have crossed the river and will come south, catching any fleeing refugees to keep them from spreading the alarm. As soon as the mounted forces have swept the western bank, they will cross in force and link up with the land invasion. The combined force will then march on the capital, which is still Gasam's strongest base. As they near the city, the mounted corps will split in two and sweep in a great circle, catching any land forces in the field and crushing them. When our infantry have the city thoroughly invested, the mounted archers will sweep on in the earlier fashion, picking up any remaining forces of Gasam's between them." He drew another of the series of pincers. "This brings us to the Granian border. Twenty-five days, gentlemen, from beginning to end."

There were sighs and low whistles. By now, all of them were nearly numb with the scope and sheer audacity of the operation. But they wanted to hear more.

"The story in Gran will be different. It is a new conquest. The land will be alive with refugees, with starving wretches, runaway slaves and outlaws of every stripe preying amid the confusion. Gasam's armies are still active there and we will find bodies of his better troops everyplace. But they won't be concentrated in a single host and we can gobble them up piecemeal. Here the individual field commanders are to use their own initiative. They can fight or bypass as they wish, combine forces or split up as long as it is done with caution and as long as they keep heading east, because that is where Gasam is. We will raise the siege of Great City if the place hasn't fallen yet, and we will pin Gasam against the sea and against Mezpa. He is planning to mop up the small coastal kingdoms of Thezas and Basca. He may have them already, we haven't heard from those parts in several months. That is where we will find his islanders. That is where we will find the Shasinn. We will have him by surprise. No one has ever committed aggression against him. He has always acted on the belief that others are weak and stupid and will always allow him to take the initiative. One morning soon he will come out of his tent, blinking, and will see us in array against him. We will smash him before he can formulate a defense. He can stand and die, or he can flee with his tattered remnants into Mezpa. Those are his only choices.'' He worked the long-handled brush into the eastern coast, leaving a great smear of chalk, as if a large insect had been squashed. He looked up at the assembled officers.

''Questions?''

A man in the rich robes of a councilor stood. ''King Hael, I hate to interject a political note into these stirring military proceedings, but when this . . . what shall we call it? . . . this 'liberation' of Chiwa is complete, who is to rule there? Gasam is said to have exterminated the royal family, and that of Sono as well.''

Hael shrugged. ''Chiwa is your neighbor, not mine. I will not presume to tell Queen Shazad how to proceed. Doubtless there is some refugee pretender here in Neva who can be persuaded to take the throne of Chiwa with certain stipulations. Or the queen may wish to install a military governor, or she may prefer to annex Chiwa to her own dominions. It is entirely up to her. When this campaign is over, my warriors and I ride home. I want no land in this part of the world.''

''Very good, Majesty,'' said the councilor, resuming his seat and beaming. Hael could see that he had struck just the right note.

''King Hael,'' said a Nevan general, ''you have mentioned the possibility that Gasam could flee into Mezpa. Would it not be possible to send a force ahead to cut off any such retreat?''

''It would be,'' Hael said. ''But it is always best to leave an enemy a route of retreat. He will fight stubbornly to the death if he sees no escape. If he flees, he will be in a hostile land with the shredded remnants of an army and his reputation for invincibility equally tattered. He will be reduced to what he once was, a mere bandit chief, with no way to repair his fortunes. I, too, would like to see him dead. But I will be satisfied to see his power destroyed and his empire stripped from him.'' He did not think it a good idea to tell them that what he desired most was that Gasam should flee into Mezpa, so that he and Deathmoon could rip one another to pieces. Gasam would be finished, Deathmoon would be damaged, and without an ally against the plains.

There were many more questions, but they were questions of logistics, not strategy: How was the army to be provisioned? What size of garrison was to be left behind in each liberated territory? And so forth.

Hael answered all questions patiently. They were to live off the land as much as possible, he explained. They were to be generous to the defeated and maintain the best possible relations with the native populations. If the local people were happy to be out from beneath Gasam's yoke, there would be little need for occupying troops. The lame and wounded could be left behind for these undemanding duties. No one questioned the validity of his strategy. All of them seemed enthusiastic for this unprecedented war.

''If there are no more questions,'' he said at last, ''this conference is ended. At first light tomorrow I want to meet here with all the field-force commanders. We shall break the army down by units and issue orders for each unit's objectives and route of march. We shall establish a message chain so as to avoid confusion. The entire royal messenger corps will ride with us to maintain continuous contact between the scattered elements and with my headquarters." He turned to Shazad and bowed. "Your Majesty, I have finished here for this night."

She rose and everyone in the room stood. "I thank King Hael. This campaign shall be the salvation of our nation and of the civilized world. You are dismissed."

When the others had filed out she descended the dais, smiling, and took his hand. "That was the most splendid performance I have ever seen. It's hard to believe you are that primitive boy I found in the public square, gaping at all the new sights, with a great, barbaric spear over your shoulder."

"As I recall, you were sprawling on your rump after being dumped from your litter."

She swatted at him playfully. "You shouldn't remind a lady of those embarrassing moments. Besides, I did see you earlier, when I was being carried through the square. You've just forgotten."

They left the chamber and found Kairn and Ansa waiting for them. As royal princes, they had been allowed to attend the council of war.

"Come, lads, we have to ride to camp." He turned to Shazad. "Your Majesty, you will find nothing of interest to you in the morning council. It is just boring logistical work."

"Nevertheless I shall attend. I want to know what is going on."

"As you will. However, there are important political matters to be discussed. Perhaps in the afternoon we can speak with your councilors. *Somebody* is going to have to rule those nations after we've kicked Gasam out."

"I have plenty of royal relatives living off me since Gasam invaded. I'll find somebody suitable who will be glad to have a throne handed to him if he'll just sign my treaty and take my advice. Neva is a big enough headache. I have no ambition to rule an empire."

"Until tomorrow, then," Hael said.

"I wish you would reconsider and stay here in the palace. These two big, strong boys can handle your army."

"But I must keep an eye on them. Their mother made me promise. Good night, Shazad."

She sighed. "Good night, then."

As they rode back to their encampment, Ansa studied his father with an arched eyebrow. "Did my eyes deceive me, or does that queen want to take up where you two left off twenty-odd years ago?"

"Nonsense," Hael said. "We're just old friends."

"Oh, yes," Kairn said. "She just wants to talk over old times." Both young men laughed.

"That's enough out of the two of you. I can't help it if women think I'm handsome. It comes of being Shasinn," he added complacently.

"You had them eating out of your hand like tame cabos," Ansa said. "Even those self-important old lords gave you no problems." He shook his head in admiration.

"That's because they were stupefied at the ambition of the plan," Hael said. "They'd have chewed me up like longnecks if I'd tried to tell them how to fight an ordinary war. And I'll have to keep it up. If I give them any time to think, they'll get scared. But once we're committed to action, they'll have no chance to back out."

They rode the rest of the way to their camp in silence.

SIXTEEN

The conference was a new experience for Larissa. The Mezpans were unlike any ruling class she had encountered previously. They did not stint the hospitality and entertainment, but they were brisk and businesslike to a degree she had never before experienced. In the lands of the west and south, the entertainment was interminable and the representatives of power got to the actual business of the meeting so slowly, and by such indirection, that even one as acute as Larissa could be unaware when a serious proposal had been made.

The first evening had been devoted to a banquet and entertainment, her hosts apparently thinking she needed time to recover from the rigors of her journey. This suited her, for it was often a helpful thing to be underestimated. The next morning, during a hunt in the island's small forest, Death-moon began to broach the subject on his mind.

"Queen Larissa," he said, "in recent years your esteemed husband has extended his empire eastward almost to the borders of Mezpa."

A small curlhorn broke cover twenty feet in front of her cabo. She rose in her stirrups and hurled her small javelin, catching the beast in mid-bound, just behind the foreleg. It landed, staggered and collapsed with a muffled bleat.

"Excellent cast," Deathmoon commented.

"Thank you. Yes, we have expanded, and rightfully so. The rulers of the southern nations behaved insolently toward us. These petty princelings have long outlived their viability in the new and changing world. Better the world should be dominated by strong empires than by weak nations."

"That is our way of thinking as well," he said, placing a priming pellet beneath the striker of his short firetube.

"And you need have no anxiety concerning our expansion. We have no designs against Mezpa. It is right that the strong should dispossess the weak, but we respect true strength in others."

"Just so." A beater started up a large waterfowl and Deathmoon raised his firetube. The abrupt *bang*, sounding so close, made Larissa wince. This show of weakness embarrassed her and she assumed that was why he chose to use the noisy weapon, when the javelin or bow were so much more elegant and they better displayed hunting skill. She determined not to let him upset her poise.

They turned to ride back to the pavilions, where a lavish luncheon had been set out against their return. Larissa dismounted and took her place at the table, noticing as she did so that Deathmoon's aides, four high assemblymen, were trying hard not to stare at her. That explained it. Deathmoon had been popping away with his firetube practically in her ear all morning to repay her for flaunting her near-nudity before them. She smiled to herself as she sat. It was an understandable but almost feminine reaction and it told her much about the man she faced.

"Upon the subject of expansion," Deathmoon said as the servants began to fill their cups and plates, "there is no reason that our two empires should not continue to expand while maintaining the friendliest of relations."

This was what she had been expecting. "How do you mean?"

"From the great river eastward is all Mezpan territory. The Hegemony extends from the Gulf of Imisia in the south to the frozen lands of the north, where there are no true kingdoms, only the small settlements of hunters and trappers. On the east we are bounded by the sea. Already we have expanded to the western bank of the great river and placed it under Mezpan domination. Our next expansion must be to the west. To expand to the southwest would bring us into unwanted conflict with our esteemed friend the Emperor Gasam. There is, however, nothing to prevent our expanding into the northwest. Nor is there anything to prevent your husband from extending his borders northward."

"The lands you speak of belong to King Hael," she said.

Deathmoon gave a snort of contempt. "Ah, yes. Hael, the vaunted Steel King. He is no true king, but some sort of holy man and sometime war chief. The land is by no means a genuine kingdom, but rather a series of petty chiefdoms populated by tribes that know no true nation save the back of a cabo! They are primitive, contemptible savages and they deserve to be ruled by a civilized nation."

"There are those who call me and my husband primitive savages," she pointed out.

"They are fools. Your husband is a man of rare vision, a man of destiny. Place and people of origin are irrelevant where such men as he are concerned."

"It is good that you understand that. About this proposed expansion: I presume that you have some knowledge of how King Hael's armies fight? They are very fluid, all mounted and in constant motion. They rain storms of arrows from all directions. It has proved disconcerting for more than one army."

"He has never encountered such weapons and tactics as ours."

"Then you have our best wishes. Good fortune to you." She raised her cup and watched him over its rim.

"It strikes me," Deathmoon said, "that the nuisance of

Hael and his savage army can be halved for both of us, if your magnificent Shasinn move north at the same time as my armies sweep west. He would have to fight on two fronts and could take personal command of only one army.''

''But I have not said that we wish to expand northward,'' she pointed out.

''You have little choice. Fair words are wonderful things, but only strength matters to conquerors. Mezpa is too powerful for you to invade and King Gasam has shown a marked disinclination to sit still. Unless he plans to set sail upon the trackless ocean in search of a new world, the only direction left to him is north.''

He was certainly being forthright, so she decided to be as blunt.

''You propose an alliance, a coordinated attack against King Hael. Very well, we will consider it. But a number of things must be understood: First, we have no way of knowing that your armies will perform as you hope they will against Hael's. I have seen your men work their firetubes and, frankly, I was not impressed. I know that Hael's tactics work very well indeed.''

''I believe that I can set at ease any fears you may have on that score. A demonstration can be arranged.''

She raised her cup again, this time to hide her elation. One of her prime objectives handed to her without effort! She set the cup down.

''Then I will be allowed to see your soldiers maneuver?''

Deathmoon smiled his chilly smile. ''Oh, we can do better than that. You have already witnessed a little naval skirmish. How would you like to see a land battle? Just a little one, of course.''

For one of the few times in her life, Larissa was caught with her mouth half-open, unable to think of what to say.

''But—but, with whom? Surely you won't set two of your regiments to fight one another for my benefit?''

''Oh, no, that would be wasteful. The Thezans have been most unreasonable lately. They have refused to cede land that rightfully belongs to Mezpa and they are in need of chastisement. Tomorrow, if it suits you, we shall sail to the mainland and meet one of their border garrisons, giving them a salutary lesson and you a demonstration at the same time. We Mezpans appreciate efficiency.''

She favored him with her most dazzling smile. "Lord Deathmoon, I like your style. This is going to be so much more entertaining than I had anticipated!''

"I am only too happy to be at your service. You mentioned that there were other points you wished to have clarified?''

"Yes. As you launch your offensive from your northwestern territories, you will be in favorable land—land for which you have an immediate use, is that not so?''

"It will take some time to make it productive in our fashion, but yes, it is valuable land to us.''

"And it is good land to campaign in? Plenty of grass for fodder? Game to feed the troops? Well watered?''

"Yes. Your point?''

She leaned forward, placing her elbows on the table. "To the north of our dominions is a great desert wasteland. To launch an attack in that direction means a long, long march through arid country, the trek all the more slow because we will have to carry water with us. We will arrive in the plains lands badly worn, even our finest warriors at less than their best fighting trim. This is not a campaign to be undertaken lightly.''

"I would think not. Is there some doubt that King Gasam would be eager to attack his old enemy?''

"Some. Because he would have to conduct a campaign that was far more difficult than yours, he will wish certain concessions from you.''

"Name them. We can always negotiate these things.'' Deathmoon nibbled delicately at a skewer of tender grilled sea-lizard meat.

"You have lands on the west bank of the great river. When we have finished our conquests of the southern lands, our lands will abut those territories. The Emperor Gasam is a great believer in natural barriers between nations; mountain ranges, deserts and rivers serve well in this role. We expect to be good friends to Mezpa, but we would feel better if the river lay between our kingdoms.''

''Natural barriers seem to slow King Gasam very little when he decides to annex territory. Which of our west-bank lands does he wish us to cede to him?''

''Only the southernmost, the one called Imisia.'' She saw that his aides, who had yet to speak, shifted uneasily. They did not like this. Larissa thought that all to the good.

''I must of course discuss this with the Assembly, but I think I will have no trouble persuading them that this is a wise course of action. We annexed Imisia only recently, and as yet we draw few revenues from that land. It would be merely a matter of our garrisons moving out and yours moving in. Yes, pending the decision of the Assembly, I think it can be done.''

''Then we are agreed,'' Larissa said. ''When do you propose to begin your offensive?''

''Next year, at the beginning of the dry season, at the time of the new moon.''

''Very appropriate,'' she said. ''In the islands, we called that the War Moon.''

''Then War Moon it shall be. Let us drink on it.''

Cups were filled all around and raised to toast the new alliance, one that would finally bring down King Hael.

That evening, Deathmoon and Larissa sat on folding chairs before her pavilion, alone except for slaves who plied fans endlessly. Around them at intervals were young Shasinn warriors, standing in the island fashion, one hand lightly holding the spear, the sole of one foot resting on the opposite knee.

''You came to this conference well prepared, Queen Larissa,'' Deathmoon said, fussing with the lace on the breast of his tight-fitting doublet.

''I try to be prepared. Surprises can be so unpleasant.''

''So they can. I noticed, for instance, that not once during our bargaining today did you bring up the subject of King Hael's steel mine, which is undoubtedly his most famous possession. At some time, when we have dealt with King Hael, the proceeds of that mine must be settled between us.''

"There was no need to bring it up," she said, watching him closely. "It is no longer Hael's. I located it and my husband's warriors took it. It has belonged to us for well over a year now."

His expression was dark and he appeared to be gnawing on the inside of his cheek. "So. The rumors were true. I congratulate you."

"Does this make you less eager to conquer Hael's land?" she inquired.

"No. But it should make you all the more eager to destroy him. He will cease all other efforts to get that mine back."

"And he will fail. I mentioned the great desert, did I not? The mine turned out to be near our northernmost holdings. He must take his army through that desert to reach the mine, which we have now turned into a fort. He will never get it back."

Seeing his black look, she patted his arm. "But do not despair. It produces far more steel than we can ever use. In recognition of our alliance, we will be happy to sell you all the steel you need at a rate far more favorable than we charge other nations."

"I thank you," he said, seeming somewhat mollified. "I must say, you are even more formidable than your reputation would have it. But then, you had that steel mine as your secret weapon. That, and the person who informed you of some of my plans."

"You made some such allusion in your letter," she said. "I confess I do not know who you are talking about."

He gave her an indulgent smile. "Come now, Queen Larissa, there is no need to be coy. All rulers employ spies, there is no shame in that."

"Shame? I've never felt it. And none of my spies has ever contacted you. They bring me intelligence of other lands and none has ever been able to find out much about yours."

"Oh, come now," he said, losing patience, "I might be willing to believe that, but the man was Shasinn!"

"Impossible," she retorted. "I *never* use Shasinn as spies, only mainland people. The Shasinn are pure warriors and nothing else. My husband and I will have it no other way!"

"Madame, I was not mistaken! The Shasinn physiognomy is most distinctive." He waved an arm toward the bodyguard. "The man I spoke to might have been the elder brother of these youths."

Now Larissa was not merely puzzled. She was utterly confused. "Just a moment. Tell me what happened. Start from the beginning." She had a feeling that this portended something awful.

"Very well, if you would have it so. Some two months ago, a man appeared in Crag, the capital. He posed as a dealer in objects of fine art and was able to carry it off rather well. He was a man of some education, well traveled. But his very distinctive features and coloration marked him as unmistakably Shasinn and there were odd inconsistencies in his account of himself. For some reason, he claimed to be over forty years old, even though he was quite clearly much younger. I had him arrested and questioned him. Gently, of course, for I knew him to be one of your spy corps and I desired friendly relations with you and King Gasam.

"Almost immediately, another spy was arrested—a mere boy, one of King Hael's plainsmen, a handsome youth but far too inexperienced for so dangerous a mission. He was seeking a man, and he described the Shasinn unmistakably. I brought the two together and the Shasinn said that the plainsman was there to assassinate him. This seemed plausible enough. That night, both escaped. From all the signs, the Shasinn went to the dungeon, eliminating the guards as they went, and they climbed down a makeshift rope to safety. Why the Shasinn did this I do not know. Perhaps to silence the boy, perhaps to bring him to you. Is this the story your spy told you?"

"I have no Shasinn spies," she said, an awful suspicion forming in her mind, "and I know no man such as you describe. I know you don't believe me, but humor me in this. Try to describe this man to me."

"Difficult," he said. "All you Shasinn look so much alike." He looked around at the bodyguard, studying each man, settling on one, pointing to him. "Summon that man here."

"Nasha," the queen said, "attend us."

The youth trotted over and stood before the two.

"His hair was unbound and quite long, about the same color as this youth's. His eyes were a lighter blue, his cheekbones a bit higher and wider. He looked about ten years older. He had a spear just like that one, taken apart and hidden, but my men found it. I had read descriptions of the Shasinn spears. . . . Are you well?"

Larissa was aware that she must look dreadful. "Any marks or scars?"

"Why, yes. I did not see them myself, but when we were making up descriptions of the fugitive to circulate among the police, the bath attendants were questioned. He had four parallel scars striping him from hip to knee. Very old scars, the woman said. There were others, but these were most distinctive. Why . . ."

He clapped his hands loudly. "Bring wine! The queen has fainted!"

Her eyes snapped open. "I am all right. Give me a moment." She tried to calm her breathing, then realized that she was biting on a knuckle. The blood ran down her chin. At last she had her self-possession back.

"Lord Deathmoon," she said, her voice cold enough to crack stone, "that man was Shasinn, but he was not one of my spies. He was an exile, the only Shasinn who does not acknowledge Gasam as his lord."

"But . . . I do not understand."

"That was Hael! You had King Hael in your hands and you let him get away!"

Deathmoon was dumbfounded. "I don't believe it!"

"In all the world there is no other Shasinn save myself whom you would describe as educated. We keep our tribesmen as warriors, nothing else. I know those scars, because I saw him get them. Hael fought a longneck that attacked our kagga at calving time. The longneck of the islands is a giant, five or six times larger than the mainland longneck. To us it is a taboo beast, full of magic. When he struck it with his spear it clawed his thigh. He almost lost the leg. It was he!''

"But he was not old enough to be King Hael. He was not more than ten years older than this youth!'' Deathmoon insisted.

Larissa sat back wearily. "Lord Deathmoon, how old do you think I am?''

"Well, it is scarcely polite to speculate, but . . .''

"How old?''

"I would estimate Your Majesty to be perhaps twenty-eight years old. Certainly no more than thirty.''

"If you had been trying to flatter me you would have said twenty-five, I suppose. My people do not count birthdays, but I know that I am well past my fortieth year. We Shasinn hold our age well.''

His look would have been comical had she been in a mood to be amused.

"But,'' he said, "who was that boy?''

"Some plainsman. Did he give a name?''

"He called himself Kairn.''

"Hael has a son of that name. I have met the elder brother, Ansa. He was looking for his father. He must have been as inexperienced as you say, to use his own name.''

"But, it makes no sense!'' Deathmoon protested.

"It doesn't have to, with Hael. We were raised together. Lord Deathmoon, you have to understand that Hael is insane. He talks to spirits. He has visions. It is just like him to leave his kingdom and go off on a mission alone.''

The look of mortification on his face gave her a bitter satisfaction, but her rage had abated, and she reminded herself that she had made some valuable progress here, and could not afford to let it go to waste out of spite. She laid a conciliatory hand on his arm. "How were you to know? You could not expect an anonymous king to show up on your doorstep. But what a shame. My husband would have ceded you half his empire to get his hands on Hael *and* his son.''

"Yes, and taken it back six weeks later, I've no doubt," Deathmoon said sourly. "And now Hael knows of my plans, of our alliance!"

"He'd have found out soon enough," she said. "He is mad, but not stupid, and he has his own spies. There is little that he can do about it."

"You are right," he said, seeming to shake off the black mood easily. "Our alliance stands as agreed, then, despite this regrettable incident?"

"Agreed." She rose from her chair. "And now I shall retire. I look forward to tomorrow. A little bloodletting should put us in a better mood." She gave him her hand and he kissed it. "Until tomorrow, then."

There were five troop transports, each carrying a hundred men and their mounted officers. The Shasinn sat on the deck of the lead transport and made jokes about the Mezpan soldiers.

"Do you think the Thezans will revoke my safe-conduct?" Larissa asked Deathmoon.

"You and your men will take no part in the action. The king of Thezas gave you safe-conduct and he will not violate it. The Thezans have an old-fashioned sense of honor." He said this with contempt.

That contempt came as no surprise to Larissa, who knew him to be as devoid of any sense of honor as Gasam. She, too, found such illusory scruples to be worthless.

"Will you be using the big firetubes?" she asked.

"They would be redundant for so small an action as this," he said evasively. She still did not know how many of the weapons he had, or how large they might get.

Two hours of rowing brought them to a small port similar to the one from which they had embarked for the island. There was great distress when the transports rowed in, and they saw a messenger flogging a cabo along the shore, apparently to spread the alarm.

"A pity your firetubes can't reach him," she commented.

"I'll wager one of Hael's archers could skewer him from here."

"But what would be the point?" he said. "We want them to know that we are here."

"Yes," she said, "but it would be amusing."

He gave her a doubting look, then turned to issue a series of orders. She watched as the men filed ashore in orderly fashion. They marched through the little town, while the appalled natives looked on in fear and wonderment, then out the other side. Larissa and her guard followed close behind. On the other side of the town there was an open field and on its grassy expanse the soldiers were forming up in their lines, trotting quickly into the places indicated by their officers. Larissa watched this odd spectacle with interest. Gasam's armies knew the value of battle lines and formations, and they had fought many enemies who employed formation tactics of one sort or another, but they had never encountered an enemy, even the Nevans, who drilled with such machinelike precision.

"If you wish," Deathmoon said, "our enemy seems to have provided us with an excellent platform from which to view the proceedings."

At the entrance to the little town was a rickety wooden tower perhaps forty feet tall. She guessed that a fire watch had been posted there in less troublesome times. She climbed the long ladder as easily as a man-of-the-trees, and waited at the top with some amusement as Deathmoon and his aides came puffing after her. The platform at the top had room for eight or more observers and was furnished with a thatched roof. She leaned on a rail and watched as the troops went through a drill to loosen them up for the combat to come.

"The men seem well prepared," Deathmoon commented.

"I will take your word for it, lord," said an aide, a fat man who had had a harder time of it than the others coming up the ladder.

Larissa wondered at this open declaration of ignorance of things warlike. Then she realized that none of them, neither Deathmoon nor his high-ranking aides, made the slightest pretense of military status. They wore neither uniforms, weapons nor armor, and were apparently going to leave the conduct of the battle to the officers on the field.

Once again, these Mezpans were unique in her experience. Even kings, who were never allowed to fight, would mount cabos and buckle on their armor to go out and ''lead'' their soldiers from a safe distance. High nobles derived their wealth from land, but attributed their legitimacy to their leadership in battle. She knew that it was seldom warranted, but the pretense was always made.

The Mezpans did not seem to esteem leadership in battle. They left it to professionals. The leadership was strictly civilian. She found this contemptible, but she suspected that it might have something to do with their success: They would not lose battles because the armies were led by well-born buffoons, noblemen who in reality were nothing but glorified landlords. Professional military men would prove themselves. Long ago, Gasam had decided that the Shasinn should be allowed no profession save that of warrior. These people had decided upon a similar system.

''How do you choose your officers?'' she asked.

''Most of them are from the landowning class,'' Deathmoon said, ''generally from among the younger sons who will not inherit land. We have established military schools for the education of officers and anyone may apply for admission to them. If the applicants are able to pass certain tests, they are enrolled. If they perform adequately in their schooling, they graduate to become junior officers in the active service. After that, promotion comes entirely as a result of their performance, both in war and in peace.''

It was what she might expect from these dull, methodical people, but she could appreciate the efficiency of such a system. If there was little warrior spirit among them, at least military competence could be sought out and put to work.

Within an hour, the Thezan army made an appearance. The shielded and armored warriors began to mass upon a ridgeline a half-mile from the Mezpans.

''Ah,'' Deathmoon said, ''right on time.''

A deep, rolling battle chant began to reach them from the ridgeline as more and more warriors joined those that were already visible. Just ahead of the tower, the Mezpan soldiers stood alertly, apparently not at all disturbed that the Thezan forces already outnumbered them at least three to one. Larissa was seldom nervous, but she glanced down at the reassuring sight of her bodyguard clustered around the base of the tower, their bronze-colored, plaited manes close together as they spoke in low voices. She knew they thought this was shaping up to be a slaughter, that the Mezpans had miscalculated. But their presence reassured her. If things went bad, they would get her back to the ship and fight a rearguard action to see her safely away.

Officers shouted orders, drums were beaten and there was a collective rattle as the soldiers held their firetubes high, slanting across their chests. At a trumpet snarl, the first line put the butts of their weapons to their shoulders and held them there, sighting along the smooth, white tubes.

The Thezan chant changed, taking on a new rhythm as the front line stepped off and began to come down the ridge. A few paces behind them came another line, then another and another. *This* was an army, as Larissa understood such things. Its formation was definite but not rigid, the men snarling and grimacing as they readied themselves for the terrible shock of battle, each man depending upon his own strength and courage and skill with his weapons, knowing that he had reliable comrades with him.

"They are six times your number," she said to Death-moon. "You have miscalculated. You had better order a retreat while you can still get to your ships."

Deathmoon smiled his superior smile. "No, not at all. It was this that we wished you to see. Just watch, and have no anxiety. You are perfectly safe."

"I have no fear for myself!" she snapped.

"Of course not," he said. "Ah. We begin."

A Mezpan officer shouted something and a faint, collective click ran along the Mezpan front rank. The men had drawn back the bronze strikers of their firetubes. Another word was shouted, apparently some sort of preparatory order. The Thezans were within a hundred paces now, and about to break into a run. There was a third shout and before the word was finished the front line erupted in flame and smoke. Above the smoke she could see that a few Thezans had fallen, but not many, and the lines continued to advance.

Another crash surprised her and she saw that the front rank was kneeling and the second had fired over their heads. Even as she looked, the second rank knelt. The third rank fired and by this time it was difficult to see anything through the smoke, save that the kneeling men were busy with flasks and sticks, recharging their weapons.

The Thezan ranks began to waver with the third volley. A good many bodies now lay upon the ground and the ranks were losing their cohesiveness. The abortive run petered out and even the march slowed to a plod as the men realized that neither shield nor armor could keep out the pellets from the firetubes.

The fire from the Mezpan lines was constant. Each volley inflicted more casualties as the lines drew closer. Larissa noticed an odd thing: The Thezans chanted and shook their shields, they sprang forward by ones and twos, but not concertedly, and they reeled back from each volley even though most of them *were not struck*.

"If they would just change resolutely," she said, "they would close with your men and slaughter them."

"But they never do," said Deathmoon. "There is something in the situation that prevents men from carrying out the logical action."

"Then why do they not run?" she asked. "Why just stand there and be killed?"

For by this time the Thezans had ground to a halt no more than thirty paces from the Mezpans, still chanting and waving their weapons, still a number of them falling each time the firetubes crashed. It looked to her like a waste of fine warriors.

Deathmoon shrugged. "That would be cowardice, and you can see that they are not cowards. I suppose you would have to be down there, standing in their ranks, to understand why they behave in this fashion, but warrior people behave that way when being fired upon. *All* warrior people.'' His cold look told her that his message had now been delivered. This was a demonstration all right, but it was not just to prove what a valuable ally he would be in a war against Hael.

''I take your meaning perfectly,'' she said.

''Just so we understand one another.''

Grim-faced, she turned back to the scene of pointless slaughter. Now, at last, the Thezans had lost heart and were running. This was a warning for her to take back to Gasam. This, Deathmoon was saying, was what would happen to the islanders should they ever march against Mezpa.

SEVENTEEN

Kairn rode his cabo, guiding it with his knees alone. In his left hand he held his bow. The other hand reached down for what seemed the hundredth time that day and plucked an arrow from his quiver. He laid the arrow to the string and drew the powerful bow, its multiple layers of wood, horn and sinew creaking as it flexed. He released the string and the arrow arched upward to join a thousand others dropping in like rain upon the miserable infantry, huddled beneath their thin shields. The enemy army was huge, but it had been unable to strike a single blow against the riders since the battle had begun early that morning. Kairn looked up and could not believe that the sun had not yet reached zenith. Surely it should be setting by now.

He heard the bawl of a kagga horn and his hand stopped in reaching for another arrow. There was a flash of white from among the enemy and the hundred-leaders were calling for a cessation of fire. The men halted their animals as a little group of officers, including a Nevan fluent in a number of southern dialects, rode to parley with the enemy. After a few minutes the enemy standards were thrown to the ground, quickly followed by the black shields and all weapons.

Kairn breathed deeply and realized how tired he was. His thighs trembled from the stress of riding for hours with his legs alone. His arms, shoulders and back ached fiercely from repeatedly drawing the powerful bow. He turned his cabo and trotted to where his hundred were massing around their banner. All over the field, the scattered units were doing the same. His hundred-commander rode up, a hard-faced Amsi underchief.

"Half an hour to remount and refill your quivers with arrows," he said. "Then we ride."

"Ride?" said Kairn. "When do we rest?"

The chief glared at him. "We rest when the war is over," he said without humor.

Wearily, Kairn rode to the remount herd and transferred his saddle and gear to another of his cabos. The animals were a bit restive but were quickly growing used to the smell of man-blood. Remounted, he joined the others who rode about the field, leaning from their saddles to pull up handfuls of arrows as if they were plucking grass. He separated the damaged ones to give to the fletchers later, thrusting the sound ones into his quiver. These would not be as accurate as arrows made for his own bow and for his own arm or eye, but they would be adequate for war, which was seldom a target-shoot. He kept ten of his best arrows in a small quiver behind his saddle, in case he should have need to aim at a single, distant target. All the most experienced warriors held a reserve of good arrows for this purpose, and he had decided it was a good idea. One of Hael's strict orders was that they should conserve their shafts, which took skilled labor and special materials. They were not to dip into the reserve supply until the original issue fell too low. The reserve was carried in the rear, on the backs of pack humpers of a special, long-legged breed that could keep up with the mounted armies. Hael left little to chance.

As Kairn rode to rejoin his standard, Ansa rode up beside him. The two had been placed in the same hundred, which was part of Hael's personal regiment, a double-strength unit made up of the best warriors from all his subject tribes.

"How do you like war so far, little brother?" Ansa asked.

"Exciting, exhausting, but little glory so far," he answered. "There was more of it in fighting the bandits. These people are not fighting us."

"We are not allowing them to fight us," his brother corrected. "Why should we? This is not a duel of honor, but a war. The more men they lose and the fewer we lose, the better. But cheer up, little brother, I have it from Father himself that things will get much worse for us before long. This is just the warm-up. The real fighting starts when we meet the islanders."

They joined the group around the banner. The younger men were whooping over their cheap victory. Warriors of more experience were saving their energy for the grueling ride ahead.

"What I don't understand," Kairn said as they prepared to ride, "is why they fight at all. Surely they can't love Gasam!"

"They fight because they are soldiers, and fighting is what they do," Ansa answered. "Besides, to them we are just more conquerors. How do they know we aren't even worse than the islanders?"

"Did we lose any?" Kairn asked his ten-leader.

"None from our ten," the Matwa said. "There were three accidents in other tens from falling cabos. None dead."

"I hope the rest of it is like this," Ansa said, grinning. "But I know it won't be."

They set off at a fast trot. The regiments massed into their divisions, then the divisions split from one another according to the prearranged plan. Theirs was the central corps, plowing straight through the heart of what had once been the proud and independent kingdom of Chiwa, now a slave-province of Gasam's empire. Kairn's hundred was with the division that took the northern loop of each pincers movement. He braced himself for another long, hard ride.

It was the third day of the campaign. On the first day, they had charged screaming through the border, pushing aside the flimsy defense of the border guard. Since Gasam cared only for aggression, he had never thought to strongly fortify his border. That had been an exhilarating ride, the heady excitement of charging with warlike intent through an enemy nation. Soon he had learned how tiring it was going to be. For the first two days it was hard riding to keep up with Hael's schedule. There was little fighting and they had ridden around the forts, which were to be left to the following infantry and engineers.

At night there had been a few hours to snatch exhausted sleep on the hard ground, the reins of a cabo in one hand. There had been little chance for loot so far, but Kairn already had a small pouch full of the steel arrowheads, taken from surrendered archers. The arrows themselves were useless, for the powerful plains bows would snap their weak shafts.

That morning they had reached the first of the great field camps, an earthen enclosure where thousands of Gasam's slave-soldiers were housed under sheds and tents. The division had massed on the heights and lured out the field army, then had ridden around it in a great circle, cutting it off from the camp, where they might at least have made some use of the earthen rampart. After that, it had been execution until surrender.

Now they would ride in their wide pincers to the next great field camp, encircling and cutting off any forces in between, leaving them stranded between the mounted force and the infantry. Kairn set his jaw and leaned into the wind. There was no sense moaning over his fatigue. The war had just begun.

Hael was well pleased with the progress of the war thus far. The assault had been swift and devastating, the coordination between the mounted corps and divisions faultless. The royal messengers rode swiftly between the forces, bearing news of victories, unexpected obstacles and military camps that were more heavily manned than expected, or less so.

He trusted that the infantry and heavy equipment trains behind him were moving as smoothly, albeit by necessity more slowly. He had little fear of anything other than that, though. It was the sort of campaigning at which the Nevans excelled above all other nations, and Queen Shazad had forged her military machine to the highest degree of loyalty and efficiency. And they hated and feared Gasam.

Each night, he rode among his men as they snatched what rest they could in their hasty camps. Although he did not want to make it obvious, he also wanted to reassure himself that his sons were well. It would have been dishonorable to display any excessive concern or favoritism, but he was only human. They were both young warriors on their first campaign, and it would have been out of the question for him to name them to commands even though he was certain that they were capable of carrying out the duties and possessed the qualities of leadership. They would ride as ordinary warriors until they should distinguish themselves.

Chiwa would be a relatively easy campaign in terms of combat and casualties, although it would be exhausting due to its breakneck speed. This he had anticipated. It would serve to weld his huge, disparate army into a cohesive fighting force with full coordination between all arms. The demanding pace would toughen them and get them ready for the next stages, which would be far deadlier. All of the inexperienced warriors would have been blooded and somewhat inured to the shock of battle.

It would be a tough, hardened, professional army that would pour through the passes into Sono. It would be a matchless war machine that would face Gasam somewhere on the eastern coast.

"My king," said the Ramdi guard who stood outside the tiny tent that was the only shelter Hael would allow himself during the campaign. "A messenger comes."

Hael roused himself. He had slept perhaps two hours, from the angle of the stars. The messenger led his cabo up to the tent and held out his message-tube. A number of Hael's officers gathered around to learn what this might portend.

"Where did you ride from?" Hael asked, taking the tube.

"From Puko. Admiral Saan sends you this."

"Puko!" It was the easternmost of the Chiwan ports. He tore the tube open and read the scroll, his smile widening as he read.

"Admiral Saan reports that all the Chiwan ports are now secured. Not just blockaded, but surrendered! Not a single craft has escaped to carry word of the attack. The naval phase of the Chiwan campaign has been completed nine days ahead of schedule!"

His men cheered themselves hoarse. They knew that his greatest fear had been that a ship would escape to bear the news of Hael's coming to Gasam. With sufficient time to prepare, the terrible conqueror might be able to assemble an adequate defense. So far, so good.

In the subsequent days they rode, fought, rode and fought, until they fell into a rhythm of movement and battle so seemingly inevitable that it became natural to them. The weariness and exhaustion of the first days fell away and the effects of hard riding and swift fighting became a sort of numbness that struck each night as they tumbled from their saddles to roll up in their blankets. Each morning they awoke with their energies restored.

An exhilaration gripped the entire army, like that of the opening day of the campaign, but this was deeper, rooted in their mission, their amazing performance and their confidence in their leader. They were doing something never attempted before: a campaign to sweep across half a world and smash the greatest conqueror ever known. And now they knew themselves to be invincible. Much of their confidence derived from Hael, a man audacious enough to conceive of such a plan, and visionary and charismatic enough to convince the Nevans to take part even in a subordinate role. Who could hope to defeat a king who was in touch with the spirits of earth, sky and water?

Hael reined in at the top of the mountain pass. His officers gathered round him and his sons rode up as well.

"Twenty-eight days!" the king shouted amid ferocious cheering. The lightning campaign to take Chiwa had gone even more quickly than he had hoped. Casualties remained low and he knew that he now had a real army. Not an element of it would hesitate to obey his orders instantly.

"It is early yet, my king," said a division commander. "Shall we ride on into Sono today?"

"No, not until I know that the other corps have taken the other two passes. We will descend on Sono all at once. Let's see what the flying force has rounded up."

In a meadow on the Chiwan side of the pass, they found a compound where perhaps a hundred men and women sat under guard. Their eyes had widened at the advent of the ferocious mounted force, but otherwise they seemed calm enough. Hael had issued strict orders that none were to be mistreated and that they were to be reassured that they were held only temporarily.

An Amsi officer came up and saluted. "They've given us no trouble, my king. We don't understand their talk very well, but we made ourselves understood. But two tried to escape the first night. We have them apart from the others."

"I want to question them," Hael said. "Take me to them." He followed the Amsi to a tree under which sat two men, their hands and feet bound, guarded by two young warriors with drawn swords. Hael's sons and officers stood behind him as he studied the two. They wore long, striped robes and small turbans. The pierced ears of both were decorated with numerous studs and pendants.

"Are you King Hael?" said one. "This is a mistake, Your Majesty. We are but humble spice merchants. We are not your enemies!"

"You tried to escape. Why?" Hael's voice was level and cold.

"Why? What man of spirit does not try to escape from capture? What reason had we to believe that these men would not kill us, or hold us for ransom? For all we knew they were but ordinary bandits claiming to be your men!''

"That sounds reasonable," Hael said. He turned to the chief of the flying force. "Which way were they headed when you got them?"

"Toward Sono, fast as their humpers would carry them, and not a man of us in sight."

"We heard rumors that there was war in the land. We feared that it was an uprising against King Gasam and we thought it would be a good idea to be elsewhere."

"We've been riding ahead of rumors," Hael said. "I'll wager you rode all the way from the Nevan border, buying or stealing new mounts as you rode each to death."

"You are mistaken, Majesty," said the other merchant, sweat running from beneath his turban.

The Matwa war leader named Jochim pushed forward and leaned down, studying each sweaty face in turn. "I know these two," he said. "They were at the dry season fair two years ago and they weren't spice merchants then; they were steel buyers."

"Since when do the merchant guilds allow men to change their status?" Hael demanded.

"This man is mistaken," said the first merchant.

"No, he is not. You are Larissa's spies, I've seen your breed before."

A guard thumbed the edge of his sword. "Shall I kill them, my king?"

"No," Hael said. "They have served their mistress loyally and well. I have a weakness for men who are daring and courageous."

"My king, I protest!" said Jochim. "These are not warriors, but base vermin who serve for pay! Kill them!"

There were many sounds of agreement.

"No, we have killed only soldiers in open battle so far. Let's keep it that way." He turned to the guard who had spoken. "Find a cinch-ring and heat it in the fire. Brand a circle on the left cheek of each of them." Now he turned back to the two spies. "I give you your lives. But if you ever show your faces in my lands, the first warrior who sees that mark will kill you on sight.''

''That's more like it,'' Jochim said as he left with Hael. ''For a minute there I thought you'd gone soft.''

In their camp, Hael sat late into the night with his sons, awaiting the messengers from the other corps. By midnight, both had reported their passes secured. Hael sent back word that there would be two days of rest. Before dawn of the third day, they would descend upon Sono.

''Nothing can beat us now,'' Ansa said as the three sat beside a watch fire.

''Never think that,'' Hale said. ''There is always something, and a leader must never forget it. The men are in fine spirits now, after many easy victories. They will not lose heart at a small reverse, but a big defeat could ruin it all. That was the Nevan strength, back when Shazad's father was king. They did not lose heart even after Gasam gave them a number of terrible defeats. With our help, they finally drove him out.'' He stared into the flickering pictures in the flames. ''That is because they are an ancient nation with a long tradition of victory. They never doubted that victory would eventually be theirs.

''But we are a very young kingdom, no older than you two boys, and this is our first truly great war. I cannot afford a major reverse.''

The next day they rested, the men mostly sleeping the entire day and night while the great herd of cabos grazed contentedly. Once in a while a traveler or a small group would come up from Sono, to be taken in custody and then held with the rest. Hael questioned them first. On the other side of the border there had been as yet no inkling of events in Chiwa and there was no mistaking their genuine surprise at their first sight of the great army massed in the pass.

The day after, men occupied themselves putting all their gear in order, finding that the hard campaigning had taken a toll of equipment that in ordinary times could last for years with minimal attention. Nicks were whetted out of swords and spearheads, arrow points were sharpened, worn cinches and girths were repaired or replaced, small wounds on cabos were doctored. By nightfall the men were actually looking forward to the next day's ride.

Two hours before sunup, they mounted and began to descend the pass. This was done at a walking pace, for a slope that was both steep and dark could be a deathtrap. Hael knew that Sono lay on a plateau higher than Chiwa, and the eastern slope would be far shorter than the western. By the time the sun heaved over the far horizon, they were off the mountain and on the broad, fertile plain.

The horns blew and, with a whoop, they set out at a gallop. Once again, stupefied customs officials stared at them as they rode past, ignoring all civilized amenities. The flying force broke away from the main body. They would remain miles in advance of the main force, avoiding contact with the enemy, and would ride nonstop all the way to the river. There they were to turn south and seize all bridges or ferries they could find, to prevent word reaching the eastern bank. The second phase of the great campaign had begun.

This army was different. The linkup with the northernmost corps had gone exactly as planned, with the northern corps sweeping down, pinning the small occupation army of that district between it and Hael's corps. The fighting had been brief, the surrender swift. The two corps had then combined to ride south and join with the third. But they found between them an army partially made up of islanders, partially of Gasam's more reliable subject troops. Apparently this district had not been entirely pacified, and Gasam had left this strong force behind to put down insurgencies. There were no Shasinn among them, but some of the other islanders were nearly as good: brave, skillful warriors and utterly loyal to Gasam. Their leaders knew better than to huddle in an open field so that the cabo-archers could riddle them at leisure, and the entire army retreated into a heavily wooded area that sprawled across the main road and extended to the River Pata.

"Can't we ride around them?" asked Ansa. "Leave them for the infantry?"

"No," Hael said. "An army like this in our rear is a dagger at our backs. I know these people. They'll come after us. We could stay ahead of them, but if we're held up by something else, say another army like this one, they could hit us from behind at the worst moment. We have to go in after them and destroy them utterly. They won't surrender."

Jochim spat on the ground. "How do we go about it?"

"I hate to split up into small units, but it's the only way. Each regimental commander will detail half his hundreds to go in, the other half to remain in reserve in case they attempt a breakout."

"Wouldn't it be simpler to send in half the regiments?" asked an Amsi chief.

"This way all the regiments will suffer equally," Hael said grimly. "It will be hard fighting in there, much of it hand-to-hand. We won't have it easy this time."

Kairn's heart thudded as he took his place with his squad. His hundred was one of those chosen to go into the woods. It would be a new sort of fighting for them, no long-distance archery. It would be better done by infantry, but no plains warrior would ever fight dismounted unless forced to. They loosened their swords and readied their seldom-used shields of hardened hide.

The long lines of riders extended along the treeline as far as the eye could see. They were ranked three lines deep, to keep the enemy from breaking through easily. Kairn was in the first line. The horns blew along the front, and the first line entered the forest at a walk. After they had proceeded fifty paces, the second went in, then the third. Tensely, the reserve force waited.

Arrow poised on string, Kairn looked up and down the slowly moving line, trying to spot Ansa. They were in different squads. Then he forced himself to keep his attention ahead of him. Let Ansa look after himself. The enemy was in front. All was silent in the forest, even the little creatures huddling quietly at this unwonted invasion. He heard the snapping of twigs and the rustling of leaves between hoofs, the gentle snorting and groaning of the cabos. He could see nothing ahead of him but trees and bushes.

Then the air split with high-pitched shrieking and the forest was alive with wild men. Twenty feet ahead of him, a bald man with a great purple star painted across his face stood behind a bush, his arm drawn back to hurl a javelin. Kairn was not really aware of aiming, drawing and loosing, but before the man's arm completed half its arc Kairn's arrow struck his chest. At such close range, it passed on through and shattered against a tree behind the man.

They were everywhere, leaping up, hurling missiles, thrusting with spears, snatching at bridles. Kairn shot at two more but was unaware whether he had struck any, so many arrows were flying everywhere among the javelins, throwing sticks and flung stones. There were screams of fury and of pain, and the bawling of wounded cabos.

The enemy surged forward in loose battle lines, only their tall black shields giving them uniformity. In this forest there was no scope for the complex formation maneuvers that Gasam had used to such great success. Here it was strength, skill and ferocity, with the emphasis on the latter.

After the third shot, Kairn jammed his bow into its case and snatched up his spear, swinging his shield around from his back by its shoulder strap. A black-haired man came for him with a spear as he scrambled to secure the hand-grip of his shield. He got the shield around just in time to block the enemy's spear-point, simultaneously sending his own into the man's lower belly. Screaming, the man fell off the point. It was a nasty wound, and the man would take hours to die if someone didn't finish him off. Just then, Kairn was not in a merciful mood. He had his hands full just staying alive.

An island warrior ran across his front to attack a hard-pressed comrade on Kairn's right. Kairn leaned forward and ran the man through the back. This was neither the time nor the place for niceties. Another came at him, screaming. Kairn thrust his spear through the man's chest just as the other's hurled axe crashed into his shield. It bounced away, but the spear-point hung up in the man's ribs and the weapon was dragged from his grasp. Releasing it, Kairn drew his long-sword.

Now the second line had caught up. They plugged the holes left by fallen men and reinforced the battleline. An enemy tried to grasp Kairn's reins and Kairn slashed the man's hand off. It remained where it had been, gripping the bridle. With their line strengthened, the plainsmen began pushing forward, using the bulk of their mounts to shove the enemy back, darting their lances over the wall of shields, hacking with longswords. The islanders and others snarled, screamed and died. Some climbed trees to leap upon the riders from above.

The crowd of horses became so close that the riders got in each other's way. Kairn decided that he had occupied the front long enough and someone else could have his place for a while. Carefully, he backed his cabo to the rear and paused, gasping for breath. The fighting front was no more than twenty feet from him, but by comparison this seemed like a calm place.

Abruptly, something dropped upon him, screaming and snarling. It had foul breath and enough weight to tumble him from his saddle. A knife lanced over his shoulder, but its tip caught the edge of his shield and it just missed his neck. He struck backward with his elbows and his sword pommel, but weakly. The fall had knocked the wind from him and his vision was wavering.

Then the weight was lifted from him. Kairn sprawled to see a rider holding the brown island man upright, one forearm hooked under the shaven chin while the other hand drew a knife across the exposed throat. Ansa dropped the kicking, dying man, leaned from the saddle, and hauled Kairn to his feet.

"You need to be careful, little brother," Ansa said, grinning.

Kairn found that he could breathe again. "I was doing pretty well until that one dropped from the clouds."

"I know. I saw you. Don't try to kill their whole army all

by yourself." Ansa rode a few yards and came back leading Kairn's cabo. Kairn found a dropped lance and sheathed his sword. With the lance in his hand, he remounted.

"That's enough resting," Ansa said. "Let's get back into the fight."

The skirmishing in lines went on for a long time, the enemy grimly tenacious, falling back a step at a time, making the riders pay for every yard they gained. Impatient, groups of riders would band together to hurl their combined weight against the lines of black shields. At first, these abortive charges were repulsed bloodily, but in time they began to break through, cutting the enemy into ever-smaller clumps.

They chased these clumps of spear-waving men through the woods for a while, the enemy retreating and then turning at bay to lash out viciously, inflicting wounds and death. Sometimes a few would hide, lie low until the riders had passed, then stand to hurl spears into the backs of a few riders before they were inevitably cut down themselves.

In time, though, even the ferocious islanders had had enough. In ones and twos, then by clumps and units, they dropped their black shields, turned and ran. As always in battle, when one force lost its cohesiveness and panic took over, the true slaughter began. The riders pursued, loosing arrows, plunging lances into undefended backs, slashing down at faceless heads with sword and axe and club.

Kairn was among the pursuing horde, shooting his arrows into the fleeing men as coldly and unemotionally as the others. There was no thought of mercy. The fight had been too long and hard, too many had died, too many had been maimed. This was war to the death and it would be folly to leave fighting men such as these alive to fight another day.

Kairn heard splashing ahead of them. Then they were out of the trees and on the sloping bank of the river. The water was full of bobbing heads and thrashing limbs. On the bank, weary men sat in their saddles, methodically shooting arrow after arrow into the panic-stricken, floundering warriors. On the other bank, more riders, the force Hael had sent across to sweep the eastern side, were doing the same. Kairn raised his bow, but hesitated.

"Them today, or us tomorrow, little brother," Ansa said. His brother beside him, even as he spoke, Ansa loosed an arrow. Kairn raised his own weapon and did likewise. They kept it up until the water was red and there was no motion save that of the river and the scavengers swimming to the feast.

When Hael saw the two grim-faced warriors he did not at first recognize them as his sons. They seemed to have aged ten years.

"Well, my sons," Hael said softly. "Now you know what real battle is like."

"Father," Ansa said, dismounting stiffly, "if this was an occupation force he left behind, what is it going to be like when we meet Gasam and his main force?"

"That," Hael said, "is when the true fighting will begin."

EIGHTEEN

The moment he saw Larissa ride into his camp, Gasam knew that her mission had not been a good one. He left the shelter of his awning and descended the log dais his soldiers had erected for him. They thought it incorrect that their king should live upon the same level as other men, so when their travels took them to flat country like this coastal plain, they would erect an artificial platform so that he could survey his army and all could see the god-king in their midst.

"Easy, little queen," he said, reaching up to take her by the waist. "Even if it is bad, we must show the people how happy we are." He said this through broadly grinning teeth.

She smiled radiantly. "I'll do my best." His huge hands almost met around her tiny waist and he lifted her from the saddle as if she were a three-year-old child.

Waving to the cheering soldiery, they ascended the dais between a double file of the fighting women. Larissa's guard ranged themselves around the dais and stood leaning on their spears, stern and impassive. She had forbidden them to speak a word of what they had seen on her mission to Deathmoon.

"Eat," Gasam said, "refresh yourself, recover from your ride. Then tell me what happened." Slaves brought food and wine, and as she drank the queen lay belly-down on a couch while one of her women, an expert masseuse, worked the knots and kinks from her muscles. She paid special attention to the queen's thighs, buttocks and lower back, always the places that suffered most on a long ride.

"Leave us," the queen said at last. The masseuse tucked a sheet around the queen, for the sun was down and a cool wind came off the nearby ocean. The other servants bowed their way out as well.

"So you did not see what you went to see?" Gasam asked.

"I saw everything I wanted to see, far too well," she responded.

"I fail to understand." He refilled her cup, disturbed at this odd state. Larissa was no more inclined than he to moods of melancholy.

"I'll start at the beginning." She told him of her trip to the island.

He frowned when she described the attack of the pirate vessels. "I would never have permitted you to go had I thought you would be exposed to such danger. How terrible if harm had come to you from my own pirates."

"There was never any real danger. My guards protected me and the pirates would have recognized me. But, in the event, they never got that close. This was my first demonstration of the firetubes in action." She described how the brief battle had transpired, and he frowned, then frowned all the harder when she described the effect of the big firetube.

"This is intriguing," he said. "It could force us to change the way we do things at sea."

"Not just at sea," she said. "But I get ahead of myself." She described the welcoming committee, and how her talks went with Deathmoon and his aides.

"What odd people," Gasam said. "Great leaders, yet not soldiers. They don't sound very formidable."

"So it seemed to me, at first." She went on to explain Deathmoon's proposed alliance, and of her conditional agreement.

"It seems a reasonable plan," he said. "And you acted wisely. Having him concede that territory as a condition of the alliance will be a great convenience."

"Wait until I tell you what he did. You will not believe this." She told him of Deathmoon's misadventure with Hael and Kairn. As he heard the story, Gasam's eyes at first widened with disbelief, then flashed with rage, but by the end he laughed so hard that the tears streamed from them.

"What a story! Oh, if he could just have held those two! But, then, I want to kill them myself, in my own way, and it will be much better to capture them myself than to stoop to buying them from this . . . this merchant-king."

"That is how I saw it, once I was over the shock of his blunder. Well, now you have heard the amusing part. Let me tell you the rest. I told him that I would like to see a demonstration of his soldiers' prowess, so that I could report to you that the Mezpans are worthy allies."

"And did he comply?"

"He did more than that. We went on an expedition to the coast of Thezas and his troops fought a battle with the Thezans for my benefit."

"A battle! What an excellent gesture. I would not have expected it from such kagga-spirited creatures."

"It was more than a gesture," she said. "It was a warning. I will try to describe what I saw." She launched into the tale of the one-sided fight at the little coastal town. She was an observant and intelligent woman who had witnessed many, many battles, and Gasam knew that he could not have had a better or more accurate account without being there himself.

When she finished, they were both silent for a long time. It was fully dark outside, but they did not call for candles or torches. They had been raised without such amenities, and in any case in this climate lights would just bring the insects swarming.

"This will bear some thinking," he said at last. "You remember the battle I witnessed in Neva, when Hael's riders annihilated my worthless Omian allies?"

"I remember," she said, a little sleepily.

"It was like that—entirely one-sided. Foot soldiers hit by missiles with no chance to come to close quarters and strike back. The difference here is mobility. Hael's archers simply kept out of range, shooting from a distance and keeping in constant motion.

"These Mezpan soldiers stand in one place but they have organized their fire to such an extent that it remains constant. And they can keep it up for a long time because such weapons do not tire a man like drawing a heavy bow."

"That is how it seemed to me. Can you best such weapons and such tactics?"

"I think so. Those Thezans fought, or tried to fight, bravely but foolishly. I think what is needed is more mobile tactics, using smaller, independent units hitting from many sides at once, and carefully chosen ground that allows us to get close. My warriors are the greatest hand-to-hand fighters in all the world, and it would be foolish to waste them against weapons that kill before they can get close enough to strike a blow."

He sighed. "But in time I will probably have to adopt those foul, smoking weapons too. From what you say, they are far more formidable than I had ever dreamed."

"That would be a shame," she said. "They are machines that kill invisibly. There is no flash of the spear, no gush of the bright blood, no triumphant warrior standing over the fallen foe. Just those faceless soldiers standing in their lines."

"I will devise a way to deal with them. It is not urgent. Deathmoon will not march to attack Hael until next year."

"Then you will accept his alliance?"

"I will accept," he affirmed. "Why do you seem troubled?"

"I am not certain. It seems like a sound plan, to crush Hael between our two nations."

"But?" he urged.

"It is just that, never before have you gone by someone else's plan for battle and conquest. Always you have acted on your own will according to your own plans for your own interests."

"And what makes you think I will change now, little queen?"

"I don't understand," she said.

"I said that I would accept the proposed alliance. I did not say that I would abide by his plans. Under no circumstances am I going to take my splendid army across that wretched desert to fight Hael on Deathmoon's behalf. He is certain to put off his own attack by a month or more, allowing me to draw off the bulk of Hael's army while he marches in unopposed. He would then finish off whatever was left of Hael's men and take few losses himself."

"That makes sense," she said. "What will you do?"

"I will give him a great many fair words and in time I will march west with my army, supposedly to turn north and march across the desert. But what I will actually do is march a few days inland from here and wait. When your spies report that the Mezpan army has marched north against Hael, I will give them plenty of time to reach the plains, then I shall march back here and invade Mezpa!" Even in the dimness, she saw the white flash of his teeth.

"Oh, my love! I knew you would think of something. If we move fast enough, we can seize the towns where the fire-weapons are made as well."

"Absolutely. Your spies must stay very busy for the next few months. I must know where those places are, where the crucial Mezpan forts are and so forth. In the meantime, I will have my engineers and infantry assemble in the Chiwan and Sonoan ports where they can be brought here by sea. It would arouse suspicion to bring them here too soon."

"And when word reaches Deathmoon and he marches back?"

"By then I will have his ports, his cities, his fortified places. I should have plenty of Mezpan renegades to ply the firetubes for us, and I will own his supply lines. These civilized armies are very dependent on their supply lines.''

Her mind began to work quickly, as it always did when presented with challenges like this. "The firetubes use that grayish powder. The big ones must consume a great deal of it. I'll have my spies find out if it is all made at a single location. If that is the case, we could send a special force to seize it immediately and cut off all the Mezpan forces from resupply.''

"Excellent idea," he said. "If there is such a place, and if it is too difficult for us to reach in the opening stage of my conquest, perhaps your spies can undertake a bit of sabotage. A few fires could destroy their storehouses of the powder.''

"I will make that their first order of business. Mezpa is not an easy land to get around in. They have no itinerant priests or wandering entertainers. They care only for business. But my spies are resourceful. Mezpa has a tremendous internal slave trade, because of their plantations and manufactories. Slave-trader would probably be the best cover.''

"Keep thinking that way, little queen," Gasam said, stifling a yawn. "And now, let us retire. These Mezpans will not stop me from becoming the emperor of the world. They will just make the task a little more interesting.''

Larissa felt much better the next morning. Gasam had decided upon a course of action, and when it came to dealing with his enemies, her husband was infallible and invincible. And the whole world was his enemy.

She called for her women to come bathe her, and after that they helped her dress, which in Larissa's case consisted primarily of selecting her jewelry for the day. A bowl of kagga milk and some fruit served for breakfast. Like all the Shasinn, she was abstemious with food if with nothing else.

As she left the royal tent she saw one of her intelligence chiefs, a Nevan renegade who had served her well for years. She beckoned to him and he hurried to her side, bowing deeply.

"How may I serve Your Majesty?" he asked.

"Several ways, and as always, with information. How go operations here?"

"The king is victorious as always. His armies now are mopping up the last resistance from Basca. These operations are being carried out by his subordinate commanders while the king himself prepares his main forces for the impending campaign against Thezas."

As they spoke they walked, the queen setting a brisk pace. "And the siege of the Sonoan capital?"

"It seems to be going as always, and will perhaps for some time longer."

" 'Seems to be'?" she said.

"Well, we've had almost no contact from the west for several weeks."

She stopped to watch a large group of Shasinn going through a complex and dangerous spear-dance, accompanied by ancient chants.

"That seems odd," she said.

He shrugged. "It is most likely a matter of weather. If there have been great storms to the west, the mountain passes may be little more than mud and the rivers may be swollen over their banks. So much of these southern lands is low, swampy country. It can be difficult to traverse in the best of times."

"I suppose you are right." She continued walking. Everywhere she went, people ceased their activities and made obeisance.

"I suppose this means that there is no report from my agents sent to the Canyon?" The Canyoners had politely received Gasam's envoy months before, listened to his demands, replied that they acknowledged no sovereign and sent him back with presents. Since then she had continued to send her spies but with no results. It was most frustrating.

"Majesty, none of your agents have reported in from *anywhere* to the west of here."

She stopped and turned to face him. "Not even by ship?"

"No ships have arrived from the west in several weeks as well. That is not to be wondered at. If bad weather leaves the land impassable, the storms could extend well out to sea. No skippers would set out to sea in such weather.''

''I don't like this,'' she said. ''It is as if we have been cut off from our empire, here in this miserable eastern lowland.''

''A matter of a few days, I am sure, Majesty,'' the man said reassuringly.

She found Gasam in the midst of his highest officers. He was issuing orders for an assembly of all his islander regiments. ''The rest of this little campaign can be left to my mainland levies,'' he explained to her. ''But your description of the Thezan forces was impressive. It may take first-rate warriors to overcome them.''

''Excellent, my love,'' she said. ''But now something disturbs me. There has been no word from the west for a good many weeks, neither by land nor by sea. It is as if we were isolated here. We have no idea what is happening in our great dominions to the west.''

''That is of no account. The lands and people are ours, and we left reliable persons to administer them for us. We shall return to find all well cared for.''

''I still don't like it. Perhaps you had better send some scouts west to investigate.''

He frowned. ''Scout out my own territory? Surely you are giving this matter too much weight.''

''Perhaps,'' she said, doubtfully.

''Besides, it is unworthy of us to become so concerned over land and cities. The whole world is my empire, and it is my pleasure to remind men of that. My capital is where my feet stand. My power is these warriors who surround me. What need have I for lands, peoples and cities?''

''As you say, my love,'' she answered, biting back further words. It was her eternal problem. For all his godlike qualities, Gasam was still a child, a rootless nomad who lived for conquest and slaughter and looked forward only to the next battle. For him the past was unreal. Once he had finished pacifying a place it ceased to exist for him. It was left to her to order their sprawling empire. She kissed him and walked away.

Without looking, Larissa snapped her fingers. The Nevan spy came running.

"Summon your colleagues, any of them who are in this camp. Bring them to the royal tent. *Now!*" The final word was a whipcrack that turned heads for fifty paces around.

"At once, Majesty!" The man hurried off in a flutter of merchant's robes.

A dozen of them appeared before her minutes later. They were a mixed group, from a number of nations. All were in trades that allowed them to travel widely without raising suspicion: merchants, entertainers, priests of wandering orders, even a specialist in the treatment of diseases of the eye.

"Your instructions, my queen?" asked the Nevan.

"Get fast cabos. You may requisition them from the royal herd. As many as you need, and all necessary gear. I want you to ride west, into our province of Sono. I want you to find out what is going on there, even if it is just bad weather. Once you know something, you are to report back to me at once!"

"As you command, Majesty," said the Nevan, bowing.

"Go!" she shouted.

She felt better when they had left. At least she had done something, taken some action. She could not say why she felt so uneasy, except that she did not like mystery to intrude upon her world. Things should be simple and make sense. She could not stand not knowing what was happening in her world. She needed to be in control: control of people, control of places, control of events. Gasam needed merely to dominate. This was part of what made them such a formidable pair.

What could be wrong? Was it something as simple as weather? That was the most likely explanation, which was why it had occurred to the Nevan. An uprising by the natives? They had left armies of occupation in the new territories. And if there was any such trouble, why had messengers not brought word to them?

Even more puzzling than the silence from the land was that from the sea. Sudden, violent storms were not uncommon, but she had never known them to halt sea traffic more than a few days at a time, never for weeks. It was possible that a tempest of tremendous force had struck unexpectedly, smashing the fleets in port. If so, it was of no consequence. Losses of men and ships meant nothing.

But something had unsettled her. She was a creature of instinct as well as of mind, and she knew better than to ignore her instincts.

The next days were filled with activity. The king's island warriors and his highest-quality mainland troops were summoned from the various locations in Gran and Basca where they were still fighting and they came running, leaving the inferior troops to finish the mopping up. Gasam was looking forward to a short, stiff campaign against Thezas.

"I've been telling their king for months of the brotherly love and affection I hold toward him," Gasam said, grinning. "But he's no fool. He'll be ready for us."

"They can't all be fools," Larissa said. "More's the pity.".

"No, it's just as well. If my men never have a chance to fight a worthy foe, they will become degenerate, like the mainlanders. It's what kept us Shasinn so fierce and skillful. We were always fighting each other, and we are the best warriors in the world, so we kept our standards high. This is an excellent situation: A tough, skillful enemy who can give us a good fight but who is not numerous enough to represent a real danger. I'll place the young warriors in front. They've done nothing but kill inferior mainlanders thus far. It's time they were tested."

"As you say, my love. It bothers me that you left that force of islanders back in Sono. We could use them now."

"I've sent for them," Gasam said. "They won't get here in time for this campaign, but we don't really need them. They'll be here for the invasion of Mezpa."

"That is good." She stared into space for a time, thinking. She counted the years on her fingers, ignoring the evolutions of the troops practicing their battle-drill to drumbeats and chants.

"Something occurs to me," she said. "It is time for a new crop of boys to graduate to junior warrior status, back in the home islands. If you send your ships to bring in the levy, those young men will be here in time for the invasion."

He grinned again. "Excellent! That way, all our juniors can now unbraid their hair and graduate to senior status. That will make them all the hotter for the invasion." Junior warriors could not own property and therefore did not share in the loot.

"And the new-made warriors will have a real campaign for their first blooding," she pointed out.

"And I'll have a much larger corps of Master Warriors."

In the old days, by the rigid rules of the Shasinn, when a new generation of boys became junior warriors, and the former juniors became senior warriors, the former seniors had become elders, given their weapons to the juniors, and retired to herd their kagga. Some of these seniors were yet in their early thirties. It seemed absurd to Gasam that men in their warrior prime should give up battle, so he had created the new status of Master Warrior. Those who survived to attain the status were privileged and were spared the more onerous duties of the other warriors. In battle they formed Gasam's strategic reserve, and were the pool from which he drew his officers. Like the senior warriors, they had slaves to care for their livestock and between campaigns they could sail back to the home islands, to visit their numerous wives and breed more Shasinn or other tribesmen. Gasam never could have too many of his islanders.

"What have the pirates reported of their probing raids on the Mezpan coast?" she asked.

"Their coastal defenses are weak. There are strong forts guarding the ports, but they do not seem to be well manned. When the pirates made feints toward the forts they came under much fire from the small weapons, but they encountered none of the big tubes such as you saw."

"A new weapon then. They were very cagey when I asked about them. They wanted me to think that they had many of them, and that some were far larger than the one I saw."

"They were bluffing," Gasam said. "And I spoke with the skipper who attacked the ship you were on. They had been chasing a small vessel all morning, and it managed to stay just ahead of them. They broke off the chase when they saw your ship, which looked like a richer prize."

"It was set up," she said. "I thought it took a suspiciously long time to reach the island, which I had been assured was no more than an hour's sail from shore. They knew the pirates were in the area and lured them in so they could frighten me with that oversized firetube."

"My respect for Deathmoon grows," Gasam said. "He may bluff, but he knows how to do it well. It would be a mistake to underestimate him."

"You had better call in all the pirates. The Mezpans said that they had neglected their coastal defenses because they had been preoccupied so long with their land conquests. If the raids keep up the defenses will be strengthened and we'll have a harder fight of it during the invasion."

"I have already done so. There is a port just five miles from here, named Usta. I've collected every warship and cargo ship from the coasts of Gran and Basca there. They are being converted into transports for my soldiers and the pirates will officer them."

She frowned. "It is too soon. The Mezpan spies will find out about it."

"It is never too soon to begin preparations," he said. "And I intend to tell Deathmoon all about it, even allow him to send observers and advisers."

"What are you up to?" she asked, knowing it would be something clever.

"He may consider me a barbarian, but even I know how to read a map. Look at this." He took up a broad scroll and unrolled it on a table before them, weighting its corners with daggers and handfuls of Larissa's jewels. His finger traced from the spot where they now were, along the southern coast, dipping low to avoid the southern cape, then up along the western coast to a huge river estuary that formed a minor gulf.

"What makes more sense?" he asked her. "To march for months over mountains and through a lot of pestilential swamps before we even reach the desert? Or to embark here, sail along the coast and around the southern cape, then row our way up the River Kol and disembark at the very edge of the desert?"

"It makes good sense," she said. "I think he will buy it."

"Of course he will. And when the time comes we will get in our ships and sail south, out of sight. When he knows we are on our way, he will march north from Mezpa. Then we will get back aboard our ships and invade his country."

She beamed. "No wonder I love you so much."

The sounds of hammering and sawing assaulted her ears continuously, but they were good sounds. She greatly preferred them to the grating clamor of hammers in the steel pit. The air was ripe with boiling pitch and the thunking of caulking hammers made a bass undertone. Old ships were being refurbished, new ones were being rerigged. They were being redesigned to carry a new cargo: fighting men.

"We have enough ships ready for the island warriors now," the pirate admiral said. He was a tall, thin, one-eyed man who spoke hoarsely because of an old throat wound. He wore the head scarf, vest and baggy knee-breeches common to his trade. His feet were bare. "We'll need more transports for the infantry, and for the engineers and all their gear. More yet for the packers and their animals."

"There is no rush," Larissa said. "If there are still too few transports by the time we are ready to sail, some will just have to wait for the first ships to return. It is only crucial that the shock troops be delivered with the first wave. Engineers and packers can wait."

She was satisfied. Already, she had dispatched a letter to Deathmoon, explaining the amphibious phase of the joint operation. She saw nothing here that might raise the suspicions of the Mezpan observers. She had even requested the loan of pilots familiar with the southern coastal reefs and shoals.

She mounted and rode toward the field nearby where

Gasam had set up his staging area for the invasion of Thezas. Already, the alert Thezans were massing at their border. Gasam considered this a good thing. He said this way, he would be able to bag the entire Thezan army in one battle, with no tedious mopping up to be done later. She hoped he was right.

As she rode to the king's dais, she saw a pair of riders flogging their beasts for all they were worth, coming in from the west. She wondered who these might be. She decided that she would know in a few minutes.

The queen found Gasam at the foot of his dais, surrounded by his senior commanders, islanders all. So the last of them had reported in, she thought. She saw Raba, Luo and Pendu—once members of Gasam's junior warrior fraternity, now the only members of that fraternity still living, save for Hael. They were highly privileged generals these days, and were permitted unusual familiarity with the king and queen, having known them since childhood.

"Just in time," Gasam said. "We are almost ready to march."

"Wonderful," she said, dismounting. "But someone is riding here fit to kill their cabos, and I think we should hear what they have to say."

"What?" Gasam frowned. He never liked to be interrupted when he was bent upon battle.

"Two messengers . . . here they come."

There was an approaching rattle of hoofs and men jumped aside as the pair thundered recklessly toward the royal couple. They reined in just before Gasam and Larissa, showering them with dust. As they threw themselves from their cabos, one of the animals collapsed to its side, kicking feebly, its heart burst. The other stood with its head drooping, ropes of foam hanging from its mouth to the ground. The men flung themselves at the feet of their sovereigns. She recognized the Nevan, and another man who posed as a Chiwan priest.

"What has happened?" she demanded. "What does this mean? Get up!"

The two men rose and stood swaying. "My king," said

the Chiwan, his lips moving beneath a thick layer of sweat-caked dust, "a great host comes! Hael the Steel King rides from Gran with his mounted archers!"

Gasam stood, his eyes bulging, his mouth working, unable at first to form words. Then: "Hael?" His next sound was not a word but an inarticulate screech. Like lightning, the swordlike blade of his spear flashed across, shearing the man's head from his shoulders. The king bellowed like a wounded kagga and raised his spear to skewer the Nevan, but Larissa threw herself upon him.

"No, my king! We must hear what he has to say!" She looked imploringly at the generals, and Luo and Pendu did the unthinkable. They laid hands upon their king, something they had not done since they were boys together. While the others held his arms in wrestling locks, Raba stood before him.

"The queen is right, Gasam," he hissed. "We must hear what this parasite has to report."

Sanity returned to Gasam's eyes. "He is mad! They lie!"

"Maybe not," Larissa said, quietly. "Release the king." It had been years since she had seen Gasam in such a rage, but she felt he was under control now. She turned to the Nevan. "Speak."

"We rode into Sono as you commanded, Majesty, but at the border crossing we were seized. Your officials had been replaced by strange warriors, plainsmen. We were taken to a great pen and held there, along with perhaps hundreds of others who crossed the border. We were there for days, with our eyes and ears open. The plainsmen did not think we could understand their dialect, and we heard them talking among themselves.

"My king, I know it sounds fantastic, but King Hael has seized your empire! These warriors had just ridden across Chiwa, thence into Sono. The ones who captured us were a special force, sent ahead to seize the borders and prevent word of the attack from reaching you! They invaded Chiwa from Neva, and the Nevans come behind them, infantry and engineers. These plainsmen have campaigned not at a run, as your islanders do, but rather at a gallop.

"When Hael's main force arrived, it was dark and there was some confusion. We took advantage of the fact to escape. We had seen where the animals of the detainees were kept, and we took ours back. We had thought we were well ahead of them, but they have been close behind us the whole time! Their scouts must have told them where your army lies, for they have ridden straight across Gran to Basca."

"How close behind you?" Larissa all but screamed.

"My queen," the man said, his lips trembling, "if you mount your dais, you can probably see them coming!"

Larissa stood unable to move, unable to think, while the blood of her beheaded spy made a pool around her feet. But Gasam was now calm and businesslike.

"Fool," he said quietly. "They sent no scouts. They let you escape and followed you." He thrust his spear almost casually, piercing the man's chest, giving the blade a half-turn as he withdrew it. A long fountain of blood erupted from the skewered heart and the spy collapsed, folding up like a dropped doll.

"Come, little queen," Gasam said. "Let's see what is to be seen." Numbly, she followed him up the steps, leaving delicate red footprints as she went.

There were heights far to the west, and at first they could see nothing upon them. Then they detected faint motion, which looked like a low-clinging smoke upon the bluffs. The generals had joined them and one darted into the tent. He came out with Gasam's telescope. The king unfolded it and put it to his eye.

"Riders," he reported at last. "More of them than I can count."

"How could it have happened?" Larissa asked, still dazed.

"Hael," Gasam said. "He was born to plague me, and he has done it again. He and Shazad. That pair of longnecks have been plotting against me. But the audacity of it! I had thought that only I was capable of such a thing!"

"How many?" she whispered.

"How many did your spies estimate he had?" the king asked. "I must assume that he brought them all."

"About sixty thousand, they think," she said, her composure coming back, immensely relieved that Gasam was so calm.

"He must have lost some, they have come a long way, and have been doing a great deal of fighting. But say he has perhaps fifty thousand, all mounted. The infantry must still be far behind."

"It could be far worse, my king," said Luo. "The cream of your army is right here with you. Just a few days ago they would have caught us scattered."

"That is true," Gasam said.

"And they have been fighting nothing but inferior forces," Pendu pointed out.

"I left a good regiment in Sono," Gasam said. "But there were not enough of them to handle this army, even if they are wretched, cowardly, arrow-shooting plainsmen."

"Look!" Larissa said. The facing slopes of the bluffs began to darken, as if a shadow crossed the sun and came toward them.

"Like ants on the carcass of a dead kagga," Gasam commented.

"My king," Luo said, quietly, "you must give us your orders. They will be here soon."

"Form the men up and fall back to the east at a run," Gasam said crisply.

"We have never run from an enemy!" said an Asasa general.

"And we are not running now," Gasam said. "We must put our backs to the sea. Above all, they must not encircle us! That is their favorite tactic! We have already allowed them to decide the hour of battle. Let's not let them choose the place as well."

With the queen, he hurried down the steps of the dais. All around them orders were being shouted. The men were confused, but that was unimportant because their superb discipline was unshaken and they responded faultlessly, forming up in their units, facing east, and setting off at an easy lope.

Larissa's mounted bodyguard arrived, the lead man trailing her favorite cabo by its bridle. Gasam lifted her into the saddle.

"Keep well to the rear of the battle lines, my queen. This is at worst a nuisance, a setback. Eliminate Hael, and all our lands will be in our hands again."

She leaned down and kissed him hard. Then she rode east as fast as she could flog her beast. She was not merely going to stay behind the battle lines. She was going to have some words with that pirate admiral.

NINETEEN

"**B**ad luck," Hael said. They sat their cabos on the bluff and saw the vast enemy camp spread out below them. "They are all together. I'd hoped to catch them piecemeal, but things don't always fall out as you want them to in warfare."

"Consider what we've accomplished already," said Jochim. "You've little to complain about."

"What do we do now?" asked Kairn, who had ridden up next to his father.

"Everybody change to fresh mounts and attack," Hael said. "There's nothing to gain by waiting, but much to lose. Do it now."

Within minutes, all his men were on fresh animals.

"There is still plenty of daylight left to finish this," Hael said. "Jochim, take the first corps in."

The Matwa commander shouted his orders and the riders descended the slope, careful of their animals, for this would not be the time to lame one.

"What are they doing?" Ansa asked. They could see that

the black-shielded legions were changing formation. Then there was a swirling of dust. "They're running!"

"They aren't running," Hael said, studying the enemy through his telescope. "That is, they aren't running *away*. Gasam just wants more favorable ground than that flat plain. My guess is the sea. If there's a peninsula where he can put the bulk of his army while shortening his battle line, we may be in for a long, hard fight."

"And after you promised this would be so much fun," said Kairn, rubbing his sore behind. Even two months of solid campaigning in the saddle had not completely numbed him.

"Suffer now so you can brag later," said a seam-faced Amsi chief, swinging a long-handled, stone-headed warhammer. Some still preferred the traditional weapons.

"Second corps down," Hael called. With a cheer, the next wave descended the slope. The first corps had already wheeled and ridden to the north. When the second corps had reached the level ground and progressed about a quarter-mile, they too wheeled and rode south.

"Third corps with me," Hael called. "Bows ready." The last of the riders cleared the crest. This maneuvering was done at a quick walk. Hael had given strict orders that there was to be no galloping until battle was joined. He did not think that this fight would be over in a single charge, and he did not want his men behaving as if it would be. The third corps filled the wide gap between the first and second. For a moment they paused. Hael raised his spear and brought it down in a slow arc. When it stopped, it pointed rigidly toward the place where Gasam's army had disappeared to the east. On a broad, curving front, the great mounted army of King Hael moved out for their final battle.

Furiously, Gasam ranged up and down his battle lines. He seldom rode a cabo, but this time he had no time to arrange things on foot. His men were not happy with the way he was ordering this battle, but they obeyed. It galled him to be forced into a defensive fight. Never before had his men fought in such a fashion, but they had never faced what they were facing now.

It was a good position. The north end was anchored upon a forested knoll, and between the trees was such a tumble of boulders that only madmen would seek to ride upon it. The far end of the knoll tapered into the waters of the bay. The south end of the line was at the very edge of the water.

He had the men heaping logs of driftwood and storm-wrack into a breastwork, cutting stakes to pound into the ground with points slanting outward and other expedients calculated to slow down riders and keep them at a distance. Shading his eyes, Gasam glanced at the angle of the sun. It was well past zenith. The later the better, as far as he was concerned.

Far in the distance, he saw the lines of riders coming closer. They extended far down to the southern end of his line. The northern end was thinner and left a wide gap between Hael's left flank and the sea.

"They're weak to the north," said one of his generals.

"Deliberately so," Gasam told him. "Hael is leaving me a place to run, like a good general. He's hoping I'll lose my nerve and flee that way. He must not know that there is a whole Thezan army up there and I'm not the least inclined to run in that direction."

"How are we to fight them?" asked Raba.

"We must hold a defensive position here, until dark," Gasam answered. "After dark there tactics are of little use to them. Then we go on the offensive and attack them. Tell your men to pay little attention to the riders. Use their spears to gut the cabos. On the ground, these plainsmen are less than contemptible."

"As you command, my king."

Gasam caught sight of men coming down the road from the little harbor. They were carrying bulky objects, and he could see nusks and slaves hauling on wagons as well. He rode through his lines to see what this might portend. He saw that Larissa was organizing this odd expedition, haranguing the men in her loudest voice, waving the miniature spear he had given her. It was smaller than a javelin, made entirely of steel, and it symbolized her authority, which was second only to his own.

"What are you doing, Larissa?" he asked. "I don't want a lot of noncombatants getting in my men's way."

"They bring shields," she said. "I've stripped the shipyard of everything useful: hatch covers, the walls and roofs of sheds, scrap lumber, anything that will stop an arrow. The men can lean them against spears and cover themselves, like those mantlets the archers and engineers use when they work directly beneath fire from city walls."

"A good idea," Gasam said. "We might as well dismantle the ships."

She shook her head. "We may need them."

"No! I will not run from Hael again!"

"Fight as long as you can, my love, and then we'll decide what must be done. But we must not deprive ourselves of any course that makes sense."

Gasam knew better than to argue when she took that tone, so he turned to the more agreeable prospect of battle. While Larissa got the makeshift shields distributed, he went again to his front lines and observed the enemy. It was an amazing sight. Never had he seen so many mounted men before. He dismounted and a young warrior led his cabo to the rear.

"There he is," said Luo, one of the few present who knew the enemy commander personally.

And it was he. Right in the middle of the enemy line, and now a little in front of it, was Hael. He was mounted on a beautiful cabo, his long bronze hair blowing in the light, offshore breeze. Propped before him on his saddle he held his Shasinn spear. It offended Gasam that a renegade like Hael should flaunt the very symbol of Shasinn greatness. Gasam's guard arrayed themselves around him. To each side of him handpicked warriors held shields of double thickness ready. All their shields had been strengthened since he first saw the plains bows demonstrated.

"Best step back, my king," said a shield-bearer. "We have your battle tower almost finished. You are too close here and they are already in arrow range."

"Not yet," he said. "He'll want to talk first." He smiled scornfully. "Hael always wants to talk."

Hael's signaler fingered his horn. "Shall I ride out and arrange for a parley, my king?" he asked.

"Nobody ever had any profit from talking with Gasam," Hael said. "Shoot!"

The signaler raised his horn and winded a long blast. Instantly, a cloud of arrows rose from his lines. As they ascended, he imagined that he saw the look of consternation that came over Gasam's face. But the distance was too great. He saw the enemy army turn into its own shadow as the warriors covered themselves with their black-painted shields.

The arrows fell, and a few moments later there came a sound such as the pecker-bats make when they rap at tree bark in search of insects. It was the sound of thousands of arrows landing on shields. Another cloud rose, then another. Hael gave a new command and the signaler blew a complex call. The first line rode forward at a trot, shooting as it went. As they neared the enemy line they split at the center and each half-rank pivoted on its flankers, swinging in a huge circle that took them to the rear of Hael's ranks. The maneuver was calculated to let the riders shoot from close range while staying out of javelin range of the enemy. Hael studied the action through his telescope. In their eagerness for a close shot, some of the warriors had ridden too close and were struck by javelins. A few cabos lay kicking on the field and some men were now riding double.

The second rank rode forward and repeated the maneuver. This was not as good as a complete encirclement, but it kept a sustained fire on the enemy while keeping his own men out of danger as much as possible.

"It's not as good as a complete encirclement," said Jochim, who had just taken part in the maneuver.

"It would have been overly optimistic," Hael said, "had we expected to encircle an army led by a warrior like Gasam. He is mad, but he is no fool. He has avoided open battle with us for all these years precisely because he knows that his sort of tactics are futile against ours.''

"What will he do now?'' asked an Amsi general. "Surely he will not just huddle there and die.''

"He will wait his chance and strike when he has the opportunity.'' Hael turned in his saddle and scanned the bluffs behind him. Men were leading nusks onto the plain, their backs loaded with great heaps of wood and brush. Far behind, on the horizon behind the bluffs he saw a low, dark line. The sight made him hiss through his teeth and the others turned to see what he was looking at.

"Big storm coming,'' Jochim said.

"Perhaps,'' a Ramdi chief said hesitantly, "you could speak with the spirits.''

"The spirits don't intervene in natural affairs on my behalf,'' Hale said.

"They don't?'' said the Ramdi, surprised.

Hael looked back toward the battle. The constant trampling of hoofs had raised such a cloud of dust that he could see nothing of the fighting. Above the dust he saw Gasam standing on his rickety observation tower. From time to time an arrow arched toward Gasam, but his shieldmen intercepted it easily. Then he saw someone else climbing the tower's ladder and he trained his telescope on the tiny figure. Larissa. So she was here, with Gasam, as always.

Kairn rode up, dusty and sweaty. "We are shooting a great many arrows,'' he reported, "but I can't tell whether we are hitting any of them!''

"You are hitting many,'' Hael said. "These men do not scream when they are wounded. How are they acting?''

"Huddling under their shields. It's all they can do. But they've rigged up makeshift mantlets of planks and they're piling heavier timber in front of them. Where can they be getting it?''

"I don't know,'' Hale said.

"Will they break to the north?'' Jochim asked.

"I've left him the opportunity,'' Hael said. "I think he will take it, but Gasam is mad and he may have other plans.''

"What else can he do?" Kairn asked. "Just die where he stands?"

"He could do that," Hael said, "but it would be unlike him. I wish we knew where all that timber was coming from."

Gasam watched the progress of the battle grimly, for it could scarcely be termed a battle when one side inflicted all the hurt while the other side suffered it. He felt a hand on his shoulder and looked to see Larissa standing by him.

"You shouldn't be up here, you are too exposed," he chided.

"I am a smaller target than you and your shieldmen are very expert. How goes it?"

"Not to my liking. The best spearmen in the world are huddling beneath their shields like Nevan ladies caught in an unexpected thundershower." He looked down to see the black roof covering his army, the men clustered as closely together as possible so that their shields could overlap, giving a double thickness. Some of the shields were nailed together by arrows.

"Are we losing many?" she asked.

"It could be worse." He looked up to judge the angle of the sun. "It will be down in an hour. Another hour and it will be fully dark. Then we strike."

"Can we last two more hours of this?" she asked.

"Through lack of any alternative, yes. Look." He pointed to the legions of the plains, going through their charge-split-wheel maneuver. "That is very pretty to see, and doubtless they can keep it up for a long time, but already the arrows fly less thickly. Either their quivers are running low, or the men are getting tired. Those are powerful bows and a man can draw one only so many times before his hand begins to shake and then he must have rest. I think they counted on slaughtering us with their first volleys and encircling us to finish us off.

"But we had just a bit of warning, and we got to this spot which is hard to assail, and your quick thinking provided us with enough extra protection to make a crucial difference. All this has thrown Hael's battle plan off balance. Look there—'' He pointed far to his right, where the enemy presence was weak. "He's left me a route of retreat. Right now he's wasting time and thought, planning how he is going to maneuver his forces to harass and destroy me when I run that way tonight.''

She nodded. "You are right, as always." She was silent for a while, watching the battle. She did not take her usual pleasure in the sight, for this was not the Shasinn slaughtering a lesser people. "Hael," she said at last. "How could Hael, of all people, have done this? How could that dreamy, foolish, spirit-speaking buffoon have taken our empire away from us?''

Gasam gripped the rail of his platform with his free hand, the other gripping his spear of steel. The knuckles of both hands were white.

"Hael and I," he said, "were born to kill each other. Tonight I shall do just that.''

The sun was down, but there was still light to shoot by. The volleys had become ragged and spotty as more and more men had to break away and ride back to the pack nusks to replenish their arrow supplies. Hael turned in his saddle to study the nearing storm. The black line was high now, and lightning flashed along it continuously.

"Look! To the north!" someone shouted. Hael turned that way to see a hundred riders approaching. It was the flying force that had secured the passes and border crossings during the campaign. He had sent them north to scout out Gasam's probable route of retreat. The Amsi leader rode up and reined in beside the king. His other officers drew aside to allow the man to report.

"We found something we didn't expect up there, Spirit-King," the Amsi said.

"This is a day for surprises," Hael said. "What did you find?''

"A whole army drawn up for battle. The land of Thezas

is just a few miles from here. Their army is massed on the border, tough-looking men, armored like turtles. They didn't know what to make of us and we couldn't talk their language, so they must still be wondering.''

Hael slapped the pommel of his saddle, a rare gesture of frustration for him.

"He was getting ready to invade Thezas! That is why we found all his islanders gathered in one place!" he thought for a while, reminding himself that there was no need for distress, that Gasam was still stymied, helpless. Or was he?

"Jochim?"

"Yes, my king?"

"Take your regiment and reinforce the north flank. Bring it around to touch the water. Gasam is not going to retreat that way and I don't want a weak spot."

"At once, my king!" The man rode off. Hael gave his signaler an order and the man blew a series of high trills, which were taken up by the regimental and then by the hundred signalers. The last wheeling line fired its arrows and rejoined the mass of the army. Fifty thousand tired men and animals waited by the heaps of dry brush while the lightning of the approaching storm flashed behind them and the enemy before them prepared its counterattack. The southern nightfall swept over them with its accustomed swiftness and the men put away their bows and drew their swords. Then they waited.

Gasam grinned with ferocious exultation when he heard the horns sound and the last line of the enemy returned to its ranks without another taking its place.

"On your feet!" he shouted. The men below him lurched upward amid a great snapping of arrow shafts as shields were wrenched apart. Even in the dimness he could see that there were far too many sprawling on the ground. Among warriors such as these, it could only mean injury or death. He turned to Larissa.

"Now I will crush him, my queen! Wait here. The next great sound you hear will be Hael's army screaming as I fall upon it and crush it.'' He descended the ladder, followed by his shieldmen.

How like Gasam, she thought, to ignore the fate of his wounded warriors, men whose support he would need later. She went down the ladder and beckoned to the chief of her guard.

"Stay by me. When the king launches his attack, you are to stay here.''

The man looked stricken. "Are we not to follow the king into battle?''

"No! As soon as the others have gone, you will drive these sailors and workmen like slaves. I want every wounded man evacuated to the ships. Don't worry, there will be plenty of fighting for everyone before this night is over.''

"Yes, my queen!''

Gasam's fingers flexed on his spear as he inhaled the sweetest smell of all—fresh-spilled blood. It detracted somewhat from his pleasure that it was the blood of his own warriors, but that would change soon.

"We are ready, my king,'' said Raba. Behind them, in the darkness, came the rustling and rattling of his eager men, their weapons ready. They had suffered for hours. Now they would have revenge. Gasam raised his voice.

"We go north, circle, and fall upon their weakest flank. We will roll them up like a mat! We fight Shasinn style at the run! Follow me!'' With a shattering war cry, they set off, leaping over the hastily-piled timber breastwork and the bodies of their slain. He knew that most of his men could not have heard his words, but those in front had, and the rest would follow. Put an enemy in front of these men, and they needed no further instructions.

His feet seemed not to touch the earth as he ran, so great was his desire to kill his enemy. Before him he could see vague shapes, illuminated by the flickering lightning, flashing and disappearing. He kept the mass of the enemy to his left until the lightning flashes revealed that the mounted forms were thinning, then he turned left. Behind him, the men followed. The next flashes revealed that they were almost upon the enemy.

"Kill them!" Gasam screamed. Behind him the war cry erupted again, and this time it did not cease, but rose to a roaring pitch and stayed there as his men collided with the enemy.

Gasam saw a mounted man raise a long-handled axe and he speared the man easily, tossing him from the saddle like a farmer lifting a forkful of hay. All around him, men were stabbing with their spears as the mounted man milled, slashing with sword and axe. A lurid light spread over the field. Everywhere, it seemed, bonfires were springing up. More of Hael's foresight, Gasam guessed. He had prepared fires against the likelihood of a night attack.

"We can see to kill them better!" he shouted, unheard.

The momentum of his attack slowed. There were more riders here than there should have been. Hael had reinforced the northern flank. No matter, they were just plainsmen, and now they did not have the advantage of their bows. Something whizzed past his ear and he realized that some of the riders were using the light to ply their bows after all. He saw a Shasinn tumble to the ground with a pair of shafts through him. Other shafts thunked into black shields.

"Push on!" he screamed. "Get among them!" His men surged forward, sending the plainsmen reeling back. Brave though they were, the riders were concerned for their mounts, so easy to spear compared to a fighting, flailing man. The cabos squalled and kicked and tried to gore with their small, curling horns. But the islanders were herdsmen, unafraid of animals.

"Find Hael!" Gasam screamed. "Kill! Kill!"

Hael heard the tremendous clamor to the north just as the first chill gusting wind hit his back.

"He's fallen on the left flank!" Hael said. "Did Jochim close the gap in time?"

"I do not think that he could have," said a chief. "There was no time."

"Could it be a feint?" said another. That was exactly what Hael wanted to know. He could meet this threat, if only he knew that it was the principal danger. All over the field the bonfires were lighted. By their glare and the flashing of the lightning, he could see that there was no body of islanders between his army and the barricade. He looked to the north, and saw that his left flank was crumpling in upon itself. The flash of weapons was continuous as the lightning had become continuous.

"Pivot on the center!" he shouted to his officers. "Pivot on the center and wheel the southern half of the army to face north! We will fall upon them and encircle them!" The horns began to blast and the ponderous movement began, slowly and raggedly, as tired men and tired animals carried out the difficult maneuver in the bizarre, uncertain light.

"Hurry!" Hael shouted. "Your friends are dying!"

At last the line faced north. Hael galloped across its front and stationed himself in its center. The men cheered to see his raised spear. The moment he was in position he wheeled north and brought the spear down, pointing to where he knew Gasam had to be.

"Charge!" he shouted. With a whoop, they did as he ordered. It was not the breakneck charge of the plains, for on this ground, in this light, more cabos would have stumbled and fallen than would have reached the enemy. But it was inexorable, and it picked up speed and momentum. It gathered up scattered men of the northern corps, and they fell in with the charging lines joyfully.

When they reached the huge, roiling mass of the island army, they fell upon it like a wave breaking over a reef.

"Gasam!" Hael shouted, spearing an Asasa beneath the chin. "Where are you?"

The two masses of men, mounted and on foot, were inextricably mixed now. The lines had lost all cohesion. It was no longer a true battle, but a monstrous brawl in which each man sought to kill until there was no enemy left to fight.

Hael felt a sort of strange, elated sense of freedom. There was nothing for him to do now, the time of generals was over. It was the hour of the warrior. He was free to seek Gasam and kill him.

"Gasam!" he screamed. "Where are you?"

"Where is Hael?" Gasam screamed. "Find me Hael!" But his men could not hear him now. The roar of battle was too loud and the blasts of thunder blended into one another. The first heavy drops began to fall. A Shasinn nearby raised his spear and it drew down a bolt of lightning. He screamed once and fell to the ground smoking, his glowing spear still clutched in his sizzling, crackling hand.

Gasam blocked an axe with his shield and speared the axe-man through the belly, then he saw a gleam of bronze among the riders: bronze spear and bronze hair—Hael!

Gasam began to trot toward the vision, chuckling as he went. The ground was clearing out now as the battle tore itself open from sheer ferocity. He could hear his old enemy, and he was calling for Gasam to come to him!

"Here I come, Hael," he chuckled. "Here comes death!" He broke into a run and saw Hael's head whip around, saw him try to wheel his mount, but it was too late. Gasam raised his shield and rammed the animal with all his strength and weight. It toppled over and as it fell he dragged the edge of his spear across its throat. Hot blood fountained high and he raised the weapon to spear Hael on the ground, but Hael had kicked free of his stirrups and was rising even then, thrusting with a spear that darted swiftly as a serpent's tongue. He had swung his shield far to the left, preparing to thrust; now he had to parry the other spear with his own. They clanged together and Hael charged instantly, leaping across the dying animal, unshielded, gripping the spear in both hands and hewing at Gasam's side. Gasam sprang back, frantically bringing his shield across to stop the spear. It connected and Gasam thrust back but was parried.

Gasam knew that he had let others do his killing for too long. Hael had always been a magician with the spear. They seemed to be fighting in an empty field in the increasing rain. Where were his men?

* * *

"Find the king," Larissa cried. With her bodyguard of junior warriors she scrambled over the remnants of the barricade, which the sailors and workmen were still tearing down. She felt sure that the army would be coming back this way soon, and would not want to be slowed down.

The battle was utterly chaotic, having spread all over the field; here a cluster of Shasinn surrounded by plainsmen who riddled them with arrows, there a crowd of plainsmen futilely trying to defend themselves, standing atop their gutted cabos. And everywhere, duels between two, or three, or a dozen enemies.

Someone grabbed her arm. "The king!"

She followed the direction of pointing spear and saw him. "And Hael!"

She began to run and her boys fell in beside her, casually spearing wounded plainsmen as they ran.

"Where is Father?" Kairn cried. The rain slashed across his face, washing the blood away as fast as it gathered on his face.

"He was in the center of the line," said Ansa, equally bloody. "Keep going north, we have to find him!" Lightning was striking all around, sometimes downing riders in groups, sometimes taking a single islander by the spear.

Sane men would dismount and throw away their metal weapons, Kairn thought. But there were no sane men on this field. He had never dreamed of such a battle even in his most fevered warrior fantasies. The two sides tore at one another without thought of surrender or retreat. They would fight until annihilation.

"There he is!" Ansa cried. They began to ride toward the duel. Kairn saw his father engaged in single combat with a big Shasinn.

"That's Gasam!" Ansa said. He had seen the man up close. They flogged their weary cabos to top speed. Another body was closing in from the opposite side, a great mob of fresh young warriors with what appeared to be a woman in their midst.

"Save the king!" Ansa bawled. He slashed at riders as they passed, even dismounted ones. "Save the king!"

There were a great many words Hael wanted to say to Gasam, but he had no breath to spare for them. The time had come to pay him back for the years of youthful humiliations, for the treachery that had made him an exile, for stealing Larissa, for the murder of old Tata Mal, for taking the splendid Shasinn and turning them into a race of mindless murderers. He savored the desperation on Gasam's face as the man understood that he was beaten, that with spear and shield he was no match for Hael armed only with the spear.

Gasam raised his spear for one last, desperate thrust, his weary shield arm swinging a little too wide. Hael's spear darted through the gap and went through Gasam's chest. Hael felt the shock of splintering bone surge through his arm. He pulled the spear out and a flood of blood and pulpy tissue followed it. Gasam stood glaring at him for a moment, then the great frame toppled. Hael raised his spear for a final thrust.

"Now it ends, Gasam!" A strange, high-pitched scream made him check his arm before he could thrust. He looked up and there was Larissa, her arm coming forward just as if she were throwing something. Something silver streaked toward him but his mind would not register what it was until he felt a shock in his own chest and he looked down to see the little steel spear impaling him.

"Father!" Kairn screamed, throwing himself from the saddle across Hael's falling body.

"Kill that woman!" Ansa shouted, leading a mass of mounted warriors against the Shasinn. But the Shasinn had thrown themselves and their shields over their fallen king and before their queen. Many sought to thrust their spears at Hael, but his own warriors likewise covered him with their own bodies.

The fight raged furiously for minutes that seemed endless,

but the bravery and fury of the plainsmen was futile against
the greatest hand-to-hand fighters in the world. And these
Shasinn were fresh, uncommitted to battle that day. In the
end they broke off and brought their fallen king to safety.

"Let that be a lesson to you, boys," Hael said, weakly, to
the sons who supported him on either side. "Never pause to
watch your enemy fall. Run him through again before he hits
the ground."

"Hush, Father," Ansa said. "You've lost too much blood
to talk."

"Talk? I've never done much else. Stop." They halted by
a fallen warrior. "Bring a torch here."

"Just a dead Shasinn, Father," Kairn said. An Amsi lowered the torch toward the dead man's face.

"Luo. He was my good friend, many years ago. A brother
in the fraternity of the Night-Cats . . ." The words trailed
off as the king lost consciousness.

"Back!" screamed Larissa. "Carry the king back to the
ships! Everyone fall back on the ships! This day is lost, but
we'll fight another day! Fall back! Help the wounded get
back! I want every sound man to cover us!" Like a herdsman
getting a scattered mass of kagga rounded up, Larissa flailed
at the men, driving them back through the now-demolished
barricade.

"Larissa!" She looked up to see a familiar face.

"Pendu!" Behind the man, to her amazement, was a small,
compact band of Shasinn in perfect order and discipline. They
trotted out toward the enemy, chanting in low voices. They
were Gasam's incomparable Master Warriors, and Pendu was
leading them.

"We'll keep the livestock off you, my queen. Get back to
the ships." She could have wept with relief, but she had no
time. Shouting herself hoarse, she gathered the remnants of
the army, whole, wounded and inert, and drove them back
to the ships.

She trudged back beside a litter of spears and shields upon
which lay Gasam. He was still breathing, and blood still

welled from the terrible wound, but he displayed no other signs of life. She directed the bearers to take the king aboard the largest transport, then she boarded herself. She beckoned and the pirate admiral ran to her side.

"Do we sail, my queen?" he asked.

"No," she said tiredly, almost in a daze. "As each transport is loaded, let it stand out into the bay. All but this one."

The sails of the ships, tightly furled against the storm, were shaken out. The rain had slackened and the wind was dying. In the light of the early morning she saw something coming down the road toward the ships.

"Shieldmen to the rails," she said calmly. "If it's the plainsmen, they'll come shooting."

But, to her amazement, it was the much-diminished band of Master Warriors. Trotting along as they had when they joined the battle, they boarded the ship. Every man's spear was bloodied its whole length. Every man's spear arm was bloodied to the elbow, or farther. Last of all came Pendu, swaggering like the junior warrior he once was, a spear in each hand. As he stepped aboard, the gangplank was drawn up and the ship began to back from the dock under oar power.

"Do they follow?" she asked him.

"No. They're whipped. They have no stomach for a fight today."

"We're the same," she said. "We've lost everything, Pendu. We've lost a battle, our empire, we may have lost our king. I've even lost my little spear."

"Then here's another," Pendu said. He leaned over the side and dipped one of the spears he carried into the waters of the bay. When he raised it, the rising sun sparkled silver from its flats and edges and spirally-fluted butt-spike. It was Gasam's famous steel spear. Pendu handed it to her.

"Does the king live?"

"Just barely. Breathing is living, of a sort. If only it had not been Hael who gave him his death-wound."

"But you slew Hael, my queen!" shouted one of her guards. The rest growled their ferocious approval.

"My queen," said the admiral. "What are your orders?"

She leaned on the spear, looking down at her husband who would issue no more commands.

"How is the morning wind?" she asked.

"A fair one, my queen."

"Then set sail for the islands." She looked wearily at Pendu. "Let's go home."

"What a slaughter!" Kairn said, as the sun rose over the battlefield. Dead men and dead cabos were everywhere. The ground was a litter of bloody mud and shattered weapons and every man who lived had haunted eyes.

"Well, Father said we would learn what war was all about on this campaign," Ansa answered.

"Did we win?" Kairn asked.

"We broke them. They ran, as Father said they would." He was silent for a while. "They made us pay, though," he admitted.

"I didn't think it would cost so much," Kairn said. "What happened?" They wheeled their cabos and rode toward the bluffs, where their father lay on a pallet. He had not spoken since identifying the dead Shasinn, whose name they had already forgotten.

"There are many things that can go wrong in a war," Ansa said. "What Father calls the imponderables. We had the whole campaign our way, then at the very end all our bad luck caught up with us at once. The invasion plan that brought them all together in one place, the Thezan army that kept Gasam from fleeing north as Father planned, the ships we didn't know they had, the terrain that favored their defense. Worst of all was the storm. It gave them an advantage in their counterattack."

"No," Kairn object. "Worst was losing Father."

"He was a warrior," Ansa said. "I don't think he ever intended to die in bed."

But the king still lived when they returned. The little steel spear had been withdrawn from the wound and lay on the ground beside him. Kairn dismounted and picked it up.

"King Hael could not have been felled by such a toy," he protested.

"It was Larissa's scepter of power," Ansa said. "And that woman can kill with anything that comes to hand. With words, most often."

"What are his chances?" Kairn asked the Nevan physician who had followed the army with his team of surgical assistants. The man straightened, satisfied with the king's bandages.

"It is mortal. This wound takes a long time to kill. The king is very strong, so he could last a long time. Weeks, perhaps a month or two. But he will die."

Kairn drew his brother aside. "The woman Star Eye, in Mezpa. She healed my wounds. It was all but miraculous."

"She is in enemy territory, little brother. All the worse because when Deathmoon learns of this, he will attack. With neither Gasam nor Hael to trouble him, he will invade the plains."

"What can we do?" Kairn asked.

"My woman, Fyana, is a healer. We have to take him to the Canyon. The Canyoners have powers no one else has. They may be able to heal him."

"It's half a world away!" Kairn said. "Can he survive the journey?"

Ansa shrugged. "He cannot survive mere time, if what this physician says is true."

"We must do something." Kairn looked out over the battlefield. "We've no work left to do here."

"We might as well ride back to the plains," Ansa said. "And we can go back by way of the Canyon."

They supervised, with great care, as the king's litter was fitted with long poles to be carried between specially-harnessed nusks. Hael's Shasinn spear lay beside him on the litter, near to his hand. When the army was mounted, they rode west in silence.

Behind them the battlefield was silent, and above it swarmed carrion bats in countless thousands.

CONTEMPORARY FANTASY
FROM TOR

☐	50824-6	LIFE ON THE BORDER Edited by Terri Windling	Canada	$4.99 $5.99
☐	51771-7	SWORDSPOINT Ellen Kushner	Canada	$3.99 $4.99
☐	51445-9	THOMAS THE RHYMER Ellen Kushner	Canada	$3.99 $4.99
☐	55825-1	SNOW WHITE AND ROSE RED Patricia Wrede	Canada	$3.95 $4.95
☐	54550-1	TAM LIN Pamela Dean	Canada	$4.99 $5.99
☐	50689-8	THE PHOENIX GUARDS Steven Brust	Canada	$4.99 $5.99
☐	50896-3	MAIRELON THE MAGICIAN Patricia Wrede	Canada	$3.99 $4.99
☐	53815-3	CASTING FORTUNE John M. Ford	Canada	$3.95 $4.95
☐	50554-9	THE ENCHANTMENTS OF FLESH AND SPIRIT Storm Constantine	Canada	$3.95 $4.95
☐	50249-3	SISTER LIGHT, SISTER DARK Jane Yolen	Canada	$3.95 $4.95
☐	52840-3	WHITE JENNA Jane Yolen	Canada	$3.99 $4.99

Buy them at your local bookstore or use this handy coupon:
Clip and mail this page with your order.

Publishers Book and Audio Mailing Service
P.O. Box 120159, Staten Island, NY 10312-0004

Please send me the book(s) I have checked above. I am enclosing $ _____
(please add $1.25 for the first book, and $.25 for each additional book to cover
postage and handling. Send check or money order only—no CODs).

Names _____
Address _____
City _____ State/Zip _____
Please allow six weeks for delivery. Prices subject to change without notice.

MORE CONTEMPORARY
FANTASY FROM TOR

☐	55852-9	ARIOSTO Chelsea Quin Yarbro	$3.95 Canada $4.95
☐	53079-9	A MIDSUMMER TEMPEST Poul Anderson	$2.95 Canada $3.95
☐	51919-1	THE ARMIES OF ELFLAND Poul Anderson	$3.99 Canada $4.99
☐	53353-4	SEVENTH SON Orson Scott Card	$3.95 Canada $4.95
☐	53359-3	RED PROPHET Orson Scott Card	$3.95 Canada $4.95
☐	50212-4	PRENTICE ALVIN Orson Scott Card	$4.95 Canada $5.95
☐	55607-0	THE HALL OF THE MOUNTAIN KING Judith Tarr	$3.95 Canada $4.95
☐	55621-6	THE LADY OF HAN-GILEN Judith Tarr	$3.95 Canada $4.95
☐	55644-5	A FALL OF PRINCES Judith Tarr	$4.50 Canada $5.50
☐	55815-4	SOLDIER OF THE MIST Gene Wolfe	$3.95 Canada $4.95
☐	50625-1	SOLDIER OF ARETE Gene Wolfe	$3.95 Canada $4.95

Buy them at your local bookstore or use this handy coupon:
Clip and mail this page with your order.

Publishers Book and Audio Mailing Service
P.O. Box 120159, Staten Island, NY 10312-0004

Please send me the book(s) I have checked above. I am enclosing $ _____
(please add $1.25 for the first book, and $.25 for each additional book to cover
postage and handling. Send check or money order only—no CODs).

Names _____
Address _____
City _____ State/Zip _____
Please allow six weeks for delivery. Prices subject to change without notice.

FANTASY BESTSELLERS
EDITED BY ANDRE NORTON

☐ ☐	54715-2	MAGIC IN ITHKAR 1 *edited with Robert Adams*	$3.95 Canada $4.95
☐ ☐	54745-4	MAGIC IN ITHKAR 2 (Trade Edition) *edited with Robert Adams*	$6.95 Canada $7.95
☐ ☐	54749-7	MAGIC IN ITHKAR 2 *edited with Robert Adams*	$3.95 Canada $4.95
☐ ☐	54709-8	MAGIC IN ITHKAR 3 *edited with Robert Adams*	$3.95 Canada $4.95
☐ ☐	54719-5	MAGIC IN ITHKAR 4 *edited with Robert Adams*	$3.50 Canada $4.50
☐ ☐	54757-8	TALES OF THE WITCH WORLD 1	$3.95 Canada $4.95
☐ ☐	50080-6	TALES OF THE WITCH WORLD 2	$3.95 Canada $4.95
☐ ☐	51336-3	TALES OF THE WITCH WORLD 3	$3.95 Canada $4.95

Buy them at your local bookstore or use this handy coupon:
Clip and mail this page with your order.

Publishers Book and Audio Mailing Service
P.O. Box 120159, Staten Island, NY 10312-0004

Please send me the book(s) I have checked above. I am enclosing $ _____
(please add $1.25 for the first book, and .25 for each additional book to cover postage and handling.
Send check or money order only—no CODs).

Name _____
Address _____
City _____ State/Zip _____
Please allow six weeks for delivery. Prices subject to change without notice.

FANTASY ADVENTURE
FROM FRED SABERHAGEN

☐ ☐	55343-8 55344-6	THE FIRST BOOK OF SWORDS	$3.95 Canada $4.95
☐ ☐	55340-3 55339-X	THE SECOND BOOK OF SWORDS	$3.95 Canada $4.95
☐ ☐	55345-4 55346-2	THE THIRD BOOK OF SWORDS	$3.95 Canada $4.95
☐ ☐	55337-3 55338-1	THE FIRST BOOK OF LOST SWORDS	$3.95 Canada $4.95
☐ ☐	55296-2 55297-0	THE SECOND BOOK OF LOST SWORDS	$3.95 Canada $4.95
☐ ☐	55288-1 55289-X	THE THIRD BOOK OF LOST SWORDS	$4.50 Canada $5.50
☐ ☐	55284-9 55285-7	THE FOURTH BOOK OF LOST SWORDS	$4.50 Canada $5.50
☐ ☐	55286-5	THE FIFTH BOOK OF LOST SWORDS	$4.50 Canada $5.50
☐ ☐	51118-2	THE SIXTH BOOK OF LOST SWORDS	$4.50 Canada $5.50
☐ ☐	50855-6	DOMINION	$3.95 Canada $4.95
☐ ☐	50255-8 50256-6	THE HOLMES-DRACULA FILE	$3.95 Canada $4.95
☐ ☐	50316-3 50317-1	THORN	$4.95 Canada $5.95

Buy them at your local bookstore or use this handy coupon:
Clip and mail this page with your order.

Publishers Book and Audio Mailing Service
P.O. Box 120159, Staten Island, NY 10312-0004

Please send me the book(s) I have checked above. I am enclosing $ _____
(Please add $1.25 for the first book, and $.25 for each additional book to cover postage and handling.
Send check or money order only—no CODs.)

Name _____

Address _____

City _____ State/Zip _____

Please allow six weeks for delivery. Prices subject to change without notice.